LESSONS IN LOVE

Kate Lawson was born on the edge of the Fens and is perfectly placed to write about the vagaries of life in East Anglia. In between moving house, raising a family, singing in a choir, walking the dog, working in the garden, taking endless photos and cooking, Kate is also a scriptwriter, originating and developing a soap opera for BBC radio, along with a pantomime for the town in which she lives. As Sue Welfare, Kate published six novels, two of which are currently under development for TV.

For more information on Kate go to www.katelawson.co.uk and visit www.Author-Tracker.co.uk for exclusive updates.

By the same author:

Mum's the Word

KATE LAWSON

Lessons in Love

AVON

AVON

A division of HarperCollins*Publishers*
77–85 Fulham Palace Road,
London W6 8JB

www.harpercollins.co.uk

A Paperback Original 2008

1

First published in Great Britain by
HarperCollins*Publishers* 2008

A catalogue record for this book is
available from the British Library

ISBN-13: 978-1-84756-092-6

Typeset in Minion by Palimpsest Book Production Limited,
Grangemouth, Stirlingshire

Printed and bound in Great Britain by
Clays Ltd, St Ives plc

With thanks to the guys at Avon, to Keshini Naidoo for her insightful comments and light-handed editing, Sammia Rafique for chasing everything up and of course the inimitable, enthusiastic Max Hitchcock for being so encouraging and supportive.

Special thanks to Maggie Phillips, my agent at Ed Victor whose friendship, sense of humour, thoughts, comments and encouragement I truly value.

To the men in my life – Phil, Ben, James, Joseph, Sam and Oliver, who between them continue to give me all the lessons in love a girl could ever need.

Chapter One

'Dear Ms J. Mills, we are delighted to inform you . . .' Jane Mills read the letter again. Apparently she had won an all-expenses-paid trip-of-a-lifetime for two to a destination of her choice from one of the following . . .

Or at least she would have done if the letter had been delivered to the right Ms J. Mills at the correct address. It had arrived, along with a new cheque book and card, three store-card bills – the other J. Mills appeared to have a penchant for shoes and handbags, so they did also have that in common – and a dental appointment for two fifteen, Thursday week.

Jane hadn't meant to open them. The post had arrived first thing Saturday morning, while Milo and Boris, her cats, had been mugging her with a mixture of impatience, persistence and some very overdone fawning, and she had been caught in the no man's land between a can of Felix, the kettle and tea bag dunking, and most certainly not within striking distance of her glasses. So, while the kettle was boiling she'd opened the letters with a paper knife. Someone else's letters. All of them.

The paper knife, with its plump little kissy Cupid for a handle, and a blade meant to represent his bow and arrow,

1

had been a Christmas present from Steve and still had a phoney evidence tag tied to it with white string. It read:

Steve Burney, in the library with the dagger.
Merry Christmas, Sweetie.
I will love you for ever. S. xxx

Which he had to have given to her at around the same time he had been sleeping with Lucy Stroud and Carol what's-her-face from Requisitions, and very possibly Anna, although nobody was quite sure if that was just Steve's wishful thinking, and as Anna had now moved to Shrewsbury they might never find out. It had occurred to Jane that he had probably bought the knives as a job lot and had the evidence tags photocopied to save time.

She glanced down at the paper knife on the kitchen table. Damned shame she *hadn't* stabbed him in the library.

She had found out about Steve a couple of weeks ago, actually 11 days, 18 hours and 51 minutes ago, when Lucy had taken her to one side at work, and said, 'Actually, Jane, there is something I think that you ought to know,' in a way that Jane knew wasn't about paperclip allocation. Apparently everyone already knew about Steve, from the man on the mop in Janitorial Services, right through to the heads of departments. Humiliating didn't even come close.

Steve had probably been rolling around on the natural cream wool carpet in front of his bloody woodburner with one of them while Jane's perfectly wrapped present sat there, all innocent and unaware, under Steve's delightfully decked, colour-coordinated, non-shedding lodge-pole pine. The bastard.

Steven James Burney – Jane let the name roll around her mouth even though the sound of it made her feel sick. They had been together almost a year and in quiet moments she had got to the point of trying out her name with his: 'Mrs Jane Burney, *Mr and Mrs Burney Mills*, Mr and Mrs Mills Burney. Mrs Jane Burney-Mills' – although she had drawn the line at actually practising her signature, at least in public where anyone might see her. There was still a photo of them on a weekend break in Rome tucked under a magnet on the fridge door. Side by side at the Trevi Fountain. She couldn't bring herself to take it down. Not yet.

Moving to Buckbourne had meant to be her bright new start. Her mother had suggested it a couple of years ago when Jane's life had seemed to have lost direction.

'Janey, what you need is a change, darling. Take a new job, rent your house out, sell your house – do something, anything. Go travelling, be feckless. You need to go wild, get drunk, let your hair down while it's still your natural colour. You know what your trouble is, don't you? You've always been too good, too steady, too bloody sensible. I really don't know where I went wrong.' At which point her mother had paused and looked at herself in the glass door of the kitchen dresser, turning to try to catch herself in profile. Then she said, 'I'm thinking of getting my nose pierced, what do you think?'

'Don't,' said Jane, not looking up from her lunch. 'They look like you haven't wiped your nose, and besides, you fainted when they gave the cat its injections.'

Her mother sniffed. 'You should be living with someone by now, married even. I'd like to be a grandma some day.' She'd paused. 'Obviously not for a while yet but I'd like to at least have the chance. What is it with you and men? Give you a room full of men to choose from and you'll pick the bastard every time. What about the one who was married with five kids? Will we ever forget Edward and that wife of his and those little ginger mop-tops chasing you through Debenhams, screaming, "That woman is sleeping with my daddy"?'

'He told me he was separated,' Jane had said, while attacking a big bowl of nachos, sour cream and guacamole.

'Shame that he hadn't mentioned it to his wife.'

'Oh, right, and you're so successful with men. What about André?'

Her mother had sniffed and topped up their wine glasses. 'Which of us truly knows our own minds at twenty? And he was terribly sweet.'

'His mum came round to help collect his things when he moved out.'

'Charming woman. I've still got one of his Airfix kits somewhere.'

'And Geno? The transvestite kleptomaniac?'

'That's the trouble with you, Jane, you've always been so damned judgemental; he was lovely – fabulous taste in shoes, and look at the sitting room. I'd never have put those colours together. He still sends me letters from San Francisco. He's in an open prison now, which is so much nicer for him. They let them shop on the Internet and everything. He bought the most fabulous ball gown on eBay – although the UV is playing havoc with his skin, apparently. I've been sending him Nivea.'

'We are talking successful relationships here, Mum, not skin care. You know, years of fidelity, Mrs and Mrs Right wandering off arm in arm, sharing their golden years, shuffling round garden centres, blocking the roads with touring caravans. Happy ever after.'

Jane's mum had sniffed. 'At least my relationships are colourful. If you're going to have your heart broken at least do it with some panache, some *élan*. It's time you got a life.'

'Mum, I'm twenty-seven. I've got a few good years left in me yet.'

'Um, that's what we all say,' said her mum, topping up her wine glass again.

And so, for once Jane had taken her advice, sold her house, got a new job in a half-decent town, had a makeover at Curl Up and Dye, and *voilà* here she was, back to square one with a good haircut.

Within three months of moving to Buckbourne, billed as an up-and-coming market town on the edge of the fen by the estate agents, Steve Burney – six foot something, with broad shoulders and a big crinkly smile – had dropped into the library. He worked at County Hall in Human Resources and had come to check up on how she was settling in. Fifteen minutes later he asked her out for coffee and the rest was history.

She glanced up at the clock, trying to ignore the great raw pain in her chest: 11 days, 18 hours and 56 minutes of history. Apparently he was notorious, Lucy said.

'Look, I'm really sorry to be the one who tells you this, Jane, but everybody knows about Steve,' she'd explained, handing Jane a tissue. 'Really.'

Today Jane and Steve had planned to have lunch at the pub in Holkham and then walk his Labrador, Sandy, on the beach to Wells. That was a proper relationship. Lunch, long walks, Labradors.

Jane sniffed back another volley of tears. Bastard. And then she turned the letter over and took another look at the address on the prize offer. It read: 'Ms J. Mills, 9 Creswell Close.'

It was an easy mistake to make. Jane lived at 9 Creswell Road, which was about two miles away from Creswell Close, a new exclusive executive housing development being built right on the edge of town, in the mature parklands surrounding Creswell House, and about two million miles away in terms of income and aspiration.

Creswell Close boasted elegant, architect-designed town houses, integral garages and individually landscaped gardens, solid granite worktops and *en suite* everything, while Creswell Road boasted about how hard it was and how it could burp the national anthem after eight pints of Stella, and had a man who slept in the end terrace, the burned-out one with boarded-up windows, who could be found most mornings eating out of wheelie bins.

Jane, totally house-detailed out, having gone round and round looking for somewhere to live on endless cold wet days the previous year, had bought number 9 after the man at the estate agents had bandied about words like 'undiscovered treasure', 'colourful', 'bohemian', 'urban renewal' and 'ripe for gentrification'. Which her mum pointed out, after she'd exchanged contracts, meant shabby as hell and dirt cheap.

Even so, it all fitted in with her plan for a bright sparkly new life, although despite numerous attempts and an Arts Council grant to paint a mural on the bus shelter Creswell Road remained resolutely feral.

As had her life.

The house in Creswell Road and the job as community

project development manager in the new regional library were meant to mark a brave bold new beginning, not another dead end.

Jane glanced out of the kitchen window across the towpath that backed on to Creswell Road. On the far side of the river, out beyond the galvanised iron railings topped with razor wire, and the skip full of brick rubble and shopping trolleys, lay the municipal playing fields, mature trees, the cricket pavilion – almost the open uninterrupted views promised on the estate agent's brochure. The one notable interruption was Gladstone, the tramp who was currently sitting on her garden wall, humming a medley from *Cats* while unwrapping the ham roll Jane had left in tinfoil on the top of her wheelie bin for him. OK, so one could reason it only encouraged him to be feckless but it was so much less stressful than seeing him sift through the detritus of her life to find a square meal.

He'd already told her she ought to eat more fruit and vegetables. 'Those ready meals, they're all additives and E-numbers, you know. Tartrazine, monosodium glutamate,' Gladstone lingered lovingly over the words like jewels in a box, 'and Lord only knows what else they put in there. And you realise that that isn't real meat, don't you? They shape it out of all the stuff they scrape and blast off the carcasses with a power washer,' he'd said cheerily one morning, as she passed him on the way to catch the bus to work. 'Meat slurry.'

It had come to something when tramps commented on your dietary habits. Especially when they spent the rest of their time talking to God and any number of imaginary friends.

Jane glanced down at Ms J. Mills' post. She could hardly

just put it back in the post box now it had been opened, could she? How did that look? Maybe she ought to nip down to the post office and explain.

'So, you've opened them *all*, have you?' asked an imaginary clerk suspiciously. 'Would you care to explain exactly why you did that? Make a habit of opening other people's post, *do you*?' Jane turned the letters over; opening someone else's mail was probably illegal as well.

Who was going to believe she had opened Ms J. Mills' post by accident? There had to be – she counted – eight letters here. They'd take one look at the new credit card and assume Jane had already booked a holiday, bought a sofa and had her legs waxed.

The other Ms J. Mills was ex-directory, which really left only one option: Jane would have to drive over to Creswell Close to deliver the post herself. She would explain, and then grovel and laugh and make light of it – possibly.

'You see, it was all just a silly mistake,' she'd twitter in a gushy falsetto to a woman who looked uncannily like the clerk in her previous fantasy encounter. Jane paused; even her imagination was cutting corners. What hope was there?

She went upstairs, peeled off her jarmies, had a quick shower and slipped on jeans and a shirt. From the landing window Jane could see that Gladstone had already moved on to number 5. (The people at number 7 were away, possibly on holiday, possibly on remand. Jane had heard a lot of banging and shouting a few nights earlier but hadn't liked to look.) Number 5 usually put out a couple of slices of fruit cake and an apple. Why Gladstone wasn't the size of a barrage balloon God alone knew.

8

Balanced on top of the bin behind number 3 were a large carton of orange juice, an overripe banana and a bag of crisps. Beyond that, down past number 1 where Creswell Road turned abruptly into Lower East Row, it was hard to tell. Jane screwed up her eyes. It crossed her mind that what she really needed was a pair of binoculars. The leafy suburbs had badger watch, while out here on the towpath behind Creswell Road they had tramp watch. Right on cue Gladstone shuffled slowly downstream on his dining foray. He appeared to be singing and grooming his whiskers. Bill Oddie would have been so proud.

Jane picked up her handbag and the letters, and then as an afterthought clipped her library security pass to her top pocket. At the very least it would help prove she was who she said she was.

As Jane drove across town, Buckbourne basked under a cerulean sky. The tightly packed Victorian and Edwardian terraces corralling the town centre rapidly gave way on the far side of the inner ring road to smarter semis and then 1930s detacheds trimmed with trees, then seventies estates and finally nineties and new millennium neo-quaint, with their double-glazed leaded lights, gingerbread-house-style dormers and matching fibreglass chimneys. They in turn opened out on to the new bypass, a series of interlinked mini roundabouts and the out-of-town retail park. Another mile or so round the bypass and Jane was skirting the walled edge of the Creswell Gardens Estate.

She took a left off the next roundabout, down through lush woodland to an impressive set of gates, where a sign printed in swooping copperplate print advertised the development, along with an artist's impression of the finished area.

Creswell Gardens
*Elegant Homes, sympathetically created to
reflect the Gracious Living of a Bygone Era.
Viewing by Appointment only.*

Jane drove into the estate. Beyond the sales boards and a row of mature lime trees that scented the morning air with their heady perfume, stood the old manor house. It was a great rambling mongrel pile built from red brick, over-egged with towers and turrets, castellations, crenulations and fabulous Georgian windows, clashing deliciously with Elizabethan chimneys and gothic Victoriana, and had been converted into half a dozen elegant apartments. There was a corporate flag fluttering in the morning breeze from a pole on one of the turrets.

Beyond the main house, the stable block and various outbuildings had also been converted, whilst the rest of the estate was further away, along a tree-lined avenue. The first phase had been completed, show houses and a dozen or so other homes laid out around a wide sweeping crescent, their well-manicured gardens set with planters and wrought-iron railings, and other houses already under construction beyond them, carefully screened by boards. Number 9 was easy to find, an elegant detached town house with a large garage and neatly clipped front lawn, which, even though it was brand new, fitted discreetly into the landscape like a well-cut jigsaw piece, its large windows and carefully chosen brickwork echoing the main house and the stables across the way.

Jane sat for a minute and wondered what it must be like to live somewhere so beautiful. The other J. Mills, whoever she was, couldn't have chosen a more perfect spot. Beyond the crescent, acres of ancient parkland rolled away to a stream, crossed by a little bridge, trout lake and established woodland. A herd of deer grazed on the far side of the glittering water. The board on the building site offered twenty-five prestige homes for sale, sharing a hundred acres of mature parkland and landscape of a far grander time, all for a small annual service charge.

Jane sighed. All right for some.

'Hello?' Someone rapped on her car window. Jane jumped. A slim blonde woman dressed in a smartly tailored navy suit smiled at her, although the smile wasn't so much a greeting as a barely veiled threat. 'May I help you?' the woman mouthed through the glass.

Jane lowered her window. 'I'm sorry?'

'I wondered if I might be able to help, only we don't encourage parking on the roadways. Viewing is strictly by appointment, and I'm afraid these properties have already gone. All these properties along here.' She gestured at the other houses along the crescent as if selling them was a personal triumph.

'Ms J. Mills,' said Jane, picking up the bundle of letters.

The woman stared at her. 'Sorry?'

'Number nine. I've come to—'

The woman looked at her and then at the badge clipped to her shirt. 'Jane Mills,' she said, the smile suddenly warming a degree or two. 'Jane? Oh, I'm so sorry. Gosh. Well, how very nice to meet you at long last. How are you settling in? Presumably the showerhead in the guest bathroom is OK now? I had Barry pop over and take a look.

11

He's naturally terribly versatile and, let's be honest, even in properties of this calibre there are always going to be a few little snags, but anything you need, anything at all . . . Oh, apologies,' she said, in response to Jane's bemused expression, and held out her hand. 'I'm Miranda Hallsworth. We've spoken on the phone a couple of times. I'm only in the show house at weekends—'

Jane took a breath. 'Actually,' she began, 'I'm not J—' but before she could explain who she wasn't, a souped-up low-slung Ford Escort, with flames custom-painted onto the metallic blue bodywork, growled to a halt alongside them, bass beat pounding away inside.

'Oh, for heaven's sake,' said Miranda. 'You know we applied to make this a gated community? Why do these people insist on coming in? I mean, honestly, do they look as if they belong in Creswell Close?'

Jane turned to look. A large man with a belly like a well-upholstered fireside chair eased himself slowly out of the driver's seat. He was very tall, and wearing a spotless white singlet, a pair of very shiny navy-blue tracksuit bottoms, and white trainers – all immaculate. His companion was tiny, a pocket Venus, with breasts like ripe melons and a waist that couldn't have been more than twenty-two inches, above an impressively pert bottom. She had an unmoving burgundy-coloured bob, a tight peach-coloured top, cropped spray-on denims, raffia-heeled espadrilles and an ankle bracelet strung with tiny silver bells. Both of them were tanned the colour of Caramac and both were a long way the other side of fifty.

They were tasteless to perfection. Miranda Hallsworth's outrage was tangible.

'Number seven, Tone and Lil,' said the man, extending hand as Miranda glared at them.

'What?' snapped Miranda.

'Number seven.' He peered myopically at her name badge. 'Miranda? Oh, right. You're the bird in the brochure; you don't look nuffin' like yer photo,' he said, catching hold of her fingers in his great hairy paw. '"Our well-trained staff will be only too happy to answer any questions." Pleased to meet you, darling.'

Alongside him Lil nodded. 'Likewise. It's lovely, isn't it? We saw this place on the Internet. And I says to Tone, I says, "you know I'd love a little place like that," I says. Little place in the country – nothing flash, so's we can pop over from *España*. Didn't I, Tony? I says—'

'Number seven,' Miranda managed as Tony continued to pump her hand.

He nodded affably. 'That's right. Six beds, three baths, master bedroom, with spa-pool bath *en suite*. We've come to pick up the keys, but there weren't nobody over in the show house. We wanted to have a little butchers before the furniture van gets here tomorrow. We're staying at a hotel in town tonight. The Metropole, booked the honeymoon suite, didn't we, Lil?' He winked salaciously and when Miranda didn't instantly react continued, 'Tony and Lily Butler. Pleased to meet you.'

Miranda almost choked.

'Seven's Lil's lucky number.'

But not apparently Miranda's. 'Anthony and Elizabeth Butler?' Miranda said slowly, her face a picture.

'That's right. See, there y'are, you've got us now,' said Tony.

'We've got a lovely place in Spain,' said Lil, to no one in particular, while pulling a packet of cigarettes out of her handbag and from it, with impossibly long acrylic

French-manicured nails, produced a cigarette that had to be six inches long. 'Great big pool, Jacuzzi, loads of land. I says to Tone, I says, "I reckon there's room round the back for a pool and a hot tub here." What do you reckon?' She lit up, then, looking at Miranda through a rolling boil of cigarette smoke, said, 'Oh my God, sorry – what am I like?' And offered her the packet. 'What must you think?'

Jane didn't hang around to hear what Miranda thought. Instead she turned the key in the ignition and pulled away, heading through the open front gates up the drive to number 9, her spirits lifted by the encounter.

Number 9 had a dark green wooden door under the lee of an elegant little portico, with brass door furniture and a bell push like a big white chocolate button, set on one side of the wall in a silver and ceramic bowl. Jane rang and waited. She couldn't hear the bell ring but then maybe the bell was quiet, or the walls were thick, or – she thought about Barry's natural versatility – maybe it didn't work at all. She waited a minute more and then pressed the button again. She couldn't just post the letters and leave them – after all, they were all open. She needed the chance to explain. Across the road Miranda was heading back towards the show house, flanked by Tony and Lil.

Lil was telling Miranda about her plastic surgeon, and asking Miranda if she'd ever thought about having a little lift.

Jane looked away. Maybe she should just write Ms Mills a note and pop the post through the letter box.

Jane glanced at the door again and wondered if she might have more luck round the back, or maybe knocking. She lifted the brass knocker and, as she did, the door swung open silently on well-oiled hinges.

14

Jane took a step back in surprise. This wasn't meant to happen. This was the sort of thing that happened in horror films. People who lived in houses like number 9 Creswell Close most certainly did not leave their doors open. Actually, looking back over her shoulder it struck her as odd that the gates were open too.

The front door opened directly into a large hallway with a wooden floor, a long cream runner emphasising the elegant proportions. A curved staircase rose from the centre of the room to a galleried landing above. There were half-glazed double doors each side of the hall and a corridor heading towards the back of the house. The huge hall was panelled to waist height and, above, the off-white walls were hung with modern abstracts, which looked as if they might be originals. Jane felt her pulse flutter. No, this wasn't right at all. This kind of house should have alarms and locks and CCTV, not open front doors.

Jane glanced back over her shoulder again, this time to see if she was being watched. Miranda had vanished into the show house.

'Hello?' she called self-consciously. 'Hello?' Nothing. Jane leaned inside. 'Hello. Is there anybody in? Hellooooo?'

Zilch. Zip. Nada.

The long hellooooo echoed down past the handsome hall table and the perfectly arranged white lilies, flowing unheard over the floor-length cream drapes and the beautifully designed lighting.

Jane bit her lip. How bad did it look to be standing by the open door of a house that didn't belong to you, with a handful of opened post that didn't belong to you either? What the hell was she supposed to do now? Jane looked round and considered her options.

Across the road Tone and Lily were respectively ambling and teetering out of the show house brandishing their keys. Any minute now they would drive up to number 7 and see her standing there on the threshold, maybe Miranda too. Should she get in her car and go? Come back another time? Shut the door behind her and head home?

Jane hesitated. Then again, what if Ms J. Mills was in trouble? What if she had fallen over, slipped while checking the showerhead in the guest room and knocked herself out cold? What if . . . Before she had really thought about the repercussions Jane stepped inside, pushed the door shut behind her and called hello again as she walked deeper into the house.

The place was fabulous, a handsome modern reinterpretation of Georgian proportions, a mix of English oak, cream walls and huge floor-to-ceiling windows with a stunning view from every one of them. The hallway opened up on the right into an airy sitting room with wooden floors and exquisite rugs, a long navy-blue sofa pulled up in front of a marble fireplace, flanked by matching chairs. French windows overlooked the park. To the left was a dining room with antique furniture and a handsome gilt-framed mirror above an open fireplace. There was a TV and music room, another sitting room and a garden room, again with floor-to-ceiling windows. Beyond that was a state-of-the-art kitchen that wouldn't have looked out of place in *Homes and Gardens*, – but there was one thing that *was* missing. There was no sense at all that this was anyone's home. Everywhere looked and smelled brand new. Jane had no idea when Ms I. Mills had moved in but surely even after a week there ought to be a cushion or two out of place, or a jacket slung casually over the back of a kitchen chair, a mug on a table or a dirty plate in the sink. Surely there had to be something, anything, to suggest that real people lived real lives there.

Beyond the kitchen was a utility room that adjoined the garage. Inside was a black Mercedes convertible, a silver BMW and a nippy little black 4x4. Nervously, Jane peered inside the cars, half afraid she might come face to face with the other Ms J. Mills, cold and stiff and far from well. But, no – still nothing. The house was like the *Marie Celeste* with down-lighters and expensive furniture.

Even so, empty or not, with every passing moment Jane was getting more nervous about being discovered exploring, and anxious to find out what the hell was going on – but also aware that the longer she stayed in the house the more suspicious she looked.

In her head an imaginary police officer, with the face of the imaginary Post Office clerk, was saying, 'So, Ms Mills, you spent ten minutes in the property. Did it never occur to you at any time that you had unlawfully entered the premises and that you were in fact *trespassing*?'

Grimly Jane went on, ignoring her inner policeman. Through the windows she could see the garden rolling gently down towards the lake, the way marked by a gravel path edged with flowerbeds, shrubs and a trail of lights. As Jane looked again she saw that there was a little pagoda, a white wooden summerhouse affair tucked into the lee of the hedge – and the doors were open. Maybe she had finally found Ms J. Mills.

Jane pushed open the door and headed out across the lawn towards the summerhouse, and as she did she could hear someone talking.

'This is ridiculous,' a woman snapped. 'Totally bloody ridiculous. I've had enough, Augustus – or maybe that's it, maybe I haven't had enough at all. I'm not sure that I can go . . .'

But before Jane could find out where it was the woman couldn't go, she rounded the corner and found a handsome woman in her late forties, long hair caught up in a clip, sitting on the edge of the deck, barefoot. She was wearing white silk pyjamas and was talking to an elegant oriental cat, who watched Jane's arrival with all the distain of an archetypal English butler. The woman looked pale and was cradling a glass of water in which something was fizzing unpleasantly.

She stared at Jane in surprise. 'Who on earth are you? And how the hell did you get into my garden?'

'Your front door is open,' said Jane lamely, glancing back towards the house

'Oh, and that's an invitation to just stroll right in, is it?' growled the woman, and then winced.

'Well, no, obviously but—'

'So did you close it?' the woman snapped, and as she did the wince hardened up into a grimace, as she made every effort to sound angry. 'God, my head hurts. I really didn't ought to drink,' she said, rubbing her temples. 'What do you want?'

'Well, nothing actually, I just brought your post over,' Jane said, holding the letters out in front of her like an offering.

Gingerly the woman glanced up and then took them. 'Thanks.' And then: 'But they're all open,' she said, turning the envelopes over.

'Well, yes,' Jane began. This wasn't going very well. 'I know.

That's what I came over to talk to you about, to explain really. You see, they were delivered to my house by accident. My name is Jane Mills, I live in Creswell Road, at number nine, and these are addressed to J. Mills, nine Creswell Close – and I hadn't got my glasses on – and, and, well, I opened them . . .'

There was an odd little silence as the woman looked first at the post and then up at Jane.

'By accident, obviously,' Jane added in case there was any doubt.

The woman turned the letters over again.

'But that was all,' Jane continued hastily. 'I mean, once I realised they were yours, I didn't read them, or anything.'

'Really?' said her inner policeman. 'Then how do you explain the fingerprints on the credit card bills and the grudging admiration you have for your victim's choice in shoes?'

On the deck Ms J. Mills was still turning the letters over. 'You opened all of them?' she said.

Jane nodded. 'Yes, by accident. We've got the same name,' she pulled the badge off her shirt and showed it to her.

The older woman stared blankly at the little square of laminated plastic.

'I'm sorry,' Jane continued brightly. 'It was just a mistake. I thought I'd just pop over and explain . . .'

'And my front door was open so you thought you'd just pop in, did you?'

Jane shifted her weight. 'Well, yes. When I saw that the door was open I worried. It didn't seem right, the door being open, and I . . . and I thought something might have happened to you.' It sounded lame but it was also true.

The woman looked her up and down and then nodded.

'Oh, something happened all right. Carlo threw a hissy fit and stormed off. Again. He is so tiring, to be perfectly honest I really can't be bothered any more.'

'Right,' said Jane, not quite sure what else to say. She was still trying very hard to keep the lid on her feelings about Steve Burney. 'Well, I know how much that kind of thing hurts. I'm really sorry.'

'Don't be, he was thirty-four, sunbed tan, beautifully capped teeth, body to die for – vainer than any woman I've ever met. He used to watch himself performing in the mirrors on the wardrobe doors. I caught him once tilting the dressing-table mirror so he could see his arse in a better light.' She paused and took a sip from the glass. 'Nice arse, though.'

Jane looked at her. 'OK.' After all what else was there to say?

The other woman nodded awkwardly. 'Thank you,' she held out the letters, 'for bringing these. By the way, my name is Jayne, Jayne Mills,' she said, and extended her hand.

'Pleased to meet you,' Jane smiled. 'And it's fine. About the letters, I mean. I just wanted to bring them over, you know. I couldn't just pop them back into the post really.'

Jane looked at Jayne Mills, who sighed. Then, as if Jane hadn't spoken, got up and wandered barefoot over the lush grass down towards the lake. Jane wasn't sure what to do, maybe this was her cue to leave. Although it struck her that maybe Jayne might just keep on walking.

'Are you sure you're all right?' asked Jane, hurrying after her.

The other J. Mills didn't even look back. 'Do you ever wonder what you do things for? I'm forty-seven, I've worked all my life to get to where I am now, I've got a great business, great cars, good holidays, a farmhouse in France, a *pied-à-terre* in London, and you know what?'

Jane shook her head even though Jayne couldn't see her.

'I don't know why I'm doing it any more. It doesn't feel right. It feels like I've woken up in someone else's middle age. I've worked hard to get something and somehow I think I've missed it. Missed the point. I used to feel like every day was a clean sheet – a challenge – you know? Whatever happened to that feeling? I haven't had a relationship that's worked in twenty years. I've got no children, no family except for my little brother, and I haven't seen him in God knows how long. There's only Augustus.' She looked back at the cat, who was now sunning himself on the deck and licking his crotch. 'And let's be honest, he really only wants me because he can't undo the cans himself.'

This wasn't quite the conversation Jane had been expecting at all. She had no idea what to say. 'You've got a beautiful house,' was the best she could come up with.

The woman looked at Jane as if she had only just realised she was still there.

'Yes, but it doesn't mean anything. Don't you ever think that sometimes it would be nice to just step away from everything? Just walk away from what you've got and have another life? A different life – start over. Mind you, you're young, you probably haven't got that far.'

Jane, trying hard not to think about Steve and how much that hurt, said thickly, 'Well, yes, sometimes. Doesn't everybody? I don't think it's got anything to do with age. But then again we have to play the hand we're dealt, don't we?'

Jayne smiled. 'If I believed that I would just keep walking straight into the lake. There has to be a way. There is always a way. What did you say your name was again?'

'Jane Mills.'

Jayne Mills laughed. 'Oh, yes, of course – sorry. It was good of you to bring the letters over. Thank you.' She turned away, and Jane thought now really was the moment to leave.

'Close the door on the way out, would you, please? It's my housekeeper's weekend off,' said Jayne, her back turned.

Jane drove home thinking about her namesake. How could her life be that bad?

As she got to Creswell Road Jane slowed down, looking for somewhere to park. It seemed a terrible shame that all those wonderful things – lots of money, cars, a house-keeper and a fantastic home – didn't really seem to help, although surely it had to be better to be unhappy and rich than unhappy and—

At which point Gladstone stepped out from behind a skip. He was wearing a grimy pink feather boa over his usual raincoat and multiple jumper ensemble and was clutching a Harrods carrier bag that looked as if it was crammed full of wire coat hangers. His face was a picture of contentment. Jane sighed. Maybe happiness was a simpler thing than everyone thought.

Chapter Two

'Ah, Jane, there you are. Do come in. Thanks for coming down. Nice to see you. If you'd just like to take a seat.' The first floor of the new library was dedicated to Human Resources. It said so on a shiny brass plaque as you stepped out of the lift.

Mrs Findlay waved Jane into her office. Just inside the door a large tank of tropical fish basked and bubbled under the glow of a daylight strip lamp.

Mrs Findlay was a plump woman in late middle age, who wore various pairs of spectacles on a tangle of chains around her lard-white neck, had an office full of begonias, and was something big in internal human resources, which always sounded a bit medical and slightly unsavoury to Jane.

'Well, here we are then,' said Mrs Findlay brightly, easing herself in behind the desk and settling herself down. 'Now, as I'm sure you're aware recently we've been looking at ways to restructure and improve our current levels of service. And I think we are developing some exciting strategies to meet that challenge.' She had a file with Jane's name on it spread out across the desk. 'I've been looking at the projects you've been involved in since you began working with us here at Buckbourne and some of the things you've initiated – and I have to say it's all terribly impressive.' Mrs Findlay smiled warmly. 'A lot of very intriguing and innovative ideas, Jane, lots of outreach to take library services into the wider community, identifying and targeting groups with special needs, good use of resources, coming in under budget, as I said, this is very impressive, just the kind of thing we want to encourage, which is why . . .'

It was the following Monday morning and it felt to Jane as if she had just survived the longest weekend of her life. It was the second weekend since Steven Burney Day – 13 days 19 hours and 11 minutes since Lucy had just popped in to her office to tell her all about Steve. The first weekend Jane had been so stunned she could barely remember it. Barely breathe. It felt like one great red raw emotional blur. But this one, the first one out of the fire and into reality, had been interminable, even given the trip over to Creswell Close to deliver the post. In quiet moments Jane reran the last conversation she had had with Steve, phrase by phrase, syllable by syllable.

He had turned up at her house after she rang him. He'd brought flowers and a balloon and some ridiculous card shop bear that had, 'Pwease don't be cross wiv lickle me,' embroidered across its T-shirt.

Now, as Steve filled her mind Mrs Findlay's voice faded to a distant drone.

'Jane, I'm so sorry, the thing is, it really wasn't my fault,' Steve had said. 'Please don't look at me like that. We were both a little bit tipsy. I didn't mean it to happen. Really. Lucy and I had been talking about the new strategic county policy document and I suggested a glass of wine. Neither of us had eaten. It could have happened to anyone. I know that is no excuse but I'd been on tablets as well – you remember, I'd had that nasty cold. And she was, well, you know Lucy – she's a lovely girl but . . . We started talking about life and all that stuff and . . . and, well, it just happened. Let's be adult about this. It was nothing. You have to believe me, Jane. We all make mistakes. It was a moment of madness. And I'm really sorry.' Steve looked down at his nice shiny shoes, the very epitome of contrition. 'Trust me, sweetie, it was an accident.'

'So you're telling me that your clothes accidentally fell off and by some miracle not seen since the days of the Old Testament, Lucy Stroud was instantly covered in Greek yogurt, chocolate sauce and strawberries?'

'Ah . . .'

'You know I've wondered for weeks what those stains were on your sofa.'

There was a very interesting pause and then Steve gathered himself together and said, 'Well, the thing is—'

But Jane was ahead of him. 'The thing is I could probably understand it happening once, Steve. It's the regular Wednesday evenings ever since that are proving a little more problematic.'

'Ah . . .'

And then Jane had trashed the flowers, popped the balloon and offered if he said pwease to insert the bear into the orifice of Steve's choice. He said she was being unreasonable.

Being in a state of shock, Jane hadn't thought to ask him about Carol and Anna. Maybe she should. Maybe she could send an email memo to her whole 'at work' mailing list asking for more details. Lucy said that she had pictures if Jane needed any further proof. The cow.

Meanwhile it was still Monday morning and despite thoughts of Steve, on the far side of the desk Mrs Findlay, big in internal human resources, was still talking.

'. . . So I do hope you understand our position in this, Jane. I have to say we'll all be awfully sad to see you go.'

Jane looked up at her in amazement. 'What?'

'I realise that it may come as a bit of shock but we're all aware that you're an extremely talented individual, Jane. I'm certain that it won't take you long to find another position. Let's look at this current situation positively – and rest reassured that we will be doing our very best to help you in your search to find another position while you're working out your notice. There may very well be something coming up within your present department. Who knows? I've had Maureen in the front office run off a list of current County Council situations vacant for you and we have prepared a very useful pack for members of staff who find themselves in this situation.' Mrs Findlay pulled a cheery yellow and navy-blue folder out from a box on the floor.

'What?' Jane said again, staring at her. 'I don't understand. What do you mean, I've got the sack? You were just telling me that I was the best thing since sliced bread. And then you follow that up by telling me I'm sacked? It's ridiculous – I'm really good at my job so *you're going to get rid of me*? How the hell do you expect me to look at that positively?'

Mrs Findlay's contorted expression took professional concern to new and dizzying heights. 'I have to say, Jane, that "sacked" is really not a term I'm very happy with. But, yes, I'm afraid we're going to have to let you go.' She held up her hands, in a 'what can I do?' gesture.

'I'm not a seal being released back into the wild.'

Mrs Findlay looked pained. 'There's really no need to take that attitude, Jane. You must understand that I find this part of my job terribly stressful and very difficult.'

If she was going for the sympathy vote Mrs Findlay had picked the wrong moment. Jane stared at her; some sort of weird benign touchy-feely PC sacking on top of Steve Burney's very public infidelity was just about the final straw.

'My heart bleeds for you,' snapped Jane. 'So what happened to how impressed you were with what I've done for the department?'

Determinedly Mrs Findlay held her ground. 'Sometimes, Jane, we need to prune a tree to ensure its continued healthy growth and when we prune a tree, some of the wood, sometimes even some of the new vigorous wood, has to be cut away. But I'm sure you'll be pleased to hear that we've decided to adopt some of your wonderfully innovative ideas, structure them into our working practice in a more permanent way.' She paused while Jane took a moment to catch up. 'We've asked Lucy to head the project up. You know Lucy.'

Jane stared at her. 'Lucy? Lucy Stroud?'

'Yes, I thought you'd be pleased. She holds you in very high esteem. Recently she's expressed a real interest in developing community links. We all thought she was a natural choice. And she comes highly recommended.'

Somewhere in Jane's head a pile of pennies dropped noisily. 'By Steve Burney?' she whispered, through clenched teeth.

'I couldn't possibly comment on that,' said Mrs Findlay, gathering Jane's file together. No, of course she couldn't; she didn't need to, it was written all over her face. 'Now with regards to passing the baton, we'll need to discuss her shadowing you—'

'Really?' said Jane, standing up.

'I didn't think you'd mind,' said Mrs Findlay, obviously pleased with how well it had all gone.

'Well, you thought wrong,' said Jane.

The self-help pack was entitled 'So You've Lost Your Job? What Next?'. Inside the front cover in a flowery font that was probably meant to look like it was handwritten from a favourite aunt, it read, 'You know, it really helps to look at this as a positive step. We have to see this as a fresh start, a chance to explore our potential, rather than taking a negative attitude.'

'Bollocks we do,' said Jane darkly, stuffing the shiny plastic folder into the fish tank as she marched out.

By the lift Jane stopped to pick up three empty cardboard cartons from the janitor's cupboard and then headed back up to the fourth floor. She didn't cry, she couldn't find the way into any more tears, adrenalin and shock holding everything tight inside her. In fact, Jane felt so numb that she wondered if she might be dreaming.

It took around fifteen minutes to clear her desk and sort the last year of her life into neat piles and a couple of rubbish bags. Jane looked at her pot plant and the boxes. There was no way she was going to get home on the bus with all this lot, so when she'd done, Jane stacked everything onto a book trolley, picked up the phone, pressed 9 for an outside line and called a cab on the library account, booking it down to Lucy Stroud.

Bad news travels fast. No one looked her in the eye as she walked back out through the office, no one spoke in the lift on the way down to the foyer, or offered to help her on the long walk through to the main front doors. It was almost as if she had the plague and they might catch it if they stood too close.

She was barely at the kerb when the cab rolled up. 'Creswell Close?' said the driver, leaning over towards the open passenger-side window.

'Road,' she said firmly.

'Right you are.' He nodded and got out to help load her possessions into the boot.

'Jane?'

She swung round. Heading across the pedestrianised area in front of the library was Lizzie, who had worked with her, and Cal from the office next door, and two or three others, all looking slightly uncomfortable and – it had to be said – shifty, every few seconds gazing back over their shoulders in case there was some chance they were being watched.

'I'm so sorry,' said Lizzie, putting her arms around Jane. 'I was in a meeting. We didn't know, we had no idea. Are you OK?'

Jane nodded. 'Bit shell-shocked but I'll survive. And don't look so worried. There's nothing you could do, was there?'

Lizzie stared glumly at the boxes. 'I thought it was going really well. I like working with you. I didn't realise that we had to leave straight away.'

Jane looked at her; the 'we' sounded too prophetic for her liking. 'We? Do you think you'll be going too?'

Lizzie shrugged. 'Who knows? It's a bit like Russian

roulette, isn't it? I mean, how are they choosing who goes and who stays? One minute you're busy planning what sandwich you're going to have for lunch and then Bang. Out. Karen Marshall's ended up on the mobile out at Fleetley on the sink estates. She'd been working in the library twenty-eight years. It's too expensive to make her redundant so they're hoping if they give her something horrible to do she'll fall on her own sword. I feel like one of those baby penguins on an ice floe with the killer whales circling. I mean, if they can get rid of you just like that *and* move Karen . . . Christ, Karen was an institution.' She let the implication hang between them. 'And I didn't think there was any chance they'd get rid of you – you were doing really well. I thought Findlay was considering promoting you, or giving you a big project, or at least congratulating you.'

Jane handed the taxi driver the pot plant. 'Oh, she did congratulate me, about thirty seconds before she gave me the push.'

Lizzie shook her head. 'It's crazy. People were talking about you.'

Jane sighed. 'That may have been the problem. Keep your head down, don't call attention to yourself – isn't that the first rule of working in a big organisation? Don't draw their fire. But then again, probably none of that counts as long as you're not screwing Steve Burney. Presumably you're not on Lucy's hit list of women who coveted her neighbour's oxen?'

Lizzie stared at her. 'Lucy? Not Lucy Stroud? Steve Burney? You are joking.' But even as she said it Jane could see her colour rising. Surely not Lizzie as well? Had the man got no shame?

Jane sighed. 'Not you?'

Lizzie's colour deepened. 'It was before you started going out with him. He always used to flirt – I mean, I just thought he flirted with everyone.'

Jane nodded. 'He probably does. Fishing expedition.'

The cab driver sighed. 'Meter's running,' he said bleakly.

'Not a problem,' said Jane. 'It's on the account. And don't forget to add a decent tip. All this loading and unloading. I'd stick a tenner on if I were you.'

'Did they say you had to get out straight away?' asked Lizzie nervously.

'No, that was my choice,' Jane said, hugging her and then Cal, and then the others. 'Watch your back,' whispered Jane as she gave Lizzie one last hug. 'Especially if you have to work with Lucy.'

'I'll phone you,' called Lizzie as the cab pulled away.

Jane was home at Creswell Road by eleven o'clock.

In her absence Gladstone had found himself a deck chair from somewhere and was sitting – in his overcoat, boa, mittens and woolly hat – in the shade of the skip, eating a fruit pie. He waved graciously as she pulled up in front of the house. She got the cabby to help carry the boxes inside.

The cats were in the sitting room on the sofa, both a little miffed at being disturbed mid-morning. Some people had no consideration.

While the driver struggled in with the plant, Jane picked up the post, went into the kitchen and plugged in the kettle. The minute the front door was closed and there was no one there to see, Jane burst into tears.

Bastards, now what the hell was she going to do? Her emotions swung backwards and forwards like a pendulum,

31

ranging from gutted, hurt, horrified and scared, through fury to despair and back again, she sobbed and swore until the kettle boiled.

How could they do this to her? Lucy bloody Stroud. Christ, if Jane had known the trouble it would cause she would have gift-wrapped Steve Burney and sent him Special Delivery. He wasn't that special, was he? Was he? She sobbed again. Yes, he was. A bastard maybe, but charming, and tall and presentable and – and bloody man – she loved him. Bastard. Jane grabbed a handful of tissues out of the box on the counter top and blew her nose.

She had worked so hard to get this far. Steve had seemed like the icing on the cake. This was supposed to be her fresh new start. And how come bloody Lucy had ended up with her man and *her job*? It wasn't fair.

The cats, Boris and Milo, ambled in, obviously hoping to pick up a little something for their trouble. They knew there was tuna in the cupboard, they'd seen her unpacking the tins, but as soon as they saw crying they backed out. No good in a crisis, cats.

Jane, meanwhile, picked up the paper knife. God, what the hell had happened to her life? She needed to get a grip and now she needed to get a job. Still sniffing, Jane opened the letters one by one. The kettle reboiled, she made tea and sat down to read them.

'Dear Ms J. Mills, we are delighted to inform you . . .' Bugger. Jane Mills read the letter and groaned. Oh, no, not again. Apparently she had won an all-expenses-paid trip-of-a-lifetime for two to a destination of her choice from one of the following . . .

Or at least she would have done if the letter had been delivered to the right Ms J. Mills at the right address.

32

If there was one Ms Mills who needed a free holiday it was her; the other Ms Mills looked as if she could afford to go exactly where she liked when she liked.

Double bugger. Jane was very tempted to throw the letters and the paper knife across the room but she couldn't really throw someone else's mail away. They were all for Ms J. Mills, 9 Creswell Close. Again. All six of them. There was nothing for it, she would ring the Post Office to complain and then drive over to Creswell Close and take Ms J. Mills her post. Again. But then maybe it was just the thing she needed to distract her from the chaos raging in her head.

Jane blew her nose, washed her face and headed back out towards the car.

Gladstone waved. He was eating something bright purple and lumpy out of a jam jar with a spoon.

When Jane got to Creswell Close, there was a large van parked outside number 7, delivering what looked like life-size statues of Greek gods. They were being lowered on a tail lift by men in brown cotton shop coats and then manoeuvred around on a large trolley. Some were being set on plinths in the front garden, some taken round to the back. There were stacks of boxes and cartons and crates in the driveway and large indefinable things wrapped up under acres of tarpaulin.

Tony and Lil were out in the front garden, having cigarettes and watching progress. They waved as Jane slowed and drew up to the front gates of number 9. Today they were firmly closed. Jane wound her window down and pressed the call button on the security system.

'Hello?'

Something somewhere in the house crackled into life. 'Hello,' said a distant voice. 'Who is this?'

'It's Jane Mills – we met on Saturday. I've got some more post for you.'

There was a short pause and then a whirr and a click, the gates jerked, and then very slowly swung open. Jane pulled up outside the front door, which this time was fully open and framing a small foreign man, dressed in a black Nehru-collared shirt and black jeans, who looked as if he was from the East, possibly the Philippines or Thailand.

'Jane Mills?' he asked suspiciously as Jane climbed out of the car. 'You said you were Jane Mills?'

Jane nodded. 'Yes, that's right. I've brought the other Jayne Mills her post. The postman delivered it to my house by accident again today.' She held out the letters. 'They did the same thing at the weekend.'

The man didn't move. 'She isn't feeling so well today.'

That makes two of us, thought Jane ruefully. All the way over in the car Jane had been thinking about revenge, something spectacular and biblical. It wasn't her normal style at all but surely, *surely*, if there was any justice in the world Steve Burney and Lucy Stroud had to pay for working her over so very thoroughly. What the hell had she done to either of them other than fall in love with Steve and be nice to Lucy? It just wasn't right.

The man was still waiting in the doorway.

'In that case maybe you'd like to take these in for her,' said Jane, proffering the post.

'She spends too much time on her own. She could do with some company. It's not right.' The man's voice was disapproving. 'I said that she should go out. Have some fun, for goodness' sake. It's not as if money is the problem.

Buy something lovely – meet nice people, fly off some-where – dump that freeloader Carlo. I keep telling her, she needs to find herself a good man. I mean, it works for me—'

'All right, all right, that's enough, Gary,' said a voice from somewhere deep inside the house. 'If you're telling my life story to the fish man again I'll—'

Jayne Mills appeared at the bottom of the stairs. She was wearing ginger-coloured linen trousers, a fitted cream shirt, brown leather belt and matching high-heeled sandals, and looked wonderful – or at least she would have done if she hadn't had that look in her eyes. It was the same look Jane had seen in the mirror earlier that morning. It was a look that said Jayne Mills was tired and sad and hurt, a little bit lost and lonely, and very much in need of a hug.

'Oh, it's you,' said Jayne, her expression unchanging. 'The letter opener.'

'Yes, sorry, I'm here again.' Jane indicated the bundle of post currently being carried by Gary.

'And?'

'And they're all open.'

'Again?' Jayne looked her up and down and then sighed. 'Well, I suppose it saves me the trouble. What's your excuse this time?'

'Emotional trauma.'

'Really.' Her tone was as dry as the Sahara.

'I got the sack today.'

'For opening other people's mail?'

Jane shook her head ruefully. 'No, unfortunately not. I'd be guilty as charged of that. No, for working hard, coming up with lots of good ideas and generally being liked, as far as I can make out.'

'Ah,' said Jayne, 'that'll do it every time. In my experience it's the quickest way to get yourself sacked. Refusing to change and being a complete bastard, on the other hand, means you're never out of work.'

'And thirteen days, twenty-one hours and –' Jane glanced down at her watch – 'nineteen minutes ago, I found out the guy who I thought was my happy-ever-after was sleeping with someone else. Well, actually, it was possibly more than one someone else, but you get the picture.'

Gary rolled his eyes and looked heavenwards.

'Rough couple of weeks,' said Jayne.

'And the woman who got my boyfriend? She's got my job now, too.'

'Really? Do you fancy a coffee?' said Jayne, taking the post from Gary and heading down towards the kitchen. For a moment Jane didn't know whether she was talking to Gary, but when she looked at her diminutive companion, the man was making an exaggerated head gesture that indicated Jane should follow.

Jane considered for an instant and then sighed. Why not? After all, what was there to go home to? She followed Jayne into the house.

They sat out on the terrace under a white canvas sail stretched over the wooden deck. Gary brought them coffee and a tray of biscuits and then made himself scarce, except at lunchtime, when he reappeared with a tray with fresh-baked bread, creamy Brie and home-made hoummos, tomatoes and sharp green grapes, and a bottle of wine, and when Jane protested, Jayne said she could always take a taxi home or that Gary would drive her.

'Seems an odd name for him . . .' Jane began thoughtfully, watching Gary make his way back into the kitchen.

'Gary?' said Jayne.

Jane nodded.

'Not if you come from Chingford. Apparently his mum was obsessed with Gary Cooper. It could have been worse,' said Jayne, filling their glasses.

'Yes,' said Gary, reappearing with a bowl of olives. 'She was a big Elvis fan too.'

So they sat in the soft shade, out of the warm summer sunshine, and talked and talked and talked, and Augustus curled around their legs and allowed himself to be fussed and adored, then curled up under the table and went to sleep.

Afterwards Jane couldn't remember all the details of how the conversation had gone, nor quite how they got round to the idea of Jane working for Jayne, but they did.

Some things she did remember.

'This is such a beautiful house. I'd love to live somewhere like this,' she had said.

And Jayne had looked out over the lawn towards the lake and said, 'I used to think that too. I'd see things and think if I had them then life would be just perfect, but it's cost me more than you can possibly imagine. Somewhere along the way I've lost sight of the reason why I was doing it in the first place. I used to feel that I was building for my future and now I realise that that future was in the past and I've got this horrible feeling I've missed it.'

'I'm sorry, but surely it's not that bad,' Jane had said, picking up a biscuit and snapping it in two.

'Maybe I need a fresh start.'

'Maybe you don't,' Jane laughed, and had told her all about her fresh new start and about Steve and the library.

'I'm sorry. How old did you say you were again?' asked Jayne.

'I'm coming up for thirty – well, twenty-eight actually – but I want to be settled, sorted, be in love, plan. I've got to the point where I really don't want to invest in something, anything, that isn't going somewhere either in my love life or my career really.' Jane picked up the wine glass and turned it in her fingertips; the bowl and stem looked as fine as cobweb. 'What I really want is nice things and no worries about money.' She sighed. 'It sounds naïve, but I suppose I want everything and at the moment it feels like I've got nothing. I've just lost my bright shiny new future. Sorry, you don't want to hear this. It's self-pity and the wine talking.'

Jayne had looked wistful. 'No, no, not at all. I remember thinking almost exactly the same thing at the same age. And I promised myself I'd never say, "When I was your age," but when I was around your age I'd just broken up with someone I really loved and I thought, damn it, it's now or never – I need to do something with my life. There's no reason why I can't have it all. I'll have a fantastic job, a great house, all that stuff and I'll find someone along the way who feels the same and we'll live happily ever after.'

'From where I'm sitting it looks like you've got most of it.'

Jayne sighed. 'I know. Don't get me wrong, I've had a great life so far. It's just I suppose that this is one of those moments when I'm looking back at all the things I've done and thinking about the choices I've made and what might have been and what wasn't to be.'

'Maybe we should swap?' said Jane jokily. They were

almost at the end of the bottle, all the bread had gone, the grapes reduced to a street map of stalks, and it sounded so easy. 'You could start all over again and I could have all this.'

Jayne looked at her. 'Are you serious?'

Jane laughed 'Hardly. Look, I have to get going. Thank you for the food and the wine, and a lovely afternoon. I've got to go and find another job.'

'You're going to start today?'

'Why not?'

'OK, I'll get Gary to drive you home.' Jayne looked at her. 'You know, maybe you were right, maybe you should come and work for me. In some ways we're a lot alike. I remember so clearly being you.' She smiled. 'And I like you, and it feels right – like fate, you showing up. Over the years I've always done best when I've followed my hunches. So how about it?'

Jane looked at her. 'How about what?'

Jayne drained her glass. 'Borrow my life for a while, see how it feels. All you would have to do is be Jayne Mills – simple. I run a dot com business from here – just me and my money and my bright ideas, and we already know you have a lot of those. You could just move in – be Jayne Mills.'

'And what about you?'

'Well, I could go and try being someone else for a change, find the old me and see how she's getting on – explore some of my might-have-beens.'

Jane had smiled, guessing it was the wine that was talking. 'Thanks, but I think I'd better be getting home.'

'I'm serious. The offer's open. Let me give you my number in case you change your mind. Have you got a pen?'

Jane nodded and pulled a biro and notepad out of her handbag.

'And while you're at it, give me yours,' said Jayne. 'Who knows when I might need someone to open my post.'

Jane smiled. 'Thanks for lunch.'

'At least think about it,' said Jayne, writing down her phone number.

Around fifteen minutes later Jane opened her front door and eased off her shoes.

She closed her eyes, wriggling her toes on the cool wooden floor, very aware of how drunk she felt. She groaned. Drinking during the day really wasn't a good idea. Although this wasn't just any day. This was the day she had lost her job, and it was – er . . . Jane tried very hard to count it up on her fingers but couldn't quite work how many hours it was since Lucy had come into her office looking all anxious and conspiratorial.

'Jane, I wonder if we could have a quiet word? I really don't know where to start but . . .'

It occurred to Jane now that amongst other things Lucy was probably casing the joint, sussing out her office, working out where her stuff could go, her collection of bears, her plants, her framed picture of Mummy and Daddy. Lucy had probably got one of Steve on her desk by now.

'It's about Steve. God, this is so hard. The thing is, Jane, everyone in the office knows what sort of guy Steve Burney is – he's notorious – and I thought someone ought to say something to you before you get in any deeper, tell you exactly what's going on. I heard you mention to Lizzie about going on holiday with him, making plans for the future. There really are some things you need to know. He's not the kind of guy who is playing for keeps, Jane. What I'm saying is that you're making a fool of yourself. Steve Burney is a serial philander – he's a dog – and I should know. We've been seeing each other for months.'

Jane shuddered as the words thumped home into her heart like arrows into a target. There had to be some way to pull the plug on the replay button in her head.

She opened her eyes. In her absence one of the cats had been sick on the kitchen floor, and on the sitting-room rugs, and on the stairs – on every other tread, to be more precise. Surely all that couldn't have come out of one cat? Or even two. God, what on earth had they been eating? The smell threaded its way across the hallway.

Unsteadily, with strange volcanic things going on in her stomach, Jane went off to find a bucket, sponge, disinfectant, bags and kitchen roll. Halfway through her dealing with patch one the phone rang.

Jane, still drunk, giddy, nauseous and on her hands and knees dealing with a puddle of cat vomit, stared miserably at the hall table. The machine would get the call, and besides, realistically, what could she possibly say if anyone asked how she was? The machine began to record.

'Hi, Janey, it's Mum here. So, how are you?' said an instantly recognisable voice.

Jane groaned.

'I know you are at work, darling, but I can't find your mobile number so I thought I'd just give you a ring and leave a quick message. I was wondering if I could come over and stay for a few days. It seems like ages since I've seen you for any length of time so I thought I'd come and stay, see what you've done to the house, see how you're getting on, hear all your news, hear about work, meet Steve – he sounds just perfect. You see, I knew a fresh start was a good idea. And I can tell you *all* about Simon – my new man. Have I mentioned Simon? I'm sure I must have. God, he is wonderful. Anyway, do you know what Tantric sex is?'

Jane groaned again, this time with more feeling.

No sooner had the machine finished recording than the phone rang again. Maybe her mother had forgotten something. She had to be told and it struck Jane that maybe drunk was probably the only way to do it. Jane scrambled to her feet and snatched up the receiver.

'Hello? Look, this is really not a good time.'

'No, I know,' said a familiar voice.

'Jayne?'

'Yes. I just rang to see if you were OK.'

'The job offer, were you serious?'

'Absolutely. Why? Have you changed your mind?'

Jane looked at the light flashing like a single red eye on the answer machine. 'Yes, I think I have.'

Chapter Three

The following morning Jane was woken by the sound of the phone ringing. And ringing, and ringing and then ringing some more. Had she switched her answer machine off? And if so why? For some reason Jane couldn't quite remember.

Being woken by the phone is a horrible way to be dragged out of sleep. And her head ached. The phone rang again, more insistently this time. Jane groaned and then, rolling over, fumbled the receiver off the hook, struggling to remember the dream that she had had. It was very vivid. Something to do with Steve Burney, and then she had lost her job, and got horribly drunk and her mother said she was coming to stay – and so Jane had opened another bottle of red, and then she froze, while the voice at the far end of the line whispered, 'Hello? Hello? Are you there?'

Not that Jane was listening. Oh, bugger. Realisation and total recall hit her like a bucket of cold water. It wasn't a dream at all. All those things were for real. Bugger, bugger, bugger.

'Hello?' hissed the voice again. 'Is that you?'

Jane glared at the phone and then tried to focus on the bedside clock. Had people got no consideration? Jesus, it was only – only – eleven. Eleven? Sweet Jesus, how the hell had that happened? Jane sat bolt upright and instantly regretted it as her brain ricocheted off the inside of her skull like a wrecking ball.

Four hours past getting-up time on a weekday, and well past Gladstone's breakfast time. She was supposed to be in work by eight today, working up a project for local schools with a horribly tight deadline. She'd be in really big trouble if she hadn't already been sacked. The phone and the sounds of her stirring summoned the cats from downstairs, who thundered across the landing and sprung onto the duvet with the vigour of trained ninja assassins.

'Hello?' said the voice again, still low, still barely audible over the mewling and purring and general feline complaining. 'Are you there?'

'Who is this?' snapped Jane. The voice was husky and low, and for one moment Jane wondered if she'd been woken up by an obscene phone call.

'It's me. Are you all right? You sound awful.'

'Who is this? You'll have to speak up.'

'I can't, I'm phoning from work. I'm not supposed to have my mobile on.'

Comprehension dawned. 'Lizzie? Are you all right? What on earth is the matter? You sound awful.'

'We've all just come out of a staff meeting. It's like the week before Christmas on a turkey farm here this morning. I'm out on the fire escape.'

'For Christ's sake, Lizzie, don't jump. A job in the library isn't worth killing yourself for.'

Lizzie laughed. 'I'm not sure I want the bloody job anyway. They've asked me to work with Lucy on the schools thing. She was already in when I got here this morning, moving her stuff into your office. She's been going through everything.'

'What do you mean, everything? There isn't anything to go through unless she's fished the bin bags out of the skip.'

'The way she was going, I wouldn't put it past her. She wanted to know where all your stuff was.'

'My stuff? There's nothing left there that belongs to me. I brought it all home yesterday. Everything else I've left is library stuff.'

'Everything?'

Jane grimaced. 'Yes, I think so. Well, everything except for a dead fern, a lot of old envelopes and advertising circulars for the recycling bin, some milk and a toffee yoghurt in the fridge.'

'She's been on the computer looking for your personal email folder.'

Jane laughed. 'Lizzie, when the hell did you turn into Secret Squirrel. How do you know?'

'Because she told me. She said she needed to get up to speed on what you've been doing and that she'd sent you loads of ideas and things since you'd started there, and that as she was doing the job now she wanted them back, that they weren't on file anywhere else so they must be in your personal files. Which, as she's pointed out several times, is completely against office policy.' Lizzie mimicked Lucy's clipped high-pitched Home Counties accent with pointed accuracy.

A hangover and blind fury were not a happy combination. 'Bloody cow, that's not true. She didn't send me any ideas. All she ever sent me were snippy little notes about photocopying. Anyway, I deleted all the personal stuff.'

'You're sure?'

'Of course I'm sure. You're making me paranoid, Liz. I forwarded all my personal email to my home email address and then binned everything that was on the office machine.'

'But *you've still got it*?'

'I just told you. Yes, I've still got it. It's just not on the library computer any more.'

'Look, I've got to go but I'd have a look through it if I were you and see if you can work out what Lucy is really after. She is desperate to get her hands on something. She asked me if I knew your password.'

Jane laughed. 'That's nuts.'

'I know, that's what I said and I think she tried it, along with "no way" and "bugger off" – but she's definitely up to something. Look, I've got to go before someone misses me. I'm busy tonight but I'll pop round tomorrow or ring from home. See you soon. Bye.'

Jane sat and stared at the phone. What the hell was Lucy up to now?

But before she could give it too much thought the phone rang again. Looked like it was going to be one of those mornings. At least this time she was awake. Ignoring the cats, Jane picked up the receiver.

'Hi,' said a bright warm voice. 'How are you this morning?'

'Jayne?'

'Uh-huh. Well spotted. I was just wondering how you were fixed for lunch today?'

'Today?' Jane glanced at the clock and tried to avoid catching sight of herself in the mirror.

'Yes. If it's inconvenient it's not a problem. We can do it another day.'

'Inconvenient?'

Jayne laughed. 'And there was me hoping to employ you for your razor-sharp mind; a brain like forked lightning. These are not the cryptic clues.'

This time Jane laughed. 'Sorry. It's all right, I'm fine. I just overslept and I'm still feeling a little fragile from yesterday. Would you like me to come to your house?'

'No, I thought we could meet at Lorenzo's. Do you know it?'

'The restaurant in Brewer Street?'

'That's it. Is one o'clock OK?'

'Sure.'

'Great,' said Jayne. 'In that case I'll see you there. Oh, and you can bring my post over, if I've got any. I know it sounds like I'm rushing you but I'd really like to sort everything out as soon as possible. And I need to introduce you to my business manager. His name is Ray Jacobson. He's my second in command; handles all the nitty-gritty for me. You'll like him. He's a great guy. See you at one, if that's OK?'

'Fine,' Jane said, as brightly as she could manage, then hung up, groaned and pulled the duvet back up over her head.

Ray Jacobson refilled Jayne's champagne glass and then lifted his in salute.

'You know, I think this is such a great idea, a kind of pilgrimage to your past. I'm almost envious. And you don't have to worry, everything here will be in safe hands.'

'I know that,' said Jayne. 'Just one thing. I've asked someone to help mind the store while I'm away.'

'Really?' He watched her face for a moment or two to see if she was joking and then laughed. 'You're serious?'

'Yes, yes, I am. I met someone recently.'

'Really?' he purred. 'How recently? I thought you were still seeing Carlo.'

She waved the words away. 'No, not like that. Her name is Jane Mills, and I met her a few days ago. She's looking for a job.'

'Jane Mills?'

'Exactly; it felt like some sort of omen. In fact, it's because of her that I've finally decided it was time for me to take a sabbatical.'

Ray set his glass down and sighed. 'Jayne, darling, how long have we known each other? How many years have we worked together? "All I need are the bright ideas and a man with an abacus and an eye for detail and I'm set" – isn't that what you used to say? I don't want to tell you how to run your business or your life, Jaynie, but do you really think—'

'Don't lecture me,' Jayne said lightly. 'I'm not stupid. I haven't just picked someone at random off the street. She's in her late twenties, working as a manager in the public sector, a very bright girl, funny, clever – in lots of ways she reminds me of me at that age. She seemed – no, she *felt* like – the last piece in the jigsaw. She's been working in community outreach development for the library services.'

'How terribly worthy.'

'Stop it, Ray. She's joining us for lunch. I'd really like you to show her the ropes, guide her through the business. I know it'll take some time but my gut feeling is that she could turn out to be a real asset.'

'You could have mentioned it earlier,' Ray said grumpily.

Jayne stroked his arm. 'I know, but the idea only really came to me yesterday, and you know what I'm like.'

'An unpredictable pain in the arse.'

'Ouch, that is so cruel. I prefer spirited.'

He snorted and refilled her glass.

Lunch at Lorenzo's. Faultless service, fabulous food, wonderful wine and a hum of conversation that implied intrigue, intimacy and money. It had been Ray's idea that they should use it for their regular out-of-office business meetings. It was a good choice.

'And what is your protégée's role supposed to be exactly?'

'I'm not sure. How about management trainee?'

'Trainee? I thought you said—'

'OK, OK, not trainee. Maybe assistant manager – managerial assistant – assistant development manager. Come on, this is not a bolt out of the blue, Ray. We've both talked about taking someone on before.'

'Hypothetically. A hypothetical assistant. And to be honest I had rather assumed I would be involved in the selection process.' He looked round. 'Can you still smoke in here?'

'Ray, you know very well you can't smoke anywhere.'

'Bloody nanny state. The thing is, we've got several good people on the staff who could just step into the role – people who already know the ropes.'

'Please don't sulk, Ray. If she doesn't work out then that's fine, but it seemed like an omen.'

'Because her name is Jane Mills?'

'It's an instinct, a hunch.'

'It's a whim.'

Jayne picked up the menu and avoided meeting his eyes. 'I thought she could start off by helping with the product selection, buying, as well as some of the day-to-day stuff. It just felt right. We need to find the right title for her.'

'How about lucky mascot?'

'Don't be spiteful.'

Ray, unable to light up a cigarette, grunted and took a canapé from the tray proffered by a passing waitress. 'So where is your lucky managerial rabbit's foot now then?'

'I told her to meet us here at one so that you and I could have a chance to talk first. I'd really like to get everything organised and leave as soon as possible. We need to go through my diary. To be honest I don't think there's that much on for the next few weeks.'

She pulled her organiser out from her bag and ran a finger down the entries.

'Damn, I'm supposed to be giving a speech at the Cassar's dinner. I'd forgotten all about that . . .'

Ray waved her anxiety away. 'Don't worry, I'll sort it out,' he said between mouthfuls of shrimp. 'When is it? I'll make sure it's covered.'

'So you'll do it for me?'

Ray just stared at her.

'OK, OK,' she said, 'I know, I can't delegate – and I also know everything will be fine and you can manage perfectly well without me. Speeches and all.'

'Is there anything else?'

'I've also arranged to see several new suppliers—'

'Your new managerial puppy can do that. It'll give her something to cut her teeth on. Don't worry, I'll walk her through it. Just relax. Have you got any idea where you're going yet?'

Jayne shook her head. 'Nope, I thought I might just turn up at an airport and see what they've got on offer.' She looked up from the diary.

'Seriously?'

'That was how I did it last time. I just need to get going before it's too late.'

Ray smiled. 'I understand that, but trust me, it's not too late. And, Jayne?' There was a little pause as their eyes met, and then he leaned across the table and caught hold of her hand. 'It's going to be fine. This thing you've been looking for – I truly hope that you find it.'

Jayne touched her glass to his. 'Me too.'

Out in the High Street, and still around five minutes' walk away from Lorenzo's, Jane took a quick look in the window of a bookshop, which was the only one on the street with a window display dark enough to let her see her reflection. What the hell did you wear to a potential dot com job with a self-made woman and her right-hand man?

The suit Jane had bought in Next was great for the library but for Lorenzo's? Nope. After Jayne's phone call she'd spent what remained of the morning soaking away her hangover in a warm bath, plucking her eyebrows, rootling through her wardrobe, pressing things, lifting cat hairs off other things with masking tape, trying on endless combinations, knowing full well that whatever she chose it would feel wrong the minute she stepped out of the door.

And Gladstone – having missed his breakfast – was nowhere in sight, which also felt like a bad omen. And despite Lizzie's phone call there was no time to go through the folder of email she had forwarded from the library – not that Jane thought there was anything in there, whatever Lucy or Lizzie thought.

As the day was warm and sunny, the sky Wedgwood

blue with not a hint of a cloud, Jane had settled on a blue and cream linen skirt, T-shirt, short fitted cardigan, straw bag, and ballet pumps as her final choice. It had looked perfect when she left the house. She stared into the shop window and tried to get a real sense of whether it worked or not. Did it make her look ditsy? Too Doris Day, too Amelie? Too young? Too casual? Maybe she should have worn heels. Did heels say sexy and confident, or did flats say sensible and reliable? Horribly aware that she was running late, Jane tried standing on tiptoe to gauge the effect – maybe there was still time to nip into Stead and Simpson and buy a pair of high-heeled sandals – while forcing herself to calm down as she reminded herself for the umpteenth time that Jayne had already offered her a job.

She didn't have to impress anyone, except she felt she had to make Jayne feel she had made a good choice and make Ray feel . . . feel . . . what was it she had to make Ray feel? Jane grimaced. God, this was awful.

Jane turned left and then right to check her profile, and her bum, then sucked in her stomach and fluffed up her hair. Behind her two Chinese people watched intently – presumably they thought she was some kind of provincial street theatre. It was nearly one o'clock already.

Lorenzo's was set halfway along Brewer Street, up a flight of well-scrubbed steps, the front door flanked by two cone-shaped bay trees in terracotta pots, which made Jane wonder if the chef popped out first thing to pick a few leaves for the fish. Unlikely.

Inside the restaurant the walls were palest yellow, the black-and-white-tiled lobby giving way to plush duck-egg-blue carpets and an air of expensive tranquillity.

'How can I help you?' said a woman on the desk, whose expression suggested she could spot a Primark T-shirt and the wrong shoes in her sleep.

'I'm meeting someone.' The woman glanced down at her bookings list. 'Jane Mills?' Jane said

Like open sesame or shazam the name had the most amazing effect. 'Certainly, Miss Mills is already here,' she said. As she spoke the woman's smile warmed and she waved a boy in uniform over. 'Could you take – I'm so sorry I didn't catch your name?'

'Mills, Jane Mills,' Jane said quietly.

The smile faltered. 'Oh, so sorry, I thought you were here to *see* Jayne Mills.'

Jane nodded and blushed although she wasn't quite sure why. 'I am. Same name, it's all a bit confusing, sorry.'

The smile snapped back. 'Not at all. If you'd like to follow Terry, he'll take you through. Miss Mills is in the bar.' Jane did as she was told.

'There you are,' said a voice Jane recognised. Jayne Mills was on her feet before Jane was halfway across the room. She and a man in a suit were sitting at a table in a little bar area adjacent to the main dining room.

'I thought you might have had second thoughts,' Jayne said smiling broadly, catching firm hold of Jane's hand. 'Come and join us. Ray's already broken out the champagne to celebrate me finally buggering off and leaving him in peace.'

A waiter appeared with a third glass as Jayne made the introductions. 'Jane, this is Ray Jacobson, my right-hand man. Ray, this is Jane—'

Before anyone could come up with a definition of what Jane was, Ray clasped her hand in a firm presidential handshake. 'Hello, Jane,' he said warmly. 'Nice to meet you. Welcome aboard. I hope you'll be very happy with us. Jayne has just been telling me about you. We go back a long way, Jayne and I.'

'Let's not bother working out how long exactly,' Jayne joked. Jane smiled and nodded as the waiter filled up her champagne glass.

Ray was small – no more than five foot five or six, his broad shoulders giving the impression he was almost square. He looked as if he was in his fifties, hair thick and grey, combed back off strong features and a deeply tanned face. He wore a tight professional smile.

'I thought we'd break you in gently. I'm not sure how much Jayne has told you about her organisation but I do most of the hands-on administration, turning Jayne's bright ideas into reality and generally oiling the wheels of the corporate machine. We've never had anyone with us on the front line before but I'm sure we'll both rise to the occasion. Jayne suggested you might be able to start Monday morning. Maybe you'd like to spend a few days in the office to get the feel of the place before you hit the road.'

'Hit the road? But I thought it was Jayne who was hitting the road?' said Jane, looking from face to face, panicking, realising that the champagne was already rippling through her bloodstream like quicksilver, rehydrating the previous day's wrinkly dried-up alcohol molecules and that she hadn't had any breakfast and that she had no idea at all exactly what it was she had signed up for.

'True, but you're off to see new suppliers,' Ray was saying.

'I am?' Jane hissed.

Jayne grinned and patted her arm. 'Don't look so worried. It'll be fine. Come round to mine tomorrow morning. I'll talk you through my diary and explain what I do.' She giggled; obviously Jane wasn't the only one affected by the champagne. 'Actually, I suppose that as of now it's what *you* do.'

Ray smiled wolfishly. 'And then you can come and see me first thing on Monday morning and I'll show you how we make order out of madam's high-octane chaos.'

Jayne laughed, Jane didn't.

When Jane got back home at around three thirty the house was quiet, the cats sound asleep in the sunny garden. She put her bag on the kitchen counter and plugged in the kettle. Lunch hadn't been all that bad. And at least working for Jayne would give her something to tide her over until she worked out exactly what she wanted to do next.

Picking up the local paper Jane turned to the situations vacant column, slipped off her shoes, padded through to the sitting room and settled down on the sofa. Sunlight filled the room. She thought she might just close her eyes for a few minutes, not long . . .

When she opened them again it was almost nine. She yawned. No phone calls, no Lizzie, no Lucy, no Steve, no Mother. Maybe there was a God after all.

'So, what do I have to do exactly?' asked Jane the following morning, staring at the exquisite Apple G5 perched wirelessly on a slab of toning grey slate in Jayne's office, upstairs in the house in the Close. There was a picture of a tropical beach hut on the edge of an azure sea as a screensaver . . . and a date from a digital camera on the bottom right-hand corner.

Jayne slipped into the seat alongside her. 'First of all, try not to look so worried. It will give you wrinkles. The company is like a cross between being a landlord, owning a farm and running a department store. I collect rent from people whose websites I host.' Jayne clicked the mouse and the screensaver and straw huts dissolved into something altogether more work-ish. 'At least my company does. I employ a posse of geeks to keep that up and running. Then there is the purchasing department, various call centres to handle the ordering, and then I have a few sites of my own.' She clicked again. 'Here we are.' A pale cream page rolled across the computer screen with links to various companies. 'We sell all kinds of things – last-minute trips, organic produce, meat, wine and cheese delivered to your door. There's a catering company, kind of dial-a-decadent-dinner.com – your dinner party is just a mouse click away. Then there are flowers and plants. Animal sitting,' she looked across at Augustus, who was currently curled up on the windowsill, sound asleep, 'oh, and housekeeping. That's how I first met Gary. He applied for a job. Two or three guys showed up, all with great references. I took Gary at face value, working out the mileage in having an inscrutable oriental housekeeper for hire. I hadn't thought about him working for me. Anyway, as part of the interview I asked them all to cook me something. Comfort food after a long day, I said. Something that reminded them of home. I can't remember what the others did, but they missed the point completely. And then Gary whipped up a plate of pie and mash.' Jayne laughed. 'He said, "Ever been to Southend?" as he slid this tray in front of me.'

Jayne's smile held. 'And then he said, "And you want to get those shoes off, girl. I can see from here they're killing you." I hired him on the spot on a month's trial; we've never looked back.' Jayne paused and sighed. 'All seems a long time ago now,' she said. Jayne turned her attention back at the screen.

'OK, right, well, there are a couple of property sites, mostly executive houses and apartments, dealing with people who've been relocated by their companies and don't want the hassle of finding somewhere suitable either to rent or buy. We have a company that sorts out everything including the move, redirecting their post, setting up their utilities, the whole nine yards. Then there is an online furniture store and one that does really nice rugs, bed linen, and towels. Think of it as problem-solving for strangers.'

Jane stared at her. 'I thought you said this was simple.'

'It is when it's going all right. All the companies are more or less self-contained. Over the years it occurred to me that everything I have ever struggled with, everything that has been a total pain in the arse, is probably just as big a pain in the arse for other people, and so I set a company to sort it out, make life simpler and see how it worked. Some flew, some crashed and burned, some made money, some scraped by. Some were ahead of their time, some past their best-before date.' Jayne grinned as she scrolled down the screen. 'Oh, one thing you might be interested in . . .' She clicked the mouse. 'Here we are.'

Jane read over her shoulder. 'A dating agency?'

Jayne nodded. 'Uh-huh, men on tap.'

'If you've got access to all this how come you're still on your own?'

Jayne winced. 'To tell you the truth it's a bit like working in a chocolate factory. You stuff yourself silly for the first few weeks but after that the last thing you want is to pick anything off the conveyor belt, however tasty it looks.'

'You did to begin with, though?' asked Jane, running her eyes down the rows of thumbnail profile photos staring back at her from the computer screen.

Jayne nodded. 'Oh, yes, I completely pigged out.'

'Is that where you met Carlo?'

Jayne sighed. 'No. We met at a gallery owned by a friend of mine. It was only once I got Carlo out in public that I realised that he wasn't quite what he appeared – nice to look at but, my God, the running costs.' She laughed. 'Enough of that. Have you got any questions?'

Jane felt a wave of panic as she sat back. 'Only, are you stark staring mad? Are you seriously expecting me to run all this? I mean, it all sounds fantastic, it looks great – and I'm impressed – but I've had no real commercial experience.'

'It's not as complicated as it looks. Most of the companies are headed up by people who've worked for me for years. People I trust. Every six months we get together for a strategy meeting. I've just finished doing the rounds. Ray keeps his hand on the tiller – and a lot of my income comes from the servers, which are no trouble at all, and property, and there's an estate manager to deal with all that, so unless there is a huge crisis most of the work is really simple – and fun.'

'And if there is a crisis?'

'I'll be a phone call away.'

'Promise?'

'Promise.' Jayne nodded.

'How will I know if it is a crisis?'

Jayne laughed. 'Trust me, you'll know. But it'll be fine. For the last few years I've spent most of my time sourcing new suppliers, looking at new products, talking to producers and manufacturers – and most of them don't know me from Adam anyway, except by reputation, so you can do that. Use your initiative, pick things you like, things that you'd like to use or eat or wear, and don't be afraid to say no, or to ask if they can change it. I just need life to tick over till I get back. Ray will help until you get into the swing of things. He can give you some idea of how many of anything we're likely to shift, and what to pay and if they fit into the product range we've already got. All the business stuff. Just use your nose.'

Jane wasn't convinced her nose was that hot. 'And you're going to let everyone know you're away?'

Jayne paused. 'Actually I'd prefer not to. I was hoping to just slip away without a lot of fuss. They won't know – most of the time they barely see me as it is. We have an office locally. Ray runs the business on a day-to-day basis. Now, about your salary. I thought if initially we match the one at the library, plus say fifteen per cent and then review it after—'

Jane didn't move. 'You changed the subject.'

'I did?'

Jane nodded. 'You did.'

'OK, well, that's because I think that if everyone in the company thinks everything is running as normal then it will. If they know I've bunked off then they'll panic, think there is something going on, wobble, and then things *will* go wrong, things that are working just fine as they are at the moment.'

'I can see that, but what if they find out?'

'I can't see how they will, but if push comes to shove you can say I'm away on business if you want to. Oh, one other thing I was going to ask you. Most of the time I work from home so I wondered if would you consider moving in here while I'm away? You said you loved the house.'

'Really? Wow, I hadn't thought about it – I'm not sure, I've got the cats—'

'They could come here too. I'm sure Augustus wouldn't mind. And it would do me a colossal favour. Gary can look after you, which will keep him out of mischief, and it means I haven't got to worry about the place. You can use the cars. I'll make sure we insure them for you to drive. And it makes all kinds of other stuff straightforward. After all, J. Mills already lives here. I'll have Ray and the bank sort out cards and contracts and signatures. You'll need passwords to access the sites – have you got a pen?'

Jane stared at her. 'Are you completely barking mad?'

'Possibly, but you'll need all those things and don't worry, I'll have all the right people investigate you, take up references, check your credit history. Besides which, you won't be able to do anything critical without Ray's consent and probably his signature. And you won't have access to everything, just a housekeeping fund to keep the house running till I get back.'

Jane blanched. 'Seriously?'

'Seriously.'

'And when will that be?'

Jayne hesitated. 'I don't know, but don't worry. Ray is a good guy, but in some ways what I really need – and don't take this the wrong way – is a figurehead, a lucky penny. You're OK about taking this on? If not, say so. I've waited this long, another few months won't kill me . . .' Her voice faded.

Jane considered for a few seconds; the library had already emailed her a list of vacancies. Mrs Findlay had sent a sugary little message saying that she was there if Jane needed to talk and she could completely understand her distress and pain. Perhaps she might like to come in and discuss her feelings with someone in Human Resources?

Jane glanced at Jayne's computer screen, now back on the image of the tropical beach. What had she got to lose? Even if Jayne's job lasted only a couple of months it would be way cosier thumbing through the job ads here, with a regular pay cheque, than sitting at home without one. And wasn't this the kind of lifestyle she had always dreamed of? A fabulous house, wonderful furniture, great cars, a housekeeper – why on earth was she hesitating?

'Yes, yes, I'm fine about it. Just a bit nervous.'

'Well, don't be. When did your mother say she was coming?'

'As soon as she can pull herself out from under Simon, by the sounds of it.'

Jayne lifted an eyebrow but didn't comment. 'Well, when you've got it sorted out, ask Gary to get the guest room ready. He adores company.'

Jane looked round the elegant office with its view out over the garden, the lake, the deer. 'No. No, actually I think I'll tell her I'm too busy at the moment. I've never been a lucky penny before. And, to be frank, I'm not sure I'm ready for Simon, my mother and the whole Tantric sex conversation.'

Jayne laughed. 'Fair enough, but please, use the place as if it was your own. If you want her to come and stay, well, it's up to you. Meanwhile, what I suggest you do is go through the sites while I go and get us some coffee; they're all bookmarked. Get a feel for what the companies do and sell and handle. Ray can help you with anything you don't understand, and he knows which fork to use, even under pressure.'

Jane looked at the screen. 'If you've already got Ray why do you need me?'

Jayne paused thoughtfully. 'I don't know. In theory you're absolutely right, I could have stepped away from all this months ago – but I had this feeling that the time wasn't right, that *it* wasn't *the* moment but that I would know when to go. The other day when you turned up, it felt like some sort of sign. You having the same name – oh, I don't know, I just had a feeling, and like I said, over the years I've learned to trust my instincts, at least where business is concerned, so I feel like now is just perfect.'

'And while I'm busy trying not to ruin all this for you what are you going to be doing?' asked Jane.

'I want to make sense of what I missed first time around.'

'And what was that?'

'How would I know if I missed it?' Jayne laughed. 'OK, I suppose I was about your age; I'd done all kinds of dead-end jobs, saving furiously, saving up to travel. And then . . .' She paused.

'And then?'

'Well, I was backpacking with a guy named Andy Turner. I suppose it was in the early eighties. Anyway, we were sitting on a beach in Kos, sharing a couple of bottles of beer. Andy had built a fire out of driftwood and there was the sound of waves washing against the shore, night sounds, but otherwise we could have been the only two people on the planet. It was getting cold and I remember leaning back against him to keep warm and he put his jacket around me and then his arms. And as we watched the sun set over the ocean, as the light faded into this soft peach and purple glow he said, "Jayne, I want to ask you something."

'I knew what he was going to say. He held me closer. I can still remember looking over my shoulder and seeing the reflection of the fire in his eyes, and then he asked me to marry him.'

Jayne sighed. 'It has to have been the most romantic moment in my whole life, and then all of a sudden that wasn't what it felt like at all. Suddenly I could see this path stretching out in front of me. Andy's mum knew my mum – we'd grown up within a few miles of each other, been to the same school, had the same friends. And you know what? I panicked. I couldn't breathe. I just thought that there had got to be more to life than this – more than getting married and living a mile away from my mum and dad, taking turns to go round for Sunday lunch, and having kids and – and the sun set in the ocean. And he said, "So what do you think?" And I said, "No."'

'Wow.' Jane stared at her. 'And is that what you want to go back to, to that moment?'

'Good God, no,' said Jayne, heading towards the door, the moment broken. 'I'll go and get the coffee.'

'Oh,' Jane said, 'but it sounds so romantic. I thought you meant that you loved him and you wished you had married him and lived happily ever after, raising small Andy Turners a few miles from your mum and dad.'

Jayne shook her head wistfully. 'No – no, but there is a part of me that wishes I had been strong enough to say, yes I love you but I'm not ready to settle down yet and I need to explore some more – maybe we both do and how about we do it together? But things were different back then, or at least they were where I came from. I grew up in a little village near Ely, where, if you weren't engaged by the time you were sixteen they thought there was something wrong with you. My mum was convinced that I was on the shelf by the time I was twenty. And Andy wouldn't have seen it as a positive thing at all. He would have thought I was rejecting him, fobbing him off.'

'And were you?'

'No, looking back I don't think so. I just wanted more than what my mum and dad had settled for. It's so much easier now but then it was still a struggle for someone like me: a working-class woman, trying to build a business. And the other thing was, if I'm honest, I wasn't sure then that Andy was the one. I thought I'd be able to find just as much love somewhere else. And you know what?' She paused, her smile faltering just a fraction. 'I never did.'

'Oh, Jayne.'

Jayne waved the words away. 'Don't. It was entirely my own fault. I had it, I knew it, and I threw it away.'

'So what happened to Andy?'

'We carried on travelling together till the end of the trip and then when we got back he went off to a job in Manchester. We vaguely agreed that we'd travel together again sometime but I think we both knew we wouldn't. Last time I saw him was when I was waving him off at Euston. Ten minutes later I headed across London to Liverpool Street, went home and started my first business. Monday, the eighteenth of April 1983.'

'As?'

'Owner, only employee and chief cyclist of Sandwich City. Firms would ring their orders in before eleven thirty everyday and I'd pedal like hell round Cambridge to all kinds of offices and shops, with rolls and homemade soup in the winter, salads and stuff in the summer. With the profit I put a down payment on a house and converted it into flats for students.' Jayne grinned. 'My mum and dad thought I was totally mad but I just knew that it would work – and I wanted to be free and thought if I worked hard and got rich it would give me my freedom, give me choices, let me buy nice things.'

'And did it?'

'Most certainly it did. I built up the sandwich business, franchised it, sold that on. Met Ray – bought more houses. For the first few years it felt like Monopoly for real. I still get a buzz out of watching when it goes right.'

'And Andy?'

Jayne sighed. 'You know, I don't know. I suppose without meaning to, he got lost in the rush. At first we spoke a few times on the phone. He's still in Manchester some-where, an accountant. Happily married, probably, two point four children. God, he might even be a granddad by now. Lots of times I've thought about looking him up, contacting him. I mean, how hard would it be? And yet I can't quite bring myself to do it.'

'Why not?'

'Oh, I don't know. I've moved on, years have gone by. In my head he is still tall, blond, tanned and gorgeous. What if he's bald now – or fat? What if I made a terrible mistake back then? What if he never got over me? Worse still, what if he did?'

Chapter Four

Later that evening, 15 days, 4 hours and who gave a stuff exactly how many minutes it was since Lucy had detonated the bombshell under her life, Jane was back at home, sitting at her computer in Creswell Road, flicking through the list of eligible men on Jayne's personals site with Lizzie from the library for company. It was called Natural-Born_Romantics and Jayne was right, it was just like being let loose in a chocolate factory. It was just such a terrible shame that there were so many misshapes.

'So, you're going to be in charge of all this?' asked Lizzie in amazement, looking at the screen over Jane's shoulder while helping herself to one of the all-butter biscuits Jane kept on standby for emotional emergencies. 'Isn't it a bit like letting the lunatics run the asylum?'

'Always seemed to work OK in the library,' Jane said, clicking onto another web page.' Actually, I think I'm more of a figurehead – being groomed for greatness.'

'Right . . . But is it kosher? I'm mean, you will be paid and things?'

'Oh, yes, it is most definitely a real job with real money, and I really start on Monday morning. Oh my God, will you just look at the state of him?'

'And you can get on to all the sites?'

'I've got one password that just lets me browse and then I've got two others that let me tinker.'

'I'm impressed. Tinkering is good.'

'Tinker *and* order.'

Lizzie grinned. 'Can we order a selection?'

Lizzie had dropped in on her way home from work, the plan being to commiserate with Jane and get her up to speed on all the latest intrigue at the library. Apparently Jane's folder-and-fish-tank trick had impressed everyone in Janitorial Services, which meant – even in her absence – she was likely to come top in the employee-of-the-month poll. Lucy Stroud was a paranoid power-crazed two-faced cow who liked to keep a posse of novelty bears on her desk, and thought most of the community weren't worth outreaching to, her preferred solution being culling, and she'd made Lizzie go out and buy the lunchtime sandwiches two days running. Janitorial Services already had a lavatory seat laurel wreath hanging up in their tea room with Lucy's name painted on it. On a less personal front, all the staff were terrified that they were going to lose their jobs, despite a meeting meant to allay fears, which had actually made everyone more paranoid. And there were so many rumours going around about who would be next in the firing line that normal work – other than stamping dates in the in-and-out sections downstairs – had all but ceased. There were so many people watching their backs it was a miracle people weren't falling downstairs, and nobody was taking decisions at all about anything, just in case. So, no change there really.

'So, from where I'm standing it looks like you've actually fallen on your feet,' said Lizzie, picking a troublesome crumb out of her cleavage.

'Got to be better than falling on him,' said Jane, staring at the screen. 'Golly, it says here that he's only thirty-five.'

Lizzie peered at the image and winced. 'Maybe that's in dog years or maybe in a universe far, far away. You'd think he'd get something done about his teeth.'

'Possibly get some? Whichever way you look at it, gummy is not a hot look, is it?'

'How long are you going to spend checking the stock?' asked Lizzie.

'Long as it takes. It's dirty work but someone's got to do it. Why? Oh, look, he's not bad.'

'I'm hungry. I was going to suggest we rang for a takeaway.' Lizzie picked up a menu from the desk. 'Oh, have you had a chance to look through the email that Lucy was so worried about?'

Jane nodded. 'I've had a quick flick through the file before you got here, but I can't see anything she would want, or worry about. Although there were several veiled threats regarding the amount of coloured copier paper we were using.'

Lizzie shrugged. 'Don't worry, she is weird. Oh, he's nice – there, the one in the middle without a squint.'

'I'm supposed to be going through all this lot so I'm up to speed on the kind of things Jayne is involved in.' Jane nodded towards a pile of box files and two ring binders on the sofa. 'I've got those to plough through and then the websites. I'm just hoping that there isn't going to be a test at the end.'

'So what else have you looked at so far?'

Jane grinned. 'Younger men, older men. I haven't got as far as the rugs and curtains, and dinners delivered in dry ice yet.'

'And are you really going to move into her house then?'

'Jayne's? I'm not sure. It makes sense. All the business stuff is over there in her office, but it feels odd moving into a house full of someone else's things. Like camping out. Mind you, you should see it – it's like something off *Grand Designs* – low lighting, good furniture, acres of bare boards and wonderful rugs – the odd sculpture here, original painting there – lots of natural fibres. I don't think I'd be able to relax in case I spilled something. Or one of the cats threw up on the Berber kelims. Although I have to say cruising around in a soft-top Mercedes has a certain appeal.'

Lizzie considered the idea for a few minutes. 'You get someone to clean, cook and all that stuff too?'

Jane nodded. 'Uh-huh. He's small, oriental, sort of dangerous-looking in an underplayed kung fu way, and called Gary. Did you ever see that film with Peter Sellers – *Inspector Clouseau*?'

'I think you should give it a try. I'm sharing a house at the moment and it's driving me mad. The idea of someone else clearing up behind me and the animals I live with sounds like heaven. And I could always come and live here while you're away if you wanted. Mind the fort for you.'

Jane looked at her. 'Really?'

'Why not? Why risk Boris or Milo hocking up a fur ball on a priceless rug? It would be brilliant. I could feed the cats, water the plants. And I'd pay you rent.' Lizzie was warming to the idea.

'And you could always do a little window-shopping on Natural-Born_Romantics if you got bored.'

'Really?'

'I don't see why not. Feel free to take the tour – oh, and you could feed Gladstone.'

Lizzie sniffed. 'Oh God, do I have to? He was fishing something out of the skip when I got here.'

'I know – such activities are part of his natural charm. Besides, if you don't he just grazes through the leftovers in your dustbin, which is far worse, trust me.'

Lizzie pulled a face. 'That is just so gross. Which reminds me, did I mention Mrs Findlay is planning to get in touch? She said she was hoping that you'd still be coming back and letting Lucy shadow you for a few weeks.'

'Don't you mean stalk?' said Jane, helping herself to a biscuit.

Meanwhile, in her flat in Buckbourne Lucy Stroud was in the bath, in a face pack, shaving her legs, waiting for Steve Burney to pop by for his regular Wednesday evening visit. She'd got a big pot of Greek yoghurt, a punnet of raspberries and a pair of handcuffs on standby. She would have liked to talk to him about Jane Mills but decided she might wait until after the main event.

In Creswell Close Jayne Mills, accompanied by Augustus, had been up in the loft looking for her old rucksack. She knew that she'd seen it somewhere; whenever she moved house it came with her like a touchstone. The night was as black as ink through the dormer windows, the stars like fishscales in a dark ocean. Jayne opened the floor-to-ceiling cupboards, eyes wandering along the rails of

71

clothes, across the shelves, past winter coats, boxes of books, her record collection, lampshades and things stored and saved just in case. In one cupboard was a pile of cartons stuck down with brown tape and carefully labelled 'Store/Sentimental'. Each label was topped with a big red stick-on heart.

Jayne smiled and lifted the top one down. Inside the box was a photo album covered in battered fawn leatherette, labelled '1980–83'. Tucked inside the cover were all sorts of letters and cards and tickets and things she had completely forgotten about. Very carefully Jayne carried everything downstairs to the sitting room, poured herself a large gin and tonic, and settled down on the sofa. Augustus took his cue, curled up in the box lid, and went to sleep, purring softly.

On the first page, sitting on a rucksack almost as big as she was, was a younger, leaner, far skinnier Jayne Mills wearing cut-off jeans, hiking boots, a long-sleeved paisley T-shirt and a toothy grin that stretched from one ear to the other. The caption, written in big bold rounded hand-writing, read, 'Finally – we're off!!'

Jayne felt a lump in her throat and turned the page. It was going to be a long night.

Bright and early the following Monday morning Jane Mills pressed the call button on the security panel below an elegant brass plaque that read, 'Waterside House. J. Mills Enterprises'.

'Hi, it's Jane Mills here,' she said into the speaker. Looking up into the single unblinking eye of the CCTV camera Jane smiled brightly to hide a flicker of nerves. She had spent Wednesday, Thursday and Friday reading and taking notes from the websites and box files and Googling up on Jayne Mills' business style and practice. Intuitive, perceptive, hands-on, and robust with a good management philosophy seemed to be the general consensus. Saturday and Sunday she had pined for Steve Burney, his cooking, his company and his bloody Labrador.

Jane squared her shoulders. Intuitive, perceptive, hands-on – she could do that. Jane had decided on her suit today – it seemed right.

There was a little whirr and then the heavy plate-glass door silently glided open. Jane stepped into the elegant flag-stoned foyer of the converted granary, with its view out over the canal. It was only a few minutes' walk from Buckbourne town centre and full of original features, soft red brick and oak beams mellow with age. It was hard not to be impressed.

Seconds later, Ray Jacobson, dressed in a white polo shirt, penny loafers and faded blue jeans, jogged down the steps to meet her, looking as if he was fresh out of the shower. 'Hi, morning. Did you find us OK?' he said. He looked younger out of his suit, and today was all smiles and warm handshakes. 'Come on up, great to see you, coffee's on.'

'I can smell it. I've never noticed this place before.'

'Beautiful, isn't it? Tucked out of the way but still really central.' Ray, guided Jane inside. 'One of Jayne's bright ideas. She bought it as a shell a few years ago. The ground floor we rent out to a whole range of alter-native practitioners. The first floor is mostly offices for Jayne's business interests, and then I use the top-floor flat when I'm in town. Takes working from home to a whole new level. Come on through.' He smiled, opening the inner door into the stairwell and stood to one side to let Jane pass. Through tall thin windows that ran from the floor right up to the pitched roof, the warm morning sunlight reflected and shimmied across the water in the canal, filling the well with glittering golden ripples.

'I'll make sure you've got the security code for next time you're in. Did you take a look at the files and the websites?' Ray asked as they made their way upstairs.

'I did, every last one of them. I'm still not altogether sure why Jayne wants me here.'

Ray's smile broadened out a notch or two. 'Ours is not to reason why. Jayne's got a nose for talent. I think we should just both relax and just get on with it. This is the office.'

As they reached the landing he pushed open a door into a warm sunlit room. Inside the walls were unfinished brick, the floor gorgeous old, time-mellowed oak floor-boards, and on two long wooden trestle tables stood a row of flat screens, a couple of wireless keyboards and matching mice, with an office chair at each. On the opposite wall in a deep alcove with a view out over the canal, were two cream linen sofas with brown suede cushions and a long low table, on which stood a bowl of pebbles and a vase of lilies. Behind it was a wooden cupboard in the same style with a coffee machine on top.

Jane smiled appreciatively. 'Wow. This is amazing. How on earth do you keep it looking so tidy? Where do you keep everything else? You know – all the chaos. The muck and bullets?'

Ray laughed. 'Oh, don't worry, we've got plenty of those – they're all in the back room. If you'd like to help yourself to coffee and pull up a chair, I'll just be going through a couple of things that I thought you might do over the course of the next couple of weeks and then my plan is leave you to it. You can work here or at Jayne's home office – either is fine by me, although to be honest I'm not used to having someone about the place. We outsource all our services, and I don't usually see Jayne from one week to the next. We lunch a couple of times a month if she's in the area but we usually communicate by phone or email. We talk most days.' Ray shifted his weight as if he was slightly uncomfortable with what he was telling her.

'So what you're saying is that you would prefer me to work from home?' Nothing like being wanted. Jane managed to hold on to her smile. Just.

He pulled a face. 'Her home, actually. Jayne's office is all set up with everything you'll need. It would be far easier than coming into town every day. Anyway – your call. Maybe if you wanted to come in until you get the hang of things . . .' He moved the mouse alongside the nearest computer and the screen flickered into life.

'Anyway, here we are. We've got new web pages and catalogues going live at the end of the month on all the current sites. Most of the donkey work has been done by our design team, graphic artist and the geeks, but I thought you could go through them – see what you think, any suggestions, you know, any little tweaks and see if there are any errors. I'd value your input.'

Jane stared at him, trying to work out if he was telling her what she thought he was saying. 'You want me to proofread the web pages? I've just spent all weekend going through the existing websites.'

'I know, bit of a pain in the arse but these are the new

shop fronts and I really do need someone with a bit of savvy to check them over. Feel free to make any suggestions. Might seem like the bottom rung, but actually I think it will give you a really good feel for what's current and up and coming.' He smiled brightly.

Jane nodded. It wasn't that she minded doing it, but she couldn't work out why he or Jayne hadn't told her that the websites she'd spent hours going through were about to be taken down – nor whether he was being serious or taking the mickey – so she smiled back and then turned her attention to the images.

'And then,' Ray said, biting his bottom lip as he stared at the screen, then clicking on a button, 'we're also currently in the process of updating all of our current customer records and product codes. There's all kinds of information on the data base that needs sifting through. We've outsourced most of the data entry but it's really important we go through all the customer details as well as the list of products we sell, and check nothing vital has been missed off. It would be really useful to cross-reference the information to see if people are buying from more than one site and, if so, what. There's a little bit of software here for that. Oh, here we are . . .'

Ray looked back over his shoulder at her and smiled again, all big blue eyes and bonhomie. Jane still couldn't quite call it one way or the other.

'Let's just sort out that coffee and then we can get you started. Oh, by the way, I've had our guys draw up your contract and there are a few other things for you to sign. There are different levels of access online. Jayne's got most clearance obviously – presumably she set you up with a username and password?'

Jane nodded.

Ray paused. 'Good. How are you fixed for supper?'

She stared at him. 'I'm sorry?'

'I thought we might pop out after work today for an early supper. I booked us a table at Carters – thought it would be nice to celebrate your launch.'

'Well . . .' Jane began.

'Nothing too late – say six thirty?'

Jane didn't know quite how to respond. Which Ray took as a yes.

'Good. Oh, and while we're on the subject of food, Jayne is supposed to be going to a dinner later in the week – Thursday, I think. You don't mind going, do you? I think she's expected to do a little presentation. I've got the script here somewhere. It's just a trade thing.'

Jane hesitated but was determined not to look rattled or outgunned. 'Oh – OK . . . I've done presentations before at the library. But I'm not sure that I can . . .'

'It'll be fine. I'll email the speech over to you with the details. I wouldn't labour the point about Jayne not being there.' He paused. 'I'm sure she's already told you that she's a little wary about letting people know she's taking a sabbatical so unless someone asks directly . . .' He smiled. 'Although I suppose technically you are Jane Mills.'

'Will you be there?' asked Jane.

'If I can, but it looks like I'm probably double-booked. It'll be fine though. They'll send a car for you.' He smiled again. 'So here we are – your first day with us.'

Jane nodded; her first day as a junior officer, she thought ruefully looking at the screen Ray had opened up on the computer. Data input, checking names and addresses was a bit like stuffing envelopes, and that, along with the proofreading, was the kind of thing you'd give someone on work experience from the local comprehensive. She felt she couldn't say anything, however. After all, how would it look if she moaned about the first job he gave her?

Something didn't feel right but she wasn't sure what. Maybe it was that she was feeling overwhelmed. Or maybe it was just first-day nerves; maybe she was up herself; maybe Ray was being genuinely kind – maybe. He poured her a coffee from the machine.

'There we go. Milk's in the fridge. That's the thing that looks like a cupboard under the coffee machine, and sugar is in the drawer there. Do you mind if I smoke?' As he passed her the cup his hand seemed to linger for just an instant too long on hers. Had she imagined it? Jane suppressed a shiver.

'No, you're fine,' she said.

Ray's smile held. 'Not cold are you, m'dear?'

'No, just a bit nervous, that's all. First-day nerves – you know.'

'Well, don't be nervous. We run a very happy ship here. Jayne's always seen to that. I don't know how well you know her but she is the most amazing woman.'

Jane added a little milk to her coffee, not quite sure what he was expecting her to say.

As if reading her mind he continued, 'I know what I've asked you to do looks like pretty menial stuff but as far as I'm concerned your being hired has come out of the blue – not that I mind; oh, no, with Jayne I've had to learn to be flexible – but if I'd known Jayne was bringing someone in we could have devised a more coherent strategy. So, this will help you suss out Jayne's business until we work out exactly what to do with you. To be perfectly honest I don't really know how she fills her time on a day-to-day basis, so if you start with something that really needs doing, we're both going to have to make the rest of it up as we go along.'

He lifted his coffee cup in salute. 'To the new Jane Mills.'

Jane tried out another smile and Ray beamed back. Maybe she was being oversensitive, worried that the job was too good to be true. Maybe it was going to be all right after all.

'To the other Jayne Mills,' she said.

Meanwhile, the other Jayne Mills set her handbag down on one of the unforgiving airport seats and stared up at the departure board to check the flight times. She felt strangely nervous. Although she'd been flying round the world for the best part of twenty-five years, this flight felt special. She smiled. Twenty-five years – it seemed impossible. Then she had never imagined herself ever being this old.

The airport clock rolled over another minute. Another fifteen minutes and they would start boarding. Jane tucked the boarding pass into her jacket pocket and then glanced over her shoulder, half expecting to see Andy loping towards her through the crowd, in his famous baggy blue shorts, a rucksack slung casually across broad shoulders, long blond hair flapping like unruly wings. Catching herself, Jayne smiled and let the ghost fade away. There was no Andy, no long blond hair, just an appraising and appreciative look from a good-looking guy in a suit from behind a copy of the *Telegraph*.

She smiled back while reminding herself that this

wasn't about the past, it was about the future. Her future. A bright shiny new future. This was about looking at where she had been to try to make sense of where she wanted to go next, and where better place to start than in Kos?

Kos – Jayne let the word linger in her mind and then very slowly roll over her tongue. It was a word heavy with memories of newly baked bread, and honey and olives and creamy feta cheese. Kos, so very ordinary now, but so unfamiliar then. Hardly a great adventure, hardly exotic in the twenty-first century, but all those years ago it had seemed so very far away, and so very foreign. Now it was just another short-haul flight, barely a hop across a globe that she had crossed and recrossed God knew how many times since. But then it had seemed a million miles away for a hick from the sticks.

So, while Greece might not appear the bravest of starts to an outsider, it had been the first step on her journey all those years ago, so what better place to start again now?

In a homage to travels past she had booked into economy class, and having toyed with the idea of taking pot luck on arrival, in the end had succumbed and booked into a little hotel in Kefalos old town, at the far end of the island of Kos, a steep climb away from the night life and the bars.

The taxi dropped her off at her hotel in late afternoon, and once she had booked in Jayne dropped her things in her room, and made her way back down the hill, down steep flights of steps to the beach, past the little church with its white walls, pale blue dome and roof, surrounded by trees and a field of what looked like cotton. Everywhere was remarkably green, despite the heat, the steep hillsides covered in low bushes and shrubs that followed the sharp rocky contours of the bay. She had forgotten how breath-taking the view was.

Below the old town of Kefalos, new bars and tourist restaurants lined the beach like a string of bright beads, colourful flotsam and jetsam stranded at the high-water mark, and windsurfers and sailing dinghies cut back and forth across the glittering water on the edges of the sun-warmed wind.

Once she got onto the coarse gritty sand Jayne slipped off her sandals and walked along the water's edge, down past the sleeping cafés and shady restaurants, down past the boat-hire shops towards a little island caught in the curled arm of the bay. Although the sun was well past its zenith it was still wonderfully warm, the waves reflecting the sunlight like the shards of a broken mirror.

The beach was completely empty except for a handful of locals swimming and windsurfing on the wind-ruffled sea where the harbour met the beach.

Jayne stretched, relishing the sensation of the warm breeze on her face, dropped her towel onto the sand and, slipping off her sandals and thin cotton dress, stepped naked into the welcoming water. Not that anyone saw or cared.

It felt like a cool caress over her body and was the perfect antidote to the long wait at the airport, the flight and the taxi ride from Kos town to her hotel. Jayne sighed and shimmied beneath the waves, the chill making her shiver, and then very slowly she rolled over onto her back, looking up into the cloudless azure blue sky. Kos. Still here after all these years. It felt as if her soul was slowly uncurling. She smiled, with an odd sense of coming home. It had been a good choice.

*　　*　　*

In Buckbourne, Ray helped himself to another olive from the little dish on the table and smiled. The restaurant was quiet.

'So, why don't you tell me some more about yourself?' he asked. 'What sort of things do you enjoy?'

Jane blinked as he carried on topping up her wine glass. She didn't make a habit of drinking straight after work and this was her second, but after a day spent crosschecking names and addresses and postcodes for customers with special interests, unusual delivery instructions and various complaints, she hadn't refused when Ray suggested they share a bottle and a toast to her first day with the company. The first glass had slipped down nicely, and – with Jane having had only a sandwich for lunch – had gone straight to her head.

'Jayne tells me that you worked in the library before joining us. What brought you to the area? Is your partner local?'

The glasses seemed big and Jane was almost certain Ray hadn't topped his up.

'No, actually I don't have one,' Jane heard herself saying. It felt like he was asking way too many questions anyway. 'Not at the moment.'

'Really? I find that very hard to believe,' said Ray, beckoning the waiter over. Since they had arrived the menus had sat unopened between them on the table.

'Actually I've just come out of a relationship,' Jane said, not meeting his eye.

'Really? Ah, well, may I offer my condolences. But you know what they say about getting back in the saddle. I'm sure you won't have any trouble finding a replacement,' Ray said brightly.

Jane stared at him. He made Steve sound like a washing machine.

'Now, what do you fancy? The seafood here is absolutely superb.' He barely paused for breath. The waiter stood by the table, with his pen hovering over a pad, and Ray's next remarks were aimed squarely at him.

'How about we start with the goat's cheese soufflé – for two – and then we'll have the paella. And I think we'll have another bottle of white with that – the Chenin Blanc – and salad, maybe the green salad with poached nectarines – that sounds rather nice, don't you think?'

It was entirely a rhetorical question. Jane stared across the table at him; she hadn't even had a chance to look at the menu, let alone choose. Meanwhile, the waiter was busy scribbling down the order, and far from feeling flattered or protected or in safe hands, Jane felt annoyed – or at least she would have been if it hadn't been for the wine. Before she could protest the waiter had vanished off towards the kitchen.

'Now,' said Ray leaning a little closer, 'where were we? Oh, I know, you were going to tell me all about what brought you to Buckbourne.'

'Was I?' snapped Jane.

Ray laughed. 'I can see why Jayne thought you'd fit in,' he said.

Jane stared at him, wondering what the hell he was going on about.

The meal was delicious but he seemed odd. For a start Ray appeared to be totally enthralled by her every word. He insisted she have a liqueur after dinner, and although Jane declined she had a strange feeling that there was booze in the coffee. This was hardly the nice shiny start she had anticipated. Looked like getting drunk during the day was getting to be a habit.

'How about I call you a cab?' Ray said while he was settling the bill. 'Unless of course you'd prefer to come back to the office and have some coffee? You look like you could use some.'

Jane hesitated for a moment or two as Ray waved the waiter over to take his card.

Chapter Five

Jane very, very slowly opened her eyes, struggling to get her bearings. It was almost dark and she had the most terrible hangover. Even her eyelashes ached. Although as she looked around the room it occurred to her that that might very well be the least of her worries. Oh my God, moaned a voice in her head, when she found she was naked in a strange bed in a strange room with the headache from hell.

Oh my God, oh my God, screamed her conscience, never one to hold back on melodrama when the occasion warranted it. Surely to goodness she hadn't gone back to the office with Ray? Surely, even given her patchy track record *vis-à-vis* men she hadn't ended up stark naked and blind drunk in the boss's bed on her first day in a new job? Surely not.

Jane scurried through her memories, trying desperately to recall exactly what had happened. She could remember the wine, remember eating supper, remember coffee, although that was slightly fuzzier, remembered thinking she felt sick – hopefully she hadn't been. And then? And then . . . nothing.

Surely she couldn't have slept all night? She ought to get up. She ought to get up, get dressed and go home.

Jane looked around for her clothes and spotted her suit and blouse hanging neatly over the back of a chair under which were tucked her shoes. Did seducers hang up your clothes? And where the hell was her underwear? Was it clean? Did it match? While her brain busied itself panicking over trivia she heard footfalls on the stairs.

'Oh my God,' whimpered her conscience. 'Oh my God . . .' It took Jane a second or two to realise it wasn't her conscience but her whimpering aloud.

She fought the temptation to hide under the duvet, while across the room the door swung slowly open.

'So you're awake then?' said Gary. He was carrying a tray on which a glass of something opaque and white hissed and bubbled. Beside that stood a pot of tea. 'You still drunk?'

Jane was torn between resenting his tone and wanting to hug him. Gary didn't wait for an answer. 'Drink this and have a shower. I'll get you something to eat. There's a robe, and everything else you'll need is in the bathroom.'

'How did I end up here?'

'Because there is a God,' said Gary grimly, plumping the pillows behind her as if Jane was an invalid. 'That and the cab driver dropping you off. You were completely off your face. Oh, and before you ask, you undressed yourself. I just tidied up behind you. Has anyone ever told you you're a messy cow?'

'I thought I'd gone home with Ray,' Jane said, concentration elsewhere.

Gary glanced down at her. 'I must be a terrible disappointment.'

'God, no – no, not at all. I just can't believe I got that

drunk. I don't think I've ever done anything like that in my life before. I don't know how I'm going to face him.' And then she paused as a thought blossomed, closely watched by Gary. 'You know, I think he got me drunk.'

'You don't say?' said Gary, in a voice heavy with sarcasm.

Jane stared at him. 'Why didn't Jayne warn me?'

Gary shrugged. 'Who knows? Maybe she thought you two would be perfect for each other.'

Once Gary had gone, Jane very gingerly eased herself out of bed, head pounding, put on the bathrobe and looked at herself in the mirror. Her hair was all over everywhere, her skin looked awful and her eyes looked worse. Much worse. She considered the row of expensive unguents and creams lined up on the dressing table for a few seconds and then padded silently into the bathroom, turned the shower on full, hung the robe on the door and stepped under the warm bubbling torrent. It hurt. She stood for a long time in the shower, willing it to wash her hangover away.

'You drowned yet?' called a familiar voice after ten minutes or so.

Jane swung round, instantly regretting moving so fast. Jayne's elegant *en suite* had been built as a wet room, with a big daisy-head shower and a bluey green obscure glass block wall snaking across the room, separating the shower area from the rest of the bathroom. Gary, looking rather like a benign bat through the distortion of the glass, was on the far side clutching the huge fluffy white robe.

'No, but I wish I had. Have you never heard of invasion of privacy? Do you know you're worse than my mother?' she said, reaching around the glass partition and taking the robe.

'Pity you didn't take more notice of her then, accepting drinks from strange men. Anything could have happened.'

'Rather naïvely I didn't think Ray was a stranger,' Jane snapped right back, slipping the robe on and tying it tight. It was warm as well as being thick and velvety.

'In my experience they don't come much stranger than Ray Jacobson.'

'Now you tell me,' she said, padding out through the bubbly water. 'He's Jayne's right-hand man. She said so.'

Gary rolled his eyes heavenwards. 'Um, yes – Jayne's got a blind spot when it comes to certain people, Ray being one of them.'

'I've got to work with him.'

'You should work from here. That way I can keep an eye on you.'

'Thanks for the vote of confidence. Have you told Jayne about Ray?'

'She thinks it's just sibling rivalry. They've been together for so long that they finish each other's sentences. Years. Too many years for her to have any sense of perspective.'

'Romantically?'

'Good God no, he likes his meat young and tender.' As he spoke Gary lifted an eyebrow.

'That is disgusting.'

'He doesn't seem to think so. His last serious girlfriend was nineteen.'

'Yuck. Because . . . ?' said Jane, taking the towel Gary handed her for drying her hair.

'Because any woman over thirty-five can see straight through him. He's all slime, style and no substance.'

'And you're telling me this *because*?'

Gary shrugged. 'Because Jayne won't listen to me. And besides, he's more likely to jump you.'

Jane groaned. 'Oh, please, don't. I'm feeling delicate enough as it is.'

'Although actually you're probably a little long in the tooth for him,' Gary continued, looking her up and down.

Jane glowered at him, or at least would have done if it hadn't made her headache worse.

'Then why did he get me drunk?'

'He probably pulls the wings off flies as well. Food is in fifteen minutes,' said Gary, on his way out of the door.

'I've already eaten.'

He pulled a face.

'What?' asked Jane, gently towelling around her hangover.

'You don't remember being sick?'

Jane groaned. 'Oh, no, don't.'

When she had finished getting dressed Jane headed downstairs. As she crossed the landing she hesitated. Jayne's office door was ajar.

Jane opened the door wider still, stepped inside and looked around. The room was awash with mellow starlight.

Although she had seen it the previous week it felt different now – calmer, more peaceful. So this was where Jayne worked; this was where Jane could work and live if she wanted to. She switched on a lamp, the room instantly warmed by its soft golden glow, and then gently ran her fingertips over the broad slate desktop. The room was painted the softest cream, with a natural coir carpet and matching linen full-length curtains, pulled back wide to reveal as much of the view out over the park as possible.

Beyond the picture windows in the moonlight, the herd of deer were gathering around the lakeside, the rippling water backed by a stand of trees picked out in silhouette against the skyline. It was an image that wouldn't have looked out of place on a painting.

Around the room there were cupboards to waist height along one wall, neatly arranged with books and stationery, and box files neatly labelled. Above them hung a Tabitha Salmon painting of gondolas on the lagoon in Venice and a whole gallery of photographs.

Along the other two sides of the room on the slate desk-tops stood plants, books and catalogues, and Jayne's Apple Mac. The final wall, with its two large picture windows, was empty, although the deep windowsills were uphol-stered and had a scatter of gold, blue and red cushions picking up the colours in the painting. Jane looked around, drinking it all in. Working here just had to be better than driving into town every day by about a million miles.

She switched on the lamps above Jayne's workstation. On the pin board above the desk, between a couple of post-cards and some theatre tickets, was a faded black-and-white photo with curled edges; it was of a good-looking guy with shoulder-length blond hair and a smile that lit up his face like a spotlight. It was impossible not to smile back. Without thinking Jane reached out and took the photo down. On the back someone had written, 'Andy Turner, Beach-Bum of the Year 1982'. Jane's smile broadened. So this was the man Jayne had run away from. Hard to see why. He was beautiful in a rugged way, and had the kindest eyes.

'So there you are,' said Gary, making Jane jump. 'What do you think then?' he said, indicating the room.

'It's beautiful.'

'I think you'll be happy as a hog in biscuits here,' he said. 'But don't mind me. Your chop's congealing.'

Jane nodded, not wanting to say that she felt so hung over that she would rather gnaw her own leg off than eat anything, particularly something greasy. She shuddered. 'I'll be down in a couple of minutes.'

Once Gary was out of the room Jane propped Andy's photo where she could see him and made a decision. Wasn't this just the kind of life she had always dreamed of living? Realistically a chance like this would probably never come her way again. She picked up the phone and tapped in a local number. 'Hi, Lizzie? Is it too late to ring?'

'No, the animals are out and I'm watching the big TV in peace. Are you all right? You sound rough,' said Lizzie.

'Thanks for noticing.'

'Flu?'

'The hangover from hell.'

'Really? So tell me all about it. How did your first day of being groomed for greatness go? Did you get pissed to celebrate or to forget?'

'Don't ask. I was just ringing to see if your offer of house-sitting was for real?'

'Oooo, hang on, let me turn the TV down. Yes, it most certainly is. When I came home from work today someone had eaten all my bread, finished off the milk, leaving the carton in the fridge door *and* broken into my extremely expensive organic yoghurt collection. Besides which, the whole place smells like a hamster cage. Why, when do you want me to start?'

'Now would be good.'

'Really? Are you sure?'

'Uh-huh – although I realise it's late. Maybe tomorrow.'

'No, no, now is just fine. They've just gone down the pub for a quick pint and then apparently it's back for a PS2 session, and I'm not sure just how much more Lara Croft I can cope with. Are you all right? Where are you?'

'I'm over at Jayne's house at the moment. I just don't think I'm going to make it home tonight.'

'Oh, really?' Lizzie purred. 'That sounds more like it. You need to find a bit of a diversion to get you over the Steve the bastard Burney thing. Who's the lucky man? Anyone we know? Oh, no, don't tell me you found someone on that website?'

'Nice try, but no, no one at all. I just got caught up in what I was doing,' Jane lied. 'You know how it is. Do you know where my spare key is?'

'Under the chipped dwarf at the end with the red hat, the one that looks like he's on drugs?'

'If you could let yourself in and feed the mogs. The food is in the cupboard under the sink. And I'll be back tomorrow some time to pick some stuff up.'

'You're serious about this? About me house-sitting?'

'Yes. It makes more sense if I'm going to work from here. Oh, and there is some ham and Branston pickle in the fridge for Gladstone's sandwiches tomorrow morning.'

'I thought you said we were going to go into the office every day?'

For a few seconds Jane considered the prospect of going back to spend more time with Ray and then shook her head. 'No, I don't think so. This will work just fine if you're happy to mind the fort.'

'Happy? I'm bloody ecstatic. Presumably you don't want me to pass your whereabouts on to the library.'

'Not if you want to house-sit.'

'Consider it done. The noise you can currently hear is me throwing my smalls into a holdall.'

Meanwhile, in Kos, in a beachside café, under the shimmering light of a string of tiny silver lanterns and the starry night sky, the other Jayne Mills had finished her supper of grilled fish stuffed with fresh herbs, served up with a green salad and a carafe of house wine. It was the end of a long, long day. Blissfully tired, Jayne watched the world go by, toasting the sounds of the sea, while enjoying a little light flirtation with a gorgeous waiter who was no more than nineteen if he was a day.

Along the strand, families and couples wandered by, hand in hand, side by side. Jayne sighed. It was perfect. The night wind carried the sounds of a band from somewhere further down the coast, the lilting rhythm of horns accompanied by laughter and the soporific rolling breath of the sleepy ocean.

Jayne caught a cab back to the hotel, carrying her sandals in one hand. She opened the shutters in her room to let the warm velvet darkness in before falling into a deep dreamless sleep.

In Buckbourne Jane was woken at seven the following morning by Augustus, Jayne's cat, leaping onto the bed, followed seconds later by Gary handing her a glass of orange juice and waving the phone under her nose. The cat stared at her, eyes narrowing as if wondering who she was and why she was in his bed.

'Who is it?' Jane mouthed as she sat up, rubbing her eyes. They still ached.

'Ray.'

'Ray?' Jane stifled a moan; she had hoped it might be Jayne. Gary put the handset down on the bedside table and flicked it on to speakerphone.

'Hi,' said a bright, cheery and far from hung-over voice. 'Just thought I'd ring to see how you were this morning. Hope you didn't mind me calling so early but I wondered if you were planning on coming in to the office today, only I've got an eight o'clock breakfast meeting.'

'No,' said Jane more firmly than she meant to. 'No, I think I'll take your advice and work from Jayne's place. It makes more sense.'

'Great. In that case I'll email next week's schedule over to you. Gary told me you'd been up for hours. Working out, in the gym, fantastic. Important to keep in shape if you want to get on in life.'

Jane stifled another groan while on the far side of the bedroom Gary, who was busy opening the curtains, shrugged philosophically.

'If you have any problems, just call me or leave a message on my machine. I don't want you to feel that you've been left out in the cold. I've added some notes and the door codes on the email I've just sent that I thought might help. OK?' Ray was saying.

'Great,' said Jane as brightly as she could manage.

'Anyway, I'm out of here. I'm going to be gone most of the day.' He paused. 'I just wanted to say it was good to spend some time with you yesterday. We must do it again, soon . . .' For the last sentence he dropped his tone to a conspiratorial purr.

'Sure,' said Jane. Over my dead body, she thought grimly as she hung up. And then she looked across at Gary. 'Working out?'

Gary shrugged. 'What can I tell you? That man is so up himself he can barely see out. He told me he'd been for a jog first thing and had his personal trainer round for an early session. Bastard. I had to say something – which reminds me, there's a tracksuit here, if you don't fancy putting that suit on, and I'll put breakfast out on the deck for you.'

'You know you're a total control freak.'

Gary paused for an instant and then said, 'And your point is? It's what Jayne pays me for. I'm Mary Poppins for grown-ups. Now get up – you'll take root if you stay in there much longer.' It was Jane's turn to lift an eyebrow. 'One other thing, how come I ended up here yesterday? I can't believe that I gave the cab driver Jayne's address.'

Gary paused midstride. 'It could have been like with the letters – you know, maybe the guy heard you wrong. Your speech wasn't exactly crystal clear when you rolled up at the front gate.'

'Sorry about that,' Jane said, avoiding his gaze. The cat was still watching her closely in case she tried something tricky.

'Could have been worse. At least you weren't sick over the cabby,' said Gary.

In Kefalos, Jayne, still in her robe, was enjoying a continental breakfast out on the roof terrace of her hotel. She was deciding what to do next while slowly working her way through a pot of black tea, served with warm new bread, soft creamy white butter and blackcurrant comfiture, all enjoyed under the shade of a rustic pergola heavy with greenery. Above her, curled around the rough frame, were sugar-pink bougainvillaea and pearl-white jasmine, their perfume heady in the morning air. In the top of a huge flowerpot close by, enjoying the sunshine, a large tabby cat watched her thoughtfully while licking its paws. Jayne smiled; Augustus would have approved.

Jayne stretched; maybe she should write a few postcards, wander around the town, explore before it got too hot and the world closed down for a siesta.

From her vantage point on the terrace Jayne could look down towards the harbour where the white- and blue-painted buildings shimmered in the sunlight, and beyond them, along the jetty, vessels bobbed at their moorings like kites on a string. The water was so clear that even from this distance she could see the rock and shoals of glittering fish below the surface.

Jayne cradled the cup between her fingers, watching a tiny boat make its way in to shore, the wake a white arrow in the azure sea, and considered her options. Should she stay on Kos? And if she stayed, how long should she stay for? And if she stayed, should she do something, go somewhere; or should she just lay out on the terrace or the beach with a book and relax? She sighed; she knew from experience it would take a while before she stilled her natural desire to be busy, although in an odd way it felt as if her brain had already stalled.

Back home that would have been a disaster. There were always things to do, people to ring, places to be, pieces of paper, emails and faxes to chase, consider, answer and return. But here there was nothing, nothing to worry about or think about, nothing but how to fill the rest of the day and the day after that and the day after that, and relish the scent and sensation of the warm wind on her skin.

It was the most peculiar feeling for someone whose whole life was focused on being busy and productive. This wasn't like a holiday with a natural and prearranged end in sight. Every day, for as long as Jayne could remember, her life had been filled to capacity, even while on holiday she often sourced new products or saw something that inspired her and at least with a holiday she could gauge how long she would have to be idle. Not having a framework or a goal was disturbing, almost frightening.

Jayne realised with a sickening start that she didn't know what to do, and for a split second felt totally lost and panicky, wondering if it was too soon to break the promise she'd made to herself and ring Ray to see how things were going at the office. Just a quick call. Five minutes, less. Or maybe she should just send a text or an email; there was bound to be a cyber café somewhere around. For a split second she even considered ringing Carlo. Maybe she had been too hasty, maybe she would fly him out. Maybe she should ring Jane, make sure she was coping.

Jayne took a deep breath, trying to quell the rising panic, and poured herself another cup of tea. It would be all right. She just had to relax, deep breaths.

While Jayne was lost in thought one of the hotel staff appeared to clear away the remains of breakfast. Jayne smiled up at the girl, who set a tray down on a side table and began packing the crockery onto it.

'So what do you think I should do today?' Jayne asked, not really expecting an answer.

The girl, who looked as if she might be a student helping out for the season, looked up in surprise, and then smiled and considered the idea for a few seconds. 'Today?' she asked in perfect English.

Jayne nodded. 'Yes, today – what would you do if you had a day off?'

The girl laughed. 'Me? I would stay in bed and sleep until supper time, but I am not you. Today is the first day of your holiday, so you should do nothing in a better way. Maybe lie in the sun for a little, read a book, doze. I'll bring you a drink later – something long and cold with an umbrella.' She paused for a few seconds, looking at Jayne as if assessing her, and then said, 'But you want something to do, yes? Maybe you should take a boat trip out around the islands – go to see the sponge divers, have lunch on the beach, swim in the sea. There is a boat that leaves from Kos town, from the harbour. You would like me to book you a taxi?'

Jayne dropped her napkin onto the table and nodded. 'Why not? Sounds great.'

The girl smiled. 'Good. But you must take something warm too – the wind is cold on the boats sometimes – and something for the sun too . . .' She mimed rubbing suntan lotion into her arms. Jayne nodded and then smiled to herself; her waitress and Gary would get along just fine.

In Creswell Close Jane decided that this really was the perfect way to start the day – eating breakfast that you hadn't prepared out on the deck, served by your house-keeper, watched by your cat, looking down through the garden towards your lake under the palest of early summer skies.

Just as Jane was finishing a bowl of toasted almonds, fresh raspberries and yoghurt, a disembodied voice said, 'Morning, fancy coming round for a drink, do ya?'

Jane looked up. Over the fence Tony Butler from next

98

door was up a ladder in the garden, busy threading a string of garden lights into one of the trees.

'What, now?' asked Jane, in astonishment, slightly nauseous at the idea of the hair of the dog.

'No, not now,' Tony snorted with laughter. 'Don't be daft. Sun's barely up, let alone over the bleeding yardarm. No, I meant, d'ya wanna come round tonight? We've more or less got the place straight now. Why don't you pop round and give us a look? Be nice to have a bit of company. Lil's missing her mates – you know how it is: new place an' that.'

Jane smiled. 'Glad to hear that you're settling in.'

'We're getting there. New place like this needs a few personal touches – you know, we need to put our mark on it, make it home. We've got a bloke coming round later to see about sorting us out with a pool. You want to think about having one an' all while he's here. I reckon we could talk him into giving us a decent discount if the pair of us had one at the same time. You wanna think about it.'

'Yeah,' said another voice that could only have come from Lil, presumably holding the bottom of Tony's ladder. 'Tone's good at that sort of thing – negotiating, sorting stuff out. I mean, even if you don't want a pool them Jacuzzis are lovely. Maybe we could try and get him to do us a buy-one-get-one-free deal.' She laughed throatily at her own joke.

Jane's smile held as she wondered just how Jayne would feel if she came home to find a Jacuzzi and Olympic-size swimming pool instead of the calm greens, whites and mellow colours of the borders, edged by shrubs and the carefully landscaped beginnings of what would eventually mature into a classic English garden.

'So, you coming round tonight then?' pressed Tony. 'Lil's

a great little cook. We'll open a bottle of bubbly, christen the new house – 'bout seven? How're you fixed? Bring your bloke, if you like. More the merrier, eh, Lil?' He peered down through the great veil of lush greenery.

'Be lovely to see ya,' said Lil from somewhere down below. 'I was saying to Tone, must be lonely for you rattling around in the great big house all on your own. We asked that girl from across the site office to come an' all but she said she was busy.'

Jane tried hard not to meet Tony's eye. The idea that they thought Miranda might pop over and party with them was very endearing. 'Maybe she's got a family,' Jane said.

'Nah, when I went over there yesterday she was saying to some woman on the phone she couldn't find a decent man for love nor money.'

Jane made a mental note to drop in a flyer for Jayne's personals site to the show home.

'Nice girl like that,' said the Greek chorus from the bottom of the ladder. 'Seems such a shame. I was saying to Tone, it's not like she's really ugly or anyfink.'

'Well, she's no oil painting, sweetheart, but she's not bad. Bit tight-lipped for my taste.' Tony took a moment to scratch his belly contemplatively. 'I was just saying to Lil, it's a shame really that we haven't got some of the old crowd down, couple of nice single blokes in there, Ronnie and Phil, suit her down to the ground, wouldn't they, Lil? Which reminds me – house-warming. Saturday night, how're you fixed? Stick in your diary.'

'Yeah, that's right,' said Lil brightly. 'We've got loads of people coming, caterers. That's what Tone's doing these lights for – likes to do some of the stuff himself, don't you, Tone? Going to be a good do.'

'So how about it?' said Tony. 'Come round and have supper tonight? See what you reckon.'

Jane considered her options. Realistically she hadn't got anything much to do other than calculate the days, hours and minutes since Lucy Stroud had told her about Steve, and devising interesting and increasingly gothic ways to wreak revenge on the two of them.

Tony's grin held. She didn't have to stay long and they were Jayne's new neighbours, after all, so she said, 'Yes, thank you, sounds like a great idea. Seven will be fine.'

'You want me to fix some nibbles?' asked Gary as Jane made her way back through the house towards the office.

'Have you got the deck bugged?'

'No, I'm psychic,' said Gary, snapping on a pair of Marigolds.

Jane worked all morning on Ray's data processing, in between proofreading copy for the new websites, and going through the press releases he had sent her. They looked great, although there were just enough little errors and tweaks needed to make Jane feel her job was worthwhile.

There was some email for the company, which she opened and then forwarded to Ray, and some email that looked personal for Jayne that she didn't. And as she read and worked Jane made a list of things she didn't know or understand and questions to ask Ray, or Jayne when she phoned home. Gary brought coffee and cake up at eleven. The morning passed quickly as she began to get some sense of Jayne's business. Being in her office helped.

The phone rang a few times.

'Hello, Jane Mills,' she said without thinking, not that anyone seemed to mind or notice.

'Oh, hi, it's Miranda here from Creswell Associates. We met the other day?' The voice and the introductory laugh was as bright and brittle as puddle ice.

Jane hesitated, wondering who it was Miranda had actually met and then the woman said, 'I was just checking to see that you were happy with the shower head in the guest room, and that it's all going well over there.'

Bingo, the woman from the show house who couldn't find a decent man.

'Actually, I haven't had time to check it out yet,' Jane said.

'OK, well, I'm in all week this week as the usual girl's away – and as I said before, we're here to help. Anything you need,' she said. Miranda would no doubt ready Barry and send him straight over.

'Good morning,' said the second caller a little later, a plummy-sounding woman with a high-pitched nasal laugh. 'Victoria Hartman? I'm just checking up to see that everything is still OK for next week?'

Jane looked down the schedule that Ray had emailed her. 'Victoria Hartman, luxury preserves and all sorts of bottled organic fruit?'

The woman laughed. 'Gosh, yes, that's right. Fancy you remembering. We do vegetables too – lovely chunky jars of baby carrots and peas, courgettes, peppers. Anyway, I spoke to some chap last time; it was last week or the week before. I was just wondering if the samples had arrived and how you'd got on with them?'

Jane glanced at Ray's email; it didn't mention anything arriving or anybody getting on with anything. 'When did you send them?'

'Last week.'

'By post?'

'Yes.'

'Right, well, I'm awfully sorry but I haven't actually seen them yet,' Jane said cautiously. 'We've been having a lot of trouble with the post just recently. I'll see if I can track them down before we meet. They may be at the office.'

'Oh, gosh. Well, that's a shame. I was rather hoping you'd have a chance to try some of the range out before our meeting. Usually, I have to say, our products really do speak for themselves.' The woman sounded genuinely disappointed.

'I'm sure they do,' said Jane warmly, scrolling down to see if there was anything else about Ms Hartman in the email or on file on Jayne's database. A search for Hartman on the computer brought up a file of product images, letters, price lists, comments from customers and Jayne's thoughts, with some suggestions on improved packaging and some marketing angles. All of them sounded favourable.

'Actually I've got your file here in front of me.' From Jane's point of view the good news was that Victoria had never spoken to the real Jayne Mills. It looked as if she had mailed one of Jayne's websites. 'Everything looks delicious, but I agree it would be better to try it,' said Jane. 'Let me check up on the delivery and I'll get back to you. What was it you sent?' she asked, pulling a pen out of the jar on the desk.

'Our top sellers: black cherries in kirsch, whole peaches in cognac, some red onion marmalade, oh, and a rather nice redcurrant and raspberry preserve that we've been working on.'

Jane laughed as she scribbled the list down. 'Sounds

wonderful. Can you just give me the address you sent them to?'

The woman gave her Jayne's home address. Jane sighed. It occurred to her that the parcel could very easily have rolled up at Creswell Road, although it beggared the question who had it. Beggared? Jane paused for a few moments. She had a vague recollection of Gladstone eating a very purple something out of a jar with a spoon – not that she had looked that closely to see what the something might be. 'Leave it with me and I'll get back to you,' she said. 'Looking forward to meeting you next week.'

'Gosh, yes, me too,' said Ms Hartman in a way that suggested they were meeting up for a brisk game of tennis and possibly Pimm's.

Besides checking up on Gladstone, Ms Hartman's call made Jane realise she ought to go through the list of potential new suppliers she was meeting and see what it was she was supposed to be looking at – not least in case anyone else rang.

The morning seemed to go very quickly; just before lunch the phone rang again. 'Hello, Jane Mills,' she said, phone nipped between her ear and her shoulder.

'Hi,' said a warm, husky male voice. 'How're you doing?'

Everything about the tone implied that the caller knew her – or rather knew Jayne – very well.

'I thought I'd better ring up and just sort out the arrangements for meeting up. Times and all that stuff.'

This was bound to happen. Jane just wished she had had the savvy to realise and come up with a strategy before it did.

'Oh, OK, not a problem, just let me check the diary.'

She slid it across the desk as they were talking. 'Who am I speaking to, please?'

There was a peculiar little pause at the far end of the line and then the man laughed and said, 'Oh, meow – bad joke. What do you mean, "Who am I speaking to"? I know it's been a while. It's me, Kit.'

'Kit,' she repeated and pulled up the 'find' menu on the computer screen.

'What's the matter, Jai?' her caller said. 'Are you OK? You sound odd.'

'No, I'm just fine,' she blustered. 'The thing is . . .' Bugger, damn, blast. Big mistake. She shouldn't have gone this route; she should come up with another way of answering the phone. There was nothing on the computer, no Kit, no Kitty, no nothing.

'This isn't Jayne, it is?' he pressed.

'Yes, well, no. No, she's not here at the moment. I'm taking her calls. At the moment,' she blustered.

'Then why did you just say you were Jayne Mills?' asked the man, not unreasonably.

'Well, er, slip of the tongue.' Jane paused, trying to find some way to prevent herself digging an even bigger hole, busily considering her options and kicking herself from sounding like such an idiot. Under different circumstances Jane would probably have made a joke, even it was a lame one, and tried to explain, but Jayne had specifically said she didn't want anyone to know that she was away. Jane had to think on her feet, and back-pedal fast.

'Sorry, Kit, it's been a bad day here. I'm afraid Jayne's not in the office at the moment. Would you like to leave a message?' was the best she could come up with under pressure. Why didn't she just say she had made a mistake, say that she had misheard him?

'But you just said that you were Jayne Mills,' insisted the man.

'Would you like to leave a message?' asked Jane, trying to sound cheery and businesslike.

'No I wouldn't. I'd like to speak to Jayne, please.'

'I'm afraid she's not in at the moment.'

'When will she be back?'

At which point Gary peered round the door. 'You want some lunch?'

'Well?' snapped the man.

'I'm not sure. Would you like me to get Jayne to call you when she gets back?' said Jane, as politely as she could manage.

He hung up. Jane sighed. God, what a twit. Never mind, next time she'd be ready. She just hoped he wasn't someone important, and hurriedly scrolled back through the list of previous calls on the phone, hoping it would give her some kind of clue as to his identity but instead, frustratingly, the call list just said, 'International'.

'Problems?' asked Gary.

Jane shook her head. 'No, no, not really. I just need to work out a ploy for people who want to talk to Jayne personally.'

But before she could follow the thought through the phone rang again. Jane picked it up. Maybe it was Kit again, armed and ready for the second round.

'Good afternoon, Jayne Mills' office?' she said brightly. That was better.

'Jane?'

'Oh, hi, Lizzie. Are you all right?'

106

'Yeah, I'm fine. I just wanted to let you know that Steve is busy trying to track you down.'

'Steve? Steve Burney?'

'Do you know any other Steves with a vested interest in your whereabouts?'

With all the excitement about the new job Jane had almost pushed Steve to the back of her mind. Now, the sound of his name made her feel hot and unsteady, somewhere unpleasant between sick, sad and weepy, and worse, a feeling she was right back at square one.

'What did he say?'

'He's been round this morning trying to find you.'

'Surely he knows that I got the push from the library?'

'He didn't go round to the library – well, at least I don't think he did – he came round to the house.'

'The house? How do you know if you're at work?'

'Ah.'

'What do you mean, "Ah"?'

'I'm off sick.'

'You don't sound very sick to me.'

'Don't you start. I've already had to cough and wheeze to order for some woman in Human Resources.' Lizzie paused and then said more slowly, 'It's the bed in the spare room.'

'I'm not sure I follow? It's new – but then again maybe you're allergic to the cats. I can't see—'

'No, that isn't what I mean. I made it up with nice clean sheets from the airing cupboard – God, even the words "airing cupboard" make me happy – and then I snuggled down with the cats and a book last night. It was fantastic, nobody fell up the stairs drunk as a skunk at three o'clock in the morning, there was no one telling anyone they loved them and they were their best mate in the whole wide world, there was no one singing, no people having sex in the room next door, there are clean pillowcases, hot water, milk – peace. And when I woke up this morning I thought: I need more of this, so I rang in and told them I'd got a bug. A nasty fluey kind of bug – lots of it going about, apparently. I said I'd try and get in after lunch, after I'd been to the doctor's.' She coughed, managing to sound all weak and wan, adding in a completely normal tone, 'And let's be honest, it was a bonus I was off really, or I'd have missed Steve, wouldn't I?'

'Bit of a mixed blessing, if you ask me. Did he say what he wanted?'

'Not really, just that he needed to talk to you, that's all. I told him I'd pass the message on. The thing is . . .' Lizzie paused.

'What thing?' asked Jane nervously.

'He caught me at a bad moment. I was in my jarmies. I thought maybe it was Gladstone wanting to know where his breakfast was.'

'And?'

'And I gave him your new address.'

Jane sighed; what could she say? He'd probably have found out sooner or later. 'Don't worry about it. I'll maybe ring him later. How did he look?'

'Gladstone?' There was a pause. 'No, all right, if you're hoping Mr Burney's torn apart with grief and pining I think you'd probably be disappointed, but if it's any consolation he does look a bit peaky – bit harassed, bags under the eyes.'

'Maybe Lucy is giving him a hard time. And if you were thinking of going for the joke there, don't bother.'

'As if,' Lizzie sighed theatrically. 'Jane, that woman would give the Pope a hard time. She's totally pissed off that you won't come and hold her hand through the changeover process. She thinks you're being very unreasonable and is trying to make sure everyone else thinks so too She's refused point-blank to join the sandwich rota and the bloody bears are already taking over every available flat surface. Oh, and she so hates the community. You should have seen her face when Long-haired Lonny from the drop-in centre dropped in to talk about getting some books and magazines for the place. After he went Lucy got a pair of rubber gloves from the janitor's cupboard, sprayed the office with half a can of Just Musk she pinched out of Lost Property, and then wiped the chair down with an antibacterial wet wipe.'

'He's a vicar.'

'She washed his mug up in bleach.'

'He works with the poor.'

'I think that was the trouble. He had a little whiff of the poor about him when he came in. Lucy prefers her vicars doing proper things, like opening jumble sales and running harvest festivals.'

'So what did you tell Steve?'

'That you'd dropped feet first into this fantastic new job, and that I was house-sitting because you were away on a training course.'

Jane was impressed. Obviously Lizzie was far better at lying under pressure than she was. Apart from giving her address away, obviously. 'Well done,' she said. In the background Jane could hear her doorbell ringing.

'Oh, I've got to go,' said Lizzie. 'I think that's probably Gladstone.'

109

'He doesn't usually ring the doorbell,' Jane said. 'You just put his stuff in tinfoil on top of the—'

'I'll call you back later,' said Lizzie, sounding distracted.

'So, about lunch?' growled Gary. 'You want some or do you want me to stand here all day?'

Jane, realising that she was hungry, nodded. 'No – I mean, yes, please.' She stretched and rubbed her eyes. 'I'll be down in a minute, I just need to save all this stuff to the main website.'

She peeled the Post-it note that she'd stuck on the edge of the computer screen and tapped in her username and password. 'Jane2 . . . switch,' she mouthed, working her way around the keyboard, careful to make sure that all the digits were in the right box and in the right case. Jane pressed return and waited.

'Username and password not recognised,' said a little error message on a natty little dropdown menu.

'Bugger.'

'Problems?' asked Gary.

'The password doesn't work. I'm sure Jayne said that this was all set up.'

'Maybe you typed it in wrong. Happens all the time to me.'

Jane retyped it. Same message. Damn. 'It's all right, I'll save all the things I've done to a separate file. It just won't let me alter the records on the main site and that's the place where all this stuff needs to be stored. It's annoying. Maybe I'm doing something wrong.'

Jane opened up the email Ray had sent her and read through the notes and the protocols for the websites. Everything seemed all right. She typed the password again.

This time the message read: 'You have exceeded the

number of attempts permitted to gain access to this area of the website. Please contact the site administrator.'

'Bugger,' hissed Jane.

Gary peered over Jane's shoulder and looked the screen over. 'Isn't there some sort of button you can push when you've forgotten your password? They've got one on Yahoo. You need your mother's maiden name and things.'

Jane glanced across to see if he was serious.

'Apparently not. I can't see what I've done wrong, though.' Jane peered at the screen, trying to work it out and then had another look through the instructions. 'I wrote it down exactly as Jayne said. I'll give Ray a ring.'

Jane tapped in the office number and was instantly redirected to the answer machine, which was annoying. Ray had already told her he was out of the office for most of the day.

'Hi, I'm afraid no one can take your call at the moment,' said Ray's recorded message, sounding all charm and superefficiency. 'If you'd like to leave a message after the tone then someone will get back to you as soon as possible.'

'Hi, Ray, it's Jane here. I wonder if you could give me a ring when you get back. I've got some sort of problem with the second-level password for the website administration. Can get on site but I can't edit anything. Thanks.'

Jane pushed herself away from the desk and looked up at Gary. 'So, what's for lunch?'

'See, I just knew you'd get used to the idea of being waited on hand and foot. You're a natural. You can have salad. I was thinking maybe goat's cheese, baby new potatoes and red onion on mixed leaves, or mixed vegetable gazpacho – and before you ask, yes, it's meant to be cold – or a sandwich . . . we'll need to talk menus.'

'At this rate I'm going to need a treadmill and a personal trainer.'

Gary grinned. 'There's a home gym upstairs in one of the loft rooms; you want me to kick-start the rowing machine for you? Oh, and by the way, these came for you.'

From out on the landing Gary produced a great bunch of cream roses, greeny-cream lisianthus, claret-red freesias and a mass of dramatic dark twirling greenery.

'For me?' whispered Jane.

'Apparently,' said Gary. 'I suppose you want me to stuff them in a vase for you? Here.'

Jane opened the card. It read. 'I'm so very sorry. Can you ever forgive me? x.' Her heart did a funny flippy backward somersault and she felt her eyes filling up with tears. Oh my God; Steve Burney had come through at the eleventh hour.

As she reread the card, Jane's mobile beeped a text message alert. It was from Steve. It read, 'Jane, we really need to talk. S.' She smiled. It was perfect timing.

Down by the harbour in Kos town, Jayne handed the good-looking guy on the booking desk another credit card from amongst those in her wallet.

Out of the window she could see *Spirit of the Waves*, a luxury day cruiser, moving gently at her moorings, one of the many day boats that sailed between the outlying islands around Kos. The boat was already loading. A steady stream of well-heeled passengers ambled up the gangplank, clutching towels and hats and all the paraphernalia for sunbathing, swimming, snorkelling and sightseeing. Part of the broad upper deck was covered with a sail, which created a cool puddle of shade, the free edge rippling in the warm breeze, while the rest of the boat was set with chairs and benches and reclining sunbeds, open to the already fierce sun.

A few of the crew, tanned lean young men and girls, dressed in blue and white striped T-shirts and white shorts, were smiling and joking with each other while welcoming the passengers aboard and directing them to the seating, the bar, and the different decks.

'No, I'm very sorry, madam,' said the man behind the desk, handing the credit card back. 'But this one has been rejected too, although I shouldn't worry about it; this machine it is always playing up. Have you got anything else?'

Jayne nodded and tucked the card back into her bag. 'Yes, I've got traveller's cheques, will those do?'

The man nodded, and smiled up at her flirtatiously from under thick lashes. If she hadn't felt embarrassed about the credit cards Jayne might have appreciated it a little more. He was around fifty, with a handsome lived-in face, dark brown, almost black, hair, shot through with grey, and a smile that cut his broad face in half like a melon slice. A white polo shirt and navy shorts worn with deck shoes emphasised his deep tan, and a body muscular and taut from living an outdoor life.

'Yes, of course, cards, cheques, cash . . .' He paused, brown eyes twinkling. 'We're always willing to consider alternative ways to pay.' And then looked her up and down appreciatively, smiling mischievously. As their eyes met they both laughed and then Jayne handed over the cheque and picked up her itinerary before joining the rest of the passengers on board.

'You'll have a great time,' he called after her. 'I promise.'

The wind nipped and tugged at her hair as Jayne found a seat under the shade of the canvas awning. A few minutes later the guy from the office joined the rest of the crew and signalled that it was time to leave.

As they cast off from the quayside and pulled out of Kos harbour the sun shone, gulls circled, sounds of bouzouki music bubbled up from the ship's PA systems and one of the boys behind the bar began handing out bucks fizz.

Jayne smiled; the girl in the hotel had been right. This was the most perfect way to spend a day.

Chapter Six

After lunch – the goat's cheese salad – Jane jogged back upstairs to the office, sat down at Jayne's desk, picked up her mobile, and called Steve. As she waited for him to answer she let her eyes move around the office, over Jayne's photos, the view from the window and the flowers, making an effort to compose herself. She had spent lunchtime pondering the bouquet and the card.

'I'm so very sorry. Can you ever forgive me?' Did that mean, I'm so very sorry, I want you back, or was it more, I'm so very sorry, but it's over now, I just don't want you to think badly of me?

Jane had decided to stay calm, stay bright, breezy and tried hard to concentrate on the tone she wanted to adopt. *'Oh, hi, Steve. Thanks for the text and the flowers. Lizzie said you'd been round to the house. Fancy hearing from you. Wow – gosh, you know I'd almost forgotten you were alive,'* was the one she was aiming for. Let him do the work, let him chase. Let him think she didn't really care, that she was over him. And it would most probably work except for the fact that it was all total lies and she had this great big hurting burning ache in her chest that from time to time made it hard to breathe. The flowers really hadn't helped.

In bad moments the sense of loss came in great rolling waves and was triggered by a totally random thought or an object that made her think about him, or something they had done, or that he had said. A private joke, a little look – oh, but her brain had its finger pressed hard down on the replay button.

In an odd way being sacked from the library was almost a godsend, soaking up some of the excess emotion like a towel. When she wasn't thinking about Steve screwing Lucy on the rug in front of the fire, Jane missed him so badly that she thought she might die from twenty-four-carat misery, although in the same breath she also wanted to punch him hard until he cried like a girl, and find a way to make him suffer for being such a total and utter shit.

She looked at the flowers; trust him to choose something tasteful. The bastard.

As her mobile began to ring Jane started having second thoughts. Did ringing Steve back so quickly make her look desperate or needy? Maybe she should have waited; maybe ringing tomorrow would be a better idea – make it look as if calling back was a casual thing, or maybe it would be better if she hadn't rung him at all. Maybe she should wait for him to call her, although as he had turned up at her house without ringing first, and then there was the text and the flowers, it suggested something big was afoot. Maybe he did want her back.

Jane pressed the handset tight against her ear, fingers white with tension. At the far end of the line the phone was still ringing.

What if Steve had been coming round to Creswell Road to tell her that he loved her? What if he had turned up at the house with a Pickfords van *full* of roses? What if he burst into tears on her doorstep and said that rubbing Lucy down with half a tub of low-fat yoghurt was the worst day's work he'd ever done in his life and that he really truly wanted Jane back more than anything, more than Lucy, more than life itself? Then what would she say?

The phone rang on and on, and despite Jane's best efforts any possibilities of bright and breezy were fading fast. What if he had come round to tell her that he and Lucy were blissfully happy, that they were getting married in the Seychelles and that he was really glad that Jane had dumped him? What if the call clicked on to voice mail and the bastard didn't pick the bloody phone up at all? What if—

'Hi there, Jane,' said Steve, cornering the market in bright and breezy. 'How are you? Nice to hear from you. How's it going?'

By the fact he knew who it was meant he must still have her number in his mobile directory. Maybe she should have rung him on Jayne's landline so that he didn't recognise the caller; got Gary to say, 'Mr Burney? Would you please hold? I have a call on the other line for you.' Make him wait, make him sweat. Make him suffer.

'Really well, thanks, and you?' she said, swallowing down the tremor that threatened; hearing his voice made her feel odd, weepy and unsteady.

'Not so bad, not so bad at all,' he replied. 'Really busy, you know how it is.' At least he didn't add, '*what with all the staff cutbacks and all.*' 'Lizzie told me that you'd found yourself a new job already, which is great. Well done, you – sounds like you've fallen on your feet.' He spoke as if they were strangers, all neat and formal, with no raw edges visible that she could pick at and pull open. His hearty tone closed them off from each other as surely as barbed wire. 'Makes me wonder if you'd got wind of the planned rationalisations,' he said, laughing without humour. 'Insider information, eh?'

'Well, you know how these things go,' she said, holding the line. 'You win some, you lose some.' Jane certainly wasn't going to give him the satisfaction of letting him know that the only insider she had on library politics had been him. After all, what bloody help had he been other than helping to pull the rug out from under her? 'I just wanted to thank you for the flowers.'

And then she fell silent and let the gap open up. Like prize-fighters, it felt as if they were manoeuvring around each other, weighing up the opposition, looking for an opening. Jane wondered who would break first, swinging an unguarded punch that would take them away from the social niceties. She was determined it wasn't going to be her. Letting Steve struggle, she stayed silent.

'The flowers?' He sounded uncomfortable, wrong-footed. 'Righty-oh . . . Well, the thing is . . .' Steve began after a second or two more.

Jane bit her lip; she was determined not to make it easy for him. His tone was fixedly neutral. Maybe he had sent them when he was drunk or low – or . . .

'. . . the thing is, I was wondering if we could maybe meet up some time, go out to supper. Talk things over. If you're free.' He said it quickly as if he had been practising.

Jane's stomach did a very impressive back flip, double salchow and splits. Was this the preamble to: '*I've made the most terrible mistake, Jane, and I'm so very, very sorry. I want—?*'

But before her imagination could complete the line, the

real Steve Burney said, 'I want us to be friends, Jane, I don't want there to be any ill feeling.'

Damn. That wasn't what he was supposed to say. 'Friends?' she repeated.

'Yes, friends. I know we can't go back to what we had, and to be honest I don't think either of us wants that, do we? I understand that you're hurt and I'm sorry about that. But I feel that we just need to talk, need to sort things out. Clear the air. As I said, I don't want there to be any lingering ill feeling between us. We don't want any repercussions, do we? After all, we're all adults.'

All? Jane felt Lucy elbowing her way into the conversation. He was pussyfooting round something. 'Steve,' Jane said, 'I have absolutely no idea what you're talking about. What repercussions? What things do we need to sort out?'

Steve sighed. 'Look, I've already said I'm sorry . . . I *was* hoping that you'd see sense, Jane. I mean, I understand that you're hurt, but I think you're behaving very unreasonably.'

'Unreasonably? Steve, will you please stop talking in riddles and get to the point? Is this about me not letting Lucy shadow me at work?'

He snorted. 'No, of course not, although I have to say I feel that that was very petty, dropping her into the deep end like that. What has Lucy ever done to you?'

Jane couldn't believe what she was hearing. 'Well, for starters she managed to end up with my job and my boyfriend,' she snapped.

Steve made a peculiar little sound at the far end of the line as if she had stamped on his fingers and then continued, sounding uncomfortable and slightly flustered, 'I was hoping we could sort this out like adults. I thought we could do it amicably.'

'We did sort it out, Steve. I can't see that we've got anything else to say or to sort out. I finished with you when I found out you were cheating on me, and amicable is not what I feel at all. I feel angry and hurt and humiliated. Oh, and by the way, I am an adult. I wasn't the one sneaking around smearing members of the library staff with yoghurt.'

'You won't let that go, will you?'

'I have to say it's a pretty hard image to shake. I don't really see the point of meeting you. And as for being friends with you, you've got to be joking. Real friends don't screw you over, screw your life up, or screw your friends behind your back. You've got Lucy, she's got my job – I hope the two of you and the fucking bears live happily ever after.'

Steve made a strange choking sound. 'I had hoped we could sort this out.'

'Sort *what out*?' Jane screamed in frustration; she was losing it and didn't care. Steve deserved everything he got. 'Will you please tell me exactly what is there to sort out? If it's about your Mary Chapin Carpenter CD, as soon as I find it I'll put it in the post.'

'Please calm down, Jane. I don't want to talk about this over the phone. Can I come round and see you?' He sounded almost conspiratorial.

Jane still had no idea what was going on, but had no sense that he was going to go away, so finally, in exasperation, she said, 'Oh, for God's sake – OK.'

'Can I come round tonight?' Whatever it was, it was really bugging him. 'Will Lizzie be there?' he asked.

'No, no, I'm not at Creswell Road at the moment. I'm—'

'I know – Lizzie gave me your address – you're on a course.'

'No, I'm not on a bloody course,' Jane snapped, wanting to shut him up and let her win for once. 'I've got a house with my new job and I'm staying there at the moment.' Damn, she suddenly remembered that she had arranged to go round to Tony and Lil's for supper. 'How long do you think this is going to take? I've got a supper date at seven.'

'I don't know,' Steve blustered, obviously not expecting her to be so direct. Or maybe so busy. 'It depends really.'

Jane couldn't bring herself to ask on what. 'If you could be here by six that would give us an hour, or would you prefer to come round another time?'

'No, no, six will be fine,' he said quickly.

'Right,' said Jane, 'I'll see you at six,' and hung up. A split second after the line went dead Jane burst into tears and threw the phone across the room as hard as she could. It hit the wall and exploded into its component parts – battery one way, cover and body another, while the sim card pinged out and flew down the back of the radiator.

'Bastard,' Jane roared. 'Bloody sodding buggering bloody bastard.' Not that it made her feel any better.

If Gary heard he said nothing, nor did he appear. Jane struggled to compose herself and sat down at the computer. She jiggled the mouse so the screensaver faded and stared at the screen, hoping it would help.

Instead, in the centre, an error message read, 'You have exceeded the number of attempts permitted to gain access to this area of the website. Please contact the site administrator.'

'Bollocks', she growled under her breath. There was nothing she could do about getting on to the website until Ray rang her back. So now what?

Grimly she flicked to the next batch of customer data and spent the rest of the afternoon feeding in names and addresses and saving them on a backup copy of the database, periodically trying to type in her password and getting the same message popping up like a cork in water. From where she was sitting she could smell the freesias in the bouquet. It didn't help her mood one little bit.

Finally, at just before five o'clock, Ray rang. He sounded unpleasantly bright, in stark contrast to her mood. 'Hi, Jane, just got out of a meeting and picked up your message. How's your day been?'

'Well, I've done a lot of the work and read through the new copy, and I've got a few questions. But I've got one major problem.'

'OK, shoot.'

'My password doesn't seem to work on the main website so I haven't been able to save any of the work I've done.'

'Um, right.' He made a thoughtful sound. 'That's odd.'

'I'm using the ones Jayne gave me. I'm not sure whether it was you or Jayne who set them up.'

'And those are the ones that failed?'

'Yes, unfortunately they're the only ones I've got.'

'Okey-dokey, no problem. Leave it with me, there's a copy here of your details. I'll get it sorted and then get back to you as soon as possible. What have you been using as a name and password?'

'"Jane2", and the password is "switch". I wrote them when Jayne gave them to me.'

Ray laughed. 'Oh, yes, I've got those ones written down here. I'll reset them as soon as I get back into the office and, if not, I'll mail you new ones first thing. Other than that, how's it gone?'

Jane considered for a few seconds. Her mobile was in bits on the office floor and in less than an hour she would be coming face to face with Steve Burney for the first time in . . . her brain rushed round trying desperately to calculate exactly how many days, minutes and seconds it was. Jane wrestled it firmly away from her inner abacus and said, 'Fine, a couple of the potential suppliers rang up. Which reminds me,' she picked up the note she had made to herself on her desk, 'are there any black cherries in kirsch, whole peaches in cognac, red onion marmalade or redcurrant and raspberry preserve knocking about the office?'

'Not that I've noticed. Shame, sounds delicious. Mind you, there are a couple of parcels that Jayne brought in last time she was here and left in the store room – samples, presumably. Could be one of them?'

'It's one of the people I'm seeing next week. The producer wanted to know if I'd tried them yet.'

'Right, well, I'm sure Jayne told you that she always makes a point of trying everything personally if she can.' He paused. 'Unfortunately I'm out of the office for a day or two, possibly till the end of the week or I'd offer to run them over to you. If you want to come by and pick them up you could.'

'Where are they?'

'If they're here they're in the storeroom behind the main office. There's a cupboard just behind the door, with filing drawers and stuff. You've got the code, haven't you? Oh, and there is post for you there too. Company credit card and stuff. I'll leave it by the work station you used yesterday. There's some paperwork Jayne wanted too. It's in the cupboard with the samples. You can't miss it. It's a manila file. If you could take that as well it would be a real help. Anyway, look, I've got to go now. I'm taking a client out for a drink and an early dinner. I'll sort the password situation out a.s.a.p.' And then he was gone.

Jane hung up. Well, that was that sorted out, although she wished Ray had mentioned that he was going to be out of the office for a few days before. She looked at the pile of paper on the desk and then up at the screen. What if she ran out of things to do?

She glanced up at the clock. It had to be knocking-off time. In less than an hour Steve would be arriving and at the moment she was dressed in a pink velour tracksuit that Gary had given her that morning. Jane stood up and caught sight of herself reflected in one of the windows. With her scraped-back hair and not a scrap of make-up she hardly looked like a woman who had just bagged a top-notch executive job with an innovative quirky go-getting company.

Shit – Jane looked at the clock again, willing the hands to stop moving. What she really needed was to go home to Creswell Road and grab a change of clothes. Maybe she could wear the clothes she had arrived in the night before? Or her suit – it looked businesslike, competent.

Jane hurried across the landing into the bedroom and looked around; now if she could just work out what Gary had done with her clothes . . .

'Gary?'

Meanwhile Ray Jacobson closed his mobile and glanced down at the note he had made on the napkin. 'Janetwo, switch.' They would come in very handy. Smiling he folded the serviette and slipped it into his pocket. He was at a little bistro down by the Cam in Cambridge, ordering dinner for Lulu. They'd met at a nightclub where Lulu was pole dancing to help pad out her student loan. She didn't need anything else padding. At twenty-two, Lulu thought Ray was the best thing since sliced bread. She wasn't old enough to have discovered that most sliced bread lacked any real character, was available everywhere, seldom had much taste and went off quickly.

Ray topped up her wine and smiled. 'You know you look great, sweetie. Have you done something different with your hair today?'

This was the first time he'd taken her out on a proper date; mostly they just went back to his flat. Lulu blushed; it was nice of him to notice her hair and it was lovely how he called her 'sweetie'. It made her feel special – although she had no idea it was because he couldn't always remember her name.

In the balmy waters around the Dodecanese the late afternoon sun dipped down lazily towards the horizon, painting the wake of the tour boat with a broad red-gold brush. Up on deck Jayne sat by the bar under the awning, tired in the warm pleasant way that comes after a day spent exploring and swimming, and eating wonderful food outdoors under a cloudless blue sky. She sipped an ice-cold white wine spritzer, aware of the tingle of sunburn on her shoulder, nose and neck.

'So,' said her companion, topping up her glass, 'you have had plenty of time to consider my offer. Will you join me for dinner?'

Jayne smiled and took another sip of wine. It was the culmination of a day's gentle persuasion that had begun since their eyes had met over the ticket machine.

'I'm very flattered, Miko. And it's been a while since I've been so thoroughly and expertly chatted up.' She tapped her glass to his.

He aped deep hurt and then laughed, gaze holding hers. She noticed that he swung between speaking the most impeccable English and a kind of cod, cartoon Greek – and since taking her money, the handsome Greek had barely left her side.

His expression suggested he was still waiting eagerly for a reply.

'I'm also very tired,' Jayne continued, pulling her pashmina tighter as the wind from the sea cooled her skin. 'At the moment my plan is to go back to the hotel, have a long warm shower and fall into bed.' There was a tiny glittering pause. 'Alone,' she added as his eyes sparkled.

'What a terrible waste of a good woman.' He was still smiling. 'Never mind. How about tomorrow then? I have the day off – we could go for a picnic, to the temples. I will bring a picnic – good wine, cheese and grapes – or maybe we could find a little hillside taverna up amongst the cypress trees. I know just the place. Cool, beautiful, just like your eyes,' he purred.

'Why am I not surprised?' Jayne laughed. 'Miko, all this attention is very flattering but I'm far too canny to fall for the whole holiday romance thing.'

'Take a chance, live a little. What have you got to lose?' he said, sipping his wine, eyes not leaving hers.

'Would you like me to write you a list?' Jayne said, looking him up and down. 'How many women has this worked on?'

He shrugged philosophically. 'I don't know. I lost count

around 1980 but trust me, it would be a great day out. We could have good fun, you and I.'

Jayne's expression didn't flicker.

'OK, OK,' he said, holding his hands up in surrender. 'No strings, I swear on the life of my poor sweet sainted mother. Come and explore the island with me, we will look at all the wonderful things – no strings, I promise, cross my heart. See, look, I'm doing it.'

'And exactly how long has your poor sweet sainted mother been dead?'

He threw back his head and laughed. 'You are a cruel and beautiful woman, Jayne Mills. If I wasn't already married I would marry you myself.'

Jayne smiled ruefully. 'Well, there's an offer I don't know how to refuse, Miko. I'm very touched and I'm sure it would be great fun but I don't make a habit of getting into cars driven by strange married men.' Not these days, anyway, she thought.

'In that case you can drive – or hire a car if you're worried about getting into mine – and I will be your guide. And I promise no monkey business.'

Jayne considered for a few moments. Every instinct told her that a trip out with Miko would be just fine and if today's boat ride was anything to go by, great fun.

She looked out across the waves towards the harbour, already picked out in lights against the early evening sky. Another half an hour and they would be landing, and Miko would be gone.

Last time Jayne had travelled to Greece, she and Andy had bummed around the islands, taking ferries, hitching or taking local buses. They had climbed fearlessly aboard ramshackle lorries full of goats and chickens, sharing rusty trucks and cramped cars with plump Greek wives and their bright-eyed children, sat in the back with old ladies dressed entirely in black. They had explored Kos town, the coast and the mountains. They had wandered along Bubble and Magic Beaches, drinking ouzo and cheap wine, getting stoned on the place, the booze, the sex, the dope and the easy life out under the stars, sleeping curled together in sleeping bags in amongst the dunes, waking covered in fine sand, trapped, crunching and coarse in their eyelashes and hair, the surrounding beach too hot to walk across in bare feet.

For an instant Jayne felt a great wave of grief for all the time that had passed and all the might-have-beens that had slipped through her fingers.

'Actually, Miko, that sounds great,' she said, not quite able to keep the sadness out of her voice.

Miko's expression softened. 'I make you promise, no strings. I'll tell you what – how about I bring my daughter along too? She is home from college working for the summer,' Miko added.

Jayne nodded. 'Fine. In that case it's a deal.'

'Really? Good, what time would you like me to pick you up?'

'I'll hire a car and come and pick you up.'

He chuckled. 'OK, I have a cousin in Kamari who does car hire. I get you a very good price.'

'Why am I not surprised?' Jayne said, pouring a little more soda into her glass. 'Your daughter doesn't happen to work in the Helena Hotel, by any chance, does she?'

Miko shook his head. 'No, that's not my daughter – that is my niece.'

* * *

Meanwhile, in the utility room in Creswell Close, Jane peered into the soapy bowels of the washing machine. 'So how long will they be before they're done?'

Gary shrugged. 'Maybe half an hour. I'll pop them in the tumble dryer as soon as they've finished. They'll be ready in plenty of time for you to go to supper next door.'

'You washed my suit?' said Jane incredulously, staring at the swirling mass.

'No, just your shirt and your underwear and that cardigan thing you were wearing under the jacket. The suit went to the dry-cleaners.' Gary glanced at his watch. 'He'll bring it back around, six, six thirty on his way back from the shop. He's very good.'

'Um,' said Jane.

'Um?' said Gary. 'There were stains on the jacket and something very nasty on the back of your trousers.'

Jane stared at him; actually he was probably right. Never mind any fresh stains, sponging only went so far.

Trouble was that there was no time to drive home and be back before Steve arrived. He was almost always early. 'Steve, my ex-boyfriend, will be turning up at around six.'

'The one with the yoghurt?' Gary said thoughtfully.

'That is in no way connected with the stains on my suit, OK?'

'Whatever you say,' said Gary, holding his hands up in surrender.

Jane looked back into the machine, wishing she had thought about clothes earlier. Still not used to hired help, it had never occurred to her that Gary would hijack them. 'Is there anyway we can stop that?'

'No. Anyway, they still need to rinse and spin, unless you want to see lover boy looking like you've just been

129

dragged out of a pond. You're about the same size as Jayne,' said Gary thoughtfully, looking her up and down.

Jane shook her head. 'Don't even go there. I'll have to see him like this. I'll have a quick shower and put some make-up on. It'll be fine. He's seen me looking worse.'

Gary held up a hand to stop her. 'Just hear me out. Jayne sorted out a whole stack of things to go to a nearly new place that sells them on line.'

'I've got my own clothes, thank you.'

'Not here you haven't,' Gary said sharply. 'I was only trying to help, and if you want to meet him wearing *that* it's no skin off my nose. No, really – you look fine.' He turned away all huffed up.

Jane glanced down at the pink tracksuit. Presumably that too belonged to Jayne as well, unless Gary kept something on standby in case of emergencies. It had an oily patch of salad dressing on it from lunch.

'What had you got in mind?'

'Honey, you could really do with a make-over. Over the next few weeks you've got to go out and represent Jayne's company and look the part. She's got more clothes, shoes and bags here than most London department stores. You need to relax and enjoy being here. She really won't mind. If you are worried, borrow outfits from the nearly-new rack, unless of course you want to go out and blow all your money on clothes. Use it like a lending library and then I'll get it washed or dry-cleaned and put it back.'

'What if I spill something?'

Gary eyed the smear of oil. 'How about I don't give you anything messy while lover boy's here?'

* * *

At five fifty-two the front doorbell rang. Twice.

'Would you like to follow me? Ms Mills is expecting you,' Jane heard Gary say from the front door. She was waiting upstairs on the landing, biding her time, and although it was childish and petty Jane had every intention of making Steve wait a bit longer. Not too long, but enough to let him clock the house, the furniture, the whole shebang. Make him truly think that she really had fallen on her feet.

'Can I get you something while you wait? Tea, coffee – a glass of wine?' Gary was saying.

Jane didn't bother listening to Steve's reply. She and Gary had spent about fifteen minutes going through the clothes in one of the spare bedrooms. This was what having lots of money was about, Jane thought, as she'd thumbed through the free-standing racks, aided and abetted by Gary whose taste was as impeccable as his tongue was sharp.

In one box – marked 'Samples' – was a whole stack of underwear. Still in their packaging in all sorts of styles and sizes there were bras, knickers, teddies, basques, thongs and tangas, so there was no question of that being a problem. From amongst the rails of things destined for upmarket recycling Gary picked out a long-sleeved soft-pink cashmere top with a deep V neck under which he suggested Jane wore a spaghtti-strapped white T-shirt, together with a pair of tailored cream linen trousers. Jane looked at the labels in the top and the trousers and realised they probably cost more than she spent in a year on her entire wardrobe. Neither appeared to have been worn.

Meanwhile, Gary, rummaging through a box in the bottom of the wardrobe, came up with a pair of high-heeled sandals, which he handed to Jane for inspection. 'What about those?'

Jane turned them over and looked at the soles. 'These haven't been worn either.'

He nodded. 'I know. Half this stuff hasn't. If Jayne likes something she'll buy it in half a dozen colours. What shoe size are you?'

'Six and half, seven.'

'Bingo. Jayne's a seven. Try them on – if they don't fit I can probably find another pair.'

By the time Jane had showered and fixed her hair and face, the clothes were all laid out in the bedroom, along with the sandals and underwear.

Now, listening to Steve being shown into the sitting room, Jane waited. And then waited some more. Her heart ached for him even if he was a bastard. And she hated him and she missed him and she still loved him. Bugger, bugger, bugger. Finally Jane took a deep breath, and walked very slowly down the stairs, all ready to make her grand entrance.

Meanwhile, Steve, cradling a glass of wine, was standing in front of an alcove, admiring one of Jayne's paintings.

He turned as she stepped into the room and smiled. Jane swallowed down the little flurry of excitement at seeing him and thought instead about Lucy, and the yoghurt and the bears.

'Well,' he said, drinking her in. 'You look wonderful, and what a fabulous house – great paintings. Certainly one of the nicest tied cottages I've come across in a while.' He indicated the canvas and then turned his full attention back to her.

Jane saw, with a sense of satisfaction, that whatever else

he had come to discuss, the house, her appearance and her new job had piqued Steve's curiosity.

'Yes, it is, isn't it? It's a Mehrutu.'

'Really,' he said, leaning closer to look at the canvas. 'I didn't know you were interested in contemporary art.'

'I'm not, but my new boss is,' Jane said. 'I had a guided tour when I got the job. Now what was it you wanted to talk to me about?' She made an effort to sound calm, even, steady. God, it was a struggle. Why did her body still fancy him? How cruel was that?

'Well . . .' Steve shifted his weight slightly, obviously uncomfortable and then apparently decided to change tack. 'Actually, I'll come to that in a minute. I don't like to pry, Jane, but I just wondered, about this new job of yours – it's nothing dodgy, is it? I mean all this . . .' He held up his hands, his eyes and the gesture encompassing the house, the art, the furniture, the whole thing.

'It is all perfectly above board, Steve.' He didn't look altogether convinced but Jane was having none of it and pressed on, 'Now, what is it you want?'

He shuffled again. 'Well, the thing is, Jane . . .' He set the wine down on the mantelpiece and pulled nervously at the cuffs of his jacket. 'Well, to get straight to the point, Lucy and—'

But before he could get any further the doorbell rang. Furiously. Steve's face was a picture. 'Damn,' he mumbled.

'Yes?' said Jane, hoping he would go on. After all, she wasn't expecting anyone. 'What about Lucy?'

'The thing is I wanted to—' Steve began again. At which point the doorbell rang again, if anything with more vigour, and they both heard Gary scurrying down the corridor, mumbling to himself.

133

It was hard to concentrate with the prospect of someone else joining them. For one awful moment Jane wondered if it might be Lucy. On the far side of the room Steve looked as if he might burst with frustration.

Seconds later there was a great commotion out in the hall and then the sitting-room door burst open, framing Tony Butler from next door, his hair awry, eyes wild and glassy. He looked dreadful.

'Jane, sorry to burst in like this,' he said, nodding to acknowledge Steve, 'but I didn't know what else to do. It's Lil. She's fallen over in the garden. I think she might have broken somefink. Can you come and take a look?' And with this he headed back towards the front door.

Steve stared first at Jane and then at the retreating form of Tony, who, besides looking slightly crazed, was resplendent in a black muscle vest, green silky jogging bottoms and gleaming white trainers teamed with an awful lot of bling that was obviously meant for their supper date. Given he'd worn more or less exactly the same outfit first time they'd met, it occurred to Jane that this was Tony's favourite look.

'I think I'd better go as well,' said Gary, following behind him.

'Who is that?' asked Steve, looking bemused as Jane headed after the two of them. 'He looks very familiar,' he added, keeping in step.

'Really?' Jane couldn't imagine a scenario where Steve and Tony's worlds might naturally cross. 'Steve Burney, this is my neighbour Tony, Tony Butler,' she said distractedly, more concerned about what they might find next door than any in-depth introductions. Tony was more or less oblivious to the social niceties, his thoughts on Lily.

As Jane said Tony's name, to her amazement Steve's face lit up like a Belisha beacon. 'Not *the* Tony Butler?' he said in an undertone as Tony and Gary hurried out of the door.

'I don't know.' Jane swung round. 'You know him?'

Steve nodded. 'God, yes, everyone knows Tony Butler – if it is him. He's a rock legend, singer-song writer, played bass with all the greats, fronted Paper Tiger – fantastic band, you must have heard of them – used to be all over the *NME* when I was a kid. Seminal album *Tiger Tiger* came out April 1971 – same week as the Stones released *Sticky Fingers*. They reckon if it hadn't been for that, well, they could have been just as big – bigger, huge. They were musos' musos. God, Tony Butler, fancy that. Bloody hell. Who would have thought . . .'

Jane stared at him; he was coming over all whimsical and nostalgic, which was slightly unnerving.

Jane didn't like to point out a) that Tony might very well not be *the* Tony Butler, and even if he was, b) that she wasn't even born in 1971, so instead she headed out through the door hot on Tony's heels.

Outside Tony guided them down the path that ran down beside the house to Lily, who was out on the patio, propped up against a large stone statue of a man with a bowl of fruit and very little else; Lily was looking considerably more embarrassed than in pain.

'I just slipped,' she said, as Tony flapped around behind them, looking anxious. 'I says to Tony, good job we hadn't got the pool in yet, I might have bleeding drowned.'

'Should we get her up, get her in the house?' said Tony, panic squeezing his voice into an endearing falsetto.

Very gingerly Gary pulled up the leg of Lily's blue silk palazzo pants. Jane stared at the damage. Lily's left ankle, swollen up like a football, was already the colour of a ripe damson, and whichever way you looked at it ankles weren't meant to bend that way. He glanced up at Jane and shook his head as their eyes met.

'I should stay right where you are, if I were you,' said Jane to Lily, taking her cue from him. 'We'll get you comfortable. Tony, go inside and find a blanket, will you? Have you called an ambulance?'

Tony shook his head.

'I didn't want to be any trouble,' said Lil. 'I thought maybe if I got it up on a stool, maybe an ice pack. It's these bleeding shoes. I'm fine in high heels but stick me in somefink sensible and I'm a total nightmare.'

'We should call an ambulance,' said Jane. 'It looks as if it might be broken.'

Tony let out a strangled sob.

'I'll go and do that,' said Steve who, having followed them to number 7, was keen to prove himself useful.

'And I'll fetch a blanket,' said Tony.

'I'm so sorry about this,' Lily said, looking up first at Jane and then Gary. 'I feel such a bloody fool. I was just going in to check on the supper. Hadn't touched a drop – my foot just slipped out from under me, just like that.'

'Don't worry,' said Jane. 'It'll be fine. Does it hurt?'

'Nah, to be honest it's kind of numb. I think you better go in and see to Tony, though. He's gone a funny colour.'

Steve, meanwhile, was heading into the house – presumably to find a phone, although it struck Jane as slightly odd that he didn't use his mobile.

'Do you think they'll take me in?' Lily was saying. 'Only Tony won't come if they do. He hates doctors and hospitals.'

'I think they might, but don't worry, it'll be all right,' said Jane.

'Tony won't come with me,' she repeated. For the first time since they'd arrived Lily looked a little tearful and shaky. 'He loathes them and ambulances. He's such a big baby. I'll have to go in on me own.'

'No, you won't, don't fret. I'll come with you,' said Jane, taking the older woman's hand. Lily squeezed it gratefully. Gary got to his feet. 'In that case I'll go and get your handbag and lock up,' he said.

A few moments later Tony appeared through the French windows carrying a fluffy tigerskin-print blanket and two black shiny silk pillows, with a gleeful Steve almost skipping along at Tony's elbow. He was nodding and mouthing, '*It is him, it's him,*' as they headed back towards Lily. '*And her,*' he continued, mugging a great wide-eyed gesture. Tony and Gary arranged the pillows while Steve whispered to Jane. 'Elizabeth Lucas.'

Jane pulled an expression of non-comprehension.

'Glamour model,' he said salaciously. 'Page three,' he added before miming the necessary attributes. 'Back in the seventies she had to beat the blokes off with a stick.'

Jane stared at him. The man really was a complete moron.

After what seemed like an age an ambulance finally arrived.

'We're private,' said Tony, as the crew gently lifted Lily onto the stretcher.

'I'll make sure they know that,' said Jane. Tony handed her a scrap of paper. 'What's that?'

'Our telephone number. Ring me.'

Jane nodded and tucked it into her purse. 'I'll ring as

soon as I know what's going on. And don't worry, I'll take good care of her.'

Lily's stoic front was rapidly beginning to crack. 'He'll be dreadful,' she said as they slid her into the back of the ambulance. 'He can't manage on his own. He's such a baby. Oh God, I don't think I've turned the oven off.'

'It'll be all right, Gary will take care of him,' Jane said, looking back over her shoulder towards Gary, Steve and Tony.

'Like I haven't got enough to do already,' Gary grumbled in an undertone.

As the ambulance doors closed the last thing Jane heard was Steve saying. 'I think we could all use a drink, don't you? So, what was it like playing with old Slowhand, then, Tony?'

Jane sighed. The man truly was a self-seeking insensitive moron but then again maybe Tony would be pleased to have something to take his mind off Lily, who was looking very tiny and vulnerable under the Witney blanket in the back of the ambulance. The ambulance man was busy putting a line into the back of her hand and as he did Lily whimpered, her bottom lip starting to tremble.

'I hate needles,' she whispered.

'Are you sure that I can't tempt you to join me for supper?' Miko said, helping Jayne down from the gangplank. Around them the other passengers were fading away into the half-light, heading off towards the bars and cafés. 'My brother has the most wonderful restaurant, fresh seafood, wonderful wine, with a view out over the ocean that would break your heart.'

'If you don't do it first. You should really go home to your wife.'

He winced. 'She does not understand me.'

Jayne laughed out loud. 'Miko, where did you learn to speak English?' For the first time she had a sense of wrong-footing him. 'Well?' she pressed.

'London School of Economics,' he said with a grin.

'And presumably all the rest of the heavy-duty flirting comes naturally?'

'Oh, you are so cruel,' he said with a thick Greek accent. 'I am just a poor lonely sailor.'

'Uh-huh, and I'm the Pope.'

He laughed and continued in impeccable English, 'Actually, I'm looking after my brother's business. He's been in hospital having a bypass. And you know, I'd forgotten what fun this can be. To be fair, I'm only fulfilling people's expectations. The punters love it – they want Greek and I give them Greek. Now, how about dinner? This restaurant is really special and I promise not to pounce.'

'Or turn into a Disney Greek.'

'You really are cruel, aren't you?'

Jayne smiled slightly. 'Absolutely. What about your wife?'

'Currently living in London with my eldest daughter. She is English. My youngest is here helping out in the family business for the summer. And actually, we're divorced.'

Jayne fixed him with her stare. 'I don't care – any pouncing and I'm out of here.'

'Scouts honour,' Miko said slyly, sliding his arm through hers.

He was right, dinner was fabulous.

It was late when Jane finally got around to pulling Tony's phone number out of her bag and finding a place to ring.

Mobiles were banned in the hospital so she had to stand outside the main doors with the smokers and tap in the number. She was a bit surprised when, on the third or fourth ring, Gary answered.

'Good evening, Butler residence,' he said primly.

'What the hell are you doing there?'

'Keeping an eye on things.'

'Do you always answer the phone like that?'

'No, but then again I've never worked for a rock legend before,' said Gary.

'So how's it going?' Jane asked.

'I was going to ask you the same thing.'

'Not bad. Lily's fine – we've been through A&E, X-ray, seen a really nice doctor and met the anaesthetist – all the usual stuff. They've just wheeled her down to theatre to set her ankle under general anaesthetic and then they'll take her into the private ward for the night. They said she should be out tomorrow morning as long as there are no complications, and the doctors don't foresee any. I'm knackered and am about to grab a cab home. How's Tony coping?'

'Oh, he's fine. I've fed and watered the pair of them and they're tucked up in the den at the moment with a bottle of single malt, a plate of ham sandwiches and about four thousand albums from the golden age of rock and roll. It's no wonder they all go deaf.'

'They?'

'I'll give you three guesses.'

Jane didn't need three. 'No, not Steve?'

'Oh, yes. He said he thought it was important that someone stayed with Tony and kept him company.'

'That man is all heart.'

'How long are you going to be?'

'I'm not sure. Depends how long it takes me to get a cab. Twenty minutes maybe. Can you tell Tony that Lily's all right and that she sends her love?'

'Leave it with me.'

When Jane arrived back in Creswell Close, on the wrong side of midnight, Tony's house was in total darkness, Jayne's porch light was on and all appeared calm. Jane realised as the gates swung open that she was really glad to be back.

Gary was waiting in the kitchen with a pot of tea and a ham sandwich on standby.

'I don't know how I've managed without you all these years,' said Jane wearily, pulling up a stool at the break-fast bar. 'I'm totally shattered. How on earth did you get rid of Steve?'

Gary laughed. 'I asked him if he was planning to stay the night.'

Jane pulled a face. 'And he said?'

'"Oh my God, is that the time? I said I'd be gone only an hour," and then I told him that his mobile had been ringing all evening. He'd left it in his jacket pocket in the hall so I pulled it out when it rang for the fifth or sixth time – that wasn't counting the text messages. It was someone called Lil' Lucy-Bear, apparently. Well, at least that's what it said on the caller display.'

'What did Steve say to that?'

'He went very pale and said "Oh God, oh God" a lot. Apparently Lil' Lucy-Bear would probably have his balls in a bucket.'

Jane took a big bite out the sandwich and smiled; she felt almost sorry for him.

* * *

In his office Ray tapped in the username and password he'd got for Jane and got into the administration area of the site straight away. Odd. Maybe she had typed it in incorrectly. Or maybe there was something wrong with Jane's computer. Whichever it was, it suited him down to the ground. He looked down through the current catalogue, wondering what Lulu would buy if she had half a chance – and then in the box marked 'authorisation' he typed Jane's code.

Chapter Seven

Jayne looked at the plump Greek man in the car-hire office, smiled and took the debit card back. 'I'm really sorry, this happened yesterday as well,' she said, tucking it back into her wallet and pulling a traveller's cheque out of her bag instead. 'I'm not sure what the problem is. It's a new card. Here – is this OK?'

He took the cheque and nodded. 'No worries. It could be the phones; it happens all the time. Me too when I was on holiday. So embarrassing. I had taken my new girlfriend. She think I am this big hotshot and ends up paying for dinner.' He laughed. 'But it's all right. If Miko says you are OK, then you're OK with me too.' He dropped the keys into her hand and then slid the paperwork across the desk for her to sign. 'It's the blue Rav4 on the end. Nice car – very sexy, goes with your eyes,' he purred, as his gaze moved appreciatively over her body.

Jayne kept the smile to herself, deciding not to comment or react. When she had been in her twenties the Greek men had been just the same. Back then she hadn't known how to react, blushing furiously at every turn, so it was rather endearing to discover that they appreciated older women with the same indiscriminate passion; flirting appeared to be the national pastime.

With the company's owner firmly at her elbow Jayne headed out of the chilly blast of some very overenthusiastic air conditioning to the beaten earth forecourt where an open-top Toyota hunkered down under the morning sun.

'It has a full tank of fuel, there's no excess mileage charge, just bring it back full tonight,' said the man, opening the door for her. 'My number here is on the paperwork if you have any trouble. But Miko, he knows – eh?' the man winked conspiratorially. 'You enjoy your dinner last night?'

Jayne didn't give him the satisfaction of looking sheepish. 'I certainly did. It's a wonderful place, great food. Do you eat there?'

The man raised his shoulders and pulled a face. 'Phuh, on the money I make?'

Jayne laughed; he was as plump and well groomed as a fishmonger's tabby.

'You should get Miko to take you,' she said, clambering into the driver's seat. 'Apparently he knows the chef – his cousin, I think.'

As were the headwaiter, the doorman and most of the clientele, thought Jayne ruefully, as she waited for the man to go back inside before firing up the engine. Driving on the right was something she needed to settle into gently.

She took her time, twisted her hair up into a knot, pulled her sunglasses out from her bag and then hesitated. Maybe she ought to stop by the bank on her way to meet Miko, pick up some cash and try to sort out her cards. It was a damned nuisance; she'd brought three with her. Her company card, a personal debit card and a credit card.

All three of which had been refused in the last twenty-four hours, which was annoying.

Jayne took the first few miles towards Kos town slowly, letting herself get the feel of the car and settling into driving on the right. After a while she began to enjoy the view, looking out over the olive groves and dark dusty scrub, past rocky outcrops and deep gullies, over low fields with rows full of produce, here and there catching glimpses of the sea through gaps in the rough terrain. The island was barely awake, still soft and fresh under a sparse blanket of morning mist. It was going to be another beautiful day.

By the time Jayne got to Kos she was relaxing and looking forward to exploring. She'd arranged to meet Miko in a car park on the outskirts of Kos town, and as she pulled up she saw him waiting for her by his car, basking in the sunshine.

'You look fabulous,' he said as he strolled over. Jayne smiled at the compliment. She was wearing sage-green pedal pushers and a fitted cream shirt that showed off her figure, along with soft leather sandals and a matching belt and bag, and he was right – she did look good. Miko didn't look so bad himself in a white cotton shirt, sleeves rolled up to show off muscular arms and a deep even tan, cream chinos, penny loafers, designer sunglasses tipped back to sit in amongst his dark curly hair. He took her hand and kissed it. 'Looks as if you are ready for your day out.'

Jayne glanced over his shoulder towards the car. 'And how about your daughter?'

Miko waved the words way. 'Don't fret. She will meet us for lunch. Have you ever been to the far end of the island? There is the most wonderful café there, overlooking the most fantastic rocky coastline. Big waves, great views, big sea – you will love it.'

'And how about your daughter?' she repeated wryly.

'Pah, you know what girls are like – she said she is helping in my cousin's shop this morning.'

Jayne stared at him.

'What?' he asked, eyes wide with something Jayne suspected he hoped might pass for innocence.

'You wouldn't lie to me, would you, Miko?' she said, voice full of humour.

He pulled a face and then shrugged. 'Quite possibly – but in this particular case no, Nina will meet us later for lunch, I promise. She is really busy and I thought after last night you would know it was OK.'

Jayne conceded. They had had a great evening, and once they had got beyond the Greek lecher act Miko was good company. They'd spent the evening in a little taverna full of locals, who all seemed to know Miko. They had laughed and sang and eaten and drunk wine all evening. She was weary after the boat trip and around eleven she had felt herself beginning to flag.

At which point Miko had leaned across the table and, touching her hand, said, 'You look tired. Rather than you finding a cab, I've arranged for my cousin to drive you back to your hotel. He runs a top-class car service from the airport. He's good driver and a nice guy, and I can vouch for him. I'll call him.'

'Thank you.'

Miko grinned. 'Oh, don't worry, I have ulterior motives.'

Too tired to protest Jayne had just smiled. Fifteen minutes later he'd waved the waiter over and paid the bill, while Jayne collected her things together and they had headed outside, despite the protestations of the rest of the company.

Outside, under a great flurry of stars the night seemed very quiet in contrast to the raucous good-humoured sounds from inside the taverna. The air was warm and heavy with the perfume of the vines that framed the entrance. In spite of herself, Jayne felt a little thrill of expectation that almost made her giggle.

'Miko, are you trying to impress me?' she said with a smile.

On the far side of the road, a sleek silver Mercedes was waiting by the kerb, music playing low on the stereo. The driver was wearing a uniform, which Jayne thought was a nice touch.

'Has it worked?' Miko asked.

Jayne laughed, and then they stood for a few seconds on the pavement, eyes adjusting to the gloom. She could feel the little crackle of mutual attraction. Now was the moment. Jayne looked up to find Miko looking down at her, eyes dark with desire.

As their gaze met she smiled. 'Thank you for a lovely evening,' she said, leaning closer to shake his hand and give him a kiss on the cheek. 'I had the most wonderful time.' And then before he could say or do anything else Jayne hurried across the road towards the taxi, as the driver hopped out smartly and opened the door for her. Jayne climbed in.

When she looked back towards the taverna, Miko was smiling and waving as the car pulled away from the kerb.

'See you tomorrow,' he called. 'Bright and early.'

And here he was.

'So where to first?' he said. 'Hills, history, the beach? Your choice.'

'Well, in that case, can you show me where the nearest bank is? I need to get some cash out.'

'A little more down to earth than I'd anticipated, but OK. We'll park here and walk into town. It's not so far and the town is lovely. Did you explore last time you stayed here? You want a coffee? How about a frappé? We can look at the boats. There is a tree where Hippocrates, the father of medicine, used to teach – or we could go to the agora, or the castle if you like. There are many beautiful places.' And with that Jayne let Miko direct her into the town centre so she could use the ATM.

He stood to one side, watching the world go by while she queued. Jayne slipped her card into the slot; the screen gave her a choice of languages. She selected English, punched the PIN in and the amount in, and waited. There was a soft mechanical whirring and a little click and then nothing. She pressed enter again. There was another whirr, another click, but no card or money appeared.

Jayne sighed; this was getting beyond a joke. She waited a moment or two longer and then tried to retrieve it by pressing cancel. No whirr, no click, no nothing. Damn. She tried again. A message came up that suggested she call her branch or ask a cashier for assistance.

Jayne opened her bag, pulled out another card and then stopped an instant before putting it into the slot, deciding not to risk it. She'd had problems with all the cards since arriving. There could be a fault with the machine or a glitch with the cards. Realistically the last thing she needed was to lose another one.

'Miko?'

He looked across. 'You OK? Is there a problem?'

'Yes, unfortunately. Can you go inside and explain that

their machine has just eaten my card? I've tried pressing cancel but it won't let me have it back.'

'Sure, was it the same one you used yesterday?'

Jane nodded. 'The one that was rejected for the boat trip? Yes, but I don't understand why.'

'Maybe it's damaged,' said Miko.

Jayne followed him into the cool confines of the bank and waited by the counter while he explained to the cashier what had happened.

The girl at the desk nodded and then went away to talk to someone more senior. The two cashiers vanished into the back of the bank, deep in conversation. When the girl returned a few minutes later she spoke in low voice, giving Jayne the occasional suspicious glance from the corner of her eye. It didn't give Jayne a very good feeling at all. Miko meanwhile nodded and listened and then added his sixpenn'orth before turning back to Jayne.

'She said unfortunately she can't return the card to you, the one you were trying to use has been cancelled.'

Jayne stared at him. 'Cancelled? I don't understand. What do you mean? Who cancelled it?'

'Apparently someone has reported it lost or stolen.'

Jayne felt her jaw drop. 'What do you mean, lost or stolen? It's my card, how can it be lost or stolen?' she protested, looking directly at the cashier, while Miko continued, 'I have already explained that there has to have been a mistake and that I could vouch for you, but the girl was just saying that their usual policy is to call the police if someone tries to use a stolen card.'

Jayne stared at him. 'But it isn't a stolen card. It's my card.'

He touched her arm. 'I know. Don't upset yourself. This

is a holiday island. Credit card fraud is rife. I've explained that there has to have been a mistake.'

'I'm not trying to do anything fraudulent. That is my card,' Jane repeated.

He nodded. 'The girl wants to know if you have got your passport with you?'

'No, it's in the safe at the hotel.'

Miko nodded. 'Well in that case we'll go and get it and then come back and try to sort it out. OK?'

Jayne felt hot and flustered. There had to be some kind of mistake. 'This is ridiculous. I'll ring my bank in the UK. There has to be some kind of mix-up. They guarantee getting a new card and cash here within twenty-four hours.'

Miko thanked the girl, explained Jayne's reply and then – leaving the card inside the belly of the cash machine – guided her back out into the sunlight. 'You look like you could use a coffee,' he said as they hit the street.

Jayne looked at him and sighed. 'I'm so sorry; thanks for your help. I didn't mean to snap at you or drag you into this, but it's crazy – and so annoying. I just need to get it sorted out. It should be fairly straightforward. The thing is this is just the first stage of my trip. I'll ring my business partner and get him to find out what's going on.'

Jayne opened her bag and looked inside. 'What worries me is that all three cards have been rejected. So does that mean they've all been cancelled? What the hell am I going to do if they're all duff?'

He took hold of her arm and guided her into a pavement café. 'For a start, don't worry. We'll have a coffee. I'll get them while you ring.'

Jayne nodded. She pulled out her mobile, called up Ray's number on the menu and pressed call. It rang once and then beeped before a recorded message said, 'Sorry, this service is unavailable. Beep. Sorry, this service is unavailable . . .'

Jayne tried the number again; one thing she was certain of was that the phone would work from anywhere. She had used it all over the world, from Iceland to the Himalayas. Maybe it was just Ray's number; maybe there was no signal despite the three bars on the screen. She flipped further down the menu and phoned home. The same message played. Jayne looked up at Miko and shook her head.

'I don't know what the problem is. I don't seem to be able to get a signal here. I'll just go and buy a phonecard.'

Miko handed her his phone and before she could protest, shook his head. 'It's OK.'

First of all Jayne rang the office in Buckbourne and got the machine, so she rang Ray's mobile. It was off and directed her straight to voice mail. Damn. With an increasing sense of frustration Jayne left him a message: 'Hi, Ray. I need you to contact me as soon as possible. I've got a problem with my credit card and the company card. As soon as you get this message can you give me a ring at the hotel and organise to get replacements sent out a.s.a.p.? You've got all my details there. I think they courier them to the nearest bank but if not, I'm staying at the Helena . . .' She reeled off the address, thanked him, and then tapped in her home number. Surely there would be someone there?

The answer machine for the house cut in after the fifth ring and Jane wasn't on the office number. Where the hell was everybody? Jane wasn't in the office, Gary wasn't on the home line. Ray was God knows where. What a great moment for everyone to be out.

*   *   *

In the little terraced house in Creswell Road Jane closed her suitcase and looked round the bedroom, wondering if there was anything else she needed to take back with her to Jayne's house. Lizzie, true to her word, appeared to have gone to work. The cats – now that they had been placated for her shameless neglect with a plate of tuna chunks and half a pint of full-cream milk – lazed in the middle of her bed in a great puddle of summer sunshine, licking their lips and purring their approval. No one seemed to have told them that milk was bad for adult cats.

Jane went across the landing, opened the bathroom door and took a look inside; the truth was she could nip back if she needed anything else, but Jayne's house in Creswell Close seemed an awfully long way away from the cosy little house backing on to the canal.

Jane glanced at the clock. She had offered to go and pick Lil up from the hospital, but they wouldn't discharge her until after the consultant had done his rounds, so Jane had plenty of time to check her email, go through the post and pack.

The only messages on the machine were from her mother, suggesting Jane might like to ring back with a date when she could come and stay, and an invitation from the Mrs Findlay in Human Resources at the library to call and have a little chat about her mental health, her back-to-work plan and her offering to coach Lucy on the finer points of outreach. Jane deleted both without a moment's hesitation.

Walking from room to room Jane felt as if she had been away for weeks. Other than making up the bed in the spare room and leaving a robe in the bathroom there was almost no trace of Lizzie, but somehow the house felt different, as if something had subtly changed in her absence.

Carrying her case downstairs and standing it in the hallway, Jane considered what else needed doing. She really ought to nip into Jayne's office in town while she was this close, go up to the storeroom and collect the samples so that she could be ready for meeting the clients the following week.

She'd need to track down the whereabouts of the bottled black cherries in kirsch if they weren't in the office store-room, but as yet she had seen no sign of Gladstone. She had no proof that he had had them but it seemed the only alternative. Although she and Gladstone had never actu-ally had a proper conversation, and she wasn't sure how he would feel about direct questions, particularly direct questions about possible misappropriation of bottled fruit, or, come to that, whether he took any notice of voices that weren't inside his head. Maybe she should just mark the peaches and cherries down to experience and put in another complaint to the Post Office?

Jane stood for a moment and listened. The hall clock ticked. The little house stretched and creaked in the summer heat. Everything in the house was neat and tidy. Downstairs in the kitchen the washing-up was done, draining board cleared, sitting room all plumped up and pristine-looking. Lizzie was obviously taking her care-taking duties seriously. On the kitchen table, wedged between a bowl of fruit and the salt and pepper, were a pile of letters, which she'd thumbed through while waiting for the kettle to boil. Some were for her, some for Jayne. It seemed odd that even though she had now moved the letters were still arriving at the wrong address.

She peered into the garden, wondering where Gladstone was. There was nothing on the bins, but then breakfast had long gone.

Once she'd locked up Jane headed back to the shiny new BMW parked in the street and slid her suitcase into the boot. There was a deck chair by the skip and alongside it an occasional table stacked with old newspapers but no sign of its occupant. She turned on the engine and drew away slowly, relishing the soft almost inaudible purr of the top-of-the-range Beamer – slowing at the corner, in case Gladstone was still in the garden of the burned-out house on the end. It was in shadow and she had noticed he was a bit of a sun worshipper so the likelihood was he was out somewhere.

Just as she was about to give up Jane spotted him on the other side of the canal bank, sitting on an upturned milk crate, watching the world go by. 'Morning,' she called, stopping and then getting out of the car, waving to him.

He didn't say anything or appear to notice she was there. Maybe he was asleep; maybe he couldn't hear her. She turned to go back to the car.

'Moved out, have you?' he said the instant she looked away. He had quite a low and very cultured voice.

'No – no, I haven't.'

'Lovely car. I nearly didn't recognise you. The girl in your house gave me a nice cup of tea and an egg and bacon sandwich this morning, said you told her to give me breakfast. Said I was to ring the bell, eight o'clock weekday mornings and she'd have it all ready. By appointment.' He smiled.

'She's a nice person.' Jane smiled. She'd have to have a word with Lizzie. There was a world of difference between leaving out the odd sandwich and cooking to order.

'She certainly is. So . . .' He looked up at her, as if waiting for her to tell him to what he owed the pleasure of this visit.

'I wonder if you've seen a parcel. It had black cherries in kirsch in it and some other bottled things – peaches . . .' Her voice trailed off, wondering how far she could go before he realised she was more or less accusing him of theft.

'Really? I like peaches,' he said conversationally. 'And nectarines and plums, oh, and those little oranges, clementines. And what are those little Chinese fruits called? White, like eyeballs?' He rolled his eyes upwards in a nasty approximation of a human lychee.

'They came in the post,' pressed Jane, inching forward with the words. 'Only they weren't meant for me. They may have been delivered to my house by accident. Someone had to take delivery of them – they wouldn't have gone through the letter box.' It was probably as far as she dared go.

Gladstone stared thoughtfully for a few minutes at the inky black waters of the canal where the shoulder of a shopping trolley peeked out from amongst a fringe of reeds.

'I like peaches,' he repeated.

'I just wondered if you'd seen then. You know – seen the postman.'

'I see him most mornings. Nice chap, always got lots of elastic bands.' Gladstone looked up at her with big and very clear brown eyes and then he nodded as if finally the question had made its way along his wiring. 'Ah. You mean did *I* take delivery of them?' He sounded horribly lucid.

'Well,' Jane began, 'I mean – well, yes, I suppose I do.'

Gladstone looked at her for a moment or two and then shook his head in disbelief. 'I know the postman round here is a bit slow but I don't think even he would let me have a parcel addressed for you.'

'I suppose not,' Jane began, embarrassed now, but Gladstone wasn't finished.

'After all, you live at number nine and he knows that I live at number one.'

Jane nodded. 'Right . . .' There was no arguing with that.

'I'd ask the people at number seven, if I were you,' he said conversationally, while sorting through the contents of his beard. 'They're a funny lot. Light-fingered, if you ask me. I saw them looking at my trolley last week. I like peaches.' And with that, whatever window had been opened closed tight shut, as Gladstone began to hum something classical and started conducting.

Jane nodded and made her way back to the BMW. After all, realistically she didn't even know for certain if the parcel had been delivered to her house, she was just adding two and two and making eight. And he *was* right about the people at number 7.

In Buckbourne town centre Jane parked the car behind the office in Jayne's space and headed round to the front door. She had the strangest feeling as she walked into the lobby, as if she didn't quite belong anywhere at the moment. Going back to her house had made her realise that nowhere felt like home any more; most certainly not Ray's den. Jane glanced up at the CCTV camera as she tapped in the door code. The lens watched her impassively as the doors slowly swung open. Jane stepped inside. The place felt deserted. Beyond the connecting door she could see the receptionist for the alternative health clinic working the phones but couldn't hear anything, giving the odd impression to Jane that she was watching TV with the sound off. Going into a building she barely knew didn't help at all with the sense of rootlessness.

Upstairs on the first floor the office was empty, immaculately tidy and totally soulless, with no sound except the low soporific hum of the computers, idling on the desktop.

Alongside the machine she had used on Monday morning were several envelopes addressed to her. There were also bank cards and a pass for parking in the car park behind the building. Others contained a brief outline of her job, along with details of her salary and terms of employment and in the last two were the PINs for the bank cards. Jane tucked the letters in her handbag and went off in search of the packages and the file that Ray had told her about.

The parcels were in a stationery cupboard in the storeroom, along with the manila file, just as he'd said. Jane decided it made more sense to open the parcels once she got back to Jayne's, closed the office door and – glad to be out of the silence – headed off towards the hospital.

'You are a real sweetheart,' said Lil, over her shoulder as Jane guided the hospital wheelchair, with Lil in it, out between the electronic doors of the main reception area and headed across the ambulance park towards the patient pickup point.

'Don't mention it,' said Jane.

Lil was clutching her overnight bag on her lap and looked tired, pale and slightly grey around the gills, despite wearing full make-up, lip gloss and with not a hair out of place.

157

'I dunno how we would have managed without you, I really don't. There is no way Tony woulda come and fetched me, he's such a big wuss. He rang this morning, said he was going to send a cab or hire an ambulance.' She chuckled. 'Or leave me here and get a little blonde in. I said bleedin' good luck to him, save me the aggravation. Great big ox.'

Jane smiled. The idea that Tony – who had to be six foot four in his white sports socks, if he was an inch – was too scared to come within spitting distance of the local hospital was rather endearing.

'You don't have to worry about Tony. Gary was on his way round there this morning when I left. He'll feed him. Tony thought it might be an idea to have a bed downstairs.'

'For him or for me?'

Jane laughed. 'I didn't ask. Do you want to sit in the front or the back?'

'Front, I reckon. Nice jam jar.'

Jane nodded. 'Goes with the job. OK, let me just push the seat right back.'

Lil looked around thoughtfully as Jane manoeuvred her into position. 'Me and Tone was planning to see a bit more of Buckbourne but I didn't have the hospital on me list,' she said, pulling her cigarettes out of her bag. 'You mind if I have a fag? I'll open the window.'

'You're fine.'

Lil lit up and took a long drag like it was a life saver. 'God, that is better,' she said, her expression beatific.

Once they were set, Jane took the armrest off the wheelchair and very gently helped Lil slide across – she couldn't weigh more than seven stone – and settled her cast in the footwell. Her toes peeping out from under the plaster were all shades of blue and purple.

'How does it feel?' Jane asked, handing her the seatbelt. 'Are you OK?'

'Bloody sore and I feel a bit delicate, but what can ya expect? I would feel better about it if I'd of been off me face. Anyway, I'll be fine once I get home. It's a bloody nuisance. We've still got loads to do in the house. I've dozens of boxes to unpack. What with the house-warming an' everything—'

'Don't worry, we'll give you a hand,' said Jane, loading the wheelchair and a set of crutches into the boot.

'So how long have you lived in Creswell Close then?' asked Lil conversationally as they pulled away from the parking bay.

Jane laughed, wondering if Lil had any idea how big a can of worms her casual question might open, but then again what would it matter if Lil and Tony knew? Realistically if they were going to be Jayne's neighbours it would make things a whole lot easier if they knew the truth.

'Can you keep a secret?' she said, pulling out into the flow of traffic.

Lil snorted. 'Me? Christ, you wouldn't believe what I've seen in the years I've been with Tony. If I ever wanted to kiss and tell, darling, I'll tell you now, I could make a bloody fortune.'

'OK, well, in that case this is peanuts; I've been there since Monday.'

Lil swung round and stared at her. 'You're having me on, aren't you? I saw you there the day before we moved in.'

Jane shook her head. 'No, honestly, and also I'm not Jayne Mills either. Well, actually I am, but I'm not *the*

Jayne Mills. Not the Jayne Mills who owns the house. I was delivering her post when you saw me.'

Lil's face brightened. 'Really? Fantastic. I like a bit of intrigue and mystery me. You're not hiding out, are you – or on the run? Not witness relocation – spies? You're not a sleeper, are you? KGB?'

Jane laughed. Lil was obviously in her element. 'Nothing nearly as exciting. I'm an ex-librarian who's just started a new job.'

Lil's sighed. 'That's a bit of an anticlimax. I could have done with a bit of excitement. Where are we going now?'

'Home. I just need to get some petrol,' said Jane.

'So come on then,' said Lil. 'You can't stop now. Tell me about not being Jayne Mills.'

After that it didn't take very long to explain at all.

In the café in Kos, Jayne handed the mobile phone back to Miko and rubbed her hands over her face.

'Well?' he asked, looking concerned. Jayne sighed and accepted the iced coffee he handed her. 'I can't get through to anybody in my office. And there's nobody at my house. It's completely ridiculous,' she said grimly. 'Looks like the bank have cancelled all my cards – that's all the cards I've got with me, and all the ones in my safe at home – and they've already issued new ones.'

Miko pulled a face. 'Why? Who to? I don't understand.'

'No, me neither. Someone asked to have the new cards sent out to my office, apparently.'

'Well, can't you cancel those ones and get new ones issued and sent here?'

Jayne took a long pull on her coffee, wishing it was something alcoholic. 'The new cards have already been used, along with my PINs – and whoever cancelled them also changed my password too. I got through to the card people and then after a few minutes they put me through to the supervisor and this woman said, "I'm terribly sorry but this password is no longer being used on this account. If you would like to contact your branch when you get back . . ." I mean, how bloody mad is that? How the hell am I supposed to manage out here until then? It's nuts. I need to talk to Ray.'

'Your husband?' asked Miko, raising an eyebrow.

Despite feeling horribly stressed, Jayne laughed at his blatant fishing. 'No, not my husband. He's my business manager. I took a new girl on just before I left. It's a long story but, in a nutshell, she's got the same name as I have, and I think that may well be the problem. I asked Ray to get her a company card and another one for the house-keeping account – she's staying in my house while I'm away – and I'm assuming that they've issued her my cards by mistake. Which is a bloody nuisance but it shouldn't take a lot to put right once I get through to Ray.' She sighed with frustration. 'This is so silly. If I was at home I could sort it out in a few minutes. Have you got access to a computer, Miko? Maybe I can get on line, send a few emails and sort it out.'

'Sure, not a problem. We'll go back to my office and try from there.' He laughed and shook his head. 'Some day trip this turned out to be, huh?'

Jane sighed. 'I'm really sorry. You are a saint, Miko. I promise to repay you.'

He waved the words away. 'For what? It's OK, it was a joke. Tell you what, we get this sorted out and then I'll take you for a wonderful lunch.'

'If I get this sorted out, I'll buy it.'

'You're on.'

Ten minutes later they were down by the harbour where Miko pulled a key out of his pocket and unlocked the office door. 'Phone, computer,' he said, waving towards the back desk, picking up a pile of post and starting to sort through it as he did so. 'Help yourself.'

'I'm surprised you're closed during the day,' Jayne said, settling down at the keyboard.

'*You're* surprised? What can I tell you? When my brother went off sick a couple of his staff walked out. There's lots of work on the island; I've got the girl who works in the office cooking on the boat again for me today. I'm interviewing for new staff next week.'

'For a cook or a receptionist?'

Miko laughed. 'Whatever I can get my hands on. Anyway, let's get you sorted out. You'll need a password to get into the computer.' He leaned over the desk and logged on for her. 'There you go,' he said. He was so close that Jayne could smell the subtle mixture of sun and sea and man on him. As if he could read her mind Miko looked down her and smiled wolfishly.

'Thank you,' she said, trying to ignore him. She pulled her glasses and a notebook out of her bag.

'You OK?' said Miko.

She shook her head. 'No, not really. And the whole of my support network seems to be out for the duration.' She could feel her eyes filling with tears. 'This is nuts. Damn, I'm going to cry now. If you were angling for a bit of a holiday romance, Miko, you must be hellishly disappointed. You're not seeing me at my best.'

Miko slipped his arm round her and laughed. 'Don't

worry. I have always wanted to be a knight in shining armour. This guy Ray – if you get through to him, he'll be able to sort it out?'

Jayne nodded, immensely comforted by Miko's arms in spite of herself. 'If I can get hold of him, yes, absolutely. He deals with the financial side of my company. If the worse comes to the worse I'll get him to wire me some money here. I've got my passport as proof of identity. I just need to get through to him.'

She turned her attention back to the screen. Miko slipped away and she pulled up the front page of her main website, pressed the contact button and wrote the same message that she had recorded for Ray. If all else failed, surely to God someone was picking up the company emails?

'Try ringing again,' said Miko, indicating the telephone.

Jayne nodded, and tapped in the number. On the third ring the call went through to voice mail. It took her all her energy not to throw the handset across the room in pure frustration.

'Ray,' she said, 'if you get this message can you please ring me a.s.a.p.? I've just emailed you. I'm having problems with my mobile phone and my credit cards. You've got all my details there. Can you please ring me as soon as you get this message? I can be contacted at this number . . .' She read Miko's office number off the headed notepaper on the desk. 'Or at the Helena Hotel. I've tried your mobile, my home number and the office number, and haven't managed to speak to anyone yet. At the moment this is just bloody annoying, but I really need to get it sorted out. Will you—' But before she could say anything else the machine cut her off. Jayne looked across at Miko.

'Bugger,' she snapped. 'There's still no one there.'

Miko took the phone out of her hand and set it down in the cradle. 'Is that unusual?'

Jayne sighed. 'Probably not. I'm just annoyed.'

'Let's go and have some lunch and then you can give it another try. How much have you got left in travellers' cheques?'

Jayne laughed. 'I can probably run to a sandwich,' she said, pulling them out of her handbag and counting them. 'A couple of hundred pounds. I really only brought them in case of emergencies. But I've got my hotel bill to pay.' Suddenly Jayne had the most awful rush of panic and looked up at him. 'Jesus, what am I going to do if I can't get any money out here?'

'First of all, don't look so worried. We can sort it out,' said Miko. 'Let's go and eat. There is nothing you can do until Ray rings you back. And the answer machine will pick the call up if we're out. Come on, things will look better when you've eaten.'

In the sitting room of the stylish top-floor apartment in Waterside House Ray's phone rang. It had been busy all day. After a second or two the answer machine clicked on to record for the fifth or sixth time in under an hour. The glittering patterns of reflected water shimmered across the high-vaulted ceiling, the sound of the voice loud in the still air.

'Hi, Ray,' said a husky male voice. 'This is Kit. I really wanted to talk to you, but looks like we're playing telephone tag. I tried to ring Jayne yesterday.' The caller paused. 'It was a bit odd. I've been thinking about it and I just wondered if you could call me.'

Ray lay back, staring up at the ceiling, and smiled.

They'd just got back from a day out in Cambridge. On the coffee table, over the sofa and spread out across the carpet were some of the things Lulu had bought on Jane's new credit card; chip and pin made it so much easier than the whole signature thing if you had the numbers you needed. There was an explosion of pale pink tissue paper and bags all over the place. She'd bought new shoes with slingbacks and bows, perfume, a couple of dresses, a hat, a leather bag and some wonderful underwear from a little boutique they had found. Lulu loved shopping – she had real gift – and was currently in the bedroom preparing to give Ray a little fashion show. She was so very grateful and he was certain she would look wonderful in the red satin corset he'd picked out for her.

'Don't look,' she called from the bedroom doorway. 'No peeking,' she giggled.

Ray smiled and gamely covered his eyes. He'd call Kit back later.

Chapter Eight

Once she'd got Lil settled in number 7, Jane drove the Beamer back round to number 9, carried her holdall upstairs and then went into the office to unpack the samples she'd brought back from Ray's.

It felt a bit like Christmas. Jane sat cross-legged on the office floor, peeled off the tape and paper, and the paper straw packed inside. The would-be suppliers, eager to make a good impression, had exquisitely wrapped all the samples in baskets and little boxes.

In one parcel were tiny hand-made soaps, bottles of bath oil and shower gel scented with sandalwood and lemon and vanilla, which filled the room with perfume. In another was a selection of hand-made paper and envelopes, some bound around with raffia and others with leather ribbon. Everything looked and felt and smelled incredibly sensual and luxurious. Jane could see exactly why Jayne loved her job.

More pragmatically, once she'd looked through all the products Jane went through the paperwork that came with them and found the names on the list of would-be suppliers with prices and margins and what kind of numbers they could supply, what Jayne thought they might be able to shift, along with where she thought they might fit into their existing ranges.

Jane scanned down the list. She was meant to be visiting these suppliers over the next couple of weeks. But there was still no sign of the products from Victoria Hartman.

Once she'd tidied the packaging away Jane started to catch up with the morning's work. There was post to go through, more data to sort out, she needed to email the edited copy off to the website designer and send a copy to Ray. As Jane considered what needed doing first she picked up her voice mails at the same time as checking the day's email.

'Hi, this is Miranda from the show house. I have a gentleman here who would like to speak to you, but apparently he can't make anyone hear. Carlo De Vine? He says he is a friend.' She paused. Jane could hear a voice in the background, masculine but high-pitched and anxious. 'Apparently he says he is an intimate friend. I just wondered if you might like Barry to pop over and check the intercom? If you could ring me back.' Jane skipped to the next. 'Hello, it's Jayne,' said a familiar voice. 'I've got a slight problem here.'

Jane turned to listen to the message as an email from Jayne dropped into the company inbox. As soon as she'd scanned the mail, Jane picked up the phone and tapped in the number of the Helena Hotel.

Somewhere on Kos the phone rang on and on. Jane was about to hang up when finally someone answered.

'Hello, Helena Hotel,' said a young woman with a heavily accented voice. 'Can I help you?'

'Oh, hello, I hope so. I'm trying to contact Jayne Mills. She is staying with you at the moment.'

'Jayne Mills, Jayne Mills,' the girl repeated. Jane was

unsure whether the girl was trying to recall the name or whether she was looking down the hotel register.

'Yes, an English woman, she's on holiday,' Jane prompted. She didn't know whether describing Jayne would help or whether it would be lost in translation and muddy the issue.

After a few more minutes the girl said, 'I am very sorry but they are not here now. Not at the moment. They go out.'

They? thought Jane. Oh, well. 'OK, well, can you give her a message, please?'

'Uh-huh,' said the girl, which Jane hoped meant yes, so she continued, 'Can you tell her I rang? My name is Jane—'

'Yes, of course,' said the girl. 'You want to book?'

This was not going quite how Jane had planned. 'No, I don't want to book. I want to leave a message for Jayne Mills. Is there anyone else there I can talk to?'

'Andrea, she speak English, mine is not so good. They are not here now. Not at the moment. They go out,' said the girl.

Which basically told Jane everything she needed to know.

'Thank you. I'll ring back later.'

'Thank you,' said the girl brightly and an instant later was gone.

As soon as she'd hung up Jane rang Ray just in case he hadn't got Jayne's messages. He must still be out of the office because the call went straight to his voice mail.

Just as she was finishing recording Gary came in. 'You got Jayne's message?' he said, nodding towards the phone.

'Yes. I've tried to ring her hotel and I've called Ray, but

he said he might be away for a couple of days, so I'll give him another try later.'

Gary nodded. 'She doesn't sound best pleased.'

'I know but I don't know what's going on with the credit cards – and I'm not sure what else we can do. I'll keep ringing Ray and there's an email here as well so I'll let her know that we're on the case. How's Lil getting on next door?'

'Oh, Lil is just fine,' said Gary wearily. 'She's had lunch, taken her painkillers and is about to go for a nap. It's Tony who is flapping about like a headless chicken. They've got this house-warming on Saturday night.'

'Can't they cancel it?'

'Apparently not. There are caterers booked and someone's on their way to put a marquee up tomorrow. They've got people flying in from Spain, and some band I've never heard of, and God knows who else. Tony is running around whimpering and making a fuss. I thought I'd nip back and give them a hand later, if you don't mind?'

'No, that's fine. I've still got a pile of work to do. Oh, and apparently someone called Carlo called today while I was out.'

Gary nodded and rolled his eyes heavenwards. 'I know. I hid – took me back to my childhood when the rent man came round. He is such a pain in the arse and he won't take no for an answer.'

'Arse?' Jane paused, remembering suddenly. 'Oh, I know – the one who moved the mirror? Jayne's ex-boyfriend?'

'Expensive ex-pet.'

'Didn't she tell him she was going away?'

'Probably not – probably didn't have the chance. He does

this a lot – storms out in a temper and then turns up expecting to be welcomed back with open arms.'

'Only this time Jayne's gone too.'

'He doesn't know that. Maybe he saw you in her car. Who knows? Very high maintenance, is Carlo. Talking of which – you want some lunch?'

In the middle of the afternoon the phone rang.

'Hello, Jayne Mills' office,' Jane said.

'Hi, I wondered if I could speak to Jayne, please?' said a low, even, male voice.

Jane wasn't going to get caught out again. 'I'm afraid Jayne isn't in the office at the moment, may I take a message?' she said, pulling a notepad closer and teasing a pen out of the pot on the desk as she spoke.

'Oh, OK. No, I'll ring back later,' the man said and then hesitated. 'Actually, on second thoughts, yes. Could you just tell her that the man in her life rang?'

'Carlo, is that you?'

The caller laughed. 'Damn, no, it's not. Sorry, obviously I've been side-lined. It's Andy. Andy Turner.'

Jane wanted to kick herself. She looked up and caught a glimpse of the black-and-white photo propped up on her desk and grinned. 'Andy Turner,' she said his name sounded so familiar.

'Yes, that's right. Has Jayne mentioned me?' he said, sounding surprised.

Jane laughed. 'Yes, she has actually.'

'Great. Well, she sent a message via my mum a little while back – said she wanted to chat. Catch up on old times. I've been away on business for a couple of weeks and only just got the message.'

'Oh, that is such a shame. She's already left.'

'Left?'

'She's gone travelling for a while.'

He laughed. 'Bugger me – that is a shame. If I'd known she was off, I might have tagged along for the ride. Did she go with Carlo?'

'No, no, he's an ex,' she said, anxious that there was nothing standing in the way between Andy and Jayne. 'He rang to see how she was. They barely talk; he didn't know she was away either . . .'

Jane tried very hard to stop blethering on, while Andy said, 'Oh, OK. When is she due back?'

'I don't know; I would give you her mobile number but she's having problems with it at the moment. But I've not long had an email from her. Can I maybe take your number and I'll pass it on?'

'Sure. It's such a pity I missed her. Did she tell you we'd travelled together?'

Jane picked up the photo off the desk and flipped it over. 'Andy, Beach-Bum of the Year 1982?'

He laughed. 'That's right. She *has* been talking about me. God, you know that seems like a lifetime ago. Where did you say Jayne had gone to?'

'Kos.'

'Really?' He sounded genuinely surprised. 'That's amazing. Did she tell you that that was where we started out from – and where we ended up before we came home?'

'No, she said you'd been there, though.' Jane didn't add that she knew it was the place where Andy had proposed.

'Fancy her going there, of all places,' he said quietly, almost as if he was talking to himself.

'Would you like me to pass your phone number on?'

'Yes, that would be great. Did you say she's got an email address? If she's off on her travels maybe that would be a better way of getting in touch?'

'OK,' said Jane. 'Hang on. I'll get it for you,' and read it out.

'That's great. How is she – you know?' he said. There seemed to be an awful lot of questions bundled up in just that one, and it sounded as if Andy Taylor might be just as interested in Jayne now as he had been back then.

'Jayne's fine. She's been very busy. I think she's really looking forward to having some time off. But I'm sure she'd be so pleased to hear from you.'

As Jane spoke, in the background she could hear someone calling him. 'Andy, are you up there? Andy?' Distant at first, and then getting closer.

'Be right down,' he said to the caller and then to Jane, 'Well, it's been great to talk and I promise I'll drop Jayne a line. I have got to go. My wife's back with the kids – bye.'

And then he was gone, just as Jane felt the words hit her like a splash of ice-cold water and the little buzz of excitement she had felt on Jayne's behalf bubbled away. Damn. He was married after all, snuggled up with his wife and kids, somewhere up North. Damn, bugger and blast. She realised how much she had hoped that Jayne would find a way back to the might-have-beens.

While she was thinking about Jayne and Andy she picked up a message from BT Callminder. Apparently Carlo was *désolé*. He didn't know how he was going to go on. He wanted to die – he *was* dying – he needed to talk, to explain, to make her understand. She couldn't make out any more for the sobbing. Jane sighed. And they accused women of being drama queens . . .

While listening to the tail end of the message Jane opened her email up. There was a mail from Steve. Apparently they still needed to talk. He was very upset by her attitude, probably *désolé*.

While Lulu went to try on another outfit, in his office Ray looked at the online banking screen for a few moments and then glanced down at the note he'd made of Jayne's new password and numerical code that he had set up. He lit up a cigarette, tapped in the numbers and then two letters from the password to open up Jayne's bank account.

It took a bit longer to execute the transfers but it wasn't hard: he had all the details he needed. Ten minutes later and it was all done. He then logged on to an online travel agent and booked a one-way ticket to Brazil – business class – on the company card. After all, once the shit hit the fan it would be silly to hang around, and if you were going on the run it would be nice to do it with a bit of extra leg room. As Ray tapped in the credit card details his mobile pinged to let him know that a text had arrived.

It was from Lulu; she was upstairs waiting for him to come and tell her how lovely she was; she was feeling lonely and bored and missed him sooooooo very much. Expressions of boredom and longing were followed by a very graphic description of how she would prefer to spend the rest of the afternoon and say thank you for her lovely shoes, although text left a lot to be desired as the language of lust. He picked up the handset to text her back; he wouldn't be long. Ray hated to think that all that youthful enthusiasm was going to waste.

* * *

173

In Kos the sun beat down relentlessly, an unblinking single eye focused on the little island. Hardly anything stirred in the heat. The air was heavy. Amongst the ruins and rocks lizards basked on, drinking in the heat, while tiny cats slept in the shade. But despite the heat, on a café terrace under the shade of a stand of trees, Jayne, glass of wine in hand, was in mid-flow.

'No, no, listen, Miko, it would be perfect. At this precise moment I need the money and you need a cook. What's the matter? It sounds like a perfectly reasonable arrangement to me. I'm a great cook – I ran a catering company years ago. I didn't always have staff, you know.'

Miko looked at Jayne and laughed. 'You're crazy. You're on holiday, for goodness' sake. I'll lend you some money.'

'Take me on temporarily. You've been so kind. I owe you—'

'No you don't. You don't have to work to pay me back. You said yourself this guy in the UK will sort everything out in a few days. And I'm very happy to lend you some money till then.'

They were sitting in a hillside café in a tiny village not far from the elegant ruins of an ancient hospital and temple called the Asklepion. Even though Jayne was worried about the money situation Miko had insisted they should still explore some of the sites, and so they had spent what remained of the morning wandering between the columns and in amongst the stone steps and statues, baths and terraces of the ancient archaeological site. Cypress trees framed the sun-bleached stones, creating spectacular views out over the island. But despite all the glorious scenery Jayne's mind was elsewhere. For the first time in years she wasn't in control and was torn between total panic and the odd sense of elation.

In the heat of the midday sun they had found a café and had been joined by Miko's daughter, Nina, for lunch. Jayne had had the lion's share of the wine, and the more she thought about it the more sense the idea made.

'Miko, you're very kind but I came away looking for an adventure – a new start – and it's just occurred to me that maybe this is it. Maybe this is what I've been looking for. Just what I need. You could at least give me a try – take me on temporarily until you find someone else. What have you got to lose? What do you think?'

'That maybe you shouldn't have so much wine at lunchtime,' he said, raising the bottle to see how much was left. They had ended up taking the Toyota back to the hire shop, reclaiming Jayne's traveller's cheque and going off in Miko's car.

'I'm a great cook,' she said grumpily, 'and a hard worker – *and* I can start straight away.'

'Are you serious about this or is it just the vino talking?' Miko said, pouring the dregs into his own glass.

'Yes, absolutely I'm serious. Obviously I'll sort this thing out with the bank over the next few days, but in the meantime I can't live on fresh air and kindness, and I'm not actually sure if I can pay my hotel bill. And I'll need somewhere to stay, so if you really want to help me, then help me do that.'

Miko grinned. 'Well . . .' he began, 'I've got this lovely apartment overlooking the sea; it's far too big for me on my own.'

Jayne laughed. 'I was going to say, before you suggest

175

anything dodgy what I had in mind was finding a cheap room or maybe a little hotel.'

'What I had in mind wouldn't cost you anything,' he purred. 'Well, hardly anything.'

'That's appalling,' she laughed again.

Miko mugged deep offence, while from across the table Nina, said, 'Dad, will you just stop with the ageing lecher thing. It's disgusting. If you don't take her on you're mad.' She looked at Jayne and pulled a what-can-you-do face.

Nina was in her early twenties, was well spoken and, despite classical Greek looks, having grown up in England she sounded as if she hailed from somewhere deep in the Home Counties. She took another spoonful of the baklava that Miko had insisted they both have with ice cream *and* cream.

'He's complete rubbish at hiring people,' said Nina, between mouthfuls. 'I've got no idea why Uncle Philippe left him in charge. I could make a better job of it. The last woman he hired couldn't cook and hated boats, and the girl he took on to do the bookings was a kleptomaniac who couldn't add up.'

Miko sighed. 'You're so judgemental, Nina. The customers really liked her.'

'You mean *you* really liked her.'

Miko reddened. 'She was very beautiful.'

'She was barking mad, she heard voices,' said Nina darkly before turning her attention to Jayne. 'If he won't offer you the job, I will, because the bottom line is if you don't do the cooking I'm going to have to go out on the boat next week, and I get seasick.' She turned towards her father. 'How my mother ever put up with him I'll never know.'

'She didn't. I had to bribe her,' said Miko glumly. 'Cost me a bloody fortune.'

'So have we got a deal then?' asked Jayne, lifting her glass towards Miko.

He sighed. 'Apparently.'

'In that case when would you like me to start?'

'Tomorrow,' said Nina, quickly.

'Whoa, wait, wait.' Miko held up his hands to stop Jayne's headlong rush towards gainful employment. 'Tomorrow, Jayne, you can come in for a little while, help get the galley stocked, we'll get a uniform sorted out and then you can go out with the boat on Friday. I need to talk to the girl in the office, sort out her rota. Last thing I want to do is offend her, and for her to stalk off in a strop.'

Jayne nodded. 'That's fine by me. I need to sort out somewhere to stay. I can't really afford to stay on at the Helena.'

'The wages aren't that bad,' said Miko with a grin.

'You can come stay with me,' said Nina. 'My aunt lets out rooms and I know she has a spare one at the moment. It's not expensive and, trust me, it would be better than staying with Papa. I had to move out in the end. It was just too much, staying at the apartment.'

Jayne wondered if this was because Nina felt Miko was cramping her style, but apparently not. 'You wouldn't believe the mess he makes. He rolls in at all hours of the night and day, drunk, singing and bringing his friends home. And not just friends,' she said archly, raising an eyebrow.

'You know, you sound just like your mother,' said Miko, blushing and looking horribly hard done by.

Nina ignored him. 'I'll give my aunt a ring as soon as I get back. I'm sure it will be OK. I will explain and let her know you're working for Miko.' She looked at her watch and started gathering her things together. 'Actually, I ought to be off. Nice to meet you.'

'Whoa, hang on a minute,' said Miko. 'Don't I have any say in this at all?' He looked from one to the other and sighed. 'Apparently not. Jayne, if you're serious you need to be down on the harbour for eight a.m. That's when they deliver the fresh food for the trip. It's simple really – you saw how it went yesterday. The bar is open all day and then we have a buffet barbecue lunch on the beach, the crew cook the meat, the cook prepares everything else. We'll go through it all tomorrow.'

'Sounds simple enough,' said Jayne cheerfully.

Nina grinned. 'Have you ever worked on a boat before?'

Jayne shook her head.

'Well, however bad you think it might be, it's worse, far worse, with big waves – although hopefully it won't be too long before your money comes through.'

Miko snorted. 'She is exaggerating, and you –' he glared at Nina, pretending to be annoyed – 'get back to work. It'll be fine.'

And that was it. By the end of the day Jayne had settled up at the Helena Hotel and with Miko's help had moved her things into a little room in Kos town on the second floor above a newsagent's, in a back street around ten minutes' walk from the harbour.

Once Miko had left, Jayne put her case on the bed and began to unpack. She looked round and grinned; from luxury hotel to galley slave in the twinkling of an eye. The room was basic, with more emphasis on shabby than chic, but it was clean and comfortable, with a window looking out into the street, a single bed in one corner, and a little table, a lamp and two chairs in the other, and along one wall was a cabinet with a kettle, cups and a couple of plates. There was a shared bathroom on the landing and kitchen on the floor below. Jayne hung up her clothes in a narrow and rather battered wardrobe. It was the kind of place she had rented when she first left home and oddly enough she felt absolutely delighted. Finally, a real-life adventure; she could barely stop smiling.

As the sun went down Jayne went off in search of supper, already with a strange sense of being part of the landscape rather than just a tourist passing through. It gave her a good and oddly peaceful feeling. On the way back to the room Jayne bought a phonecard from the newsagent downstairs. She'd ring Ray and Jane tomorrow and let them know where she was and what was happening.

Dear Steve, as far as I'm concerned we don't have anything to talk about. I certainly don't have anything to say to you that hasn't already been said. Please stop contacting me.

Jane looked at the email and let her finger hover above the send button, considering whether or not to press it. It was the end of the day, she had saved everything to the back-up files because she still couldn't access the main website, despite Ray saying he would sort it out, and had spent the last half-hour writing and rewriting to Steve. This was version twelve, and so far the most succinct version that didn't involve swearing.

She stretched and reread the email. Besides sorting out

179

the raw edges of her love life she needed to talk to Ray about the pass codes.

On the desk was the manila folder that had been with the parcels she'd collected from the office. What should she do with that? Where would it be best to keep it until Jayne came home? Without opening it, Jane slid it into one of the desk drawers so that it was out of the way, then turned her attention back to Steve's email. Maybe she should use version one: 'Dear Steve, I wish you and Lil' Lucy would, just go f . . .'

The flowers had blind-sided her, softened her up. When Jane had picked up the voice mail on her mobile she'd discovered that while she was in the hospital collecting Lily, Steve had rung twice. She was beginning to feel bullied and cornered, and with no real idea what he was up to, she felt angry and hurt. Whatever it was he wanted to say he should either forget it or have the good grace to say it straight out, face to face, or in the email or on the answer machine. This was harassment. And the flowers were just plain cruel.

When the phone rang Jane almost snatched it up off the receiver. 'Hello?'

'Jane?' said Ray, sounding concerned. 'Are you OK? You sound a bit fraught. I just picked up your messages and Jayne's. I thought we needed to talk.' Another one who needed to talk, Jane sighed.

'Have you managed to get through to Jayne yet?' asked Jane.

'No, I only got back to the office a few minutes ago and I'm turning round and going back out. I've just rung the hotel. Apparently she checked out this afternoon. I've got no idea where she is.'

'But I didn't think she had got any money.'

'I know. The thing is, you don't know Jayne like I do. She is very headstrong – God alone knows what she is up to.'

'You don't sound worried. Should we be worried?'

Ray laughed. 'No, I don't think so. Jayne is one of the most resourceful people I know. I'm sure she's fine and she'll be in touch. Until that happens I'll sort the bank thing out. Have you used the company card for anything yet?'

'I bought petrol yesterday.'

'And there were no problems?'

'None at all other than the guy behind the desk trying to get me to buy five litres of oil.'

'Good. It's got something to do with you and Jayne having the same name, I'm sure. I'll check that out first thing tomorrow.'

'OK. Oh, and I still can't get into the workings of the website to save the stuff I've done.'

He paused and then said, 'Really? OK, well, I'll sort that out too. In the meantime I've got a couple more things for you that I'll mail through. Oh, and I've got some things being couriered over to you. Can you make sure they're signed for? They're for a client and I don't want them going to the office if there's no one there.'

'Sure.'

'Can you make sure you sign for them yourself?'

'All right.' She paused. 'Why?'

Ray made an uncomfortable little sighing sound. 'I don't like to say this but Gary is notorious. I don't know whether Jayne's mentioned it to you or not, but he is always losing things.'

'Gary?'

'That's right. In lots of ways he is really efficient – but anyway, if you could tell him you need to sign for anything for the company and then keep it in the office for me that would be great.'

'And do what with it?'

'Nothing – well, not until we need it or I tell you, OK? Just keep it somewhere safe.'

'Of course.'

'Great. Well, in that case I have to be going. I've got a couple of meetings first thing tomorrow but you can leave it with me to contact Jayne. I'll sort the card thing out and wire her some money as well once I've made contact.'

'Right, OK,' Jane said, feeling a tension she didn't really know she had ebb away. Ray would sort it out and she needn't worry. Everything was going to be all right after all.

As Jane said her farewells Gary popped his head around the office door. 'Supper will be ready at seven,' he said as soon as she had hung up.

She stretched. 'Great, just to let you know that Ray is going to sort Jayne out tomorrow. Oh, and apparently he is having something couriered over here and wants me to sign for it.'

Gary shrugged. 'Whatever. Anything that lightens my load. I'll give you a shout when supper's on the table.'

Jane went back to the screen to reread the email she planned to send to Steve. Maybe it would be better to talk to him. She dialled his number and, when no one replied, was about to leave a message when it occurred to her that it was Wednesday. Wasn't that the night Lucy said they always met? The likelihood was the reason Steve wasn't answering his phone was because he was off somewhere buying yoghurt or, worse, was possibly already applying it – maybe to the sounds of Jane's voice if she left a message. She hung up quickly, feeling shaken and slightly nauseous.

At which point Gary called, 'Courier', and Jane headed off downstairs to the front door.

Framed in the open doorway was a tall good-looking guy in his late thirties with a motorcycle helmet tucked under one arm. He gave Jane an appreciative once-over as she made her way down the hall.

'Taking you somewhere nice, is he?' said the man as he handed her a thick printed envelope marked 'J. Mills. Traveluxe, tickets enclosed'.

Jane smiled as she took the pen. 'Don't ask me, I'm just the monkey, not the organ grinder. All I've got to do is sign for it,' she said.

'Shame,' said the man, slipping the pen back into his jacket. 'I was hoping that maybe if he broke a leg or something you could take me instead.'

Jane grinned. 'Well, if it happens I'll let you know.' Then she thanked him, closed the door and then took a closer look at the package. It seemed odd having tickets sent to her house, but then again, Ray had said he was out of the office. She went back upstairs, turning the envelope over wondering if it was for a client; maybe there was a website she'd missed. Making a mental note to check next time she talked to him, Jane dropped it into the drawer alongside the large brown envelope from Jayne's office and then went off to have a shower and get changed. It felt like it had been a long day.

Steve rang while she was in the shower. Apparently he

hadn't been able to get to the phone before. She didn't bother ringing him back.

The following morning, well before eight, Jayne – dressed in shorts, a T-shirt and trainers – walked down to the quayside, which was already a hive of activity.

'We need to get all this stuff into the fridges, chop chop. Vittorio and Theo, can you bring the ice? And if you could just help me bring these . . .' Miko said to Jayne, indicating the pile of boxes stacked in the back of a small white van parked alongside where *Spirit of the Waves* was moored.

She nodded, slid a tray of salad vegetables off the top of the pile and headed up the gangway, hot on the heels of Miko, while the rest of the crew carried on boxes of ice, and the meat and fish for lunch, loading everything into the chiller down by the galley.

No quarter was given for either age or inexperience, or the fact that technically at least Jayne was still on holiday. The girl Jayne would be replacing was a leggy and very curvy blonde with a tan to die for, and whether she could cook or not, she was going to be a hard act to follow with the crew. Dressed in skimpy shorts and a skin-tight T-shirt, sunglasses tipped back on her head, she stood to one side near the galley's large sink, directing operations and ticking things off as they were stowed away.

When Jayne came back with a tray of fresh pitta bread Miko was deep in conversation with her.

'Jayne?' he said as she turned to leave.

'Yes?'

'How do you feel about manning the galley today? I was planning to wait until the rota changed over but Christina is happy for you to go out today if you want to.'

Jayne nodded, trying to work out whether this was a good thing or a bad thing. The blonde, all teeth, tan and lip gloss, smiled back at her.

'I'm not really a natural cook,' she said, tucking a stray shoulder-length strand of hair back behind her ear. 'And really I was only helping Miko out till he could get someone else. I've got – how do you say? – other talents. Miko said so, didn't you?' she purred in a heavy Eastern European accent. Beside her Jayne could feel Miko cringing.

'So, Jayne, we'll need to pop back up to the office and find you a uniform,' he said briskly, rubbing his hands together. 'We've got some spares. Let's go and get that sorted out, shall we?'

Jayne grinned as the two of them headed back across the quay. 'Why on earth are you chasing me when you've got a piranha like that on the staff? *Other talents* . . .' She laughed aloud and shook her head.

Miko reddened. 'What? Book-keeping, that's what I meant,' he snapped. 'She's great on the front desk and she has a lovely telephone manner.'

Jayne raised an eyebrow and Miko held up his hands in surrender. 'OK, so she is also stunning, but trust me, when you get past that there's nothing much else there. She's got the brain of a boiled shrimp, and the crew were about to mutiny. She thought cooking for the boat would be a nice change from working in the office and that she'd get paid to swim and top up her tan.'

'Not sweating her brains out in the galley?'

'I thought you said you hadn't worked on a boat before?' he said with a grin, by now opening up the office. 'Oh, she didn't mind working behind the bar, getting drinks bought for her and flirting with the punters, but for the last three trips Theo – that's the dark-haired grumpy guy, looks like Eeyore with a tan – has done most of the cooking. They were delighted when they heard I'd got a replacement.' His grin widened. ''Specially when they discovered it was a grown-up.'

'And I'm supposed to be flattered by that?'

He shrugged. 'You haven't heard what they called her.'

'And you're coming out with me?'

Miko pulled a face. 'I didn't think you'd be going today and unfortunately I've got business to see to. So, no – but Theo will show you the ropes. He's a good boy.'

Jayne sighed. 'Maybe I'll get a chance to swim and top up my tan.'

Miko handed her a box of shorts. 'Small, medium or large?' he asked, eyeing her bum speculatively.

Meanwhile, life in Creswell Close had ground to a stand-still. The leafy roadway was completely blocked by four articulated lorries, a catering truck, half a dozen transit vans and a posse of roadies, musos and riggers, who wouldn't have looked out of place at a Black Sabbath gig, and all of whom were hellbent on negotiating their way up Tony and Lil's driveway.

Miranda had been over from the site office but had vanished once she saw the shape and size of the oppos-ition. No one who regularly cleared up after people who bit the heads off bats was going to be phased by a small peevish-looking blonde with a mobile.

It appeared to be utter chaos as a stream of people like ants unloaded all manner of weird and wonderful things from the back of the vehicles: lights, shop-window dummies, and a stuffed bear in flying goggles to name but a few. For one awful moment it looked as if the roadies might a) have to carry the marquee and everything else in by hand, or b) resite a whole pantheon of Greek gods to avoid them either being mown down or decapitated, or c) reverse over Tony, who – beside himself with complete panic as things got more and more complicated – was running in and out of the vehicles waving his arms about, on the edge of total hysteria.

Jane, who was working in the office, would have been totally oblivious if it hadn't been from Gary coming up with coffee and suggesting they pull up a chair each and watch. 'It's a complete circus out there,' he said conversationally, as he set the tray down on her desk.

'I know, but I'm sure it will be all right. They look like they've done this kind of thing before.'

'No, no, it *is* a complete circus. Tony told me yesterday – high wire, trapeze, clowns, the whole nine yards.'

'Really?'

Gary nodded. 'Themed party, very chic, very now – apparently. That and the fact Lil loves the circus.'

'Do you think we should go round and offer to help?' said Jane as they peered out of the front windows. Tony was jumping up and down now, although it was difficult to work out whether it was purely for effect. Meanwhile, Lily, wearing a huge straw hat, was sitting in a wheelchair under the portico like some frail winsome Southern Belle, orchestrating proceedings with a cigarette in one hand and what looked suspiciously like a gin and tonic in the other. Or maybe it was a mint julep.

Gary shrugged. 'Might be fun. I mean, it's a toss-up between this and cleaning out the deep-fat fryer. How about you?'

Jane puffed out her cheeks thoughtfully. 'More data entry, getting annoyed about not being able to access Jayne's website and wondering when Steve or Carlo will ring back.'

Gary sighed. 'Tough decision.'

'Maybe we could just go for half an hour or so. Check up on Lily. Watch the big parade.'

Gary was already on his feet. 'I'll lock up,' he said.

By lunchtime it was beginning to take shape, the marquee rising from the lawn like a great creamy white beast, with a ring and tiered seating, whilst men were laying cables and lights and unloading all manner of speakers and floors and staging.

Jane handed Tony a mug of tea – one of the dozens she had made since arriving. 'Looks good,' she said, nodding towards the lawn, where the riggers and erectors scuttled around like beetles.

'Yeah, I was thinking that's where we'll have the pool. Bloke was really helpful last night.'

'Oh, he came, did he? I thought you might ring and cancel him,' said Jane, as a small man abseiled down from one of the larger trees in the garden with a set of wire cutters in his teeth.

Tony nodded. 'Nah, helped take me mind off Lily, and that friend of yours was full of bright ideas. Very helpful. Very novel.'

Jane decided not to pursue Steve's gift for bright ideas. 'I don't think I've ever seen a house-warming like this before,' she said, as two men came past with the stuffed bear and a life-size model of a strongman on a trolley.

Tony laughed. 'Oh, this is small for them. It's nuffink. These guys usually do festivals and stuff like that. Nah, this is a walk in the park. They've done Wembley, NEC, Knebworth, Glastonbury, Reading – all over the States, Australia – most of the big cities in Europe . . .'

As they spoke Gary scuttled by, carrying a clipboard, followed by a procession of roadies carrying palms in pots. 'And you set up over there . . .' he was saying, pointing officiously, 'and be careful with that plinth. That's where they're going to put the ice sculpture.'

Jane glanced up at Tony. 'Ice sculpture in a circus?'

He shrugged. 'What can I tell you? I thought Lil would really like it, – bit classy, you know. She had one for her twenty-first birthday; some sheikh bought it for her when she was modelling. I saw this one in a brochure, thought it would add a bit of style.'

'What's it of?' asked Jane, watching two heavy men in boiler suits hefting the plinth into position.

'It was a tough call. I was torn between Pegasus Rising – that was lovely – an' then they do this one with two swans about to take off.' He demonstrated. Jane could see how you might be impressed. 'Or . . .' he continued.

'Or?'

'Or a life-sized replica of Elvis at his last gig, Indianapolis, the twenty-sixth of June 1977.'

Jane smiled. Well, obviously. What else . . . ?

Chapter Nine

Jane nipped back round to number 9 at lunchtime to check the phone – in between back-lighting the bear and rearranging the parlour palms to give Elvis a bit of cover – to see if Jayne had rung, and to check the email. Good job she did. There, curled up in the inbox, was a chatty little mail from Ray.

> Hi, Jane – sorry, just to remind you, as we hadn't mentioned it and I wasn't sure if you'd checked the diary – it's the Cassar dinner this evening. They'll be sending a car at around 5.00. I've attached Jayne's speech and the itinerary. Hope it all goes well. Still haven't got through to Jayne but am sorting out credit cards and money, etc. as I type – if she contacts you, will you please tell her that the matter is in hand?
> Best Wishes, Ray

Jane reread it. At least a trip out would be a change from data processing and bear back-lighting, and it was only a trade do. Ray had said so when they had lunch. She wondered if they had a stand or a table or something.

She could probably get away with wearing the smart brown suit Gary had got back from the dry-cleaners – her little cream top underneath, earrings and high heels just to give it a bit of pizzazz. Jane glanced at her watch, wondering what time it started and where it was. Probably in the town hall or one of the local hotels.

While she was waiting for the attachments to download Jane tapped Cassar into the search engine on the computer and read the first entry. It wasn't exactly what she had expected.

Started by Henry Cassar in 1975, the Cassar Club is a prestigious UK-based philanthropic charitable organisation whose membership is selected for their entrepreneurial skills and their special expertise and acumen in the modern world of business. Membership is by invitation only, notable members include . . .

Jane scanned down the list of members past and present and, as she did, felt her heart sinking fast. She recognised several names on the roll of honour – many famous, some infamous – and below that were pictures of their last social get-together. It was some kind of charity fundraiser with a champagne fountain, celebrities, and some very high-octane designer frocks. Jane stared. Her Next suit was definitely not going to do. As she read on, a copy of Jayne's speech appeared, followed by the itinerary, which popped up on the screen alongside Ray's cheery little note.

She scanned down and groaned: champagne reception on the terrace, followed by a formal dinner in the great hall, speeches, vote of thanks, black tie . . . Black tie?

Jane felt a little flutter of panic followed by a bigger one and then an even bigger one as she scrolled down the page and read the guest list. If this was his idea of a joke then Ray's sense of humour left a lot to be desired. She toyed with the idea of ringing him, but then decided she needed real help, not the kind Ray had offered her so far, and hurried downstairs.

'Gary? Gary, where are you?' Jane called anxiously.

The house seemed to be empty; there was a high probability he was still at Tony's. There had been talk of Pimm's, beer and bacon butties to keep the workers on song. She had to get him back. Anxiously Jane opened the back door, only to find Gary out on the patio sharing a joint with half a dozen roadies and a grizzled rock chick with purple hair and a nice line in tattoos.

'Oh, thank God, there you are,' she said.

'Just having my lunch break.'

'OK, I'm not checking up on you, the thing is—'

'Don't tell me,' said Gary, 'the cat got stuck in the printer again.'

'No,' said Jane, totally wrong-footed. 'When did that happen?'

Gary shrugged, implying it was just one of those things that helped make his day go with a swing. 'Lunch won't be long. Ten minutes – I was thinking chicken Caesar salad, followed by crème brûlée?'

There was a lot of nodding and appreciative noises from the roadies.

'I'm not worried about lunch; what do you know about the Cassar dinner?'

Gary considered for a few minutes and then said, 'That it's a really important annual event, and that Jayne said Ray was going to do it for her.'

'Well, apparently he lied. He's not. I am.'

'*You are?*'

'Don't say it like that. I am – and I was hoping you'd help me,' said Jane, crestfallen.

Gary handed the spliff to the guy sitting next to him. The man had so many facial piercings that Jane couldn't help wonder if, come teatime, his face leaked like a sieve.

'Best we start now then,' Gary said grimly, getting to his feet and rolling up his sleeves as if he had been asked to give a hand concreting a driveway. 'What time is the car showing up?'

'Five o'clock – why? Where is this place anyway?'

'A big country house near Cambridge. So, let's get this show on the road, shall we? Guys, I'm sorry to cut it short but I've got to get on.'

'No worries,' said the man with the ZZ Top beard and no teeth.

'So does everyone get a car sent for them?' said Jane incredulously, as Gary marched her back into the house.

He shook her head. 'Only their keynote speaker.'

Jane stopped mid-stride and stared at him. 'What?'

'They invited Jayne earlier in the year after the chairman saw an article about her in one of the Sunday magazines. It's a real coup. Bit old school, Cassar, still hasn't quite get over the fact that we had a woman Prime Minister.'

Jane stared at him.

'Yes, really,' said Gary, 'Jayne's been working on her speech for ages. Weeks, trying to get the right tone and spring it on Cassar that the world has changed. He and his cohorts are keen to listen; apparently the internet is going to be the next big thing.'

Jane swung round. 'What do you mean *is going to be* – it already is.'

'Exactly. What Jayne said was that Cassar was the kind of man who's tickled pink that some feisty gel has got her own company and that it's doing well, by jingo.' He slapped his thigh to emphasise the point.

Jane sniffed. 'Dinosaur.'

'That was exactly what Jayne said. But it was a great thing to be asked, and the fee he offered is enormous. I can't believe Ray dropped this on you.'

None of this was helping. 'They sound like something out of the Dark Ages. It says on their website they've got special expertise in the modern world of business.'

'They lied. Have you got a copy of Jayne's speech?'

'Yes, Ray sent me one over. Do you think I should ring him and say I can't do it? I mean, I can hardly give a keynote speech for a company I've worked at for four days, while pretending to be someone I'm not.'

'Why on earth not?' said Gary. 'And it would shoot Ray in the foot, for a start, if you did.'

'Meaning?'

'Well,' said Gary, guiding her upstairs. 'I'd bet my collection of Franklin Mint John Wayne commemorative plates that he's told Jayne he'll do the speech for her. It was the only big thing on the calendar for the next couple of months and if he hadn't agreed to do it then Jayne would never have gone.' Gary paused. 'So, you have to ask yourself, why is he letting you do it?'

'I've no idea. It's weird – it's crazy. It makes no sense.'

Gary nodded. 'Exactly. It's bloody ridiculous – unless of course he wants you to fall flat on your arse and make a complete fool of yourself.'

It wasn't something that had occurred to Jane. 'I don't

understand. Why on earth would Ray want to stitch me up? Or Jayne, come to that?'

'Well,' Gary rolled the word around his mouth thoughtfully for a moment or two. 'First of all, I don't suppose he was best pleased when he heard that Jayne had hired you out of the blue.'

'So this is sour grapes?'

'Could well be. I'm sure he assumed she'd just go off on her travels and leave him in charge.'

'Well, she has really,' protested Jane. 'At the moment I'm about as much use as chocolate fireguard.'

Gary nodded. 'Probably less, but you're still *here*. Presumably Ray imagined he was going to have the run of the place. You know, while the cat's away . . .'

'He wants to play?'

'Uh-huh. So . . .'

'So?' asked Jane nervously.

'So, we need to sort it out and discover what he's up to. Did you say you'd got Jayne's speech?'

'I'm just printing it off.'

'In that case you need to rehearse it, and meanwhile I'll find you something to wear, and see if I can get Jayne's hairdresser to do a drive-by cut and blow-dry. And before you start complaining, this is important; we'll charge it to housekeeping and Jayne won't mind in the least. And if you're worried about spilling stuff all down yourself, then we'll find something that won't show the stains. Come on.'

And then the phone rang. It was Lizzie. Apparently a lorry had turned up with a lot of boxes for Jane, and two red leather sofas. Should she sign for them?

* * *

On board *Spirit of the Waves*, Theo, who in Miko's absence was in charge, expertly slipped a long thin-bladed knife into the belly of a small silver fish, opened it up like a prayer book, slid the guts into a waiting bucket, rinsed the fish off and then dropped it into a tray of crushed ice along with a couple of others that he had already finished, all apparently in one single seamless movement. It was fast, impressive and Jayne guessed meant to intimidate her. It worked.

They had picked the fish up from the first island they'd called in at, while the punters were taken off by two of the crew to explore the sponge museum. When Jayne had been out with the boat a couple of days earlier she had been impressed by the idea of using freshly caught local fish, little realising that she would end up preparing them.

Theo rinsed the knife and returned it to the block; he was tall, tanned and muscular, with dark wavy hair, and probably around thirty. He also had the hump and Jayne suspected it had something to do with her.

'If we do maybe thirty more of those . . . Not everyone will want them,' he said, waving his hand in the direction of a tray of ungutted fish, glittering as the sunlight caught their sequin-bright scales.

By 'we' it was quite clear he meant Jayne. 'Just brush the skin with olive oil and sprinkle with salt and pepper. Maybe slide a few onions inside or a slice of lemon, some garlic. And then –' he washed his hands – 'while everyone is ashore looking at the scenery and all that, throw the guts over the side. But not when they are swimming. OK?'

Jayne nodded. His tone suggested she wouldn't be the first cook to anoint their passengers with fish innards. Jayne's stomach did an impressive little flutter.

'And then next we have to make the kebabs.' And with this he picked up a vicious-looking skewer, slipping it through a button mushroom before running through an unwary prawn, sandwiching it tight between the mushroom and lump of red pepper. 'If you can do sixty of these . . .'

Jayne nodded again, watching Theo's competent kebab-making whilst working on her sea legs. The combination of a heavy chopping board, skewers, a block of sharp knives and trying to prepare lunch for forty-odd passengers on what felt like the back of a truculent mule was a novel one. It had never been like this is in the sandwich business.

She swallowed hard. She wasn't normally seasick, but the pungent odour of onions, olive oil and fish guts was really not helping.

Meanwhile, Theo ran a hand along the equipment stacked in racks behind her. 'And then when we put ashore the guys will take all this, and take the chicken and steaks – those are very simple – then the breads, they go into baskets. You line them with napkins. We need bowls of mixed salad, green salad, coleslaw, potatoes salad – you know – the crew take it all ashore. You just need to make sure everything is ready for them and that they have got what they need. There is a list.' He indicated a clipboard hanging from a hook above a box of lettuces. 'If you can have it ready in an hour and half . . . OK?'

Jayne looked up at him; piece of cake then, really. The boat hit another wave and a Cos lettuce obligingly rolled across the worktop and dropped into the bucket of fish guts, followed by a whole procession of plum tomatoes.

Theo sighed. 'Choppy today. Never mind,' he said,

scooping the escapee salad up and dumping it into the galley sink. 'Don't worry, it will wash off. Oh, and when you've done down here, can you check on the bar snacks and give them a hand if they're busy?'

Jayne nodded yet again, not quite able to bring herself to speak. Her stomach was heaving in time with the engine. She had a strong suspicion that Theo was making her pay for Miko's tan-topping blonde and wanted to ensure that if Jayne had any aspirations to either swim, flirt or sunbathe that they would be short-lived. The bucket of fish guts slid along the floor towards her as they hit another wave.

'I can't wear that,' said Jane incredulously. She and Gary were in Jayne's bedroom, trying to find something for Jane to wear to Cassar's dinner. There were high heels, low heels, hangers, hats, handbags and gowns everywhere.

'It's beautiful.'

'It's backless.'

'How about this one, then?' Gary held up another hanger.

Jane's eyes narrowed. 'It's cut down to my belly button. You're winding me up, aren't you? I'd fall out of that. Jayne's got a lot more front than I have.'

'Actually you'd probably be able to see most of it in that one,' said Gary thoughtfully. 'Maybe if you wore a cardigan . . .'

'You said that you'd help,' growled Jane.

Gary sighed miserably. 'Yes, I did, didn't I? Damn it – ah, well.' He went back into the walk-in wardrobe and reappeared a few moments later with another outfit on a hanger. 'Here, now you have to admit, this would be perfect. What do you think? Subtle, conservative, elegant, understated – in fact, no fun at all, really,' he said, holding up a full-length black evening dress with a low V neck and a lower but do-able back, long sleeves, a fitted waist and bias-cut skirt with jet beading on the bodice, neck-line and sleeves that emphasised the tailoring. It could quite rightly be described as a classic.

'Oh, now that is fabulous,' whispered Jane. It was the kind of dress that grown-ups wore – a take-me-seriously-I-have-arrived kind of a dress.

'And it won't show the dirt either. Try it on; I'll go and find some shoes,' said Gary.

Half an hour later Jane stood in front of the dressing-room mirror looking like a million dollars. Jayne's hairdresser had pinned her hair up, and Gary handed her a pair of antique faux diamond earrings and a necklace borrowed from Jayne's jewellery box to set the look off. She did a little walk and twirl to gauge the effect.

'Well, bugger me,' said Gary. 'Do you know any lines from *Pygmalion*? How about a little something from *My Fair Lady*?'

Jane stared at her reflection. She could hardly believe it. The transformation was amazing. The dress was very lightly boned, giving her curves to die for. 'Wow,' she said, putting the earrings in. 'What do you reckon?'

'That you look bloody fantastic. Now we just need to find you a suit to travel in.'

'How about my brown one?'

'How about you go get Jayne's notes and read the speech?'

Jane picked up the sheet of paper from the dressing table and took a deep breath. 'It starts with a joke.'

'Well, thank God for that,' said Gary, settling himself down on the ottoman at the foot of the bed. 'Righty-oh, off you go, let's hear it.'

Jane, meanwhile, was scanning down the page. 'I can't read this. How can I say I started my first business in the late seventies? I wasn't even a foetus then.'

Gary waved the words away. 'Oh, don't make such a fuss, it'll be fine. They'll probably all be so pissed by then that they won't notice or they'll think they misheard, and those who don't will just think you've had Botox or a really good face lift, 'specially if you could just squint your eyes a bit more . . .' He demonstrated. 'They'll probably sidle up to you afterwards and ask who your surgeon is. Come on, get on with it, we haven't got all day.'

Jane read the sentence again. 'How about if I say, "The company was started in . . ." or maybe, "We started the company in . . ."?'

'OK, OK, if you must. I'll go get a pen,' said Gary. 'I just hope the joke is good.'

In the clear azure waters around the Dodecanese, Jayne was busy down in the galley covering the last of the salad bowls with cling film. The galley was hot and cramped, the air heavy with the smell of diesel fumes, fish and olive oil, and as the boat pitched again, Jayne swallowed hard, pulling the cling film taut, trying very hard not to breath in too deeply, and then eased the bowl into one of the large plastic trays that would go ashore with the rest of the crew. In another box were tools, turners, tongs, paper plates, napkins and rubbish bags. She took a quick look down the list that Theo had left to ensure she'd covered everything.

Jayne was just contemplating whether there was anything else that needed doing before she started the clearing up, when Theo shouted down, 'You done down there? Only we're anchoring in about five minutes. Can you get up here and cover the bar?' There was an edge of exasperation in his voice.

'Sure,' said Jayne, pulling off her apron and heading up the steep steps that divided her jolly little pit from the rest of the boat. Halfway up, the boat rolled and she clung to the side rails, closing her eyes till the moment had passed. As she clambered on deck Jayne pushed the stray strands of hair back behind her ears and headed through the little posse of passengers towards the bar. It was nice to be out of the heat. She didn't have time to consider what she might look like, or come to that, smell like.

The bar was busy with several pre-luncheon drinkers.

'Can I help anyone?' she said, sliding into the cramped space between the counter.

'Where's t'other lass t'day?' said a big fat northern man, eyeing her up and down. He was propping up one end of the bar, along with his male companion, who was as thin as string. He sounded deeply disappointed. They were both drinking beer and had obviously been there some time. The big man had a high gloss across his balding pate of what ought to be suntan lotion, but Jayne suspected was more likely sweat. He was wearing an England football shirt and had skin seared to a rich pink, the colour of perfectly cooked lamb. His watery pale marble-green eyes were fringed with white lashes. 'We came out today to see her. D'int we, Brian?'

'Aye, special, like,' said his companion, drinking his beer down to the suds. 'We were going to see t'temples, weren't we, Colin? Wi' guide and everythin'. By coach. All booked, paid up and everythin', but we said we'd come and see her instead. Nice lass, Christina, friendly.'

The fat man nodded. 'Said we'd come and keep her company. Have a bevvy or two. She was going to show us some special spots, wasn't she, Colin? That's what she said, special spots. She promised.'

Jane stared at the two of them, torn between laughter and bemusement; how the hell did you top that? 'Would you like another drink?' she said, indicating their empty glasses.

'So is t'other lass not on t'day then? Is she not downstairs?' the fat man pressed.

'No, she's working in the office today.'

The man sighed and took another long hard look at Jayne. 'She promised. We were going to see t'temples.'

Jayne wasn't sure she could cope with being this much of a disappointment. They were obviously not at all interested in any special spots she might have.

On the lower deck the crew were busy manoeuvring the boat up alongside a long wooden jetty on an otherwise deserted beach, while the rest of the passengers waited expectantly, carrying bags and towels, some already in their swimming costumes, some in shorts, or wrapped around with brightly coloured sarongs and long dresses, all eager to get off and explore or get into the water. One of the crew was sorting through a pile of snorkels and flippers stored in a hamper strapped to the back of the boat.

Halfway up the beach was pitched a long thin blue and white striped gazebo, offering the only shade for as far as the eye could see. Beneath it were picnic tables and stacks of chairs, and to one side a gas barbecue, everything there sun-bleached and sand-scoured to the palest pastels.

One of the boys jumped ashore and, taking a rope, pulled the boat closer to the walkway and guided it in the last two or three feet, another joining him to help tie the boat off. Theo waved to Jayne. He still looked grumpy. 'You all ready with the food?'

Jayne nodded. 'Yes, I think so. Everything on the list is done.'

'Right,' said Theo, as the boys slid the gangway out, barely waiting for them to finish, 'once we've got everything secure the crew will take the things ashore. If you give them a hand, then you can wash up –' he indicated the bar – 'and tidy the counters and the galley.'

Jayne stared at him as he swaggered off. 'A thank you would be nice,' she growled, but too late for him to catch the words. Meanwhile, the larger of the two northern men leaned over and tapped her on the arm, whilst belching, muffling the sound with a large pink fist that reminded her of a boiled ham.

'I'll have another of them little bottles o' beer while you're there, pet. Them ones there.' He pointed with a stubby finger to the bucket of bottles clinking in ice. 'T'other lass used to go on shore wi' all the cooking gear and go fer a bit of a swim. Lovely figure she'd got, fantastic legs, fantastic tan, a real asset to the crew she was,' he said mournfully. 'We'd done this trip three times this fortnight on account of her – hadn't we, Brian? We're off home tomorra. She was going to show us this special place she said she knew.'

'So you said,' growled Jayne, turning her attention to the thin man. 'Do you want another drink?'

'Aye, she were so sexy, right nice – very polite – lovely,' said the second man, shaking his head mournfully. He didn't have to add *not like you*. Jayne popped the tops off two beers, slid them across the counter and then went back down to the galley and pulled on an apron. The whole place reeked of warm fish guts, hot diesel and garlic. No wonder blondie preferred swanning around behind the bar and swimming.

'And so finally, ladies and gentlemen, I'd like to thank you once again for inviting me to join you this evening. Thank you.' Jane took a little bow and looked at Gary for applause; the housekeeper narrowed his eyes to impenetrable dark slits. 'What?' asked Jane.

'You want the truth?'

Jane considered for a few seconds. 'Probably not.'

'It's dull. Dull as . . . as . . .' He shook her head. 'To be honest, I can't think of anything that dull.'

'Thanks,' said Jane grumpily.

'OK, so tell me that I'm wrong.'

Jane hesitated. 'I thought it was a bit flat. I suppose I assumed it was because I don't know much about the company. Maybe Jayne was going to zizz it up a bit; maybe these are just working notes. The trouble is I haven't got any zizz to add because I don't know what the hell I'm talking about.' Jane slumped down miserably on the ottoman alongside Gary. 'Oh God, this is going to be a total bloody disaster, isn't it? Maybe I should just ring them up, tell them that I've got a bug, a broken leg – bubonic plague. Maybe you could ring them? You could pretend to be my mother.'

'I will do no such thing. Don't be a wimp. We just need

to work on the script. I can't believe that's the final draft. Jayne writes great speeches; she does loads of preparation. You've met Jayne, she's full of enthusiasm – she loves the business. She loves what she does. I can't imagine she would be that boring,' he said, jabbing the sheets of paper Jane was holding. 'Actually I can't imagine anyone would be that boring.'

'Maybe it was the way I read it.'

'Maybe it wasn't.' Gary sniffed. 'Maybe it was Ray punching a hole in the bottom of your life raft.'

'So where do we look?'

'Jayne's computer. Did you say you'd got the password?'

'Not to her private stuff, no.'

'Good job I have then. She gave me the administrator's password, you know, in case anything ever happened to her while she was away. Come on.'

The two of them headed across into Jayne's office. Gary sat down at the desk and typed in a series of number and letters, and an instant later the screen in Jayne's private area on the Mac blossomed into life. There on the desk top was a picture of Andy Taylor, taken with Jayne in a little bar somewhere hot and foreign. They were both sipping cocktails and looking tanned and, well, and oh so very young. Jane smiled. Obviously Jayne had moved on from the tropical beach hut picture that had been on there last time she'd seen it. God, it was such a shame he was spoken for, she thought as she stared at the photo.

'Right,' said Gary, breaking into Jane's train of thought. 'Speech, speech, speech . . . Cassar. Let's see what we've got in here.' As he spoke he shuffled down through the files, pulled a pair of glasses out of the top pocket of his shirt and then opened up the find menu. Thirty seconds later they had what they were looking for. Gary double-clicked on the one marked 'Final Draft', his eyes moving down the text.

'*Et voilà*,' he said, leaning back triumphantly.

'Well?' asked Jane.

'You was very nearly had, hon.'

'Really?'

'Certainly was. Take a look at this: snappier, sharper, and the joke is actually funny.'

Jane leaned in and read over his shoulder, and then glanced down at the sheets of paper in her hand. 'So what have I got here?' she asked.

'Whatever it is and whatever the reason you've got it, it's the wrong version. Let's print this one off and see if it works better.'

The car, driven by a man in full livery and a peaked cap, came to pick her up at bang on five o'clock.

Down in the galley of *Spirit of the Waves*, Jayne pushed the hair off her face with the back of her hand, wrung the bleach-soaked cloth out and hung it over the taps like a tattered ensign. She stretched and then winced. Her back ached, her legs ached and her head ached – in fact, it would have been easier to try to work out what didn't ache – but at least the kitchen was clean, lunch had been a great success and she had managed to dispose of the fish guts without either covering a punter or getting them over herself. Just as she was easing the tension in her shoulders and back Theo clambered down the steps into the galley. They were chugging slowly back into Kos town harbour, the sun rapidly losing its footing in the late afternoon sky.

'We've got forty-six booked for tomorrow,' he said. 'Two vegetarians, and the bar needs restocking.'

Jayne had had enough. 'Thank you too,' she said grimly, pulling off her apron and dropping it into the wash bin.

He stared at her. 'What?'

'You heard me. You are the most unbelievably rude man.'

Theo bristled and squared his shoulders.

'No, no,' said Jayne before he had the chance to open his mouth. 'Hear me out. I'm very happy to do what you ask, I'm paid to cook and clean and I will, that's what I'm here for, but I'm not here for you to be unpleasant to or to bully. Do you understand, Theo? I'm an employee not a slave, *Capisce*? Good manners cost nothing. I don't know what your problem is, but I'm happy to hear it and see if we can sort it out.'

Theo stared at her.

'Come on,' said, holding his gaze. 'Whatever it is, if I'm going to work here I need to know. Am I treading on someone's toes? Taken the job from one of your cousins?'

Theo hesitated and then shook his head. 'No, no one's toes, no cousins.' He paused and then sighed. 'I thought maybe you were Miko's latest lady friend. We have had lots of them, lots of trouble. He is . . .' Theo looked heavenwards obviously searching around for the right words or maybe something in translation.

'An old dog?' Jayne offered helpfully

Theo laughed, in spite of himself. 'Yes, yes, an old dog.'

'Well, the good news is that I'm not anyone's girlfriend,' Jayne continued. 'And I can cook and run a kitchen, and take orders, but I am used to being treated with a bit of respect. If you've got a problem with that—'

She didn't have to go any further. Theo shook his head.

'No, not a problem at all. You know, I thought perhaps you were another airhead. The last girl he got, she did nothing but pout and whine and when I complained to Miko he said, "She's young, she's just learning, and the punters like her."' He lifted his hands in a gesture of resignation. 'What can you do?'

Jayne smiled; she could sympathise with him. Over the years Ray had taken on a couple of girls as receptionists and PA, and girls Friday that had similar 'talents'.

'Well I'm not young, and I learn fast.' She didn't add that she needed the job because it wasn't altogether true, but at the moment it felt like it.

At Cassar's mansion Jane stood by the desk in the entrance hall, taking in the view and getting her bearings. Nervous didn't anywhere near cover what she felt. The house was all turrets and towers and twiddly bits; the main reception room had high vaulted ceilings, a great fireplace about the same size as her kitchen, and the walls were hung with swords, shields, lances and trophies from an earlier age. The main staircase was flanked by household colours on one side and a suit of armour on the other.

'If you would like to follow Anton, Miss Mills,' said one of the men greeting the guests, 'he'll show you to your room. Miss Mills will be staying in the Berkeley Rooms.'

Anton nodded. He was a fey man of indeterminate age, dressed in an immaculately pressed morning suit, with very taut skin and slicked-back dyed hair. He took the set of keys he was given and waited for her to follow him.

'Mm, the Berkeley Rooms, corner suite, mullioned windows, lovely view out over the grounds. First floor,' said Anton appreciatively. 'Are we waiting for anyone else?'

he asked, gazing thoughtfully around the enormous room at the arrivals.

'No, no, just me,' Jane said, trying to keep the nervous edge out of her voice.

'Lovely suite, the Berkeley,' he repeated, still lingering. He didn't add that she must be more important than she looked to be given the Berkeley Rooms but that was how Jane felt. She smiled, swallowing down a whole squadron of butterflies.

'And then, once you're settled in, if you'd care to join everyone out on the terrace for champagne and canapés . . .' Anton was saying. As he smiled he revealed a set of perfect even teeth. Veneers that impressive cost serious money.

There were lots of the other guests milling around in the foyer. Most were distinguished-looking men in late middle age or older, with a sprinkling of Young Turks making up the numbers. As one of the few women present – certainly one of the very few under fifty – Jane felt the men's eyes eagerly following her progress across the room, taking in every detail. She reddened under their undisguised interest; Gary had found her a classic Chanel trouser suit from amongst Jayne's recycling pile and Jane knew that, even given her anxiety, she looked wonderful. Elegant, slim, with just a hint of panache – the epitome of the successful businesswoman. Jane suppressed a grin; God, if only her mother or Steve could see her now.

As she followed Anton towards the stairs Jane was very aware that at the edge of the crowd was a tall, good-looking man with dark hair and bright eyes, who caught her gaze and smiled nonchalantly in her direction as she crossed the room, which made her heart flutter. God, he was gorgeous.

His smile broadened as she smiled back, while her brain firmly reminded her that she was there to work. It was going to be hard enough keeping up the façade of being Jayne Mills. The man's smile held and Jane felt her colour rising. It was one of those odd moments that seemed to take for ever. Jane looked away first, flustered and wrong-footed. He was probably in his mid-thirties, tanned, with broad shoulders, and . . . and under her breath Jane purred. Some men were just built to wear black tie.

Meanwhile ahead of her Anton swished through the assembled guests, nose in the air, Jane following.

'It's a beautiful house,' she said hastily, trying to recover her composure.

'Um,' he said noncommittally. 'Bloody nightmare to keep warm in the winter, and the dust and the stairs – don't get me started. We're up here, first floor on the right.'

Jane followed him closely as they made their way up an impressive sweeping staircase under portraits of very ugly people, then through a rabbit warren of corridors, wallpapered in an oppressive tartan interspersed with acres of wood panelling and *objets d'art* ranging from Greek sculpture, through dried flowers to more suits of armour.

'It's modelled on Balmoral,' said Anton, in answer to her unspoken question. 'Right down to the draughts. We used to have a piper but they use CDs now. Royalist, is old Mr Cassar. Cut him and he bleeds Duchy of Cornwall shortbread.'

'What about my luggage?' Jane asked, looking back over her shoulder as they took another sharp turn past a side table set with a huge bowl of china fruit.

'Don't worry, madam. One of the boys will have brought it up already and someone will be dealing with it. If you've got anything that needs pressing just ring housekeeping and feel free to use the facilities while you're here. There's a map in the desk; the grounds are beautiful this time of the year. Help yourself. We'll just get you settled in and then you can head back downstairs for some corporate mingling. Are you here for the whole weekend? They weren't sure; said "TBA" on your invitation.'

'TBA?'

'To be arranged.'

'Oh, right, no – I'm just staying overnight.'

'Shame, lunch tomorrow is always a real corker. Here we are . . .' Anton stopped at an impressive mock Tudor door, opened it for her and stepped aside. Jane made a determined effort not to look either overawed or panic-stricken as it swung open. Beyond the heavy oak door was a huge corner suite with a view out over the house's extraordinary formal gardens and boxes hedges, which were clipped to form complicated knots and curlicues, set amongst and around vast beds of blood-red roses, in acres of perfectly manicured lawns.

In the great mullioned bay was a sofa and two armchairs, a coffee table standing between them. Against one wall was a roll-top desk, while through an archway hung with plaid drapes was a queen-sized bed with a canopy, and a walnut wardrobe about the same size as Jane's bathroom in Creswell Road.

She took it all in, in an instant, let out a long breath and tried hard not to swear; she'd never seen a room like it outside stately home tours and TV programmes. In the bedroom a maid in traditional uniform was busy unpacking her case and hanging up her things. Jane resisted the temptation to run in and snatch her clothes back, and instead tried very hard to concentrate on Anton, who was busy giving her a guided tour of the room.

'And over there is the *en suite*. In the sitting room there's phone, TV, CD, DVD, satellite, and internet access – drinks cabinet, fridge, tea, coffee – although feel free to ring down for anything you want.' He drew a hand around the room like a master magician. 'And if you need anything else you can either ask Elsie,' he nodded towards the girl busy slipping Jane's smalls into the top drawer of the dressing table. 'Or ring down to housekeeping. Would you like some tea sent up? People will be turning up for the next couple of hours so there's no rush.'

Jane nodded. 'Yes, please, that would be great.'

Anton nodded. 'Would you like anything with it? Maybe some sandwiches? Or how about some cakes? Chef makes the most wonderful patisserie. Or would you prefer something stronger – gin and tonic, Scotch and soda?' he asked, opening up the drinks cabinet. 'Sun's bound to be over the yardarm somewhere. Would you prefer champagne?'

Despite her nerves Jane suppressed a grin. This was the life.

Exhausted, Jayne padded across the quay, back towards her rented rooms. She yawned. Her feet and legs were killing her. It had been a long day, with the prospect of another one tomorrow. Even though she prided herself on being fit and was always busy running the business there was a world of difference between an office job and hard physical work. Every molecule ached.

The booking office was in darkness, with no sign of

Miko or his blonde receptionist anywhere – which meant she would have to go out later to the cyber café to pick up any email. With a bit of luck Ray would have sorted out the money situation. Jayne stretched, trying to ease the ache in her shoulders, pulling the phonecard she'd bought out of her handbag as she walked. On the street corner was a bank of open-air phones. She waited until one was free and tapped in Ray's number. After four rings it redirected her to his voice mail. There was no one at her house either. For a moment Jayne felt a great wave of frustration, along with an odd sense of being disconnected. It felt as if everyone she knew had vanished off the face of the earth. Strangely enough, it didn't feel all bad. Once the frustration had passed she had a huge sense of liberation and freedom. It felt as if at the moment she could reinvent herself and be anybody, anybody at all. Who did she want to be after all these years?

How strange – Jayne looked around at the people passing by – no one knew her, what she did or what her name was. Oddly enough it felt exciting. Smiling to herself, Jayne tucked the phone card back into her bag and went off in search of supper. So this was her fresh new start after all.

Glancing out of the leaded windows of her room at the Cassar mansion Jane could see elegant people milling around on the terrace, chatting, sipping cocktails and nibbling on canapés that would probably cost the same as a steak anywhere else. People who, amongst other things, had come to listen to her speech.

As the thought passed through her head, her mobile peeped with a text that said 'Did you order a leopardskin-print dining table and chairs?'

Jane sighed and dialled her home number. Lizzie answered instantly. 'Lizzie, what's going on?'

'You tell me. The hallway is full of boxes – I thought they were samples.'

'Well, can you tell them that there has been a mistake, and to take the dining table and things back?'

Lizzie sniffed. 'The sofas are lovely, and maybe they *are* samples.'

'Maybe they are, but they shouldn't be coming to my address. What does it say on the delivery note?'

'Um, it's definitely this address and I think they're all from the company you're working for.'

'Just explain there's been a mistake.'

'I tried that with the sofas. They look great in your sitting room.'

'OK, refuse to sign the note. They'll have to take them back then and I'll sort it out as soon as I get back.'

'The man says—'

Jane sighed. This was the last thing she needed right now. 'Let me talk to him.'

'Hello,' said a gruff voice. 'You the lady what ordered a table and chairs?'

It took her ten minutes to persuade him that she wasn't and to take it away. God alone knows what she was going to do with the sofas – not to mention the boxes.

When she came off the phone Jane tried to clear her head and get back to the task in hand. It would be fine, she repeated to herself, just fine. All she had to do was use the speech Jayne had written and smile. She'd done lots of presentations at the library. But realistically Dover Street Mother and Toddler Group was a million miles away from the audience she could expect at Cassar's.

She took a look in the mirror and rang through her check list. Speak slowly, make sure she looked up from her notes and made eye contact from time to time, relax, ease into it – smile until you get cramp, that's what Gary had said. Simple. The phone pinged again. Reluctantly, in case it was Lizzie again, Jane picked it up. 'Relax, smile – you'll be fine,' it read.

She laughed, relieved and pleased; it seemed as if thinking about him was enough to summon Gary up from the depths. A split second later her mobile rang. Maybe he didn't think that a text was enough and was planning to give her a touch-line pep talk.

'Hello, don't you trust me?' she said brightly.

'What do you mean, "don't I trust you"? Is that you, Jane?' snapped Steve.

Jane moaned, wishing she had spent a second checking the caller display. Why did he have to ring now, just when she had managed to spend almost a whole day *not* thinking about him?

'Sorry, I thought you were someone else,' Jane began. Not that he was listening.

'Actually I'm glad you brought up the issue of trust, Jane, because I want to talk to you about the repercussions of blackmail. I know I might be overreacting, and blackmail is not a nice word to use.' He spoke very slowly as if she was a child or a bit slow. 'I'm not proud of what we did but I think you are behaving unreasonably. Lucy and I have talked about it a lot and we've decided to go and see someone in Human Resources next week. We're going to call your bluff, Jane. We're going to have it out. And if you don't cooperate I'm going to have no choice but to involve the police.'

'Whoa, hold on there, cowboy,' said Jane. 'I don't know what you're talking about. I haven't done anything.'

'Not yet,' he snapped right back. 'But we both know the threat is there.'

'Threat? What threat? Steve, I have no idea what you are talking about.'

'So you said the other day, Jane, but you don't fool me,' said Steve. 'Lucy said you cleared your email file and forwarded it to your home address.'

'Well, I did – it's no secret. I sent all my personal emails to myself. There's no law against that.'

'There might be,' Steve said darkly.

'Look, can you just stop all the cloak-and-dagger stuff and tell me what's going on? I'm at an important meeting. What do you mean about blackmail?'

'Call it what you like—'

'How about I call Lucy and ask her what the fuck this is about?' she shouted.

'You will do no such thing. That's harassment and if you threaten—'

Jane had had quite enough of his smug self-righteous tone. 'Oh, just fuck off, will you?' she roared and hung up, at around the same time that someone knocked on the door. 'Come in,' she called, throwing the phone onto the bed. It was amazing that it had survived given the punishment it had had over the last few days.

Anton pushed the door open. 'Oh, there you are. Just heard the screaming and wanted to make sure everything was all right. I wouldn't normally bother but last year's keynote speaker threatened to hang himself between the nibbles and dinner. Most of the guests have arrived,' he added without missing a beat. 'They'll be going in to eat in about an hour.'

Seeing the look of surprise on Jane's face, Anton shook his head. 'No, no, he was fine, had a bit of a bad week, you know how it is. His wife was furious. Apparently he does it all the time – threaten, that is, not actually do it – and people think it's only creatives that are highly strung.' He paused. 'Poor choice of words. So, all set, are we?'

Jane nodded. 'More or less.'

Anton nodded. 'Righty-ho. In that case let me take you downstairs to meet the great and good. Mr Cassar is a bit frail; he'll see you at dinner.'

Downstairs the terrace was awash with early evening light, guests mingling and sipping champagne cocktails, their glasses filled and refilled by waiters who moved with all the silent stealth and cunning of big cats. Despite Anton leaving her in the urbane clutches of Cassar's events manager, Jane managed to find herself a quiet spot to one side of the pack, letting the fresh air and the breeze clear her head. She had no great desire to speak to anyone; this whole business with Steve was getting on her nerves. She was going to have to see him again and clear matters up once and for all, whatever it was. Blackmail? God, that man was such a drama queen.

With her mind firmly on other things she watched the sea of faces passing, careful not to make more than fleeting eye contact with anyone. Jane had no intention of introducing herself in case anyone asked any awkward questions. And then the man with the dark hair and bright eyes walked by, spotted her and smiled.

'Hello,' he said, stopping midstride. 'Do I know you? I'm sure I recognise your face from somewhere.'

'Really? Do you use that line often?' she asked, holding a straight face.

He laughed. 'Nope, I can't say I do, but if it works . . .' And then he said, 'No, actually, not at all but in this case it's true. So, *do* I know you from somewhere?'

'I wouldn't have thought so. Actually I don't know anyone else here. It's my first visit.' Although there was something about him that looked vaguely familiar too. Maybe he had been on TV or in the newspapers, some millionaire captain of industry. She didn't like to ask if he'd ever been involved in community outreach with Buckbourne Library.

'It's my first time too. I'm meeting someone here,' he said, scanning the sea of faces. 'So,' he continued, looking across the little groups, 'has he gone to get you a drink?'

'Sorry?'

'Your boyfriend, or your husband, or . . .' He shrugged. 'What do people call each other these days?'

Jane laughed. 'In my case? Manipulative two-timing bastard. Don't mind me – fortunately he's an ex now. Not that I'm bitter or anything.'

He mugged a wince. 'So you're here on your own then?'

Jane nodded. 'It's that's kind of event, I think.'

The man extended a hand. 'Well, in that case maybe we should team up. I don't know anyone and this is not really my sort of scene at all. My name's Kit, Kit Harvey-Mills, pleased to meet you.'

Jane scanned the faces. 'And where is your girlfriend, or wife, or . . . what do people call each other these days?'

'Living in South America with a property tycoon last time I heard. I didn't catch your name.'

'Jane,' she said, not lingering over the details. 'What do you do? Are you in business?'

'No, no, actually I'm a photographer. I'm supposed to be meeting my sister, but I haven't seen hide nor hair of her. Mind you, she's always late. Well, at least with me she is. In business apparently she's a piranah.' As a waiter passed by Kit turned, skilfully lifted two glasses of champagne off the tray and handed her one. 'There.'

'Nicely done,' said Jane with a wry grin. 'What sort of photography are you involved in?' But something else was happening as she spoke, nothing to do with what he did, or what he was saying, or where his ex was, or what she was doing there. There was a funny little fluttering buzz in her stomach and when she looked up into his eyes she sensed he was feeling it too. Mutual fancying; Jane almost giggled and ruined it.

'Oh, all kinds of things.' His expression was bright and he was a fraction too close, and Jane was glad. 'Wildlife mostly – I've just finished a shoot for the BBC.'

'Really? That's fascinating.'

But not, thought her rogue heart, quite as fascinating as the smell of him under expensive aftershave, and the framework of laughter lines gathered around his dark warm eyes, and the way his shoulders moved under the dinner jacket, and the way his hands cradled the champagne flute. Jane shivered, trying very hard to get a grip. This was silly – nice, but silly – and hardly the right moment. As her mind warned her off it felt like the rest of her body was scanning him, drinking in every last little detail. She could feel him doing it too and blushed furiously. God, it was ages since she had flirted with anyone, and even longer since someone had flirted right back.

'And what about you? Some high-flyer, queen of industry?' he was saying. Not that she could hear him very clearly over the sounds of her heart beating in her ears.

'Me? Oh, no.' She made a dismissive gesture with her hand. 'Hardly. I've just started a new job, in an online company.' She took a sip of champagne. 'A dot com.'

'Really? E-commerce? That's a coincidence. Actually my—'

Oh bugger, that was a mistake. Jane smiled and held up a hand to stop him. 'Yes, but please don't ask me any tricky questions, I've only just started, and at the moment I feel as if I'm totally out of my depth,' she said quickly before he had the chance to carry on.

He laughed. 'That bad?'

'No, not really.' Oh God, she fancied him. Worse still, Jane knew without a shadow of a doubt that he fancied her. Oh God . . . and then Anton appeared.

'Excuse me,' he said, butting in with polite determination. 'I just wondered if you were ready?'

Jane stared at him in surprise. 'For what?'

'Dinner is in an hour. I thought you might want to –' he made a gesture that suggested fluffing and preening – 'You know, climb into a frock or something.'

'Oh, right, yes I do.' Jane turned to Kit, flustered and panicky. She had almost totally forgotten about the speech and why she was there. 'I'm so sorry. If you'll excuse me I just need to go and – and – and –' she felt herself reddening again under his appreciative gaze – 'you know . . .' she finished lamely.

As she turned to follow Anton, Kit said quickly, 'It's been lovely to meet you. Sorry, that sounds a bit naff. Are you here with someone for dinner? Your company?'

Jane panicked for a few seconds. As the guest speaker, she could hardly sit with him at dinner. 'Yes, yes, I am,' she lied.

'OK well, in that case I was wondering if maybe we could meet up later on, after dinner? For a drink – chat – you know.'

Jane hesitated – actually she did know – and said, 'That sounds lovely, and don't worry, it doesn't sound naff at all. I'd really like that. See you later. I've got to . . .' She paused, searching around for the words. How the hell was she going to explain it to him? Maybe he didn't need to know, maybe the name Jayne Mills meant nothing to him, maybe if he didn't catch the introduction he might think she was just there representing Jayne's company.

Their eyes met, their gaze lingered and she just didn't know what to say, and so Jane smiled and turned away, following Anton through the crowd, wondering even in her panic whether she had lost any Brownie points for sounding so eager, all the while aware of his eyes following her.

'Hm, well done. I think you've pulled, chuck. Nice bod,' said Anton as they headed back to her room. 'I'll be back to escort you down in about half an hour or so – or were you hoping for a bit of a soak?'

Twenty minutes and a quick shower later Jane looked at herself in the bedroom mirror and did a little twirl. The dress Gary had sniffed out looked fabulous. She added another spritz of perfume before checking her watch. So far, so good. No one had had the chance to spot any cracks in her story, meeting Kit was an unexpected bonus and she had decided she would explain everything to him later

221

over a drink. Thinking about him made her smile, not that she had thought about much else since coming back upstairs. God, he was seriously gorgeous. Fancy finding Mr Right here, while she was pretending to be Miss Someone Else. She was glad now she had edited Jayne's script so he didn't think she was old enough to be his mother, but she'd need to find him right after dinner, set the record straight.

Nice eyes. While her mind bounced around making cooing and purring noises, Jane finished her make-up and hair.

There was a knock at the door. 'All ready, pet?' said Anton brightly.

'More or less. You can come in,' she called, taking the jewellery out of its case.

Anton wolf-whistled appreciatively. 'Very nice. Here, let me do your necklace up for you,' he said. 'Love the frock. You look absolutely fabuloso.'

Jane blushed and did a final little twirl. Hopefully Kit would appreciate it too. 'Thank you,' she said, picking up her wrap and evening bag, with the speech tucked inside.

Actually Anton was right, the black dress, jewellery – the whole thing looked very understated and very classy. She might not be a successful businesswoman yet, but Jane certainly looked like one.

'Dressed like that you'll have to beat the trouser off with a stick,' Anton said enviously.

Jane giggled and without a backward glance followed him out of the room. Just get the speech over, meet up with Kit . . .

As they reached the landing Kit came loping up towards them. 'He's keen,' said Anton, *sotto voce*.

222

As their eyes met Jane felt that funny little buzzy-fuzzy thing kick in the bottom of her stomach.

'Hi,' he said. 'You look gorgeous.' Jane smiled; she wasn't the only one. And what was even better was that as he got closer he looked once and twice and then as they passed almost shoulder to shoulder, and he half turned and looked again, staring this time. Jane felt the heat furiously rising in her face.

Anton meanwhile said to him, 'Everyone is going into dinner in a few minutes.'

Kit seemed to be slightly bemused. 'I won't be long. I'm just going to find . . .' He didn't bother with the rest of the sentence, he was too busy looking Jane over, who was so red now she thought she might spontaneously combust.

Anton shrugged and pulled a what-can-you-do face. 'I wouldn't normally ask,' he said in an undertone, as he and Jane made their way down into the elegant foyer, lit by the opulent glitter of a vast crystal chandelier, 'but the place is a complete rabbit warren. People are always getting lost. Last time we had a weekend party, one man never did make it down for breakfast. We kept finding him wandering around outside on the terrace, banging on the windows, swearing at the ground staff.'

Jane looked back over her shoulder. Kit was at the top of the stairs looking down at her and then an instant later was gone. Downstairs the lobby was almost empty except for a few latecomers and uniformed staff. The doors to the main dining room stood open. To one side of the doorway were the guests who would be sharing the top table. Anton introduced Jane to her host, a tiny birdlike man with silvery grey hair, although Jane's mind was still working its way through the details of her encounter with Kit.

'Miss Mills, this is Sir Henry Cassar,' said Anton. Jane smiled and extended a hand.

'Jane, my dear, I'm so very pleased that you could make it. I've heard so much about you. Sorry I couldn't be down to meet you earlier; phone calls, you know how it is . . .' Henry Cassar was saying, taking her fingers and pressing them to his lips. '. . . I hope everything is to your satisfaction. I'm looking forward to hearing your speech.'

His words made Jane snap to. Her speech. Jane stared at him. She really needed to get a grip. Speech first and then Kit, although it was hard to resist letting her eye roam over the faces of the guests.

'It's wonderful to meet you too. It's an honour to be invited and it is the most wonderful house,' she said lightly.

Henry Cassar slipped his arm through hers as they headed into the dining room. 'I'm so glad that you like it,' he purred. 'I bought it for my late wife as a wedding present.'

Jane glanced across at him. As presents went it sure as hell beat a set of saucepans and a toaster. Henry caught her eye and winked conspiratorially, stroking her hand as they set off. Jane suppressed a stunned smile, realising the message he had just telegraphed. Despite being at least seventy, Henry Cassar was letting her know that he was single and still very much on the look out.

Beyond the double doors the enormous dining room was set with round tables, seating a dozen guests on each, the tables decked with white and pale pink linen, pink candles, silver cutlery, crystal, great bowls of summer flowers and the paraphernalia of dining at its most opulent. In one corner of the long room a string quartet played. There were flowers everywhere. The air was busy with the low hum of conversation from the diners, laughter and the clink of wine glasses.

Henry Cassar led Jane up to the top table and settled her down to his right. Jane scanned the room, but there was no sign of Kit. To Jane's right was sitting another elderly man who had already tucked his napkin into the front of his shirt collar in preparation for the food to follow. After brief introductions, the master of ceremonies stood up, projecting his deep resonant voice out into the packed room.

'Ladies and gentlemen on behalf of our host, Sir Henry Cassar, I would like to welcome you all to the Cassar Foundation's Thirty-Sixth Annual Charity Gala Dinner. We are delighted that so many of you could make it this evening . . .' As the introduction continued Jane's eyes moved around the assembled company and as she did she noticed that Kit had slipped quietly in through the double doors and was making his way slowly around the edge of the room, to his table.

Meanwhile the master of ceremonies had moved on: 'And we'd like to extend a particularly warm welcome to our guest speaker, Ms Jayne Mills, who will be . . .'

Kit was staring in her direction; and in the split second when their eyes met Jane smiled. It gave her something to think about other than the squadron of butterflies revving up for take off in the pit of her stomach. He didn't smile back.

Chapter Ten

In Kos town Jayne had had a shower and changed out of the crew uniform into a long cotton dress and was sitting by the open window of her little room watching the tourists wander by in the street below.

It was oppressively hot and she had opened the windows to catch the edge of a breeze that smelled as if it were blowing in from the sea. She was exhausted but also oddly content. She'd brought a steak home from the boat and served it up with a green salad and a couple of flat breads, opened a bottle of red and was sipping it slowly, enjoying every mouthful, whilst listening to the sounds of the evening: the voices, the music and the cars from the street below.

Despite the noise Jayne felt really peaceful, almost as if time had stopped, as if her old life had ended and a new one begun. Just like that, a few short days and everything had changed. She smiled and stretched, feeling pleased at having found her new start almost without trying.

The phonecard she'd bought was propped up on the little table between the salt and pepper shakers that she had liberated from the galley. As she hadn't got through on the phone she planned to email Ray and Jane, let them know she was all right, and where they could contact her and get the money situation sorted out, but in a strange way it didn't seem to matter quite so much today. It almost felt as if all that was about someone else. She was just nodding off in the chair when there was a knock at the door, which made her jump, instantly wide awake.

'Hello?' she called.

Nina, Miko's daughter, stuck her head round the door. 'Hi. You OK? I just thought I would check up on you. You look totally whacked.'

'Well, thanks for that. I am but I'm fine, just tired that's all. How about you?'

The girl rolled her eyes. 'Knackered. Dad can't seem to get his head round the idea that this was supposed to be my holiday as well. So far all I've done is work, work, work – which is why I'm here. Dad says he's sorry he didn't come down to meet you off the boat and asked if you'd like to come over for supper tonight by way of consolation. I think he feels guilty that you didn't just take his money and run. That and the fact he fancies you, obviously – he's always liked a challenge.'

Jayne grinned and then shook her head, indicating the empty plate and knife and fork on the little cane table. 'That's kind but not tonight. I've already eaten. I'm thinking about having an early night. Some of us have to work for a living, you know.'

Nina laughed. 'I'll tell him. Did it go well on the boat today?'

'Not bad at all.'

'You sorted the money thing out yet?'

Jayne shook her head. 'No. I'm going to email my business partner in a few minutes. Would you like a glass of wine?'

Nina giggled. 'Thanks but no thanks. I've got a date – dinner, dancing, beach walking in bare feet. It's a real job trying to find somewhere on the island to have a hot date where there are no cousins, uncles or aunts on the staff. Although I think we may have found the perfect spot.'

Jayne laughed. 'Well, in that case, don't let me hold you up.'

'Fair enough. If you change your mind, he told me to give this to you.' Nina handed Jayne a card with Miko's number on it, and with that she was gone.

Jayne closed the shutters, picked up her handbag and followed Nina down into the street.

The internet café was around ten minutes' walk away, down past cafés and tavernas and restaurants teeming with life, with music and conversation. The café was full of students and summer staff busy emailing home. Jayne realised with a smile that she was part of the same group now. The girl on the front desk nodded a welcome and beckoned her over to an empty machine. Jane logged on to her company website, typed in her details and waited, watching the little egg timer on screen that denoted the passing of time, spin and spin . . . and then it stopped.

'Username and password not recognised,' said a little error message on a natty little drop-down menu.

Maybe she had typed it in wrong. She did it again and got the same message. Maybe the site was busy. Jayne typed it in again.

The little hourglass on screen spun and then faltered and finally stopped. This time the error message read, 'You have exceeded the number of attempts permitted to gain access to this area of the website. Please contact the site administrator.'

'Bollocks', Jayne growled under her breath. What the hell was going on now? She paused, frustrated, staring at the screen. This was nuts. There had to be something else she could do, and then Jayne had a thought. Maybe there was something else. The geek who had set her company's system up had given every user different levels of access and as she was the top of the foodchain. As the user paying the bills, in theory she had got access to all areas.

Jayne paused, trying to remember what the emergency password was for the site administrator, the one that she had left with Gary in case of fire, famine, pestilence or flood, and then after a minute or two's thought, typed in another username, 'admin1' and the corresponding password, 'sesame1' and waited. This time the little timer spun for no more than ten seconds before the screen flashed up the main menu page of the company website. Fantastic. Relieved, Jayne went deeper into the site to retrieve her email from the server.

There were several messages in her inbox: lots of ads, business-related mail, and things from clients and customers that she forwarded to Jane and Ray, a note from her brother. Jayne scanned down the list of senders – there was a mail from Jane, another Ray and also one from Andy Turner.

Jayne grinned: Andy Turner. Maybe he had got her message after all. Smiling to herself she debated whether she should read Andy's first or maybe save him up as a treat. Ummmm, *Andy Turner*. She let the sound of his name roll around over her tongue like a good wine before opening her brother's email.

Hi, Honey, hope you're well. We've had to reschedule a shoot so I'll be in the UK later this week for about three weeks – so I thought I'd surprise you and drop in on my way through. I did try to ring but missed you. Just thought I'd let you know I WILL be at Cassar's dinner on Thursday to see you in action. Thanks for wangling me the invite, even if I couldn't quite make the top table. I know I said I probably wouldn't be able to make it – but, hey – look forward to seeing you there. Is it OK to bum bed and board for a few days?
All love x

Meanwhile on the dais at the top table in the opulent dining room of Henry Cassar's mansion, Jane was trying very hard to concentrate on the conversation around her, trying to appreciate the wonderful food and the superb wine and trying even harder to stay calm. All she had to do was read Jayne's notes, wait for the laughter after the jokes, smile, and try to ignore the gorgeous man on the table at the back of the hall who couldn't seem to take his eyes off her. The butterflies in her stomach had taken up tap dancing. She glanced up and looked over towards the far side of the room, almost relieved that at the moment she couldn't see Kit in amongst the other guests.

As the waiter cleared away the remains of the main course – medallions of lamb in a piquant redcurrant sauce served with a selection of steamed vegetables tossed in butter, and the sweetest new potatoes, none bigger than a marble or longer than a matchstick – which had tasted like heaven, Jane took a sip of wine and looked around her. There was just dessert to go now, and then she was on. Jane looked down at the menu, trying to ignore the fact that her hands were trembling slightly: biscuit baskets of summer fruits, sorbet and meringue pieces served with vanilla ice cream. Sounded delicious, even though it would bring her closer to the speech. Jane shivered and took another look around the table.

Henry Cassar had been flirting outrageously all the way through dinner, whilst the man on her other side had been shovelling food into his mouth as if they were about to reintroduce rationing. He belched appreciatively and licked his lips as the waiter cautiously removed his plate.

Below the dais the serving staff moved around the hall, distributing food and clearing tables as if moving on oiled rails. The long elegant room was bubbling with conversation and laughter. Everyone else except for Jane seemed to be having a wonderful time, while in the corner by the French window, music from the string quarted lifted and bobbed up every now and then like a cork above the babbling hum of the voices.

Jane felt increasingly nervous and had made a conscious effort to stay off the vino despite Henry's effort to ensure her glass was perpetually filled to the brim. Not long now and it would all be over . . .

In the cyber café Jayne was rereading Ray's email; the background noises and the street sounds fading away as she concentrated on the words.

. . . Jayne, I'm very reluctant to cast aspersions on someone's character but I'm not all together convinced that Jane is quite what she appears.

I have arranged for your cards to be reissued. But you're right, the credit cards – the ones you took on holiday – *were* cancelled, have been reissued and have

231

been used extensively since, and we have had various password problems here over the last few days.

You and Jane both having the same name was always bound to cause us some problems and it may well all be as a result of this that there are a few teething troubles. Whatever the cause, I don't want you to worry, everything is under control. I'm going to meet with Jane early next week to try to clear up some of the points. Her references check out and she seems plausible enough . . .

Jayne stared at the screen. During all the years that she had been in business one thing she prided herself on was being a shrewd judge of character. She had taken on hundreds of staff, and although occasionally people hadn't been quite what they appeared she had never been completely off beam with anyone before. 'Seems plausible enough' was not how she had read Jane at all.

Jayne reread the email, trying to work out exactly what it was that lay between the lines. Ray's nose had been put out of joint when she had hired Jane, and OK, so maybe it wasn't the most tactful thing she had ever done, but it had felt right. Had she been wrong about Jane?

By marked contrast Jane's email was all concern about her current situation, but was it a well-played bluff?

Hi Jayne,
Sorry I missed your call. I was worried when I got your message – I hope you're OK. I did try to ring your hotel but I couldn't make the girl on reception understand. I've left messages with Ray to sort out the card situation, and if you email me with contact details I'll pass them on to him. Please let me know you are OK. Other than that things are going well here. I've been through the new

catalogues and am wading through reams of data processing. I've made contact with several suppliers and plan to hit the road next week . . .

'. . . And so ladies and gentlemen, in conclusion I'd like to say thank you for inviting me here this evening. And I hope that my speech didn't send too many of you to sleep, although I suppose at this end of the evening we can always blame the effects on Sir Henry's excellent wine. Thank you.'

There was a polite ripple of laughter. Jane waited for a second or two and then the applause began to rise, slowly at first, then building to an enthusiastic roar. She smiled and nodded left and right, happy that it had gone well – and even more delighted that it was all over.

Jane sighed, took a pull on the brandy that Henry Cassar had insisted she had to accompany her coffee and sat down, dropping Jayne's notes back into her bag as she did.

A rotund red-faced businessman at the far end of the table got to his feet and proposed a vote of thanks. Jane smiled and nodded her thanks in his direction, feeling the tension slowly easing out of her shoulders and neck. Finished, done and dusted. Then the master of ceremonies rose to make announcements, although by this time Jane was no longer listening.

It was all over: Jane sighed; now finally she could relax. There would be a quick round of handshaking and thanking and lots of social smiling and then she could slip away from Henry and find Kit. She almost giggled with excitement.

As she took another swig of brandy Henry Cassar caught hold of her hand and lifted it to his lips. 'Great speech,

233

m'dear,' he said warmly. 'Well done. You had them eating out of the palm of your hand.'

Jane smiled. It wasn't true, but it was nice of him to say so. It had been fine, though, and she certainly hadn't let Jayne down. The jokes had gone well, the words flowed and at least for some of it Jane felt she had managed to convey a little of the passion and enthusiasm Jayne felt about her business interests. Jane took an after-dinner mint from the tray on the table, shoulders slumping, suddenly tired.

'Oh, goodness me, don't flag on me now, m'dear,' Henry purred, eyes twinkling. 'The evening's young and my people have booked the most wonderful band. We'll dance till dawn. And we need to talk you and I – I feel that we have a lot in common. Rags to riches, and all that.'

Jane stared at him; Henry was probably old enough to be her grandfather, not that that seemed to deter him one little bit.

'How about we top that brandy of yours up with a little champagne?' he was saying, waving the waiter over. 'I haven't had the chance to show you round the house yet. It really is the most wonderful old pile. Did Anton tell you there's a heated indoor pool, sauna and a steam room in the folly? Maybe you saw it as you drove in? Do you like to swim? I meant to ask if you are staying for the weekend? I've got some wonderful watercolours and one or two rather exciting Impressionists that I'm terribly proud of. Said in the *Sunday Times* that you're very fond of modern art. You know, you really are the most fascinating woman, m'dear. I'd like to know more about you, you know. Now, tell me . . .' As Henry continued talking Jane suppressed the urge to giggle; the waiter added champagne to the brandy balloon. She had no intention of drinking it, although at least Henry, in his on-the-spot rundown on the sights, had had the decency to leave his etchings out of the equation.

With the meal at an end the other diners began to drift away from the tables, heading off towards the sounds of dance music emanating from the open doors of the orangery, and as she and Henry joined them Jane caught a flurry of movement on the periphery of her vision and was about to check it out when a hand settled gently on her arm.

'Do you think I could have a word with you?' said a soft male voice.

Jane turned and looked up into Kit's eyes and smiled. For some reason he didn't smile back; instead his expression hardened. He had been watching her over dinner and, if anything, was watching her even more intently now.

'Sure. Are you all right?' she asked. He didn't reply. 'What's the matter? I can explain about the—'

'Can I ask you where you got the jewellery you're wearing?' he said, sounding very formal, his speech clipped and icy.

Jane stared at him in surprise, fingers lifting to the little collar and drop necklace. 'This?'

He nodded. 'That.'

'Yes, of course. I borrowed them. And the earrings,' she said, feeling more and more uncomfortable. Kit was hanging on her every word, his gaze not shifting from hers. She began to feel horribly self-conscious. 'Why? Is there some kind of problem?'

'I don't know. How about you tell me?'

'I just told you. I borrowed them.'

'You borrowed them?' he repeated.

Jane nodded. 'From my boss.'

'Right. And your boss is *who*, exactly?'

Jane swallowed hard; Henry had discreetly stepped back so they could talk but was within easy earshot. 'Well,' she began, 'the thing is—'

But before she could finish Kit continued, 'Where is my sister?'

Jane stared at him. 'Your sister?'

'Jayne Mills,' he said grimly, eyes never leaving hers.

Jane stared at him. Kit Harvey-Mills . . . comprehension dawned. He was the Kit who had phoned. She recognised his voice now. This was the Kit who had wanted to speak to Jayne. 'Oh bugger,' she whispered.

Meanwhile Henry Cassar had stepped closer. 'Are you all right, m'dear?' he said, looking from face to face.

Jane had no idea what to say, struggling to regain her composure.

'What seems to be the problem?' Henry was saying to Kit.

'I'll tell you what the problem is,' snapped Kit Harvey-Mills, finally unable to hold back any longer, his face taut with concern and fury. 'This woman is a fraud and an impostor.'

Jane stared at him in horror, willing him to be quiet, trying very hard not to panic, while her stomach did a horrible shuddering back flip. Damn, and just when it had all been going so well.

Everyone in the little group turned to stare at her, while she just wished that the floor would open up and swallow her. Jane could feel her face reddening furiously while her brain leaped around trying to come up with something that sounded plausible and eventually realised that there was only the truth.

'Actually he's right, Henry,' she said quickly. 'Although I'm not exactly an impostor and I can explain ev—' she began.

Henry looked bemused and turned towards Jane to listen, but before she could finish the sentence, Kit said, 'She's wearing my grandmother's jewellery. I left it with Jayne for safekeeping while I've been travelling so my ex-wife didn't get her hands on it. What have you done with Jayne?'

Henry peered at him for a few seconds as if trying to place Kit's face, and then shook his head. 'I'm most terribly sorry, but do I know you? Who exactly are you? Are you on the guest list?' Behind Henry, Anton had shown up, together with the in-house security guards, great lumbering men in dinner jackets, with shoulders the width of phone boxes, who looked as if they were probably ex-army or, in one case, possibly ex-zoo.

'I'm Jayne Mills' stepbrother,' Kit snapped. 'My name is Kit Harvey-Mills and I'd arranged to meet Jayne here this evening. She was the one who arranged my invitation. I want to know what the hell is going on and where my sister is. And I want to know *now*.' As he spoke his tone grew increasingly forceful, his eyes not leaving Jane's face for an instant.

Now Jane knew exactly why he had looked familiar. She was almost certain that there was a photo of him in Jayne's study. A picture she had passed over without really registering it consciously. Jayne's baby brother; why hadn't Jayne warned her?

237

'Oh God,' she whispered. She could feel her stomach sinking.

There was a moment's silence and then Henry nodded. 'Right, in that case you had better come with me and we'll try and sort this out. You can use the drawing room.' As he turned, Henry winked slyly at Jane and said in a voice barely above a whisper, 'You little minx, you should have told me you were in trouble. I guessed you were a wrong 'un from the moment I clapped eyes on you. Bit of a character. I love a damsel in distress. Like handcuffs, do you?'

Jane blushed furiously as, flanked by the security guards, she, Kit Harvey-Mills, Henry Cassar, Anton and a couple of hangers-on made their way through the crowd, which parted like the Red Sea. Jane could feel every eye in the place watching her. She had never felt so uncomfortable in her entire life. This was not how she had anticipated the evening going at all. Up until now the worst Jane thought that could happen was that the speech went down badly.

'Let's go in here, shall we?' said Henry, opening double doors into an elegant room overlooking the formal gardens.

Beside them Kit looked uneasy, not at all happy with Henry's apparent chummy tone. Jane stared at Kit; he was still gorgeous, dammit.

'What about my sister; what about the jewellery?' he repeated. 'Or would you prefer me to call the police?'

'Anton, please get some champagne and some more coffee for us,' said Henry.

How nice to have minions, thought Jane fleetingly as Anton headed off back into the house.

'Never mind coffee, I want some answers,' Kit snapped.

'Would you like me to get my lawyer?' Henry asked Jane solicitously. 'I think he's out in the smoking room at the moment but I'm sure he wouldn't mind popping in? He's very good.'

'No, no, thank you, Henry,' said Jane, and then to Kit Harvey-Mills, who was still glowering at her, 'please, Kit, there is no need to worry and there is no need to call the police. Jayne is fine, she's having a break. She's in Kos at the moment. I can explain everything.'

'I've tried ringing her.'

Jane nodded. 'I know, me too. She's been having problems with her mobile. I've got an email address for her.'

'What about ringing her hotel?'

'I've tried that. She booked out.'

'That's bloody convenient,' growled Kit.

'What on earth do you think I've done with her?' snapped Jane, getting angry now. He quite obviously hadn't listened to a word she'd said.

'I've got no idea,' he answered. 'That's the problem. If all this is true why are you pretending to be Jayne Mills?'

'Whoa, let's all calm down and take a seat, shall we?' said Henry. He indicated a chair on one side of the fireplace to Jane. 'Now why don't you tell us exactly what is going on, m'dear?' He settled himself down in the chair opposite.

Jane sighed. Here we go, she thought miserably, looking first at Henry and then at Kit. She started to explain the name situation, and then the post mix-up and how Jayne had wanted a break and had been waiting for the right moment and how she hadn't wanted anyone to know.

'I know you're not going to believe this but my name really is Jane Mills. I'm just not *the* Jayne Mills.'

Kit was about to speak.

'And I can prove it,' she added hastily, cutting him off, pulling her wallet out of her evening bag. 'I've got my credit cards and, oh damn, my driving licence is back at the house.'

'Which is where exactly?' asked Henry, head tipped to one side, a study in listening. Jane wasn't sure whether this was assistance with Kit's questioning or a blatant attempt to get her home address.

Sitting on the sofa under one of the huge picture windows, Kit was watching her, taking in every word. Jane said, 'Kit, please don't look at me like that. Jayne is just fine, I promise you, really.'

'Why did you pretend to be Jayne and why did she let you do a keynote speech?' he asked incredulously.

What could she say?

'It wasn't Jayne, it was Ray who asked me to do the speech and said that unless I was asked, just to let people assume I was Jayne. It seems weird now, but I've only just started and I was under the impression it was some sort of little trade show. I do what I'm told and I told him I'd done presentations before. I'd got no idea how prestigious an event it was until this afternoon.'

Kit's expression didn't flicker.

'So let me get this straight: you have the same name and a very similar address, and currently you are employed by the real Jayne Mills, that's right, isn't it?' said Henry.

'I *am* Jane Mills,' snapped Jane. 'But yes, that's more or less right. I'm just not the one you were expecting.'

Henry held up his hands. 'Well, that should be easy enough to check. Now tell me about the necklace?' Henry indicated the jewellery she was wearing. 'Are you telling me your employer gave you access to her jewellery too?'

'No, well, at least not exactly. For a start I had no idea they were valuable, certainly not heirlooms. Her house-keeper, Gary, found them for me to go with this outfit.'

Henry's expression suggested he approved of the outfit but had the good sense to keep his thoughts to himself. Kit's face remained impassive.

Finally Henry said, 'Right, now presumably there are people who can verify your story?'

'Of course – Gary, Ray – I can give you their phone numbers.'

Henry clapped his hands. 'Wonderful. There we are then. A couple of phone calls and we can clear the whole thing up.'

But it wasn't Henry that Jane wanted to convince. She stared at Kit. 'You do believe me, don't you?'

Kit shook his head. 'I can't believe Jayne went away without telling me or leaving some way of contacting her.'

'She didn't, I just told you.' Jane tried very hard not to shout. 'It's a problem with her phone. Why don't you ring Gary or Ray? They'll explain.'

'I've got a better idea. Why don't you give me the jewellery and then we'll drive over to Buckbourne and I'll talk directly to Gary and Ray?'

Jane pulled a face. 'Are you serious?'

He nodded and for a moment she wondered if he was trying to call her bluff. 'I'd just like to get this sorted out.'

Jane sighed. 'Fine. In that case I'll go and get changed and get my things, unless you have a problem with that?'

Kit considered for a moment and then shook his head. 'No, no problem.'

As he spoke she realised he was looking at the neck-lace. Jane instinctively touched it, as if she could feel his

241

eyes like fingertips. 'How about if I leave this with you until I get back?'

'OK. How long are you going to be?'

Jane unfastened the collar, removed the earrings and set them down on the table between them. 'Fifteen minutes.' Even though she had done nothing, handing over the jewellery gave her a peculiar feeling.

'Oh damn, you're not leaving, are you?' Henry looked crestfallen. Jane suspected he had hoped that everything would be resolved and that she – grateful for his intervention – would be eternally grateful and stay for the weekend.

'I think it would be best if I did.'

'Ah, pity, and just when we were getting on so well,' said Henry. 'Maybe we could meet up for lunch some time?'

Meanwhile Ray was sitting by the phone waiting for Kit to ring, presumably he had gone to the Cassar dinner, and presumably Jane hadn't owned up to being anything other than Jane Mills. He smiled. Surely it wouldn't be long now before he called.

Jayne was still mulling over what Ray had said when she opened Andy's email. She scanned the opening couple of lines and her spirits immediately lifted.

Hi, Hon. My mum passed your message on. I was so pleased to hear from you after all this time. I have thought about you on and off over the last few years and keep meaning to get in touch, but you know how life and the years keep on rushing past, and when you look over your shoulder another five or ten have vanished over the horizon.

I've missed you – and often wonder what would have happened if you had said yes to me in Kos, how different life would have been. Your assistant told me that you were there at the moment. I've enclosed my phone number in case you fancy a chat any time . . .

Jayne smiled and started to type. She could hear his voice, almost as if he was reading to her. Andy Taylor. Just the sound of his name gave her a good feeling.

Dear Andy,
It was so nice to hear from you. Kos is as beautiful as ever – although life's been a bit strange since I arrived . . . and actually it would be wonderful to talk to you . . .

Ray was rehearsing his big speech. It was important to get the right tone. 'The thing is, Kit, I don't now why Jayne employed Jane in the first place, it seemed . . .' Ray paused, in rehearsing what he would say and what gestures would be appropriate, then steepling his fingers thoughtfully as if trying to find the right words. 'Well, to be perfectly candid, at the time it seemed odd, out of character. Almost as if . . .' Ray feigned concern. God, this was so very much better than he could have ever hoped for. 'I don't like to say this really, but it was almost as if she had been coerced,' Ray said carefully. 'It's so out of character. I mean, we both know that Jayne can be a bit eccentric at times, but this seemed way over the top. How does it sound? I mean, for goodness' sake. Someone she barely knows shows up on her doorstep and she gives her a job managing her company while she goes off on some sort of a voyage of discovery? You have to admit it's a bit odd. And now this.' He held up his hands to emphasise the point. 'This girl is going round impersonating Jayne at public functions. I don't think she's broken the law, and at this stage I really can't see any reason to go to the police – I'll see to Jane – but I think we should both be worried about the real Jayne Mills, don't you?' Ray lingered over the word 'real' to make his point. 'She's in Greece on holiday at the moment – Kos, as far as I know. Although I have to say I'm not exactly sure where; she recently booked out of her hotel but that isn't altogether odd or unexpected. She has plans to island-hop and certainly do some travelling for the next few weeks. We've talked about it a lot just recently. She has been a bit stressed. Wants to find herself.' Ray allowed himself the merest hint of sarcasm, which he thought anyone, even Kit, could appreciate.

'To be honest, I think this is all some kind of mid-life crisis, Kit.' He slowed again. 'Although one thing that you ought to know is that Jayne has had some trouble with her credit cards while she's been away – oh, and her phone. Oh, actually, while you're here there is something else that might be of interest. I haven't thought anything about it until now. I've got CCTV here,' he said, 'and I was running the tape through . . .'

Ray paused thoughtfully; he wasn't really sure quite how to time his revelation of Jane's catalogue of apparent deceit and deception. Did he just blurt it all out – all anxious and concerned and unable to cope – or did he make Kit work for it? Which would be the most convincing? Maybe a little at a time, so that Kit didn't rock the boat. Ray considered the various scenarios. Which would be the most damning? He glanced at his watch, wondering when Kit would ring. Maybe he should ring him? Ray paused to reflect on the events of the last couple of weeks. Jane's unexpected arrival had been a gift from the gods . . .

Just then the phone rang.

He smiled and picked it up. 'Hello, Kit,' he said. 'How's it going?'

Chapter Eleven

Jayne stretched, it felt as if she had been sitting at the desk in the internet café for hours. The day was cooling rapidly and it seemed a very long time since she had climbed out of bed. With the prospect of another early start the next day it was time to head back to her room. She was just about to log off when one last thing occurred to her. Jayne tapped in and brought up her online banking, pulled out her pocket diary, and put in the account numbers, hidden amongst a list of phone numbers.

While she couldn't think of any way of directly accessing the money from Kos without a debit card, she still needed to see how things were going. Jane glanced down the list of numbers in the back of the book; it would be different if she could get through to her local branch but the calls went into a central office so there no point phoning and trying to persuade them that she really was Jayne Mills. Hopefully Ray would get it sorted out soon. It seemed bizarre to feel so impotent.

It was a relief when the screen unfolded with her details on – no password issue here, thank God; that would really have made her paranoid. On the next screen she had to put in a four-number security code and two letters from her password. She tapped in her details and waited. At the side of the screen the egg timer slowly turned.

'I ought to go to the police,' Kit said, as Jane climbed into his car. Was he thinking aloud or was he expecting her to reply? He had a cherry-red vintage Austin Healey frog-eyed Sprite which, under other circumstances, Jane would have commented on, but not tonight. She had changed out of Jayne's elegant evening dress into jeans, a shirt and a short suede jacket for the drive home, and looked cute, slim and, with her hair still up, very attractive – not that Kit appeared to have noticed. He had Jayne's diamonds in a cloth bag and Jane had very nearly had enough.

She was tired, she was stressed and, worst of all, she swung between being outraged, embarrassed, upset, indignant, thinking that Kit was making a mountain out of a molehill and the realisation that he really was genuinely concerned about his sister's safety. He was right, Jane *could* have been anybody and anything *could* have happened to Jayne. Except that it hadn't. Jayne was fine, and Jane wasn't just anybody, but convincing him of that would be an uphill struggle.

She also realised, even as she was closing the car door, that accepting Kit's lift back to Buckbourne was a mistake. So why had she accepted? Jane stared hard at him. Because she was telling the truth and had nothing to hide, because she wanted to prove her innocence and because, even given the present state of play, Jane fancied him. Damn it.

Looking across the car, Jane realised her first reaction to Kit, even now, was all chemistry and desire, even though she knew it was crazy and he still suspected that she had

247

bumped his sister off. The likelihood was that there was no way back from this, but she *still* fancied him. Which was mad, but true. Who said you could trust chemistry?

Meanwhile, Kit, anxious and preoccupied, pulled away from the house in a rip of gravel, worry and exhaust fumes. She had to be crazy. Jane looked away. Henry had offered her a car and driver or an overnight stay, although she had politely refused. Henry had pressed a little, rather taken by the idea that Jane was some sort of scarlet woman, up to no good. Although realistically, the only kind of scarlet Jane had experienced in the last few hours or so was blushing bright red with embarrassment at being unmasked and Kit accusing her of theft.

'Why don't you ring them then?' she said grumpily, snapping the seatbelt on. With the roof up the interior of the sports car felt claustrophobically small.

'Because I can't believe that Gary would be taken in by anybody.'

Jane stared at him. 'So are you saying you believe me?'

'No, I didn't say that. What I said was I believe Gary. Oh shit – I don't know. I can't work out what the hell is going on.'

'You don't have to, I keep telling you. This is all kosher and above board. Jayne wanted a break from work and asked me if I'd work for her. That's it. End of story. You're getting hooked up on the name thing. Jayne just didn't want it to become common knowledge that she was taking a sabbatical, but I've got nothing to hide. It seemed simpler not to tell Henry. I think it was Ray's idea not to say anything. Honestly. I used to work in the library, for goodness' sake. I've got references; you only have to ask Ray about me.'

There was a pause and then Kit said, 'That's just it, I already have.'

Jayne stared at the balance on her personal current account, trying hard to make sense of what she saw on the screen, trying to convince herself it was some kind of optical illusion. Her current account appeared to be empty, as did her savings account, her ISAs, her bonds, and her higher interest rate account – all of them had a zero balance, all of the money apparently gone. Vanished. Jayne shivered and looked again, wondering whether it might be a good idea to log on again. This had to be some kind of error.

This couldn't be happening. She felt a strange chill. It just wasn't possible. She was stunned – more than stunned, she was rigid with disbelief. This was ridiculous. It had to be wrong. She took a couple of breaths, trying to still the manic beating of her heart.

What was even more disturbing, if that was possible, was that the link to Jayne's business and company accounts no longer appeared on the page with her personal accounts. Without the link she couldn't get in to see what was happening in the company – and for this she had no administrator's password. Surely there has to be some mistake, her brain kept saying. Jayne scrolled down to see when the money had been trans-ferred from her account. Apparently it had been taken out after she arrived in Kos. All gone, not a penny left. Jayne took another deep breath. She needed to talk to Ray and Jane too. Whatever was going on it needed to be sorted out – now.

* * *

In Creswell Close, Gary had given himself the night off and was out on the deck at Lil and Tony's, helping himself to another glass of champagne before settling back onto a sunlounger alongside Lil, who was holding court in a peacock throne-style rattan chair, her ankle, now swathed in a chiffon scarf, carefully propped up on a pile of pillows. She was wearing a purple velvet kaftan, studded with acres of beads, miles of braid and enough tassels to keep half the strippers in the area respectable, and had taken like a duck to water, being waited on hand and foot.

'So how's it all going?' Gary asked, sipping the bubbles.

'It's like waiting for the Indians to attack, you know, like in them old cowboy films. Wagons circled, everyone watching, everyone waiting.' Lil stared fixedly out into the darkness where the roadies moved like shadows between big ice-filled dustbins of beer cans and the dull red glow of the barbecue.

Gary looked at her; maybe it was the painkillers.

The atmosphere in the Healey was so thick you could cut it with a bread knife. Kit was staring fixedly at the road, which snaked away under them like a white ribbon in the moonlight, while Jane was trying very hard not to cry or to swear or to ask him to stop the car and let her get out.

'What did Ray say?'

'I don't want to talk about it,' said Kit.

'I'm not a thief,' she said, over the sound of engine.

'Oh, right, that's got that cleared that up then. And presumably if you were you'd tell me, would you?'

'If I'm a thief and a con woman why the hell did you offer to take me home?'

He paused for a few seconds and then said, 'Because

I don't want to let you out of my sight until we get this cleared up and find Jayne. I saw the way that old lecher was eyeing you up – you'd got him eating out of the palm of your hand. Christ, he'd probably have helped you get away.'

'Get away? Get away with what? This is ridiculous. We've been over this half a dozen times. I'm not Bonnie and Clyde – I worked in a library.'

'When not impersonating other people.'

'How many times do I have to tell you: I wasn't impersonating Jayne, I was standing in for her at her request.'

'An arrangement you conveniently forgot to mention to your host.'

'Bollocks.'

There was silence for a few minutes.

'I should call the police.'

'Oh, for God's sake, why don't you just ring them?' Jane snapped, pulling the mobile out of her jacket and slamming it into his lap. He said nothing. Jane stared out of the window. Trees hurtled past; despite being so close to the ground they were travelling so fast that she had a sensation that they were flying.

'Go on then,' she goaded.

'I can't when I'm driving.'

'God, that is so weak. Pull over.'

They squealed to a halt in a lay-by, everything suddenly incredibly quiet after the animal roar of the engine. When Jane looked over, Kit was staring at her but hadn't picked up the phone.

'Well, what are you waiting for?'

'I don't know.'

'Was because you thought I was impersonating Jayne

the reason you came on to me on the terrace?' she asked, aware of the slight tremor in her voice.

'No,' said Kit. His knuckles were white as his long fingers gripped the steering wheel. 'No, it wasn't.'

'You know, you're good, I really thought you fancied me, and all the time you were busy trying to work out whether to call the police or not.'

'No, I wasn't,' said Kit. 'I didn't know who you were then.'

'So what were you doing?'

He laughed grimly. 'Chatting you up.'

'You were?'

'I was until I realised you were impersonating my sister.'

'I wasn't.'

'You were wearing my grandmother's jewellery and calling yourself Jayne Mills.'

'That's because my name is bloody Jane Mills.'

'And the jewellery?'

'I'm not going over this again, Kit.' She picked up her mobile and held it out towards him. 'Here. Ring the police.'

Silence fell like an excutioner's axe, although it was nice to know that he did fancy her. Or rather he *had* fancied her. Kit stared at her for what seemed like a lifetime. Jane held her breath.

Outside the moon hung like an all-seeing eye, and for one glorious moment Jane thought that he was going to kiss her. Instead, Kit looked away and turned the key in the ignition. The sound filled the cockpit like a storm breaking.

'I thought you were going to ring the police?' she said.

Kit glanced at her. 'So did I,' he said as they pulled away. 'So did I.'

*   *   *

In Kos under the same heavy, lazy-eyed moon, Jayne had been queuing for a phone for the best part of twenty minutes behind a gang of migrant workers and holiday-makers phoning home to check on children or pets, or brag about the weather, the booze and the tan they were rapidly developing. The late night air was hot and heavy with exhaust fumes. As her brain worked overtime on the state of her bank account, Jayne got more and more tense, and was strung as tight as a bowstring by the time she got to the front of the queue. More annoying when Jayne finally got through, she got the office answer machine.

It was almost more than she could bear.

'Ray, I don't care what it takes, get in contact with me a.s.a.p. I can be contacted by email, obviously, or via *Spirit of the Waves* Cruises.' She pulled one of Miko's brochures out of her bag and began to read off the number. But before she could finish the sentence the phone was picked up.

'Jayne, is that you?' Ray sounded almost as anxious as she felt.

Jayne felt a great flood of relief. 'Ray. Oh, thank God. I was beginning to think everyone had disappeared off the face of the earth. What the hell is going on there? I've just been online and my bank accounts are empty – I don't know what the hell is going on – and there is still no sign of my cards. Did you wire any money?' Jayne wasn't sure where to start or what to start with.

'Whoa, whoa, hang on. What do you mean, your bank account is empty? That can't be right.' Ray made her repeat what she had discovered, with Jayne hoping that they could get to the end of the conversation before her phone credit ran out.

253

'I've spoken to Henry Cassar tonight,' said Ray.

'Ray, I'm sure it's important too but can we discuss Henry later? It's hardly got anything to do with my money vanishing.'

'Well, actually it could have a lot to do with it. Apparently, according to Henry, Jane was passing herself of as you. She did the Cassar speech this evening and turned up there in one of your dresses and your jewellery.'

'What?' Jayne felt the breath catch in her throat. 'What the hell do you mean, my dress? My jewellery? Why, in God's name?' Her brain was close to overload. 'And what the hell was she doing there anyway? I thought you were going to do that talk. I thought we agreed. I thought . . .' Finally the words ran dry and she was speechless, brain stalled.

'I know, I know, calm down; there was a bit of a problem. I'd made a mistake, I'd double-booked and didn't want to let Cassar's people down. And like you I thought Jane deserved a chance. Henry rang here to double-check that we were actually employing her and then he came out with all this stuff. Apparently, Kit was there and was beside himself. If it hadn't been for Kit I doubt Henry would have guessed. Jayne, I really think it's time we thought about calling the police in. I mean, I'm not quite sure what the hell is going on here, but it seems to me that we've got a real problem and it's got Jane's name written all over it.'

Jayne bit her lip, trying hard not to panic. 'OK, but can you go online and check that the company accounts are OK? I'm not sure if you can ring me back on this number. If you can't I'll ring you back in half an hour.'

'And what about the police?' said Ray.

Jayne stared out into the night sky, not wanting to believe that this was happening. 'I don't know, Ray. I mean, I know how it looks but I still can't believe that Jane is capable of doing something like this. It's too calculating – too—'

'Oh, for God's sake, Jayne, what more do you need? A bloody flare to go up? There's something going on here and everything points to your little friend from the library.'

'But how? How the hell could she have done this much damage in so short a time? I've only been gone a few days and I met her by accident.'

There was a weighty little pause at the far end of the line and then Ray said icily, 'Are you sure about that?'

'What the hell is that supposed to mean?'

'OK, perhaps you finding Jane may have been pure coincidence, but you told me yourself that she had opened your post. So, how big a leap of faith does it take to see a pattern here?' He paused as if waiting for Jayne to catch up.

'There's got to be a thousand better ways to steal from me and not get caught. Did she think we wouldn't notice?' Jayne realised with a start she had herself made the leap to Jane being a thief.

'Lord only knows. Who knows how long she plans to hang around? She's just been fired – we don't really know why – she's just broken up with her boyfriend, and then she comes over to your house. She's down on her luck, she sees how you live – who knows exactly what went through her mind? She certainly knows that you're wealthy; Jesus, she probably read your bank statements . . .'

'Oh, bloody hell, Ray,' Jayne stammered.

'I think we should call the police.'

Jayne swallowed hard.

*   *   *

It was well after midnight when Jane and Kit finally got back to Creswell Close. Kit pressed the button on the security grille. 'Hi, Gary, it's Kit.'

'Kit?' said a bemused voice. 'Hang on a minute.'

A second later the gates slowly swung open and the garden lights snapped on. As they pulled into the driveway another went on in the hallway and in the open door stood Gary.

'Kit,' Gary said as soon as he climbed out of the car. 'How are you? How lovely to see you.'

Jane followed a split second behind. 'What on earth is going on? Jane, I thought you were staying at the party tonight.'

Kit looked back at Jane. 'Do you know her?'

Gary snorted. 'For Christ's sake, of course I know her, Kit – she's working for Jayne.'

'That's what she said,' Kit said, looking suspicious. 'So where's Jayne.'

'In Kos,' Gary replied.

'That's what she said too,' said Kit, his tone not changing.

Gary lifted an eyebrow. 'What? Oh, come off it, do you think I'm under duress or hypnotised? Come on in, the pair of you. Do you want a cup of tea? You both look absolutely shattered. Kit, stop scowling. If the wind changes you'll stay like it.'

Jane almost sobbed with relief as the housekeeper wrapped an arm around her. 'And you, don't look so worried. It's all right,' he said. 'Really. Cassar rang to see if there was anything he could do. He said you were a magnificent woman and wants to know if you're free next week for lunch.'

Jane's eyes filled with tears. 'Oh, Gary.'

'Shush, we'll sort this out, sweetie,' he said, running a hand over Jane's arm. 'Only trouble was, while he rang Jayne rang from Kos. She left a message but I can't get through on the number she left.'

'She rang?' said Kit.

Gary nodded, and as they got to the kitchen, flicked the phone on to hands free, skimming quickly through the messages.

'Gary, Jane, I need you to get in contact with me a.s.a.p. I've got a real problem at the moment.' And then there was a number. Jane sounded tense and upset, close to tears. Gary hung up as soon as the machine had coughed up the date and time.

'See,' he said, addressing Kit. 'She's absolutely fine.'

Ray paced up and down the flat for a few moments, composing himself, staring at the phone, working through his script. He then picked it up and dialled the number Jayne had given him. Once they had said hello, he barely let Jayne get a word in.

'It looks OK, Jayne. I've been through everything and from here it looks solid. Maybe she chickened out at the last minute, or maybe she is biding her time to see what happens. Maybe dipping into the company was too rich for her. Anyway, from what I can see everything appears to have been shifted into her personal current account. I'm assuming she must have thought that you wouldn't be looking at your accounts on holiday. I'm running a programme at the moment to see what she has spent on the company credit card, and I promise to chase up the card situation and get some cash out to you. I'm not sure what the hell has taken them so long, unless of course they've had some help too.' He could hear Jayne's breath, tight and anxious, and he smiled.

'Would you like me to call the police now?' Seconds ticked by. 'Well?' he asked, a little more forcefully this time.

'I can't believe this,' Jayne said in disconnected tone. 'I just don't understand. How did she get hold of the passwords and codes for my personal bank accounts?'

Ray paused for a little while and then said, 'I think she may have taken them from the office. I'm sorry, I really am. Now would you like me to ring them, or wait till you get back?'

'I need a flight.'

He could hear the resignation in her voice. 'I'll organise one at this end.'

Jayne sighed. 'OK.'

'About the police . . .'

'I don't really see what choice we have, do you?'

Ray waited a second or two more and then said, 'We could try and deal with it internally. I know what I said, but there's been no real harm done at the moment if we can stop her now; after all, we've got her bang to rights. And let's be honest, this kind of thing doesn't help customer confidence or credibility or, come to that, suppliers.' He paused again, letting the possibilities sink in. 'Maybe we can contain this ourselves. Let's be honest, we don't want her to do any more damage to the company, do we?'

'Look, get me home and in the meantime . . .' said Jayne, suddenly sounding exhausted, . . . in the meantime you're on the spot, Ray. Do what you think best.'

'Leave it with me,' Ray said, and then hung up, triumphant.

* * *

258

Jayne walked away from the phone with a strange hollow feeling in the place where her heart should be. This wasn't right. She felt sick and lost and uncertain. How could this have happened? The phone she had just hung up began to ring but Jayne was too preoccupied to go back to pick it up. How could she have been so wrong about anyone? Had she lost the knack? Was she getting more gullible as she was getting older?

She didn't want to go straight back to her room even though she was exhausted. The idea of being alone with her thoughts was almost more than she could bear. Feeling despondent she called a cab and headed up towards the hillside café where she and Miko had had supper the day she had been for the boat trip. Although it was late she guessed he might still be there – and if he wasn't she had no doubt that there was someone there who would know how to get in touch with him. Jayne pulled her pashmina tight around her shoulders suddenly cold despite the languid heat of the night. What the fuck was going on?

Gary finally admitted defeat and dropped the phone back into its cradle. 'She must have gone. I'll ring the offices of the cruise company and leave a message.' He looked at Kit. 'Unless you want to?'

Kit shook his head and turned his attention back to Jane. 'So let me get this straight. You're working for Jayne?'

Jane topped up her wine from the bottle on the kitchen table. 'Hallelujah.'

'And you lent her Jayne's clothes?'

'And your family heirlooms? That was me,' said Gary holding up his hands in surrender. 'I had no idea how precious they were. I knew they were valuable but I thought if I told madam here that she was wearing real rocks then she would refuse to wear them, and she needed something special with that frock. My fault. I am sorry.'

Kit nodded. 'So why, yesterday, when I'd spoken to you and you fudged the call and I rang Ray, why didn't he tell me the truth then?'

Gary and Jane looked at each other and then at him.

'You spoke to him and he didn't tell you Jayne was away? What did he say?' asked Jane.

'I've been trying to think what it was exactly that he said. I remember I asked him if Jayne was all right, and he said yes but he sounded a bit noncommittal. When I said I was flying home and planned to ring back and arrange to come and stay with Jayne, he said she was on the road. I'm sure that's what he said. I said she'd invited me to the Cassar thing and that maybe I'd be able to make it after all, and then he said he'd make sure I was on the guest list; said it would be a nice surprise if I turned up.' Kit laughed. 'Which it most certainly was.'

'So he meant you to discover me – meant you to, to . . . to what?'

'Call the police? Make a scene? What I don't understand is why.'

'Whatever he's up to he wants Jane in the frame,' said Gary grimly.

'OK, OK,' said Kit almost to himself. 'So why? You said, Jane, that you were having problems accessing Jayne's website – and she is having problems with her phone and credit cards.'

'And passwords. We put it down to a mix-up over names. We're both having all sorts of password problems. I gave

260

the ones Jayne gave me to Ray to try and sort it out and he said he would reset them.'

Kit nodded.

The security buzzer on the front gate rang. Gary got up and pressed receive.

'Gary had to use the administration password to get the speech for tonight because nothing else worked.'

'Um, so what do the passwords control?' asked Kit.

'I'm not sure about Jayne's, but mine gave me access to websites, site content, data bases, a housekeeping account for day-to-day stuff. Presumably Jayne can access everything, access the business, banking, site content, data – everything,' said Jane.

Kit looked at Jane for a moment and then said, 'What we need is a geek – someone who understands computers and can work out what's going on.'

'I think we might need a lawyer as well,' said Gary thoughtfully as he stepped away from the speaker.

'Why?'

'Well, the police have just arrived. They want to talk to Jane.'

Ray meanwhile poured himself a small single malt and practised his speech.

'Officer, I think there's been a misunderstanding. Yes, we do employ Ms Mills. My business partner took her on.'

He had to be prepared in case Kit rang the police, although surely they would want to try to verify that Jane was who she said she was, and surely in relation to work at least he would be the first point of call. Surely. He took another stroll across the Axminster; casual sincerity was the key.

'Yes, my business partner did employ her. It's a bit of a delicate situation.'

When the phone rang Ray jumped and then grinned. Showtime. He took a moment or two to compose himself before lifting the receiver.

'I miss you, Daddy-kins,' Lulu purred in a little-girly voice. 'I've got all my pretty new things on and nowhere to go.'

'I'm busy,' snapped Ray, ignoring the little flutter in his groin. 'I miss you' was Lulu-speak for 'Come over, I need screwing.' 'I need you to get off the line. I'm waiting for an incoming call. It's important.'

'Ohhhhhhh, and I'm not? That's such a shame,' she whispered, upping the leverage and lust by half. 'I thought that maybe we could get together tonight. I'm all on my own-some and I miss you, so much—'

'Lulu, be a love and just get off the line, will you? It's late,' he said, his tone cold as ice.

It was enough to break Lulu's simpering, horny kitten mood. 'You said we'd go somewhere nice this weekend. You said—'

'I know what I said,' Ray growled. 'And we haven't lost the chance yet, but something's come up. Do you understand? Something important.'

'So we're not going anywhere then?'

'That wasn't what I said. It's Thursday, the weekend doesn't start on a Thursday. Even you must know that,' he added under his breath.

Lulu whimpered. 'Are you cross with me?'

'No, no, I'm not cross, Lu, but I will be if you don't get off the damned phone. I'll ring you tomorrow. All right?'

He could almost hear her flinch.

'You hate me, don't you?' she said, her little-girly voice full of tears and self-obsession. 'You do, don't you?'

'No, of course I don't hate you. Look, I'm sorry, sweetie,' he said quickly, without a hint of remorse. 'I don't mean to upset you, but it's been a long day.' A long day waiting for the shit to hit the fan, a long day of knowing when to bat it back or just let it go sailing by.

'You sound really tired,' she said, softer now.

Christ, *now* she sounded concerned. How come Lulu decided *now* was the moment to reveal hidden depths?

'Maybe I should come over and give you a little massage.'

Ray groaned. 'Look, sweetie, how about I ring you back later when I've finished up here? I can't concentrate—'

'You're still working?'

'Uh-huh.'

'At this time of night? You're always working. You've never got any time for me.'

'Now you know that's not true.' Bloody woman. She whined on a bit more, although not too much because they both knew, if they were honest, that Lulu was just arm candy and if she pushed her luck too far she would be back-behind-the-bar-where-he'd-found-her candy. And with that Ray hung up and poured a little more single malt into his glass. After all, there was still time for the police to show up and take a full statement, and he wanted to have his wits about him.

In the kitchen at Creswell Close Jane looked up at the detective framed in the doorway and felt her stomach tighten.

'Good evening. I'm Detective Inspector Harry Rolf, Miss Mills. I wonder if we might have a few words with you,' he said. There was nothing about his tone that implied it was a request. Behind DI Rolf stood a female detective constable, whose expression suggested she would rather be almost anywhere else than in some posh bird's house at well after midnight on a weeknight.

'What is this about?' asked Kit, getting to his feet and standing between Jane and the police officers. Jane was touched and a little surprised that he was being so protective.

'We just want to have a few words, sir,' said DI Rolf. 'Now, Miss Mills, we can do this here or we can go down to the station if you would prefer.'

Jane stood up. 'It's all right, we can go into the sitting room.'

'Would you like some tea? Or coffee?' asked Gary.

The policeman declined with a nod of the head and so Jane led them back through the house.

Ray's plan was relatively simple. Over the last few years he had been . . . Ray paused, letting the Scotch ease into his bloodstream while trying to rationalise exactly what it was he *had* done. He had been *preparing* for retirement, redressing the balance in the work-wage ratio. Feathering his nest, lining his pockets. Ray had wanted to ensure that when the time came for him and Jayne to part company, he would be compensated for all the years he had spent tidying up after her.

Jayne was warm, bright and bold, and bound to make money. Ray had known that from the moment they'd met, however many years ago that was now. Back then he'd been an accountant in a high street firm and Jayne was a new client who had shown up with a carrier bag full of receipts, a handwritten ledger, tight jeans and an imagination geared purely and sweetly towards making money and running a successful business.

He had sat in the gloomy sepia-tinted office, with its peeling walls and ghastly chipped Formica-topped furniture and listened, astonished, at this slip of a thing with so many plans. They were about the same age but he felt so old and dull compared to Jayne. Christ, even back then her plans had plans, and what was most impressive was the way her vision worked: she never had any great desire to take gargantuan steps but rather safe baby steps, one project funding another and another – a patchwork portfolio of developments fuelled by a genuine vision and understanding of what ordinary people wanted and needed and were willing to pay for. And as she talked Ray had taken a look around – at least metaphorically – at his prospects and realised they amounted at best to a full partnership when one of the old guard finally died, membership of the local golf club, charitable work for the Round Table, a little blonde wife, a couple of kids and a Cavalier King Charles spaniel . . . and as he looked he could almost feel the boredom creeping up over him like ivy.

Jayne Mills had been an inspiration and in his way he had courted her. Not sexually – she wasn't his type – and even back then he preferred them a lot younger. He had courted her in a business sense: taken her out to lunch as a client, helped her sort out her tax, found loopholes and low-cost loans, and although he had been paid well for his efforts – eventually Jayne had stopped paying his firm's bills and offered him a job – the thing was that Ray felt she had never really fully acknowledged his guiding hand in her success, his solid worldly sensible string tied tight on her bright shiny bobbing kite. Eventually she had offered him shares in the company, but not in every aspect of the company, and that had hurt.

And so over the last few years he had been seeking some recompense for his hurt feelings. After all, he told himself, sipping the Islay malt, it wasn't as if he hadn't earned it. And so he had helped himself to a little cream off the top of every pie. His own little nest egg. His brain suggested all manner of euphemisms. Embezzle was such a nasty word.

Ray had been extremely careful to cover his tracks, hiding his activity under almost geological layers of orders and returns, handling charges and credit card transactions, and as stock moved through the system he had a way of peeling away tiny slivers of percentages, but Ray had always known that one day there would be a moment when there would be a power shift – and this he sensed was it. He had never been greedy, just thorough, going not for the quick fix but rather for the long game. Not that anyone would notice or detect or be able to follow his carefully honed plans without a lot of time, dedication and patience. Oh, no, he had been very careful.

Jayne had used the same firm of auditors for years, someone Ray had recommended, and he had made sure that he was the one in charge of systems and implementing changes, and generally seeing to the way things were done. It wasn't hard, as that was what he was employed to do.

He had fought off the geeks who had insisted they needed a fully integrated system so that he – or Jayne – could see if things balanced at the press of a key, feathering his nest slowly, patiently, with pennies rather than pounds. Even so, there was no way he could have anything in the company that attempted to reconcile stock with income, outgoings, returns and credits. At least not at the moment. Ray had been careful and now the time had come. Just as Jayne had a feeling that Jane's arrival was an omen, so had Ray. This was a chance just too good to miss.

All roads led to Rome, or in this case to Jane Mills. He just needed to make it appear that she was on the take. He would appear to be shaken – concerned, anxious that after all these years Jayne had finally lost her touch with personnel. Maybe she was no longer able to keep all the balls in the air. And the power would have shifted. On the back of all this hippy bullshit about finding herself, Jayne would doubt her judgement. It would be a real knock to her confidence – he'd make sure of that – and then, while she was down, he would suggest he step in and took more of an active role. Let her become more of a figurehead; ease the strain.

And when the time came to resign from active service, he would ride off into the sunset without anyone being any the wiser. By the time anyone got around to doing a full audit – if they bothered – Ray would be long gone.

South America had always appealed to him. He could live like a king on the money he had squirrelled away for a rainy day. Ray had accrued a portfolio of property equal to Jayne's, all manner of stocks and shares, all bought with Jayne's profit and all above board and legal with the tax man: bought with money he had laundered so well you could see right through it. Taking Jane Mills on without so much as a by-your-leave had been the final straw for Ray, and would prove to be Jayne's Waterloo.

* * *

Jane came back into the kitchen about fifteen minutes later. 'I've got to go down to the police station and make a statement. I'm just fetching my coat and bag.'

Gary stared at her and then at Kit. 'Why?' he said.

Kit held up his hands in surrender. 'Don't look at me. I don't understand why they came. I didn't call the police. Really.'

'It isn't about Jayne,' said Jane, her voice cracking with emotion. 'Apparently I'm being questioned in connection with the blackmail and harassment of my ex-boyfriend and his new partner.'

The room went quiet. 'What?' said Kit

Jane nodded. 'I know. Crazy, isn't it? Apparently someone has been sending them intimidating emails and threatening to send the head of department and about a dozen other people compromising images of the pair of them.'

'You're a blackmailer as well?'

Jane stared at Kit in amazement. 'Well, thanks for the vote of confidence, Kit.'

At which point the female police officer came in and asked if Jane was ready to leave.

Chapter Twelve

'Would you say that you were upset by Steve Burney's treatment of you, Jane?'

'Of course I was.'

'And of course at the same time you'd been through the added stress of being made redundant and discovering that Lucy, Miss Stroud, Mr Burney's new partner, had taken over your position.'

Jane looked up in time to see the uniformed officer by the doorway struggling to suppress a snigger.

'Yes, all those things are true, but . . .' Jane paused, collecting her thoughts.

'And we have a statement here from a Mrs Findlay about an incident involving a fish tank and some sort of self-help literature.'

Jane stared at him.

'So?' said Detective Inspector Rolf in a low voice, leaning in towards her, cajoling, his expression almost tender.

'So being upset, which I think under the circumstances is completely reasonable, and threatening somebody are poles apart. Yes, I was upset – I still *am* upset about the two of them – but no, I didn't blackmail or threaten anyone.'

Rolf smiled wolfishly. 'You know, I think we could all understand how upset you've been by this situation, Jane. It's a very human reaction. After all, Lucy is younger than you, attractive – sexually adventurous . . .'

Jane stared at him in amazement, wondering how he knew. Had Steve told him about the yoghurt? This had to be a yoghurt-based assumption. One way and another it had been a long day and she had had just about enough.

'Look,' Jane snapped, 'I've already told you. I didn't blackmail or threaten anyone – OK? As far as I know I've got nothing to blackmail anyone with. And you're right, finding out that Steve and Lucy were carrying on behind my back was bloody horrible, but what they did was not illegal, and however much it hurt there's nothing I can do about it.'

'Do you think it should be illegal?'

'Oh, for God's sake,' said Jane in exasperation.

'Do you want him back? Do you think threatening him is really going to help get him back?'

Before she could answer, the door opened and a uniformed officer came in and whispered something in DI Rolf's ear. He nodded and then looked at Jane. 'You might like to know that your mother has just arrived.'

Jane stared at him in amazement. 'My mother? Are you serious?' she said incredulously. 'Why in God's name would my mother be here, and who on earth told her I was here?' Jane shook her head. It felt like she had woken up inside a bad dream.

'A young woman,' he glanced down at his notes, 'Miss Elizabeth Preston, who is currently house-sitting for you, was concerned that you might be in trouble – we called there first – and she said she was going to call her.'

Trust Lizzie. 'OK, well, I've got no idea what good my mother will do. You'll understand why when you see her.'

'She would like to see you.'

'I'm sure she would.'

'What does that mean, Jane?'

She was getting deeply annoyed by DI Rolf's body language and the way he kept using her name; if it was meant to engender trust it wasn't working, mainly because none of it rang true. He had quite obviously been on some kind of course.

'You'll understand why when you see her,' Jane said, taking a sip from the little Styrofoam beaker of water that DI Rolf had provided for her.

'Would you say that you are estranged from your family, Jane?'

She stared at him and shook her head, wondering exactly what all this was meant to achieve. A teary confession of guilt? A plea for mercy? A sobbing desperate confession?

'No, I'm not estranged from my family, Inspector Rolf, although sometimes I wish that I was. Now, will you please explain to me what exactly it is I'm supposed to have done, or let me go home?'

Rolf smiled. 'Come on, Jane,' he said, his voice dropping to a conspiratorial purr. 'How long are you planning to keep this up for? It will be easier for you, easier for everyone, if you just hold your hand up and say yes it was me. I did it. We'd all like to go home.'

'Tell me.'

Rolf's expression hardened fractionally. 'Do you use a computer connected to the internet in your new job?'

'Yes, of course I do.'

'And you had access to a PC while you were working at the library.'

'Yes.'

'And you have one at home?'

'Yes, I imagine most people in the country have one or have access to one.' Jane tried hard not to sound angry or sarcastic but wasn't at all sure that she was succeeding.

He nodded. 'But not all of them have access to files and email and information from Buckbourne Central Library, do they?'

'No, of course not.'

Jane was exhausted and just wished that he would come straight out and tell her what the problem, what the accusation was. Sitting beside Rolf, the female police officer, who had been at Jayne's house earlier, picked at something troublesome on her skirt and pointedly avoided making eye contact.

'When you left the library, did you take anything with you from your office or from anywhere else in the building?'

'Yes, I did. I took all the things that were mine as I had no plans to go back. Only personal possessions, though. A couple of mugs, a plant, odds and ends – a mac and an umbrella, the things on my desk. I think most of them are probably still in boxes at my house, in the hallway and in the kitchen, if you wanted to check.'

'And what about files from the computer at the library? Did you copy any of those or delete any? What did you do with your files?'

'I deleted a lot of things, left the library policy and contact stuff on the system, along with a schedule of meetings I'd booked and business documents and the projects I'd been working on.'

'And what about personal email?'

'I forwarded it to my private email address in a bulk folder.'

'All of it?'

'Yes, as far as I know. What is this about?'

'So let me just clarify this. You forwarded all your private email to your own personal email address?'

'Yes, as far as I know, that's what I just said.'

'So do you recognise this, Jane?'

He pulled a picture out from the file on his desk and handed it to her. Jane stared in amazement. It was an A4 image on glossy photographic paper, presumably taken by Steve, although that wasn't evident from the contents. It appeared to have been shot in his sitting room, from the look of the sofa. Lucy Stroud filled most of the foreground. She was on all fours on the carpet, peering back rather coyly over one naked shoulder, her back and torso smeared with what Jane hoped was yoghurt, her medium-length strawberry-blonde hair caught up in bunches. She had pantomime freckles drawn on her nose and cheeks, and the large strawberry caught between her teeth was framed by lips painted bright red. She was wearing long white socks and had what looked like a very short gym skirt on, although it didn't so much cover as frame an ample back-side, resplendent in a pair of oversized navy-blue knickers.

As the details registered Jane felt her mouth drop open. 'Oh my God,' she gasped, stifling a giggle along with a lot of surprise. 'Where on earth did you get this?'

'Are you saying you don't recognise it?' asked DI Rolf. She was conscious of him watching her reactions.

'No, I don't recognise it.'

'How about this one?'

He dropped another onto the desk alongside the first. This one was of Steve Burney, standing in front of the fireplace in his sitting room. He was dressed in a schoolmaster's gown, leopard-skin posing pouch and mortarboard, flexing a cane – and other than that he was completely naked, if you ignored his socks and sandals.

Jane looked up at the policeman and laughed in spite of herself. 'Bloody hell. Where on earth did you find these?'

'On your computer,' he said flatly.

'No,' said Jane in amazement, 'no, that's impossible. I would have known. I don't believe you.' And then she looked at them again. 'Are you serious? You are, aren't you? What person in their right mind would send these to anyone? I mean, for God's sake . . .' And then the penny dropped. 'Lucy sent them to me, didn't she?'

This was what Lucy had been looking for; this was what had been worming away at her.

Still Rolf's eyes didn't leave hers. 'You've seen them before then?' he pressed.

Jane shook her head. 'No, I haven't. Trust me, I would have remembered. I've never seen them before in my life, although I understand now why Lucy was so concerned. I mean, would you want to know there were photos like this around of you? Or know that they were in the hands of someone you thought didn't like you? Jesus, they're dynamite.'

'So you're saying you've never seen them?'

'That's right, but now I have I understand what all the fuss is about. When Lucy came to tell me about her and Steve having a relationship I didn't believe her.' Jane paused, feeling the pain, still raw but nowhere near as acute as the sensation, like grabbing hold of a live electrical cable, that she had felt when Lucy had first told her. She looked up at DI Rolf. 'Actually, that's not true: to be honest I did believe her, I just didn't want to.'

'And?' encouraged Rolf.

'And she told me that she had proof if I wanted it. Later that day, or the day after, she sent me an email. It was spiteful and gloating and said something like, "Now you know what's going on, now you have the proof, I presume you'll just get lost and leave me and Steve to get on with our lives in peace." Those weren't the words exactly but that was the tone.'

'And?'

'And nothing. I thought that she meant that her telling me about the two of them was enough – but presumably she must have sent these as well, maybe as attachments. The thing is, I was so upset I couldn't bring myself to read all of the email – it went on and on – or open anything else that she sent me over the next few days. There were several of them but I didn't give her the satisfaction of replying.'

'But you read them?'

'No, I just said I didn't.'

'Are you saying you deleted them?'

'No, no, I was incredibly upset and she was crowing. I thought that maybe Steve was the one, you know – my happy-ever-after – and the idea that he was with Lucy was more than I could bear really so I dragged the mails into a file with all the things I'd received from Steve. I suppose I thought I'd read them later, when I felt stronger. I renamed the file in their honour.'

Rolf looked down at his notes. 'Bloody Cow & Two-Timing Bastard?'

Jane reddened. 'Yes, that's the one.'

'And then what did you do?'

'What do you mean, what did I do?'

'I'm trying to help you here, Jane.'

Jane looked at him. 'I don't know what you mean. I didn't *do* anything. I didn't know I had these pictures. If I had I would probably have been hurt and shocked and amused and stunned – actually all the things I felt when you showed them to me now.'

He handed her a sheet of paper ripped from a spiral-bound notebook in a plastic evidence bag, on which was written. 'Nice photos' in black felt tip in block capitals, and then another, the printout of an email that read, 'I'm sure that lots of people would be interested to see how you spend your spare time.' The email address at the top wasn't Jane's but an anonymous email account in the name of 'Teddypooh'.

'Well?'

'I didn't write either of these,' she said, sliding them back across the table towards him. 'And I haven't got an email account called Teddypooh either.'

Rolf sighed. 'Jane, I have to ask you. Who else would send these pictures? Who else would care enough? Who else was hurt or angry enough?'

She stared up at him. 'I have no idea, but what I do know is that it wasn't me.'

'Who else then? Who has access to your computer, your files, your password?' He sighed as if she was letting the side down by not owning up.

Jane stared at him; the trouble was he was right – who

276

else could it be? It seemed cut and dried, except that she knew she hadn't seen the emails or contacted Steve or Lucy. No wonder Steve was upset. If it wasn't so serious she would have to laugh. Those socks and sandals hardly said sex god. Crazy. Jane swallowed hard, fighting the desire to giggle. The urge got stronger and stronger.

DI Rolf looked at her while Jane wrestled with the giggle.

'So, who else could have sent these emails?' he repeated, pointing to the printout.

'There are more?'

He nodded. 'All saying more or less the same thing, all up the ante just a little – very clever. All from Teddypooh.'

As he spoke Jane was trying to work out who else *could* have sent the mail. Lucy had told her that she wasn't the only one Steve had been playing around with, but then again, surely she hadn't sent the photos to all of them? Unless of course she was mad. Was her plan to see them all off? But who else had access to Jane's computer and who else hated Lucy? Somewhere, deep in the back of her mind, a penny dropped.

'Where did you say the handwritten note was found?'

Rolf watched her face. 'Miss Stroud's pigeon hole in the library.'

'And when did you say she found it?'

Rolf frowned. 'I didn't.' He glanced down at his notes but said nothing.

'I haven't been to the library since they sacked me, not even to take my library books back. You should be able to check that on the CCTV footage. And I haven't been at home for days.' And as Jane spoke the pile of pennies grew and grew until, despite her best attempts she couldn't help but show it on her face. When she looked up Jane realised that DI Rolf was watching her like a hawk.

'Something you want to tell me, Jane?' he asked, voice so low now that she had to strain to pick out the words.

'No, but I can tell you that it wasn't me,' she said flatly. 'I've not been near my computer in days and I certainly haven't been to the library – if anything I've been avoiding it.'

'Really? Would you like to tell me why?'

'Because the way I lost my job stank. Human Resources wanted Lucy to shadow me while I was working my notice out and, candidly, I would rather eat a bucket of cat sick.'

He looked triumphant. 'You really don't like Miss Stroud, do you?'

Jane rolled her eyes heavenwards. 'No, I don't, but that's not a secret. Actually I suppose when I get over how much it hurt I should be grateful she told me. I feel a fool but what they did isn't illegal—'

DI Rolf picked up the photos on the desk and looked at them for a second or two more before slipping them back into the file. 'No it isn't, but sending this kind of material with a view to blackmailing, harassing or threatening someone is.' He paused for a few seconds waiting for her to say something, and when she didn't he continued, 'Right, well, let's go over the details one more time, shall we? When you left the library—'

Jane stared at him; surely he couldn't be serious. She was so tired she could have cried.

It was the wee small hours when they finally let Jane out; Detective Inspector Rolf said he wasn't charging her but that she shouldn't go anywhere – particularly not anywhere near Lucy Stroud or Steve Burney. As if.

Head down, heady with fatigue, Jane made her way out of the police station. She was cold and exhausted, with a thumping headache, and had completely forgotten about her mother, who was sitting opposite the loos in the reception area, wringing her hands like something out of the Old Testament.

Despite it being around four in the morning, Mrs Mills senior was wearing full make-up, hooped gold earrings, a faux leopardskin coat and some kind of mauve chenille snood that framed her face like badly drawn curtains. Under the harsh and unforgiving fluorescent light of the police station she looked like as if she might run a bordello in between reading palms.

As soon as she spotted Jane she was on her feet. 'Oh my God, Jane, are you all right, darling? They said you were helping them with their enquiries. Oh God – I always knew it would end like this. Are you going to prison? What on earth do people wear for prison visits?' she wailed, before promptly bursting into tears.

'For heaven's sake, Mother, pull yourself together, will you?' Jane said between gritted teeth, trying hard not to draw any more attention to herself, at which point the door to the toilet opened and Kit Harvey-Mills appeared, drying his hands on his trousers. Jane stared at him in amazement. 'What on earth are you doing here?' she said, feeling her colour rise.

'No need to sound quite so grateful,' he said.

Jane held up her hands in surrender. 'I'm so sorry, that wasn't very polite. I'm just surprised—'

'I was worried about you.' He shifted his weight, looking almost as sheepish as she did, and then flapped his damp hands around like flippers. 'No paper towels,' he added, which was a stupid thing to say but convinced Jane that he really did fancy her, because the only time you say totally stupid things with such gusto is when you're trying very hard not to.

'I thought you might need a lift home,' he said. 'Your mother was just telling me about someone called Edwin that you used to go out with. Apparently he was married, five children, ginger – she said she always knew you'd come to a sticky end.'

Jane groaned miserably. 'Thank you, Mother. Now do you think we can just go home, please?'

'Oh, good idea,' said her mother. 'I'm exhausted. And Kit do call me Audra. Would you be a dear and give me a hand with my suitcase?'

In Kos the night breeze rattled and tugged at the shutters of the first-floor sitting room. Through open French windows Jayne thought she could just see the first grey light of the new day.

Miko stroked the hair back off Jayne's face and smiled. 'Don't worry. It will be all right. I promise, whatever you need . . .' he said gently, kissing her lightly on top of the head.

It was such an intimate and yet oddly sexless gesture. Jayne pulled away and smiled up at him. 'Miko, do you know I've waited twenty-five years to hear that from a man and to believe him.'

He topped up her wine glass. 'In that case I shall take it as a huge compliment.'

'I didn't say that I believed *you*,' she said with a grin. 'The last one who said that and meant it . . .' Jayne let the words fade and die, wondering what would have happened if she had believed him back then. 'Ah, well, no good crying over spilt milk. I need to look forward, not back. Thanks for the wine and for letting me use the phone.'

Miko nodded. 'Tomorrow I will buy you a ticket home. I have this cousin who—'

Jayne held up a hand to quieten him. 'It's fine, Miko, really. And I owe you enough as it is,' she said, cutting him short. 'Besides it's already being sorted out and it's already tomorrow, and in about –' Jayne looked at her watch – 'God, in four hours I'm due down on the quay to help stock up the boat for forty-odd tourists, not forgetting two vegetarians.' Miko was about to say something else, so Jayne continued, 'And before you protest I think if you send your receptionist out with Theo again there will probably be a mutiny or a murder. And I'll only be prowling around if I don't go out. Waiting is awful – this way the time will fly.'

'No, Jayne, I'll cover it. I'll send Nina instead. It's high time she did something to earn her keep.'

Jayne laughed. According to Nina she hadn't stopped since she arrived on the island. 'She hates boats and she gets seasick.'

'Phuh – young people, no staying power. It will do her good and, besides, that will give Theo something new to moan about. Not that I want you to go. Why don't we just go to bed? It's late. We're both tired.' He mimed a yawn, which made Jayne yawn in sympathy. At the same time his eyes darkened with something Jayne recognised as a heady mixture of desire, lust and lechery. She smiled and stepped a little further away, glass in hand. In another time and another place it might well have been different, but the last thing she wanted now was any more complications.

'Come on, honey,' he purred.

'I'm flattered,' Jayne said gently, 'but my life is complicated enough at the moment.'

Miko shrugged philosophically. 'You can't blame me for trying. You are a very beautiful woman.' Jayne held his gaze until he grinned. 'No, no, I really mean it, it's not just another line. Cross my heart. This journey of discovery hasn't gone quite the way you planned, has it?'

Jayne laughed. 'You can say that again. I go away to find myself and end up flat-busted broke, working in a kitchen, and spending the night getting drunk with a dodgy Greek.'

Miko looked wounded. 'It's not a kitchen, it's a galley.'

Jane laughed. 'Thanks for the wine, Miko – and for letting me use your phone. Is it OK if I call a cab? I really ought to go back and get a couple of hours' sleep before work.'

'You know that you can stay here,' he said, tone light now.

'I know, and it's very kind, but despite appearances I'm really not after your body.'

He pretended to be deeply hurt.

'Andy promised to get me some money and a ticket out here by Saturday morning.' It had been so strange hearing Andy's voice after all those years. In some ways it was almost as if no time had passed at all, and yet in others it felt as if they were complete strangers.

'Andy? Who exactly did you say that this Andy is again?'

Jayne smiled wistfully, 'Andy Turner was the guy who first brought me to Kos, the guy who promised me that everything would be all right – and you know what? Back then, it always seemed to be.'

'The guy you came here to ring?'

Jayne nodded. 'I must pay you for the calls. It was just that I kept running out of credit on the phonecards and you were the only person on the island I knew who had a phone.'

He sighed. 'And there was me hoping it was my natural charm and good looks. If I'd known you were ringing another man I'd have said no,' he teased. 'Now is there anything else you need?'

Jane finished off the last of her wine. 'How about the cab?'

He waved the words away. 'Don't worry about a cab, you can stay here. There is a spare room, and I promise not to try and creep into your bed, unless of course you want to reconsider my offer. I am very happy with payment in kind.' He paused for a few moments to see if Jayne was planning to change her mind, but when she didn't jump in, continued, 'You'll find a spare toothbrush, towels and everything you need in the *en suite*. And if you are serious about working tomorrow we can always pick up a clean uniform at the office. I'll drive you down to the quay if you're sure you want to go out with the boat.'

Jane nodded. 'I do. I owe you one, and besides, it will give you a chance to find someone to cover the shifts. Andy said he'd try and get me an early flight.'

'What about your business partner?'

Jayne considered for a moment or two. Wasn't Ray someone else who had said that it would be all right?

'We've got all sorts of problems with the business at the moment. Andy said he could book somewhere on line tonight.'

'So why didn't your business partner do the same?'

Jayne shook her head. 'You know . . . I'm not sure.'

'And what about the bank and your money – what did he say he was doing about that?'

'I'll sort that out as soon as I get back.'

Miko split the last of the wine between them, his expression unreadable.

In Buckbourne Jane, Kit and Jane's mother had finally arrived back in Creswell Close.

'What a wonderful house, Kit. Did you say it belonged to your sister? What wonderful taste,' said Jane's mum as she pulled off her coat and dropped it into Gary's waiting arms. 'I could absolutely murder a cup of tea, Gary, if there's one on the go. It is Gary, isn't it? Let me introduce myself. I'm Audra, Jane's mother. I've heard such a lot about you, I couldn't bring myself to drink that stuff at the police station. It was tepid, grey – ghastly,' she shuddered.

Jane caught Gary's eye and looked heavenwards, as he followed her mother through the house towards the kitchen, followed at the rear by Kit.

Under her coat Audra was wearing a mauve tracksuit, which perfectly matched her snood.

'Oh, and I just love those curtains,' she was saying. 'Aren't they gorgeous? You know, I'm sure I saw that fabric in John Lewis in the autumn, presumably they were specially made – do you sew, Gary?'

'Mum, please,' implored Jane in an undertone, wishing the ground would just open up and swallow her whole, or if not her, then her mother.

'People like their talents to be appreciated, Jane. You know you really fell on your feet with this job, didn't you sweetie? I was wondering, you know it might be an idea for me to stay for a little while, keep an eye on you. Just till things get sorted out, obviously. Unless, of course, I'm cramping your style.' She fluttered her eyelids coquettishly at Kit and then gave Jane a horribly camp pantomime wink.

'That's very kind but there's really no need,' said Jane hastily.

'Really?' said her mother, holding Jane's gaze like a sniper with a target in the crosshairs. 'That's not how I see it at all, Jane. Just look at the trouble you get yourself into when I'm not around to take care of you. Besides, I can hardly abandon you in your hour of need, now can I?'

'I don't see why not. It's never stopped you before. We barely talk unless you want something,' said Jane between gritted teeth.

'Oh, you're such a joker,' said Audra, still with her eye on Kit.

Jane sighed. 'Gary, would you mind helping me make up the bed in the spare room for my mother?'

The little man nodded. 'Don't worry I'll do it. It's what I'm paid for.' He managed to make it sound as if he was being asked to gnaw his own leg off. That's just what she needed, more guilt.

'And what about Kit, or is he bunking down with you?' asked her mother brightly.

'Mum, will you please just shut up?' said Jane, unable to contain herself any longer.

'I was only asking, darling. I mean, we're all adults here.'

'Mum, I've had one hell of a day and if you don't be quiet and leave me alone I may say something I regret.'

Her mother looked at her in amazement. 'But, Janey, I've come miles to support you, turned out in the middle of the night. Is that the thanks I get?'

Jane nodded. 'I'm afraid so. Now if you'll excuse me I'm totally knackered. I'm going to bed.'

Outside through the blinds Jane could make out the first light of dawn.

'Well,' snorted her mother to no one in particular, 'is that any way to speak to your mother?'

Jane didn't bother answering and instead made her way upstairs to her bedroom, heavy footed and totally exhausted. She felt as if she ought to be trying to work out what was going on, find some answers, but her brain refused to play, dense as lead, a great grey mass of exhaustion.

Jane closed the bedroom door and sat down at the dressing table, taking a few minutes to scrape off the last remaining traces of make-up. Her hair looked like a nest. As she rubbed moisturiser into her face and throat, she looked round at the exquisite lines of Jayne's elegant bedroom. This really wasn't how her new life was supposed to go at all. In the last twelve hours she had met a man she really fancied, who thought she was a thief and a liar, been accused of theft and extortion, spent goodness knows how long being questioned by the police and now her mother had arrived. How much worse could life get?

Almost as she had the thought there was a gentle but persistent knocking on the bedroom door. Jane held her breath; if it was her mother she would scream. She stayed very quiet and still, wishing that she'd gone straight to bed and hadn't left the light on.

'Jane?' Kit whispered. 'Jane? Are you still awake?'

Kit? Jane smiled. He was the last person she had been expecting, and possibly – with the exception of Gary – the only person that she would be glad to see. She clambered to her feet and opened the door just a crack.

'Hi, are you OK? My mum isn't with you by any chance, is she?' she said, peering past him, out on to the landing

He shook his head. 'No, she's downstairs in the kitchen with Gary, talking police brutality, teabags and soft furnishings. Do you mind if I come in for a few minutes?'

Jane looked up at him, wondering exactly what it was he wanted. Caught in the doorway, his strong, well-defined features picked out in the lamplight, he looked mouthwateringly gorgeous. He had taken off his bow tie hours ago, his dress shirt was crumpled now and open at the neck, revealing a deep V of dark hair on a broad suntanned chest. Jane tried hard not to drool and, failing, wondered again why he had come to her room, all sorts of interesting X-rated thoughts running through her head. As their eyes met she hoped he couldn't read minds and then wished that he could. Enjoying the little shiver of desire, Jane stepped aside to let him in.

'Are you all right?' he asked, sliding past her, his body so close she could feel the heat of him.

'Not really. I just want to go to bed. How about you?' Even as she said it, Jane felt her colour rising. 'I mean, well, you know –' she said hastily – 'not that. I mean, I'm not propositioning you.'

He grinned at her obvious discomfort. 'Shame.'

Jane stared at him, trying to work out whether or not he was joking. They stood in silence just a fraction too close for a fraction too long, before Jane said, 'So what did you want?'

'I had a phone call from Jayne while I was at the police station. She left a message.'

287

'Oh, that's great, I'm glad. How is she?'

He pulled a mobile out of his pocket and flicked it on to speaker. Jayne's distinctive voice filled the quiet room. After the social niceties her voice dropped a little, her tone more guarded and intimate. 'Kit, Ray told me that you called him about Jane earlier. I don't know whether you know about the problems I've been having – there is something very odd going on. I'm not sure exactly what he's told you but I've had all kinds of trouble with my credit cards, and then this evening when I looked, my bank accounts have been emptied. Ray thinks that Jane is involved. He's checking the account numbers where the money was paid into. It all seems very strange to me. I'm coming home as soon as I can. I arranged for a friend to get me a ticket, but in the meantime,' she paused, 'just keep your eyes open and keep an eye on Jane for me. I find it hard to believe that she is on the take but . . .' she paused again, suddenly sounding tired and slightly weepy, '. . . but then what do I know? See you soon.'

Jane stared at him; just when she thought that things couldn't get worse. 'Oh, Kit. What on earth is going on?' she said.

'You tell me.'

'I don't know. I have no idea, you have to believe me,' said Jane, her eyes filling with tears as the events of the day finally caught up with her. 'I was really looking forward to this job, living here. It came out of a clear blue sky, sounded brilliant – Jayne's got such a great life – and she was happy for me to take it over for a while so she could go and explore, but instead it's been a bloody disaster.

I swear that I haven't touched a single penny of Jayne's money. I just assumed the card thing was a mix-up in the names.' A sob cut the words off. She felt cross with herself for crying but was powerless to stop the tears. 'And then you think I stole your family heirlooms and the police think I was blackmailing the yoghurt prince and his evil, bear-collecting sidekick. Christ, I feel like I've woken up in the middle of a nightmare.'

When she looked up, to her amazement Kit was smiling at her.

'What?' she snapped, angry with him for not taking her seriously or understanding how hurt and upset she was.

'I believe you,' he said, wiping one of the tears away with his thumb.

'What?'

'Well, if you really are a con woman and thief and whatever else they reckon you are, then, and let's be frank about this, you're total rubbish.'

'Well, thank you,' she said crossly, running her hand under her nose.

He pulled a tissue out of the box on the dressing table and handed it to her. 'You missed a bit.' He took another and dabbed at something on her cheek; she didn't ask what it was she had missed.

'I think there is something going on,' Jane sniffed.

Kit nodded. 'I agree. Have you checked your bank accounts lately?'

She shook her head. 'No, I haven't needed to.'

'Then maybe you should. Have you got online banking?'

'Yes, I can look now, if you like, but we need to be quiet. I don't think I can take much more of my mother.'

His grin widened. 'What do you mean? She is a real sweetie.'

'Easy for you to say.'

With that Jane picked up her bag, opened the door and they crept across to Jayne's office, pulled the door to and then woke one of the slumbering Macs.

'What do you think we should look at?'

Kit shrugged. 'We could start with your personal accounts.'

Jane took her wallet out and pulled out a slip of paper with her security code on it. Kit stared.

'What?' said Jane, as she tapped them in to the computer.

'You've got your bank details in your handbag?'

'Uh-huh, that way they're handy and I'd never remember them without writing them down.' As she spoke the banking screen unfolded as if by magic, and both of them stared at the balance in her current account. Jane felt faint. 'Oh my God,' she whispered. 'There has got to be some mistake.'

Kit nodded, pressing the scroll-down key. 'Not if you've recently won the lottery.'

'Should we ring the police?'

He looked at her sceptically. 'Bearing in mind that they already think you're blackmailing your ex-boyfriend that may not be such a great idea.' He pointed to the slip of paper alongside the computer with her bank details on. 'So does anyone else have these?'

'I don't think so.'

'How about friends or former employers, ex-boyfriends, or someone that Jayne employs?'

Jane shrugged. 'No, I gave Ray the account details for my bank account to pay my salary but this –' she held the slip of paper out towards him – 'is for my online account. It's got different numbers. One is like an account number for the whole thing and then there is a pin to activate that.

It's account management really, paying bills and moving money around. So these are the security codes, but I've memorised my password, the other numbers would be useless without that. So to move money out of Jayne's account someone would need all those things, for her account, unless they did it manually.'

Kit looked at the screen. 'But you don't need anything other than your account number and sort code to pay money in?'

Jane stared at him. 'God, no, I suppose not.'

'Well in that case we need to find the people who had Jayne's online account number, PIN and password – there can't be that many. Can you you see when the money was paid in?'

Jane selected her current account and scrolled down to the date when the money was moved. 'It was Wednesday.'

Kit sighed. 'So it could have been you?'

Jane stared at him, trying to decide if he was serious or not. 'Kit, I would have to be some kind of nutter to transfer Jayne's money straight into my current account,' she said. 'I mean, who's not going to look there? And besides, I just told you that I needed passwords and numbers to move money around in my account; the same is going to be true for Jayne – and I haven't got the pass-words or numbers to access her account.'

'You say,' said Kit.

Jane looked up at him and for one awful moment had a mental image of the photos that DI Rolf had shown her at the police station; she hadn't known she had them either. What if she *had* got the codes and didn't know about it? Whoever was setting her up would surely ensure that she had the codes somewhere, so that at least it looked as if it was possible for her to commit the crime. What had she been given that belonged to Jayne?

'You know, you're right,' she murmured. 'I bet I do have them. This only makes sense if whoever did this can say I had the opportunity.'

Jane opened up her email file and took a look at the emails Jayne and Ray had sent her; there were no banking codes there. What else? Where else? She looked round the room, trying to feel the answer as much as see it; after all, it wasn't unlikely that in her own office that Jayne had a copy of her banking access codes somewhere to hand. Jane's gaze moved slowly over photos and paintings, the in-tray, framed prints – and then down over the office drawers, bookcases and filing cabinets, which she realised now could have contained absolutely anything, her eyes settling at last on the desk drawer. Inside was the padded envelope that the courier had brought earlier with plane tickets and, underneath, the manila folder that Ray had asked her to bring back to the office for safekeeping.

'I know exactly where they are,' she said, heart sinking. She got to her feet, opened the drawer and then opened the folder. Inside – as she feared – were all kinds of things: photocopied bank statements, account details, passwords, a list of properties, stocks and shares, in fact all kinds of details about assets that Jayne held. There was everything she could possibly need to tap into Jayne's bank accounts and personal life and drain her dry. Helplessly, she handed Kit the file.

'Ray asked me to pick these up from the office. He said that Jayne wanted me to bring them here for safekeeping.'

Kit thumbed through the contents and nodded, 'And have you got any proof that he told you to take them?'

Jane shook her head. 'No, of course I haven't. He just said it in passing when I said I was coming in to the office to pick up some samples that clients had sent in.'

'And what about that?' Kit nodded towards the envelope that the courier had brought over.

Jane shook her head. 'I don't know anything about it really. I think they're plane tickets for Jayne or maybe for a client. I can't remember exactly what he said now. Ray had it sent over here and insisted that I sign for it. He said he'd sort it out later.'

Kit picked the envelope up and turned it over, examining it carefully as if there was some chance that it might explode. He pulled open the tabs, took out the contents and looked them over.

'Going somewhere?' he said, as he handed them to her. Inside, in a folder was an open ticket for Brazil in Jane's name.

She stared at him in horror but before she could speak her mother opened the door. 'Oh, there you are,' she said, then looked Kit up and down and smiled knowingly while, surreptitiously, Jane slid the tickets and the manila folder back on the desk. 'I thought you two would have been snuggled up in bed by now. I was just saying downstairs to Gary that it was high time Jane found herself a decent man.'

To his credit Kit didn't bat an eyelid. 'Well, in that case I'm glad to oblige. We were just going to bed, weren't we, Jane?' he said. 'Nice to have met you. Good night.' And with that he held out a hand to Jane, which she took gratefully and followed him out of the office.

'Oh . . . OK. Do you want me to switch the lights off?' asked Jane's mum, hot on their heels.

'That would be great,' said Kit over one shoulder.

Jane said nothing until they reached to her bedroom door.

'Thank you for that,' she whispered. 'But what are we going to do about Jayne's money?'

He grinned. 'We?'

She blushed. 'God, I'm sorry, I know it's got nothing to do with you. I'm just so tired that I can't think straight.'

'Actually, it might have a lot to do with me. At the moment – thanks to you – my sister is apparently destitute, and there's no way I'm going to keep her in shoes and lipstick. And the con woman who is robbing her blind is . . .' He paused, watching Jane's face and then laughed. 'What kind of man fancies a criminal mastermind?'

Jane didn't know whether to laugh or cry. 'Kit, I'm so sorry. You know that I didn't take Jayne's money, don't you?'

'It doesn't look like it from here, but as I'm taking your side I'm hoping that you're telling the truth.' He glanced over his shoulder where Jane's mother was apparently deep in thought over how to turn off a lamp. 'I think we should at least go in, don't you?'

As he spoke he opened the bedroom door, which from this angle gave a great view of Jayne's huge queen-size bed. Jane had a red-hot, graphic flash of what it might be like to wake up alongside Kit and blushed, while across the landing her mother was watching them like a hawk. When she caught Jane's eye she wriggled her fingers in a funny little wave.

'Oh, for heaven's sake, she is completely insufferable,' whispered Jane.

'Come on,' said Kit taking her arm, 'I don't know about

you but I'm knackered and we can't talk out here.' And then, turning, called, 'Good night, Mrs Mills.'

'Audra,' said Jane's mum, preening. 'Do call me Audra. After all, we're practically family.'

In the bedroom Jane, so tired now that her teeth ached, slipped off her shoes and padded across to the bathroom. Outside, she could still hear her mother ferreting around on the landing

'Make yourself at home,' Jane said over her shoulder without looking back at Kit. 'I don't think she'll be long,' and then closed the bathroom door. She brushed her teeth while staring grimly into the bloodshot eyes of her wey-faced reflection. God, what a day. All she wanted to do now was lie down on the bed, close her eyes and sink into unconsciousness.

A few minutes later when she opened the door it seemed as if Kit had had the same thought; he had taken off his shoes and now lay on her bed, appearing to be sound asleep.

Smiling, Jane picked up a throw from the chaise longue, lay down alongside him and carefully covered them both up. Finally, being horizontal felt wonderful, although the movement was enough to make Kit stir, and as he did he rolled over and put his arm around her.

'Why don't we just have a little nap? I mean, goodness knows how long your mother is going to be lurking about out there,' he murmured, and with that, sleep closed over him like a rising tide. Jane, still smiling, curled closer, closed her eyes and was asleep no more than ten seconds later.

Chapter Thirteen

By the time Jane finally woke up in Buckbourne, Jayne had already had a shower, driven down to the quay with Miko, found herself a clean uniform in the office, helped load the boat up with bread, salad, meat, fish and booze, speared a tray full of kebabs and was making great headway with the fish gutting. All this, and Theo was almost civil.

In Creswell Close Jane had been having a very odd dream; she dreamed she was being chased up the stairs of Jayne's waterside offices by a very large moose, complete with antlers, who was so close behind her that she could feel his breath warm on her cheek, not to mention hearing him snorting furiously in her ear. The moose seemed benign but who could truly fathom the brain of some-thing so very large and unwieldy? So in her dream Jane kicked for home and made a great lunge for the door handle of Ray's ultrachic office, and as her fingers closed around it and the door opened, she opened her eyes and realised with a start that the stalking moose was actually Kit Harvey-Mills snoring furiously in her ear.

He was curled up tight around her on Jayne's huge bed, snuggled up under the woven throw, his face close to hers, one arm under her neck, the other around her waist, holding him tight against her, which would have been wonderful except she suspected his arm was probably even more deeply asleep than he was, and the snoring was really not sexy.

Her waking disturbed him so that he spluttered, stopped snoring – fortunately – and said, 'Oh, hello. What is the time?' Which was quite cute, particularly as he looked all warm and sleepy and kind of muzzed up in a sexy way, his hair sticking up all over the place so that he resembled an older, better-looking Dennis the Menace. She would have said so except she didn't know if he was someone who woke up grumpy, and despite having slept with him, it sounded a bit over-familiar.

Jane wriggled out of his arms and across the bed with a growing sense of self-consciousness, smoothing her hair down and avoiding breathing on him.

Kit, who by contrast seemed fine with the whole thing, stretched and blinked and peered at the bedside clock. 'God, is that the time? I feel really rough,' he mumbled between yawns. He wasn't alone; Jane ached all over. She couldn't remember the last time she had slept in her clothes and felt horribly grimy and gritty, as well as tired, and was busy wrestling her brain into submission so that it didn't run off screaming in complete panic as memories of the previous day's events came flooding back in glorious Technicolor.

Meanwhile, daylight elbowed its way in through the gap between the curtains.

Kit stretched again, stood up and headed off towards the bedroom door. 'Thanks for, you know . . .' He nodded towards the bed. 'I didn't mean to fall asleep. I just didn't realise how tired I was. Did I snore?'

Jane smiled. 'Just a bit, but it was fine – long day.' Both stood for a moment or two, neither it seemed wanting to call a halt to their impromptu sleepover.

Kit shifted his weight. 'I suppose I'd better go and have a shower.'

Jane nodded. 'Be careful when you open the door. Chances are my mother will be curled up on the threshold with her ear pressed to the woodwork.'

He grinned by way of reply.

'You think I'm joking?' she said, heading slowly towards the *en suite*. She didn't want him to go but couldn't easily see a way or a reason for him to stay; they both had to get on with the day.

'Have you had any thoughts about the . . . you know . . .' He held up his hands to encompass the great whatever.

Jane was more specific. 'My growing reputation as a diamond-stealing blackmailing embezzler?'

He nodded.

'To be perfectly honest at the moment I'm trying really hard not to think about it at all.'

'So, the ostrich approach, then?'

'Not exactly. I didn't do any of those things but I don't know how to prove it at the moment. And I'm scared about what might happen if I can't. It feels ridiculous, like it's happening to someone else – but it isn't. So, I thought I'd have a shower, have a think, have some breakfast and then see what I come up with.'

'Sounds like a plan. What about your mother?'

'I'm not counting on her to be any help at all. I'm hoping she'll go home today. Realistically, nurturing and support aren't her thing and when she's finished nosing around, interrogating you and Gary, she'll get bored and be off. Anyway she won't be up till lunchtime.'

Kit pulled a face.

'What? Oh, no, don't tell me.'

'It's midday already.'

'In which case we better make it brunch and do it very quietly,' said Jane, at the bathroom door. She realised that as they were speaking, and without thinking about it, she had begun unbuttoning her shirt and was suddenly very aware of Kit's eyes following her hands.

'Unless, of course, you'd like me to hang around and wash your back first,' he said lightly.

Jane stared at him; actually there was nothing she would like more – after all, she had slept with him. Jane hesitated just long enough for self-doubt and self-consciousness to creep in, and for her to start wondering if maybe he was joking.

In the same light tone she said, 'Don't think I'm not tempted but I probably need to sort out how come I've got all your sister's money and a load of personally shot porn on my PC first.'

'It won't take that long, and we'd be saving on water,' he said, moving towards her, grinning, beginning to undo the remaining buttons on her shirt. Jane shivered as the buttons gave way and tried very, very hard not to groan as his fingers brushed across her shoulder.

'I should warn you, I don't lather well when I'm tense,' she said as he slipped his arms around her.

'Oh, I'm sure I can cope,' purred Kit, leaning closer.

Jane's pulse echoed loudly in her ears. She was just wrestling with the fact that she hadn't brushed her teeth when there was a wild and raucous knocking on the bedroom door.

'Coooeeeeee. Jane, are you awake in there? Cooooooooooooeeeeeee. It's me.'

'Mum?' Jane groaned.

'Oh, good, you're up. I've brought some tea. I just wanted to let you know your boyfriend is downstairs. Is there any chance you could open the door, Janey? You know I hate shouting but I didn't want to barge straight in.'

Kit pulled away and Jane started to rebutton her shirt as she crossed the room. 'There's got to be a mistake,' she said. 'I haven't got a—'

The door swung open, framing her mother. 'Oh, there you are. You look awful – did you sleep in those clothes? You should really brush your hair, darling, keep a little mystery in a relationship. Your father never saw me without full make-up, hair done. Morning, Kit. I just thought you ought to know your boyfriend is downstairs.'

'Mum, I've already told you, I haven't got a boy—'

'He seems terribly upset. Gary's just popped out into town to get some odds and ends. He mentioned that they're having a party next door tomorrow night so I gave him my guacamole recipe and that other dip – you know, the one with green peppers – so I'm holding the fort while he nips out to buy ingredients.' Her mother set the tea tray down on the ottoman at the foot of the bed. Jane couldn't help noticing that there were three cups.

'He cried, darling. I was moved. He said he loves you and that that other woman – the younger one, I can't remember what her name was – anyway, he said you had to understand she meant nothing, not really. It was purely physical, just a fling, and that he had made the most awful mistake and that he wants you back. I have to say he seems very sincere, although he isn't what I expected at all.' Audra stopped talking and then looked from face to face. 'What? Was it something I said?'

'Mum, can you just take the tray downstairs? I need a shower. I'll be down in ten minutes.'

She turned back to Kit, not quite able to meet his eye. He held up a hand to stop her. 'Don't mind me. I'm going to go and grab a shower too, you've obviously got things to sort out. I'll see you downstairs in a little while.'

As he went, Jane looked at her mother who aped non-comprehension. 'What? Don't look at me like that, Jane. I've done nothing. I'm just the messenger. Although really I think you should look on the bright side.'

'And which side would that be, Mother?'

'Well, hopefully this will mean the police won't charge you with blackmail. He seems so upset. I didn't mention anything about the yoghurt . . . or the photos. Oh, and by the way, the shower in my room doesn't work. Gary said I should ring Miranda.'

Jane picked up the tea tray and handed it to her. 'Out.'

Before her mother could protest Jane headed into the bathroom and slipped out of her clothes. Now, as well as feeling grumpy, she was angry and frustrated. Jane stood under the shower, letting the water cascade down over her, wondering what she should say to Steve. She hadn't expected him to show up again. Maybe it hadn't been his idea to get the police involved at all; maybe it was Lucy; maybe he was feeling guilty, contrite. But then again, even if Steve came crawling back on his hands and knees would she ever be able to trust him? She knew that she couldn't.

Jane sighed, tipped her face up into the flow of the

water, running her hands back over her hair as she rinsed out the shampoo, wondering what else could happen? An image of Steve in his headmaster's gear flashed through her mind. Jane shook her head. It was a stark contrast to the mental picture of Kit in his dinner jacket and bow tie. It was such a shame Steve had to leave it until now to be sorry, just when Kit had shown up.

Jane grinned, almost purring as she closed her eyes and replayed the way Kit had made her feel seconds before her mother had burst in. Damn – she was furious with Steve and cross with her mum for all sorts of things, frightening Kit off just being the last in a long line of grievances.

Jane dried and dressed with care with increasing realisation that if she was too long, chances were that she would end up going down into a kitchen that contained her mother, Kit, Steve and Gary.

She checked the mirror, hair still damp – jeans, shirt, a little bit of make-up, sandals – in the end the idea of Kit coming face to face with Steve *and* her mother was more than she could bear and she almost ran out of the bedroom and downstairs.

In the hallway her mother was hanging about, apparently totally enrapt by a silk flower arrangement on one of the side tables, quite obviously waiting for Jane to appear.

'Oh, Jane, there you are,' she said with surprise so very thin it almost snapped.

'Hi, Mum.' For a second they both took a long hard look at the flower arrangement of claret silk peonies, tucked in amongst straw foliage in a large Grecian urn. 'I'm sure if you asked, Gary would let you take that home,' said Jane, archly.

Her mother sniffed. 'I was only looking. Everything is so very understated, so very tasteful.'

Jane nodded. Like she would know; Audra was wearing a turquoise and silver kaftan with earrings so large they probably had their own atmosphere. Tasteful was nowhere on the map. 'Has Kit come down yet?' Jane asked, peering past Audra.

'You know, Jane, "Good morning" would be nice. "Thank you for coming. I hope I didn't worry you, Mum."'

Jane winced; for once Audra was right. She was so used to playing this game with her mother she'd forgotten basic manners. She should have said all that last night, however surprised she felt that Audra had appeared.

'Sorry, Mum, you're right. Thank you for coming. It's really . . .' She struggled, looking around for a word to describe how it felt seeing Audra. *Nice, good, lovely* – none come anywhere close. 'It's really odd seeing you – I mean seeing you here, under these circumstances to see . . .' Jane decided to cut her losses. 'So, good morning, did you sleep well?'

Her mum nodded. 'Yes, thank you. Now can you tell me what exactly is going on?'

'No.' Jane sighed. If only. 'I'm not altogether sure myself. Have you seen Kit?'

'No, I've not seen hide nor hair of him since I brought the tea up.'

'Where did Steve go?'

'Is that his name? I didn't catch it – he just burst in. I thought it was Gary coming back at first. He seems terribly upset.'

Jane paused. That didn't sound like Steve at all. Maybe he and Lucy had had a row. 'So where did you say he is now?'

303

'I made him some tea and he went out into the garden. He said you needed peace and quiet, so that you could talk. Sort things out.'

Optimistic of him, thought Jane as she headed out through the French windows into the garden beyond. The midday sunlight was so bright that she winced, the raw glare reflecting off the roof of the marquee next door, bleaching the flowers and plants to white. She could hear the sound of voices from over the fence, presumably busy making preparations for the house-warming. Jane hurried down through the shrubs and along the meandering pathways until finally she spotted a figure sitting out on the little deck by the summerhouse. He was looking out over the lake, his broad shoulders hunched defensively, and was wearing a crisp white shirt rolled up at the cuffs, and blue jeans, although all Jane could see in her mind's eye was a headmaster's gown, the posing pouch and sandals. It was a hard image to shift. She really needed to sort this out.

As Jane got closer he turned and lifted a hand in greeting.

'Hello,' she said, focusing into the sunshine as he stood up, and as he did they both gasped in unison, Jane's jaw dropping. 'Who are you?' she said before she could stop herself. Somewhere in her head she knew the answer, if she could just find it.

'I don't understand. Where is Jayne? Who are you?' he countered. Her visitor was tanned, with Latino good looks and mirror shades tucked up into his dark curly hair. He had a gym-honed body and was probably in his mid-thirties. He was also incredibly handsome, with huge liquid brown eyes and the petulant mouth of a teenage girl.

'I'm Jane Mills,' she said. 'I'm living here at the moment.'

The man frowned. 'No, you're not, you are lying. I love Jayne Mills – she is my life, my soul, my soul mate. Oh my God – what have you done with my Jayney, where is she?' As he finished the sentence his face crumpled like a used tissue and he burst into tears. 'Oh my God, my baby,' he wailed. 'I miss her so much – what have I done? What have you done with her?'

'Oh, it's Carlo, isn't it?' Jane said, almost to herself. How Jayne had put up with him she had no idea, although maybe she wasn't seeing him in his best light.

He looked at her, tears stopping instantly. 'How do you know my name?' he said, suddenly defensive, eyes narrowing.

'Jayne told me about you.'

'What do you mean, Jayne? You just said *you* were Jane.'

'I am.' Damn, why didn't she just call herself something different, lie. She spoke slowly. 'I'm working for Jayne at the moment, and by coincidence we have the same name.'

Carlo didn't look convinced. 'Really?' he said, looking, if anything, even more suspicious. 'So what have you done with Gary?' he said, looking back towards the house. 'Or has he gone too?'

'No, he hasn't gone. He's out buying green peppers, apparently.'

'So where is Jayne?'

Jane looked at him, wondering whether it might be worth getting postcards printed with the main points for all those people who were interested, when Kit appeared. 'Oh, there you are. I just came to say goodbye.'

'What?' She stared at him. 'I don't understand.'

'I thought I'd book myself into a hotel. Give you and . . .' he glanced towards Carlo, 'some breathing space.

305

You probably need some time. I'll ring later so that we can try and sort this thing with Jayne out.' He turned to go.

'Wait,' said Jane. 'I'm not interested in him.'

Carlo whined.

'Yes,' Kit answered, 'but you've still got things to sort out.'

'No, no, I haven't.' Kit was walking away now. Jane wanted to thump him. 'Kit, wait, please, you're making a mistake. What I meant is that this isn't my ex-boy friend at all. There's been a mistake. This is Jayne's ex-boyfriend.'

Carlo started to sob. 'Don't say that.'

'Oh, for goodness' sake stop whining, will you?' snapped Jane. 'Pull yourself together. No wonder she dumped you.'

Carlo wailed miserably

'Jayne?' said Kit, staring at Carlo. 'No.'

'Apparently so.'

'I've sent her cream roses – her favourite – and chocolates. She never called. I didn't know what else to do. I had to see her.'

'Oh, you sent the roses? I thought it was Steve. That explains a lot. I didn't get any chocolates.'

'My life isn't worth living. How can I go on?' sobbed Carlo.

Jane looked at Kit and cringed; it was horribly embarrassing.

'Why don't you come in and have a cup of tea, wash your face?' said Jane. 'Jayne's away – on holiday. I'm sure she'll call you when she gets back.'

As she spoke she caught Kit's expression, which suggested that if Jayne had a ha'ppence of sense she'd steer well clear.

*   *   *

Meanwhile Jayne wiped her hands on a cloth and looked around the galley: everything was clean, tidied away and all the food ready for the barbecue – salads all bowled up, bread in the baskets, kebabs done, fish gutted. She knew that given a couple of weeks or so all this would be second nature. Even the smell of the diesel engine didn't seem quite so nauseating today. It was almost a pity that she had to go home. Jayne glanced out of the porthole at the sea, wondering exactly what she would find when she went back.

As she was hanging the cloth back on its hook Theo leaned down and said, 'Jayne, would you mind coming and giving a hand in the bar, please? The crew are about to dock.'

Jayne smiled, his tone was a million miles away from that of the previous day.

'Sure, I'm on my way,' she said, and clambered up the companionway. It felt as if she had been away from home for months; maybe once she had her finances sorted out she would come back to Kos. She slipped in behind the bar and turned her attention to the first thirsty passenger; if she didn't sort them out then maybe she would need to come back and work the rest of the summer.

When Jane, Kit and Carlo got back into the house, Audra was sitting in the kitchen at the table, along with Gary, and Tony and Lil from next door. They were drinking coffee and some kind of liqueur in an ornate purple bottle. Lil was in a wheelchair but looked considerably perkier than she had yesterday.

'Oh, there you are,' said Lil with a grin that Jane suspected owed a lot of its sparkle to the glass in her hand.

'Have you sorted it all out? Your mum was just telling us about you being a blackmailer.'

But Jane was ahead of her. 'Yes, fortunately she made a mistake.' Audra's colour instantly lifted and her mouth opened, but Jane continued, 'Lil, Tony, I'd like you to meet Carlo.' They murmured a welcome to Carlo, who was still sniffing unhappily. 'He's the other Jayne's ex-boyfriend. And this is Kit, Jayne's younger brother – and presumably you've already been introduced to Audra?'

'Your mum,' said Lil. 'Yes, I was just saying that if she was staying for a few days she would be more than welcome to come to our house-warming. You too, Kit, Carlo – the more the merrier. Now, how about some coffee and a glass of . . .' She picked up the bottle and squinted myopically at the label. 'One of the guys from the band bought us half a dozen bottles as a moving-in present. It tastes like chocolate.'

'Mixed with some sort of fruit,' added Tony, who looked as if he was a couple of glasses ahead of the pack. 'Reminds me of prunes,' he said, smacking his lips thoughtfully.

'Would you like coffee?' said Gary, getting to his feet. 'Tea? I was planning on getting brunch on before the liqueur kicks in.'

'I thought you were out buying green peppers?' said Jane.

Gary, shrugged and then plugged in the kettle. 'I needed a cover story,' he whispered, turning to light the gas under the skillet. 'I was hoping she wouldn't find out that Lil and Tone were getting caterers in.'

Across the room, Carlo, possibly miffed at losing the spotlight, pulled out a huge handkerchief and blew his nose. 'Oh my God, it's awful.' He whined. 'What am I going to do?'

'No one's reacted to my cooking like that in years,' grumbled Gary, tying on an apron.

Audra sighed and pulled out a chair. 'Oh, you poor thing, you look terrible. Here –' she poured Carlo a glass of the liqueur – 'sit down and have some of this. It'll do you good. Now, what's the matter?'

Gary rolled his eyes. Jane looked away. Kit grinned.

'What?' Jane said.

Kit caught hold of her hand and pulled her close till his lips where level with her ear. 'I am so pleased that lover boy isn't pining for you. I –' he stopped and pulled back a little so that she could see the look in his eyes – 'was hoping to take a rain check on that shower.'

Jane felt a little ripple of desire and laughed. 'Interesting turn of phrase.'

'Leave it alone, you two,' said Tony. 'What's this about you being arrested, Janey?'

Gary sighed. 'The woman has got such a mouth on her.'

'You were telling me I should take more notice of her the other day,' said Jane

'Well, I was wrong,' grumbled Gary.

Kit, apparently keen on pulling the situation round to something more social, pulled out a chair for Jane. 'So, you're my sister's new neighbours, are you?' he said brightly.

Lil nodded. 'That's right. We met Jane when we were moving in – that's this Jane, not your Jayne.'

Jane smiled. 'You'll have to excuse me. I've got a couple of calls to make.' Now that she knew Steve wasn't going to back down she really needed to get on top of things – hopefully before she was arrested. Kit glanced up at her. 'Need any help?'

'Not at the moment. I'll call you if I do. You should have a glass of chocolate prune juice.'

Kit gave her a wry look.

Upstairs in the office Jane rang Lizzie's mobile. It was switched off. Jane tapped in her own home number, planning to leave a message, so she was surprised when someone picked up on the third ring.

'Hello,' said a familiar male voice. 'I'm afraid that Lizzie is in the bath at the moment but I'm happy to take a message.'

'Gladstone?' she said, unable to keep the amazement out of her tone.

There was a moment's hesitation and then he said, 'My name's Peter, actually.'

'What are you doing in my house? What are you doing answering my phone?'

'Er, Lizzie said I could. I've just dropped in for coffee.'

'Coffee?'

'And a shave and a shower. I've got an interview this afternoon at three.'

'What?'

'An interview. I know. I'm as surprised as you are. Lizzie got it for me – a vicar looking for an IT man for his community project. Some sort of drop-in centre. Lonny?'

'You're a geek?'

'My father wanted me to do something avant-garde.'

'Right. Well, can you tell Lizzie I—' Before she could finish the sentence Jane heard the sounds of water moving and splashing, and groaned inwardly.

'Lizzie? Lizzie?' she snapped, only too aware that she sounded uncannily like her mother.

'Hi,' Lizzie said, sounding as bright as a new penny.

'Lizzie, what are you doing at home, and are you in the bath with Gladstone?'

'His name is Peter.'

'I don't care if his name is Prince Ferdinand the Fourteenth, I asked you to feed him not, not f . . .' her mind stalled over a suitable F word,' . . . fawn over him. What do you think you're doing, Lizzie, and why aren't you at work?' Yep, thought Jane, she most definitely sounded just like her mother.

'We got talking and he said he'd had problems and how he had a Ph.D. in cybernetics and then he came in for coffee and I remembered that Long-haired Lonny was looking for someone to teach computer skills, and do all his IT stuff and I thought Peter would be ideal. Perfect, actually, given his personal history.'

'So you decided what? That he'd forgotten how to bathe so you ought to give him a hand?'

Lizzie giggled. 'Not exactly. Without all that hair and that beard he's kind of cute. And he's stopped eating out of bins.'

'Oh, please.'

Jane could hear Gladstone giggling in the background. It was hardly what she had expected and not really what she had rung to talk about, just another complication. 'And you called my mother.'

'The police were here.'

'So you called my mother?'

'I did try to ring you but your phone was off. They took your computer.'

'What?'

'I've got a receipt and they promised they wouldn't delete or lose anything, and that you could have it back

311

once their investigation was complete.' Lizzie had obviously memorised it parrot fashion. 'And anyway, I thought it would be all right because I knew you'd got everything backed up onto the hard drive and you'd got those little memory stick things.'

Jane took a deep breath. This wasn't going to be easy. 'Lizzie, do you know why the police wanted to talk to me?'

'No, not really. They didn't say. I did wonder whether it was about this new job. I mean, I don't mean to sound negative, Jane, but it seemed too good to be true, if I'm honest. A house, the BMW – I mean, I'm thinking drugs. Not that I wanted to say anything—'

'Lizzie, have you been on my computer since you've been staying at my house?'

'Well, yes, you said I could. You said I could look at . . .' She paused, sounding uncomfortable, as Jane remembered what it was she had let Lizzie look at, and bearing in mind she was now presumably in the bath with Gladstone.

'Jayne's websites?'

'Yes, I went window-shopping. You said I could.'

'And anything else?' There was silence. 'Lizzie, I need to know if you looked at anything else, anything in my personal email files from the library.'

The silence was so deep you could have sunk an ocean liner in it.

'Well?'

'I wanted to see what Lucy was so worried about. I mean, you didn't seem that bothered. You'd not even looked.'

'And did you find anything?'

Lizzie laughed. 'Yes. God those pictures are amazing. Why didn't you say something?'

Jane knew everything she needed to know. 'I didn't know I'd got them until last night.'

'What? Where did you see them last night? I don't understand,' said Lizzie.

'Lizzie, the reason they took me to the police station last night, the reason they took my computer away was because they think that I'm blackmailing Steve and Lucy.'

'No?' said Lizzie incredulously. 'God – I'm mean you're not, are you? You wouldn't. You don't strike me as that sort at all.'

'Lizzie, you don't get this, do you? Did you put a note in Lucy's pigeon hole and send her an email saying you'd seen those pictures?'

There was another long silence. Even Gladstone seemed to have stopped splashing around.

'It was only a joke,' said Lizzie, sounding defensive. 'I didn't mean any harm. Lucy is such a cow to work with; you wouldn't believe what she's like. I rang in sick again today; she is driving me nuts – do this, do that, fetch this, fetch that. She treats me like her own personal gofer.'

The silence spread like fog. Then Lizzie said nervously, 'It was a joke. I just thought it would stop her being so arrogant. I mean –' she paused and took a deep breath as if trying to compose herself – 'OK, they think it was you, don't they? God, I'm sorry, Jane, I didn't think it would cause you any problems. I was just trying to rattle her – she is so stuck up. Don't worry. I'll ring them. Who do I need to speak to?'

'DI Rolf. I've got his number here.'

'How did you know it was me?'

'I couldn't see how it could be anyone else.'

'What do you think they'll do to me?'

313

'Lizzie, I really don't know. No real harm's been done, I suppose.'

'I didn't mean you to get into trouble.'

'I know, but they put two and two together and came up with me. After all, I was the one Lucy sent the photos to, I'd got a grudge. It was pretty basic maths as far as the police were concerned.'

'I'll sort it out,' said Lizzie. Not that she sounded that keen.

'And about Gladstone?'

'Look, I—' she began, sounding defensive.

But Jane was ahead of her. 'I think the job with Lonny would be great for him. I think it's a brilliant idea.'

Lizzie laughed. 'Me too, and he looks really cute without his—'

'His beard. Yes, you already told me.'

'I was going to say clothes.'

Jane groaned. 'Too much information.' Behind her Jane heard the door being pushed open and turned, hoping it wasn't her mother. It was Kit.

'How's it going?' he mouthed.

Jane covered the receiver. 'OK.' And then to Lizzie. 'Have you got a pen handy?'

'Give me a break, I'm in the bath.'

'OK, well, in that case I'll text you DI Rolf's number and *please*, Lizzie, ring as soon as you can.'

'I will. I just need to get Peter to his interview and then I'll—'

'Lizzie,' Jane snapped furiously, 'Lonny will wait ten minutes. Get out of the bloody bath and ring DI Rolf now.'

'All right, all right,' said Lizzie, sounding huffy. 'Keep your hair on.'

Jane looked skyward as she heard Lizzie clambering out of the bath. 'I'll talk to you later,' she said; all she could hear were the sounds of Lizzie swearing under her breath.

Kit looked at her. 'A breakthrough?'

'I hope so.' And then explained to him about the photos.

'Great, now we just need to deal with the embezzling.'

Jane nodded. 'I want you to ring Ray.'

'And tell him what?'

'Don't tell him anything – just talk to him.'

'And what?'

'Kit, he's set me up.'

'You think?' he said, tone sarcastic.

'Who else could it be? I need you to talk to him, see what he says.'

'And say?'

Jane shook her head. 'I don't know. If I knew then I'd tell you. Just talk.'

'Anything else?'

'We need to speak to Jayne.'

She reached across and touched the mouse. An instant later the screen of Jayne's Mac flickered into life. 'I'm not sure if Ray can read the emails I send from Jayne's account or her website so I'm going to pick up the messages and then log into my own private account and send a message from there, and hope that she's getting them.'

'The one to which you were sent the porn?' he said, with a grin.

Jane decided not to answer.

'Sounds a little paranoid,' he said.

Jane swung round and stared at him. 'Kit, I'm being framed, what do you expect me to sound like? Pleased?'

'Sorry.'

Jane shook her head. 'No, it's me – I'm getting really twitchy about all this. How long before the police come back and arrest me for something else? Last month I was working in the library, walking Steve's Labrador and busy having a dull, safe little life. Now here I am, living in a millionaire's house, looking after her business and being accused of stealing, stalking and embezzlement . . .'

She flicked up her on-screen banking. The balances in her current account were still the same: according to this, she was a very rich woman.

'At least we know where it is,' said Kit.

Jane looked up at him. 'That's true, but what worries me is what about the rest of her things? I mean, Jayne doesn't just have money, does she? And what if Ray, or whoever it is, *can* access my account? What if he takes the money out of here and it vanishes – then what am I going to do?' She sounded shrill and felt powerless to stop.

'You said yourself that anyone can pay money into your account, but that they'd have to have all your passwords and things to take it out.'

Jane stared out of the window into the parkland. 'OK, so maybe I am being a bit paranoid. As far as I know Ray hasn't been through my handbag.'

All fed, watered and tired from their exertions, the passengers of *Spirit of the Waves* lazed around on the sunloungers set out around the deck, sleeping, chatting and drinking, or watching the little boat's wake cutting a trail through the sunlit waves. Tired after a long day, Jayne poured herself a glass of juice and leaned on the bar, watching the coast of Kos as it grew closer and closer. Not long now and they would be back in harbour.

316

She stretched and stifled a yawn, smiling to herself. Her legs and back ached; this really wasn't how she had seen her new life going at all. Fun, though, to be hands on, to be working under pressure and as part of a team after so many years. It was also nice not to be in charge, for once, although today as she had been working Jayne had been thinking about the day cruise packages Miko was offering. There was lots of scope in the menus and presentation.

Jayne smiled to herself as her brain skipped off with the idea. Maybe when she got the situation sorted out back home she would come back, talk to Miko about improving his product. Oddly enough the idea made her really excited.

'You finished downstairs?' asked Theo, breaking into her reverie, indicating the galley steps.

Jayne nodded. She didn't know Theo well enough to read his expression or his tone, although it seemed as close to neutral as she had seen him so far.

'Oh, yes, all done and dusted. I thought I'd come up and cover the bar while the boys got ready to dock.'

'Done and dusted?' He looked blank.

'It's just a turn of phrase; means that everything is finished, completed.'

He nodded. 'Good. A couple of the passengers said how nice the food was today.' If there was a slightly grudging tone to what he said Jayne made a point of not noticing.

'Wonderful. As long as the customers are happy . . .'

He nodded but seemed in no hurry to move away. Jayne wasn't quite sure how to broach the fact that she was going back to England so decided to come out with it. 'Did Miko tell you that I'm going home tomorrow?'

He stared at her. 'No, he didn't. I don't understand. You've only just started.' His eyes narrowed. 'Is this about me?'

'No. Something has come up that I need to sort out.'

'For a few days or for good?'

'I don't know yet.'

He shrugged, manner reverting back to the rather barbed indifference of the previous day. 'Always the same with Miko: as soon as we get good help . . . Ah, well, just tell him not to send us that blonde again. I'd rather do the food myself.'

'I was thinking I might come back.'

Theo shrugged philosophically. After all, she had hardly been there long enough to make any kind of impression. 'It would be good,' he conceded. 'Makes a change to have someone on board that isn't afraid of hard work.'

Jayne decided to take that as a compliment. 'Would you like me to get you a drink?'

'No, not until we get the passengers off. Maybe you like to join me and the rest of the crew for a beer tonight? The weekend begins here, after all.'

Friday evening. The words formed in her imagination; the days in Kos had become a blur, running one into the other and although she hadn't been on the island that long Jayne realised she had already completely lost track of what day it was. How odd, when back home her life was defined by the day and the clock and all kinds of schedules.

In the distance she could pick out the lights strung along the harbour's edge, twinkling in the early evening, the glow reflected in the water. The day was already softening into night.

Friday evening. Back home she would be turning off her computer, heading downstairs for a glass of wine and supper, listening to Radio 4 or music while Gary cooked.

Looking around the deck, life here couldn't be more different. Jayne smiled, thinking about Miko and his daughter Nina, even Theo – friends she had made since arriving on Kos, the kind of people she would never meet at home. She'd really enjoyed being part of their lives. It made her think that despite all the disasters, coming to Kos had been exactly what she needed, and that she was on the right track after all. Heading into port, with the wind mischievously tugging at her hair, she felt that her life back in England belonged to someone else.

She was aware that Theo was still beside her, waiting for an answer. 'Thanks for asking, but not tonight. I'm hoping to sort out my ticket home. I need to look at the details, flight times, pack.'

Theo nodded. 'Another time then,' he said, sounding as though he meant it, and headed back towards the wheelhouse.

Jayne wiped down and tidied the bar, hands busy while her mind worked overtime, wanting to be back in port now. Talking about leaving had made her restless. It was odd that Kos, which a few days earlier had seemed so very close to home, now seemed so very far away.

She heard the engines cut back as the boat manoeuvred into the harbour mouth. On deck and under the awning, the passengers began to collect their belongings together, the crew getting ready to come alongside the quay and make the boat fast while the gangway was slid into place.

They were probably another ten minutes away from

actually disembarking, so to pass the time Jayne went down into the galley to make sure that everything was tidy and tucked away, ready for whoever took over from her. Trays tidied, knives and skewers secured, everything clean and ready for the off in the morning. Her fingers traced along the counter top, checking, and thinking what she had to do when she got ashore.

On deck the boys were pulling the boat in alongside the dock, creeping closer, closing the last few feet. One of the crew threw the rope to a man ashore. Jayne peered out to try to see who it was pulling them in. Probably Miko – yes, it was him – and then she looked again.

Standing alongside him, catching the second rope, was someone she recognised. For an instant she tried to place the face. After all, who did she know on Kos? And a split second later the name came to her and her heart leaped. Andy – it was Andy Turner, older, still slim, his long blond hair now greying and trimmed into a respectable style, and she was damned if he didn't look amazing.

She stared at him through the porthole, almost afraid to look away in case he was a mirage, an illusion cooked up by her tired mind.

In Buckbourne Ray paced up and down the office. He had already drafted an email to Jayne: 'All is in hand, your tickets will be delivered to the office address you sent. I've booked a flight out for you on Monday late afternoon.'

Now he just needed to go through what he planned to say to Jane: 'Jane, I don't know what the hell has been going on here . . .'

She would obviously protest her innocence but he would explain he had CCTV footage showing her coming in and out of the building, taking Jayne's files, amongst other things, and that he knew it was her account the money had been transferred to because he had seen the account details, say that he was prepared to keep the police out of the situation as long as the money was transferred back. Sit with her while she did the transfer. He would say he had no idea what was going on, listen to her outrage, listen to her protesting that she didn't know anything about anything, wait for her to calm down and then suggest that there was overwhelming circumstantial evidence to suggest that she was on the take.

He must make sure he had tissues – she was bound to cry – and then he would suggest that the best course of action was for her to hand in her notice, take a couple of months' payment in lieu and get the hell out of it. Obviously she would feel aggrieved.

He would even give her a good reference. And when Jayne got home he would say it had been a bad fit, that when you scratched the surface Jane wasn't what she appeared, but that it was all sorted out now. He'd suggest he take over the day-to-day running of the business. That way Jayne could rest easy, travel more, find herself, knowing that everything was in safe hands. Ray smiled; job done.

Chapter Fourteen

Jayne couldn't believe her eyes. She hurried up the steps from the galley and practically ran across the deck to meet Miko and Andy. When she got to the top of the gangway she stopped, looked Andy up and down, and grinned at him as their eyes met.

'I didn't expect to see you here,' she stammered.

'I found him loitering on the quay,' said Miko. 'He told me he was looking for some mad Englishwoman who'd managed to get herself flat-busted broke and marooned on Kos. I figured that there couldn't be that many, so I thought we'd start with you.'

All the time that Miko had been talking Andy's eyes hadn't left Jayne's.

'Hello,' said Jayne, suddenly self-conscious.

'Well, hello yourself,' Andy said, his face alight with recognition and pleasure. 'You know, you look fabulous.'

Jayne laughed and glanced down, very aware of exactly how very unfabulous she looked. She was wearing a baggy *Spirit of the Waves* T-shirt and navy-blue Bermudas with matching deck shoes, hair scraped back off her face, although at least she had taken her apron off.

'Right,' she said with a wry grin. 'Nothing like a day

cooking in a galley to bring out the best in the girl. That smell? That's me. I wish you'd warned me you were coming, Andy, I'd have made a bit of an effort.'

'I thought you had,' he said. As Jayne made her way down towards him Andy held out a hand to steady her as she stepped ashore. 'I backpacked halfway round the known world with you, Jayne – one day in a kitchen is nothing compared to that. Remember the blue and green tent and those army surplus sleeping bags? I thought they might impound them on the way back through customs because they were a bio hazard.'

Jayne pulled a face. 'Oh yes, I'd forgotten all about that. Thanks for the memory. I can't tell you how pleased I am to see you, but I hadn't expected you to show up. I thought you'd sort it out and I'd just pick the ticket up at the airport.'

He shrugged. 'And I thought, given the current state of play, that you'd obviously lost your touch.' When Jayne looked nonplussed, Andy continued, 'C'mon, Jayne, you were the woman who managed to navigate us round the globe with a school atlas and a pile of ferry timetables. Now, have you got anything you need to get?' He glanced back towards the boat.

'I just need to grab my handbag, nip to my room and pick up my things, pack – there are only a couple of bags. It won't take very long. Fifteen minutes.'

Andy laughed. 'That's not like you, Miss Control Freak. I thought you'd be all ready for the off, all set. Up at the crack of dawn squirrelling things away neatly in your backpack – seems like only yesterday.'

'Well, yes, I would normally.' Jayne hesitated and glanced across at Miko. 'It's just that I didn't stay in my digs last night,' she began.

'Ah,' said Andy, reddening. 'Oh, I'm sorry – it never occurred to me. I didn't think.'

Jayne began to explain but Andy cut her off. 'It's all right, really, Jayne. It's none of my business. God, I feel a bit of a fool now.'

Momentarily, there was a great itchy crackling wave of discomfort. 'No, it's not like that,' Jayne said. 'Really.'

'Not for the want of trying, I can tell you,' said Miko, looking all hard done by. 'I've been all over her like a rash – dinner, champagne, day trips. Christ, you'd think at her age she'd be flattered.'

Andy and Jayne stared at him and then laughed.

'What?' said Jayne.

'Well, you're not exactly a spring chicken, are you?' grumbled Miko. 'I thought you'd be grateful. I mean, you're not bad-looking but, phuh . . .' He held up his hands. 'What can I say? Anyway, Andy, I hope you have better luck than me.'

Jayne shook her head in disbelief. 'I know you'll probably find this hard to believe, Andy, but if it hadn't been for Miko here, I don't know what I would have done over the last few days.'

'Oh, stop going on about it. You'd have been fine,' said Miko dismissively. 'You're one of life's copers.'

'He rescued me,' Jayne insisted.

Miko sighed. 'Against my better judgement, to be perfectly honest. I was only trying to get her into the sack. I think I must be losing my touch. I used to be such a bastard,' he said, almost to himself.

Andy nodded philosophically. 'Didn't we all?'

Jayne laughed; where women were concerned she doubted Andy had a single grain of bastard in him, and even Miko, she knew, was far mellower than he made out.

'What time is the flight?' she said, making an executive decision to change the subject.

'First thing tomorrow morning. I've booked into a hotel for tonight.' He smiled. 'I booked you a room too, I wasn't sure where you were staying.'

'I'm going to nip back on board and get my bag and make sure Theo is happy for me to go.'

'I should just bugger off, if I were you. That man is never happy,' said Miko. 'And now I'm one man down.' He looked so sad.

'Thank you for everything,' Jayne said, putting her arms around him and kissing him on the cheek.

'Oh, that's it – *now* you get physical,' he complained.

'I don't know how I can possibly thank you, Miko,' said Jayne. 'I'll be in touch; I've got your address and numbers. And once I've got things sorted out at home I'll send you the money I owe you.'

Miko waved the words away. 'Honey, you don't owe me anything. It has been good to have you around – and if you ever want the cook's job, it's yours.' He glanced towards the boat. 'I think even Theo was impressed.'

Jayne laughed. 'Actually I might take you up on that, once things are straightened out. I've got a few ideas.'

'Why am I not surprised?' sighed Miko.

As soon as Jayne had collected her things from the boat she and Andy made their way back into town. Jayne couldn't quite get her head around the fact that after all these years Andy was finally there. He'd just shown up to rescue her. She glanced across at him, drinking in the details and reflecting on just how good it felt to see him after all this time. He looked great for his age, dressed in jeans and a pale blue shirt that emphasised those big blue eyes of his, now framed by a raft of laughter lines.

The two of them fell into step without a word. Andy's hair was still long enough to be pushed back behind his ears, framing strong handsome features, although, far from making him look old, it gave him a distinguished, rather rakish look. He still walked with the same loping gait.

And oddly enough, seeing him there made her heart flutter in the way it used to all those years ago with a heady mix of affection and plain old-fashioned lust – amazing that it still worked after all these years. More than that, his presence was oddly comforting and familiar, and yet at the same time she was painfully aware of the gulf of time that had passed between then and now. Realistically she didn't know any more about the man she called Andy than she knew about Miko, who was still busy dealing with the boat.

'So,' she said, aware of the paradox, 'what have you been up to?'

Andy grinned. 'Oh, this and that, you know how it is.'

'Still living in Manchester?'

'I've got an office up there. I'll have you know it's very trendy these days up North.'

Jayne smiled. 'So I've heard. What do you do?'

'These days? Well, a lot of it seems to be admin and planning and trying to work out what comes next. I started up an IT company a few years back with a couple of friends, offering bespoke computers systems and troubleshooting to business clients – but all sorts of stuff really. I worked for one of the first computer companies to come into the UK and I really liked it and it grew out of that. You remember Jason Holmes?'

Jayne pulled a face. The name was familiar, the face a black-and-white image from a curling old school photo. 'Vaguely. Was he ginger?'

'That's him, although he always swore blind he was strawberry blond – well, he and I and Helen Hollingwood started up together.'

'Ben Hollingwood's sister? Was she at school with us? Couple of years younger?'

'Uh-huh. That's her. Well, Jason dropped out so she and I carried on the company. Twenty-odd years ago now.'

'Skinny with buck teeth, mousy hair – bit of a geek?'

Andy laughed. 'Yup, that's the one, although now she's tall, skinny and blonde and has had lots of very expensive cosmetic dentistry. We've got two kids. Jake is seven and Ellie's nearly ten.'

Jayne stared at him and suddenly felt a great wave of envy and sadness and regret. It was stupid. *Of course* Andy had got married, *of course* he had had children. Why wouldn't he have? He was too good a man to be on his own. She realised with a horrible start that there was some small part of her that had assumed he would be there for ever, caught in aspic, waiting for her, that no one would ever take her place.

She stared up at him, feeling the press of unexpected tears.

'Wow,' she said, with the slightest tremor in her voice. 'Well, that's great – that's fantastic – one of each. I remember you saying that's what you'd like, good planning.' She forced herself to laugh, while the voice in her head reminded her that back then he had been talking about having one of each with her, a little Jayne and a small Andy. She swallowed the tears back. It was her own fault – she couldn't say he hadn't given her the chance.

If he noticed her discomfort Andy didn't say anything. Instead he said, 'And how about you?' as they crossed the main road, heading back towards Jayne's rooms.

'Oh, you know, I've done all sorts of things. I've got a great company – a dot com.'

'Great, I think that's where the smart money still is. And how about the personal stuff?'

'Well, I travel a lot. We've just bought a cottage in France. Last year we bought a little place in New York, so if you ever want a holiday.'

'We?' he pressed.

'My company. Property is still a good investment.'

He laughed. 'That isn't what I meant. Married, kids?'

Jayne matched his laugh but didn't quite meet his eye. 'No.'

'Really?' He looked genuinely surprised.

'No, I know it sounds crazy but I just never got around to it. Time flies when you're enjoying yourself. I've had relationships but – well – as I said, time flies.' She managed to make it sound upbeat and easy, even though her heart felt as if it were about to burst. It was such a simple answer, a thing Jayne had said casually in passing a hundred times to other people in other places, but this was the one place that it truly counted, the one place that it really hurt.

Her smile held, holding him off like a shield, Jayne afraid not of his surprise at her singleness, but of his pity.

Andy said nothing for a few moments and then: 'How about we eat? I don't know about you, but I'm starving. The food they served on the aeroplane barely passed as a starter.'

Feeling as if she had been let off the hook, Jayne nodded.

'Good call. Miko showed me this amazing place. Do you mind if I have a shower and get changed first?'

Andy considered. 'How about you pack and we move into the hotel and go out from there?'

Jayne nodded. 'OK. Since when have you been the sensible one?'

Andy laughed. 'Since the kids arrived. Taking them anywhere is like a military operation. It's better as they've got older but Helen's useless at all that kind of thing. Last year we went to St Lucia. I've got a client with a house out there . . .'

Jayne nodded, trying very hard to look as if she was listening, afraid to speak. She could feel her colour rising. She didn't want to hear about Helen, their wonderful life and their beautiful children – how selfish was that?

'Jane? How nice to hear from you.'

There was a pause. 'Hello, Ray,' Jane said, trying hard to keep the tremor out of her voice. She had set the phone on to speaker so that Kit could listen in. 'How are you?'

'Oh, I'm fine. You?'

'You left me a message asking me to ring when I got in?' said Jane.

'That's right. I just wanted to let you know I've got Jayne's money and ticket situation in hand – storm in a teacup from what I can see. I just wondered if you might like to pop over to the office. There are one or two things I think we really need to discuss and sort out. Bit of a hiccup, I think, but nothing that can't be straightened out. Sounds very hollow there. Are you on hands free?'

'Yes, I'm just finishing off a few bits and pieces.'

'Problems?'

329

Jane looked at Kit. 'No, not really, but there do seem to be a few glitches – things that aren't quite right. I've still got password problems. And last night at the dinner—'

'How did that go, by the way?'

'The speech went down well. But I met someone there. Do you know Jayne's brother?'

'Kit? Yes, he rang me. Don't worry about that. I think it was a few crossed wires. We need to talk.'

'He was worried about Jayne. It totally threw me.'

'Jane, Jane, Jane, don't worry. No harm done. I've already spoken to Kit and explained the situation. He's fine with it – it's just a little misunderstanding.'

Across the room Kit's expression suggested otherwise.

Jane took a deep breath. 'I've got a problem with my bank account – someone has paid in a huge amount of money.'

There was a little weighted pause and then Ray said, 'Really? Well, in that case it's probably best not to talk about it over the phone. I think we should get together and have a little chat. Where are you now?'

'At Jayne's house.'

'OK, well, how about popping over to the office? I've got a client coming over later, or would you prefer to wait until tomorrow?'

'No, it's all right. I'll come over now,' said Jane.

Kit stared at her.

'I'll be about half an hour,' Jane said, and with that, hung up.

'What the hell do you think you're playing at? I thought we agreed I'd go and talk to him.'

'Oh, and you think he'll tell you the truth? That man is as slippery as an eel. I need to know what he is up to. It isn't your bank account the money is in.'

330

'He is way out of your league. From where I'm standing it looks as if he's trying to frame you for embezzlement. We've got no idea what he's up to. Actually, we've got no idea what's going on at all.'

'That's what I mean to find out,' said Jane, heading towards the door.

'Just be careful.' Kit pulled out his mobile and tapped in Ray's number.

Remarkably, given how elusive he had been over the last few days, Ray answered on the third ring. 'Kit,' he said warmly. Jane stopped midstride and turned back, moving in closer to listen. Ray sounded almost jubilant. 'How are you?'

'I'm just fine. I'm on my way to Jayne's house at the moment and I thought I might drop in and see you.'

There was a hush. 'Right,' said Ray after a few moments. 'I didn't realise you'd be coming by.'

'I wanted to pick some things up from my sister's; you know she's been storing my stuff?'

'No, no, I didn't. Um, just hang on – you know the girl you met last night?'

'The one impersonating my sister.'

Ray sighed. 'I feel as if I'm partially to blame for that. You see, Jayne didn't want anyone to rock the boat – she didn't want anyone to know she'd taken her hands off the tiller, so to speak. I think Jane may have taken my suggestion a little too literally.'

'Really.'

'She's staying at Jayne's house.'

'What?' snapped Kit, acting up a treat. 'But last night you told me you thought she was unreliable. You said that she—'

'I know what I said,' said Ray hastily, 'but the thing is

Jayne hired her, not me. I'd got no say in the matter. Kit, you have to understand I feel as if I'm controlling a forest fire here. Your sister – well, the last few months she has been a little confused.'

'Where are we going with this? Are we saying that Jayne is no judge of character? Or that she's lost it or is having a breakdown?'

Ray sighed. 'I don't know but she has been acting oddly, and I've got no idea exactly what this girl has access to . . . and . . . and . . .' He paused, apparently struggling with some great inner dilemma. 'Look, she is very plausible, She's coming here in a little while. Let me talk to her and I'll try and clear things up. How about I give you a ring when the meeting is over? And in the meantime don't worry, your sister is fine. There was a little hiccup over her credit cards but I've sorted that out.'

'What sort of hiccup?'

'It's this name issue, but don't worry, I'll have it all cleared up by Monday.' He laughed. 'Good job I'm here. Place would burn down without me.'

'If you'd like to take a seat . . .' said Ray.

Jane didn't sit. Instead she stood, her eyes fixed on him. 'Ray, can you explain why there is so much money in my bank account?'

Ray smiled wolfishly. 'I was rather hoping you could tell me. Jane, I have to tell you I've been thinking about calling the police ever since I got Jayne's phone call. I checked earlier and, as you know, all her accounts are empty and from what I can see of it the money has ended up in your account.'

Jane stared at him. 'I just told you that and I'm also telling you that I didn't move it.'

Ray shrugged. 'Really. Well, I have to say that's not how it appears from here. Let's have a look at this, shall we?' He pressed a button on his desk and a grainy film appeared on one of the screens. Jane stared as Ray continued. 'I've got CCTV footage showing you entering the building when there was no one else around and searching through the store cupboards. Oh, and here we are – here we have film showing you leaving the building with Jayne's personal file of passcodes, passwords and account numbers.'

Jane stared at him in horror. 'You told me to take them home. You said Jayne had asked you to get me to take them home for her. Why would I take them without permission?'

But Ray was ahead of her. 'And then this afternoon I was checking things bought on the company credit card and purchases authorised by you. Amongst a lot of other things I came across, air tickets for South America. When I rang the courier agency, apparently the tickets were signed by you. It was a special request on the order; Jane Mills only to sign and receive the package.'

Jane stared at him, her heart sinking. 'You bastard, you set me up. This is nuts. I would have to be mad to have done this. I mean surely, Ray, if I was going to embezzle a company, transferring my boss's entire bank account directly into my own would be a total no-brainer.'

Ray shrugged. 'What can I say? You tried to pass yourself off as Jayne at the Cassar dinner. You even wore her clothes and her jewellery, Jane. To be perfectly honest I wonder if you might be ill, delusional. Have you ever suffered from any form of mental illness?'

Jane's jaw dropped. 'How dare you?' she stammered.

'Look, I understand, it happens. This was a big career jump for you – stressful and overtaxing. Maybe you feel you're out of your depth? I did try to warn Jayne about taking you on.'

He sounded so calm, so very self-assured and so very, very patronising.

'This is rubbish,' said Jane furiously, 'and you know it is.' As she spoke she could feel tears pressing up behind her eyes, and was frustrated that by crying her anger could easily be interpreted as fear or weakness.

'I've already explained the situation to Jayne and to her brother. I've got copies of the CCTV video, a receipt for the flight bookings, all done with the company credit card. You know that I had to talk Kit out of going to the police about the jewellery you helped yourself to? And then this morning in the trade press and on Cassar's website there are photos of you pretending to be Jayne Mills at their gala dinner. Doesn't look good from where I'm standing.'

Jane felt as if there was a big rock pressing down on her chest. 'I didn't do any of this, you know that,' she said. 'I didn't take Jayne's money, I didn't book that flight; there must be some way I can prove this.'

'To whom?' Ray smiled, although the smile didn't warm his expression by a single degree. 'And if not you, then who else did?' he said quietly.

Jane blinked back the tears. 'You,' she whispered thickly. 'You did all this, didn't you? I don't see how it could have been anyone else, and worse than that I don't know why.'

'And who is going to believe that? I had a phone call from the police earlier today. Apparently they had you in for questioning about blackmailing one of your former colleagues.'

Jane stared at him. 'How do you know that?'

'Oh, I have ways. They rang me to check you out and I rang a friend. It would be your word against mine, Jane. How do you think you'd fare? I've worked for this company for donkey's years. Jayne trusts me, and rightly so. I have to recognise that perhaps we do need someone to help. I can see Jayne's point, but not you, not now.' He paused again and flipped through a file on the desk top, eyes moving down over the sheet of paper pinned into it.

'Right, let's get this over and done with, shall we? I've got things to do. We did say we'd offer you a three-month trial when Jayne took you on, so I've been thinking that if I gave you three months' pay in lieu of notice . . . Obviously we'll give you a good reference and I'll square things away with Jayne.' He paused, watching her face. 'So what do you say, Jane?'

'I think it stinks. What's the alternative?' said Jane.

'The alternative is simply that I ring the police and report the theft of –' Ray paused for effect – 'exactly how many thousands was it that appeared in your bank account?'

Jane felt a great wave of heat roll through her. 'I didn't take that money,' she whispered. 'You know I didn't.'

'But that isn't how it looks, now is it? Given the fact that the police are already on your case this is not going to look good at all. How is thief going to look on your CV? And I think you have to consider the wider ramifications. Reporting the theft could well have a knock-on effect on trade. Scandal and failure can easily take on a life of their own. People take great pleasure in the misery of others. Businesswoman takes off to paradise while her company is fleeced by newcomer – I can see the headlines now. You'll make Jayne look a complete fool. Don't you think you've hurt her enough?'

'I haven't hurt Jayne at all,' Jane protested.

Ray shrugged. 'That rather depends on what you do next, doesn't it, sweetie? I can make things very messy. For everyone.' He pushed the file towards her. 'All I need is for you to sign this form to say you accept severance pay in lieu of notice. It'll take two seconds, and then it'll be all over and done with.'

Jane shivered. 'Are you threatening me?'

Ray lifted his hands in a gesture that implied he was harmless, with nothing up his sleeve. Jane didn't believe him for an instant. 'Of course I'm not threatening you. What I'm saying is that we need to nip this in the bud before it goes any further, come to a sensible arrangement and move on.'

He pulled out a chair at one of the computers. 'What I'd like you to do is transfer Jayne's money back into her account, give me back the company credit cards and return to wherever it was you came from in the first place. Simple. Then I give you three months' salary and a great personal reference, sort Jayne out and you go away and find yourself another job, and everything in the henhouse is rosy.'

Jane looked at the chair, considering her options. 'Why are you doing this? What have I ever done to you?'

Ray's face was expressionless. 'This is my company. I've built it up from nothing. Jayne's fine with all her bright ideas, but without my help it would have gone down the pan. And then she hires you – I mean, what was that about? It makes no sense when I'm here.' He paused. 'What are you waiting for?' Ray's voice was barely above a whisper.

'So you're telling me you're doing this because you're jealous?' Jane said.

'Just sign the fucking contract,' he snapped.

Jane picked up the pen, hesitating above the dotted line as she scanned down the page, trying hard to work out what she was signing away.

At that moment the phone rang, breaking the tension. Ray stared at it as if willing it to stop. After the third ring the answer machine cut in and Kit's very distinctive voice filled the room. Ray stepped forward to pick it up but not before Kit said, 'Hi, Ray, I'm a little early. I'm just parking.'

If Ray was rattled by Kit's arrival he hid it well. 'Not a problem, I've got someone here at the moment, but she was just leaving,' he said, and then hung up.

Jane stared at him. 'What?'

'Have you signed?'

Jane shook her head. 'I want to read what I'm agreeing to.'

'How very sensible. It's very straightforward, Jane. Take it away, read it, and then transfer the money back into Jayne's account. I'll expect it back on my desk first thing Monday morning,' he said, closing the file on the desk. 'Simple.'

'I haven't got the account numbers,' she countered.

Ray grinned. 'Oh, I think you have. You'll find they are in the file you took home the other day.'

'I'm not using those.'

Ray continued. 'Think about it, Jane. If the cash is back where it belongs by first thing Monday morning, I'll deposit your wages and a little bonus to help you on your way. If it isn't, I'll phone the police. I'd just do as you're told if I were you.'

'Hush money?' she said.

Ray frowned. 'That's a little harsh. Now, why don't you run along while I smooth things over with Kit?'

Almost as he spoke the security phone buzzed, the sound followed by Kit's, 'Hello.'

Ray pressed the unlock key.

'Would you like to go out by the fire exit?' he asked, glancing towards an opaque glass door in the far corner of the room.

'Why would I want to do that?'

'Please yourself. I just don't think Kit is overpleased about you passing yourself off as his big sister, all decked up in the family baubles.'

'That wasn't what happened.'

Ray snorted. 'Give or take a minor detail or two, that is exactly what happened, Jane. And certainly that is exactly how Kit sees it. Now, are you going or not?'

Jane started to collect her things together. 'What are you going to tell him?'

Ray shrugged. 'Kit? I shouldn't worry about that. You just worry about getting Jayne's money back where it belongs.'

As he spoke the office door opened and Kit hurried into the room. He looked as if he had been running. Jane looked up at him and for a moment he faltered as he caught sight of her. 'Are you all right?' he asked her.

Jane bit her lip, struggling to hold back the tears that had been threatening for the last ten minutes, and nodded. She wondered if Ray might suspect anything but he was far too busy trying to get rid of her.

He caught hold of her arm. 'Sorry about that, Kit. Of course she's all right, aren't you, sweetie? We've just been tackling a few hiccups and teething troubles, but it's all sorted out now. Jane is feeling a bit overwhelmed, aren't you? I've just been explaining that we all make mistakes, errors of judgement – overreach, go outside our brief, easily done on the spur of the moment. Anyway, no real harm done.'

He paused, waiting to see if Jane was going to say anything and when she didn't, continued, 'Actually, Jane was just telling me she's decided that it's time to move on. I think joining us was a bit of a knee-jerk reaction after the débâcle at the library.'

Kit stared at Jane, waiting for her to protest. Hadn't they worked on the notion that the two of them being there together would rattle him?

Jane opened her mouth but nothing came out, no words, nothing. She was thunderstruck at being railroaded by Ray, and angry and hurt, and couldn't think what she wanted to say. Finally she mumbled, 'This isn't right. I haven't done anything.'

Ray looked at her, expression hardening. 'Now come on, sweetie, we've already talked this through. I'll sort things out here; all you have to do is sign those forms and do that little bit of banking we discussed.' His smiled widened as he got to the top of the stairs. 'Come along, Jane, time to go . . . help yourself to coffee, Kit. I'll be back in a minute,' he said over his shoulder. And then to Jane, whispered, 'And you? I'll be online first thing Monday morning to check that everything is back where it should be.'

An instant later he was gone and Jane stood alone on the landing, trembling from head to foot.

When the door closed Jane couldn't get out of the building fast enough; she felt sick and angry and outraged and impotent. She looked back at the front door as it closed silently behind her; maybe she should go to the police, maybe she should go now.

As she walked across the car park she burst into tears. What a bastard.

Kit took the cup of coffee Ray offered him. 'What was all that about?' he said.

Ray rolled his eyes heavenwards and sighed. 'Women. God only knows. To be perfectly honest she's been a walking disaster. She's managed to screw up our accounts package, Jayne's credit cards and the Cassar dinner all within a week. It's amazing. After you and I spoke I took an executive decision and asked her to leave – commerce really isn't her bag. Nice kid, wrong job. So, is there anyway I can help you or is this a social visit?'

'Jayne rang me.'

'From Kos?' Before Kit could say anything else Ray sighed heavily. 'See what I mean? Total chaos. But don't worry, all that is in hand. I've got a ticket booked. Money wired, everything shipshape and Bristol fashion.' He looked fleetingly at the door. 'God only knows what Jayne thought she was doing, taking on someone like that.'

'She seems very competent.'

'Oh, I'm sure she is, just not in this field.

Anyway, enough about that – do you fancy a drink, or dinner while you're home? How are things with you?'

340

Chapter Fifteen

By the time Kit came out of Ray's office it had started to rain. Jane sat in a café a few minutes' walk away, watching the rain trickling down the windows, feeling miserable and dejected, while part of her wrestled with the notion that if she didn't hurry home and put Jayne's money back, the next thing she would feel was the snap of handcuffs as the police arrested her.

Kit opened the café door and looked round, searching her out amongst the cluster of shoppers. 'Are you all right?' he said, sliding into the booth alongside her. 'You look awful.'

'He told me that if the cash is back where it belongs by Monday morning that he'd deposit my salary and a little bonus to help me on my way, and if it isn't, he'll ring the police.'

'He threatened you?'

Jane nodded. 'Basically I've got to play along or he'll set the police on me.' She stared at Kit. 'Trouble is, I don't see that I've got any choice.'

'Which means what, exactly?'

She looked up at him. 'That I go home and transfer the money back.' She paused. 'What worries me is, if I do that and take Ray's offer it will look as if I did steal it.'

The waitress came and took their order, killing conversation. When she'd gone Kit said, 'Well, if it's any consolation he told me you were incompetent, a total disaster. A ditz.'

Jane bristled and was about to speak when Kit continued, 'He also implied my sister was barking mad and in need of either medication or psychiatric help.'

'And is that what you think?' Jane growled.

He paused and grinned at her. 'You're way too arsy to be a ditz – and mad or not, if my sister heard him say she was one Penguin short of a packet she'd probably lay him out.'

'So what do we do?'

'Is there any way to catch him out?' Kit sighed. 'What we need is some slip, some proof that he was the one moving the money around and that he set you up.'

Jane stared at him. 'There has to be a way.'

Kit shook his head. 'I agree but I don't know how we go about finding it.'

Jane had such a sense of impotence and frustration that she could almost feel her blood pressure rising. What the hell was she going to do? This wasn't how she imagined her life working for Jayne Mills going at all. She planned to travel, do a good job, drive great cars and wear wonderful clothes – not . . .

'Jane?' Kit said.

Jane looked across the table. 'What?'

'Your mobile.' She peered at Kit as he repeated, 'Your mobile is ringing.'

'Oh, right, right . . .' said Jane, pulling it out of her handbag. It was Lizzie, her voice barely audible above the hum and clatter of the café. 'Won't be a minute,' said Jane, getting to her feet and heading outside.

'I just called to tell you that Peter – Gladstone – got the job,' said Lizzie brightly. 'Isn't that amazing?' Jane left a long cool pause which after a few seconds Lizzie felt obligated to fill. 'Yes, all right, and I went in to see the police. I've got to go back to make a full statement but the man I spoke to said I would probably get off with a caution. And then of course there's work.' Lizzie sighed. 'I'll have to go in and explain to them as well – see what's-her-face in Human Resources. I'm not sure what they'll do, although given the rationalisation . . .' She paused. 'I can hardly work with Lucy now, so I was thinking maybe it might be better to jump than be pushed. Oh, but Peter was brilliant—'

'So you said.' Jane didn't ask whether that was at his interview or at the police station while his new-found guardian angel owned up to blackmail.

'You know he was in prison?' Lizzie continued brightly.

'No, I didn't know that,' said Jane, although she thought, given his lifestyle, it was hardly surprising. Not everyone could deal with finding Gladstone sound asleep in the coal shed.

'He did some sort of computer stuff – hacking and stuff. Technogeekery.' Lizzie giggled. 'I'm not sure that'll be much help, working with Lonny, but it can't hurt. He did say that I was best to own up.'

'Good advice,' said Jane drily. 'Especially if you are the one that did it.'

Lizzie wasn't planning to rise to the bait. 'Apparently he said that if I didn't own up then they could have followed a data trail at the library, and proved the emails came from my machine.'

Jane felt her whole body respond. 'Really?'

'Yeah. Peter said that organisations often have security in place to see who's logged on and who's doing what on a network where and when, and even if they haven't, tracing that kind of stuff is easily do-able, apparently. Any defence lawyer would have known that and got you off. It makes you think, doesn't it?'

'It certainly does,' said Jane quietly, her mind already running away with the thought.

'And if I didn't own up – which I was going to, obviously,' Lizzie said hastily – 'then some geek could have tracked the traffic on my machine.'

'Your one at work?'

'Well, I didn't use *yours*. I mean, not once I'd found the photos,' Lizzie said, sounding indignant. 'It kept preying on my mind at work when Lucy was being such a cow; I wanted to bring her down a peg or two. I didn't mean to cause you any problems. It was stupid really.'

'You were,' said Jane. 'Very.'

'Can I still stay in your house?'

'For the time being,' said Jane cautiously.

'Ohhhhhhh,' whined Lizzie. 'Look, I'm really sorry, please, I won't do it again. Any dirty pictures of your ex-lover and his odious girlfriends show up again, I'll ignore them. Promise. Cross my heart.'

'Lizzie, stop begging. The can-you-stay-in-my-house question has got nothing to do with you trying to stitch Lucy up. It's that I'm just not quite sure what's happening with work.' She hesitated for a few seconds, unsure how much to tell Lizzie. Given Lizzie's current track record Jane wasn't exactly eager to take her into her confidence, but she could do with some help. 'Is Gladst— I mean Peter with you now?'

344

'Er, yes,' Lizzie said, sounding horribly defensive. 'We were just trying out your coffee machine. Did you know it made cappuccino?'

'My mother bought it for me.'

'What a lovely present.'

'It would be if I ever drank cappuccino. Can you put him on? I need to talk to him.'

'Who, Peter?'

'Yes,' snapped Jane. 'Peter.'

'You're not going to tell him off, are you? It was me who invited him in, and he's washed, and we got some cream for his rash—'

'Lizzie, be quiet. I'm sure he has scrubbed up a treat, and no, I'm not going to tell him off, but I need his help,' Jane said. 'Can I talk to him now?'

'Oh, yes.'

'Hello,' said a familiar voice. 'Did Lizzie tell you, I got the job?'

'She did, congratulations. I'm really pleased for you.'

'And Lonny said he'd help me to find somewhere to live.'

'Great. Look, Peter, I really need to pick your brains.'

'Oh, OK.' He sounded surprised.

'Do you mind?'

'No, not all,' he said and then in a lower voice, barely above a whisper, 'and please, call me Gladstone – I prefer it.'

Jane sighed and then began to explain briefly about the stunt Ray had pulled before listening to the things Gladstone had to say. Five minutes later she rang off and hurried back into the café.

'All right?' said Kit, as she slid into the bench opposite him.

Jane nodded. 'Yes, I think so. When did Ray say that Jayne was coming home?'

Kit shrugged. 'Late Monday, I think. He said he'd sorted the tickets out for her.'

'Damn, he wants me to sign the disclaimer and transfer the money back by Monday morning.'

'I don't understand?'

'I need a way to get to Ray's computers at the office and the only way I can think of doing that is to get Jayne involved. I need a witness to verify what we find – if anything.'

'Can you get in?'

Jane nodded. 'I think so. I've still got the door codes but I can hardly go in there without permission.'

Kit thought for a few moments. 'Technically at the moment you're still working for the company.'

Jane nodded. 'I know, but not sure that Ray would see it that way if he finds me poking about, and also I don't mean just me. I want to take someone in with me.'

Kit shook his head. 'I'm not with you.'

'Someone who can get me off the hook. Someone who can prove it wasn't me who took the money.'

'Are you serious? Who?'

Jane nodded. 'I need to take a tramp called Gladstone in as well.'

'Jesus—'

'No, apparently he looks nothing like him since he's cut his hair and shaved his beard off.'

'So how long do you need?'

'I've got no idea but we need to keep Ray out of the way, and I need to do it as soon as possible.'

'I could invite him over to dinner,' said Kit.

346

Jane smiled. 'I've got a better idea.'

'Which is?'

'I just need to make a quick phone call.'

'You mentioned maybe getting together for dinner while I'm home, so I was wondering,' said Kit, 'if you might like to come over tomorrow evening for some supper. It's been ages since we caught up and, besides,' Kit sounded a little uncomfortable, 'I wanted to thank you for sorting out all this nonsense with Jayne. God only know what was going through her head.'

Ray smiled to himself; obviously his ruse had worked. 'That's very kind.'

'When is she coming home?'

'Jayne? Late Monday, as far as I know.'

'OK – so about supper?' pressed Kit. 'The things is I've been invited to a party afterwards. You'd be welcome to come along too, if you like. It's a house-warming party for Jayne's new neighbours, can you remember Paper Tiger? Well, it's this guy called Tony Butler.'

'Yes,' said Ray, 'I do. I went to see them at Leeds. I thought he was dead.'

'Apparently not. Tony and his wife have moved in next door to Jayne – his wife used to be a page-three model, apparently. Anyway, it looks as if it's going to be some do. They've got a couple of live bands, caterers, booze, dancers.' Kit paused. 'I feel I ought to make the effort for Jayne's sake.'

'Well, obviously,' said Ray briskly, suppressing a grin. 'Sounds like it might be a good night.'

'OK, well, shall we say about seven-thirty for eight at Jayne's place? I'll get Gary to rustle up something half decent.'

'Sounds fine. And how are things going with the other Ms Mills?' asked Ray. 'No trouble, I hope?' He wanted to know where Jane was and what she was up to.

'She rang me earlier to say she would be popping over later to pick up her things. Said she needed to sort some things out in the office. Files and stuff? Apparently there are some numbers or something she needs.'

Ray smiled to himself; looked like Jane had seen sense after all. 'OK, well, in that case I'll see you tomorrow night.'

Andy had booked the two of them into a modern hotel on the edge of Kos town, with air conditioning, spacious elegant rooms, a pool, Jacuzzi, hot and cold running room service – pretty basic amenities really, Jane thought to herself as she set her cases down at the end of the bed – but nevertheless it felt a long way from the dog-eared little apartment she had just left.

Alone in her suite Jayne slipped off her clothes and, naked, padded across to the bathroom, which was lined with cream and pale grey-blue marble, the gold-coloured fittings making it appear tarty and slightly overdone rather than conveying the opulence and sense of luxury she guessed they had been aiming for. Whatever, the water was hot and plentiful, the rack of matching blue and ice-white towels luxurious, with a pile so deep you could probably have lost a toddler in one, and the Molton Brown toiletries, all laid out in a big palm-leaf basket, were as tempting as fresh cherries.

Jayne sighed as she stepped under the torrent, relishing the sensation of the water on her skin, letting it ease out the aches and tensions, washing away the fetid smell of the galley.

348

'Jayne? Jayne, are you OK?' Andy's voice broke into her reverie.

'Yes, I'm fine,' she called through the half-open door. 'I'm in the shower.' As if he couldn't guess. He'd booked them into adjoining rooms but it hadn't occurred to her he would use the door between. 'I'm just about feeling human again.'

'Do you want a drink?' he called.

Jayne laughed. 'Not in here. Although actually, yes, I could murder something long, cool and alcoholic.'

She turned off the shower, pulled a towel off the stack, wrapped it around her hair turban fashion, and slipped on a thick white cotton robe from the hook by the door.

'Champagne do?' he asked as she opened the bathroom door. Before she could reply he popped the cork on a bottle of Krug misty with condensation, dripping icy water onto the cream tiled floor.

Jayne took the glass proffered to her. 'What's the occasion?'

He laughed, topping his own glass before turning to offer a toast. 'Do we need one?' He paused, his expression unreadable and then, touching his glass to hers, said, 'Old friends.'

'Less of the old,' said Jayne ruefully, taking a sip.

'I realised when you phoned,' Andy said, settling himself on the sofa near the door to the balcony, 'that there was a part of me that thought I would never ever see you again and I realised how sad that made me feel. You have no idea how pleased I was to hear from you.'

Jayne sighed. 'Even if it means bailing me out?'

'Particularly if it means bailing you out. It's nice to know that the world-famous Jayne Mills is as fallible as

349

the rest of us. You know, you used to terrify me – you always seemed so self-assured, with your eye on the ball.'

'That was just a trick of the light.' Jayne stared at him and laughed.

'I was gutted when you turned me down, Jayne. I knew there was no way back.'

Jayne felt her eyes fill with tears. They'd never talked about why she had said no. 'Oh, Andy,' she whispered, 'I'm so sorry. You've got no idea. I was scared all the time. I wasn't self-assured at all, just afraid if I didn't keep things under control we'd drown in a sea of complete chaos. All those little rituals, all that neatly folding stuff up, sticking to the plan and the itinerary, were like touchstones, imposing order on chaos, charms to keep the bears away.'

He stared at her and then laughed. 'Really?' he said in amazement.

Jayne took a long pull on her glass. 'Yes, and you know what? I almost did the same thing this time, planning where to go next, working the itinerary out – taking control instead of letting things just happen. And you know what I discovered this time around? Even if stuff happens I can cope. Even without any money the bears didn't get me. I can cope – even if life throws shit I can still manage. After all this time,' she smiled, 'I've had to come face to face with something that I've always feared and, you know what, chaos won't kill me.'

Outside it was beginning to get dark; they should eat. Jayne could already feel the tendrils of champagne creeping through her veins, carried on bubbles of exhaustion. Andy leaned across and refilled her glass. 'Are you going to get dressed?'

Jayne looked down at the bathrobe, the colour emphasising the beginnings of a tan. 'I wasn't, why? Does it disturb you?'

'No, no, not at all, although I keep remembering what's under it.'

Jayne laughed. 'None of it's quite so perky now.'

He grinned. 'Looks all right from where I'm sitting, but I thought you wanted to go out and eat.'

'Later,' she said, knowing the bubbles had reached her brain. 'Tell me about Helen and the children.' And, Jayne thought, even as she was saying it, how typical of a woman – as his warm gentle reflective expression carved a hole in her heart – that she wanted to know everything about a rival and would use what she knew to torture herself with for years.

'What would you like to know?' he asked, watching her face intently.

'Everything – where do you live, are you happy? Do you have a dog? What are your children like, do you have photos? This wonderful tall thin elegant blonde you married instead of me – what's she like? I need to know all about her.' And as she spoke, Jayne cursed herself for the little splinter of pain and regret in her voice.

Andy's eyes didn't leave her face as he began to speak. 'Helen is an incredible woman. She terrified me when I first met her – always so self-assured, with her eye on the ball.'

Jayne stared at him. 'Are we talking about me here? Isn't that what you just said about me?'

He grinned. 'No, with you I always knew that there was a softer side, something less formidable and I loved you for it. For you the world was an adventure, even if you were afraid of the chaos. Can you remember when we got

351

stuck in Phuket? I remember curling up on a tiny camp bed with you in a hot little room with my arms around you and you crying because you were feeling homesick and miserable and were missing your cat.'

Jayne laughed as she remembered, and at the same time felt her eyes filling with tears. 'Oh God, Andy, that was so long ago. Where's the time gone?'

He shook his head. 'God knows. With Helen I soon realised that she didn't need me at all. Helen is a fantastic woman but she's not wired like that. There are times when I think she barely tolerates me – the wise fool.' He sighed. 'Ah, well, we live and learn.'

Jayne blinked back the tears. 'Oh Andy,' she whispered. 'I'm so sorry. I wanted you to be happy, even though knowing you married someone else is ripping me to shreds. I don't want you to be sad.'

Andy smiled ruefully. 'I'm not.'

'But you said . . .'

'I know what I said. Helen and I worked together brilliantly, we've got two fantastic kids and she is a great mum—'

'Oh God, please don't tell me your wife doesn't understand you.'

'Oh, she understands me only too well. No, Helen knows exactly what sort of person I am. Which is why we're getting divorced.'

She stared at him. 'What?'

'We've been living apart for nearly four years now. She's dating an accountant from Hove. We've got joint custody of the children. They spend half their time with me and half with her. She thinks I'm not ruthless enough, and that under pressure I let my heart rule my head. And you know what? She's absolutely right. Which is why I'm here on my slightly dog-eared white charger to rescue you from fishing-gutting and fat men from Yorkshire.' He grinned. 'So do you want to get dressed and eat or shall I see if they do room service?'

Jayne stared at him. 'Oh, Andy.'

It seemed like no more than a breath before he had his arms around her. No more than a heartbeat before her lips were on his.

'I've missed you,' she said.

'Me too,' he whispered and then, pulling back, said, 'so are we eating here?'

Jayne laughed and then shook her head. 'God knows.'

'Are you hungry?'

'Yes, and I think we both need something to absorb the alcohol,' she said.

'You've only had a glass.'

'It's been a long day.'

He nodded. 'You can say that again.' And then Andy pulled her close and Jayne melted into his arms.

'I hurt so much when you said you wouldn't marry me,' he whispered. 'I thought I would die without you.'

Jayne sighed. 'I'm so sorry.'

'Did you ever regret your decision? Did you ever think about what might have been?'

Jayne looked up into his big gentle blue eyes and smiled. 'Every day, but I also think I did the right thing, at least for back then. We both needed to grow up and do other things, go other places.'

'And now we have,' said Andy.

'It wasn't that I didn't love you,' said Jayne.

He smiled. 'You know, that's what I thought. I was

certain you did. It amazed me when you said no. I was so sure – so very sure you'd say yes.'

'I nearly did, but we both needed to do more than just go home and get married.'

He grinned. 'I'm sure we would have.'

'I wasn't so certain.' As their eyes met there was a little pause, a deep dark electric moment that flashed with desire and mutual need and a million and one unspoken thoughts and words, and an instant later was gone.

'Let's go eat,' he said.

Jayne nodded. She had a feeling that there was still time, even after all these years. Still time.

Chapter Sixteen

In Creswell Close, Audra had been persuaded to go to watch TV in the sitting room with Lizzie and a bottle of California's finest and pinkest wine, while Gladstone talked Jane, Kit and Gary, who were sitting around the table in the kitchen, through what he needed to do to track down the online transactions at Jayne's office. It all sounded very complicated.

'Maybe I should go upstairs and get a flip chart,' said Jane wrly, while passing round a dish of nuts.

'Oooh, it's just like the Italian job,' Gary said excitedly, opening another bottle of wine.

'Which bit?' asked Gladstone, eyebrows deeply knitted.

'None of it,' said Jane to Gladstone firmly. He was still gurning thoughtfully. 'Now, let's just go through it again. How long do you think it will take?'

Gladstone considered his answer while Gary complained, 'I don't understand why you want me to go with you, Jane. I mean I'd be the first one to admit there's not enough cloak-and-dagger in my life but—'

'But nothing, Gary. The thing is, Jayne trusts you and knows you wouldn't let anything bad happen to her or to anything important to her. We need to have an impartial witness to what Gladstone and I are going to do.'

'Which is what, exactly?'

'Well,' said Jane, looking towards Gladstone for support and confirmation of what she was saying, 'we're going to go in Jayne's computer system and try to trace who did what, where and when. We'll try and find out who changed the passwords, who ordered the tickets to South America, and who moved the money, by working out which machine was used, what time that person visited the site and when. And then do the same with the banking. We might not be able to say who it was but at the very least I'm hoping Gladstone can prove that it wasn't me.'

'We can easily trace activity on different sites,' said Gladstone. 'What I can't promise is that we'll be able to work out exactly what any user was doing on that site. Some of what we find out will be circumstantial.'

'But won't Ray say that as you've got the code for the door at Jayne's offices you could have gone in and done the transfers from there?' countered Kit, playing, Jane hoped, devil's advocate.

'That's true, but there is CCTV coverage at the offices. I'm not sure how long Ray keeps the tapes – we need to find out – but he said he had the film of me picking up the bank file so that suggests they go back quite a while, although obviously he did make a point of keeping that one. I need enough proof to show Jayne that it couldn't have been me. At this point it hasn't got to stand up in court. Will you come upstairs while Gladstone checks out the computers here and watch while I transfer Jayne's money back into her account?' She handed Gladstone a Post-it note. 'These should help. They're the passwords I was given by Jayne.'

As she got to her feet she caught hold of Kit's hand.

Although Kit's fingers closed around hers, he hesitated and then he said, 'Jane, I don't think that that is a very good idea.'

She stared at him, feeling her heart sink. 'Which bit?' she asked.

'Moving the money back into Jayne's account.'

'Well, I can hardly keep it, can I?'

'No, but whoever transferred the money into your account has got Jayne's passwords and details. Who's to say that once you've moved the money back that they don't move it again – and this time to somewhere where we can't reach it?'

Jane stared at him. 'I hadn't thought of that. So what are you suggesting I do instead?'

Kit sighed. 'Well, either you leave the money where it is – after all, it's safe enough there – and call Ray's bluff, or you transfer it into, say, my account, and then we'll know it's safely out of everyone else's hands.'

Jane looked up at him, considering her options. 'You're right. I could transfer it over to you, Kit, but it's not that I don't trust you, it's just that that money feels as if it has been almost accidentally left in my safekeeping and the person I want to hand it back to is Jayne, not you, not anyone else, just Jayne.'

At which point her mother put her head round the kitchen door. She was clutching an empty glass and swaying very slightly. 'All done yet, darlings?' she purred, 'only the film's just finished and we're out of wine in there, and Lizzie is whining on and on about missing Gladstone. Oh, are there more nibbles?'

'Mum, please, this is important,' said Jane, passing her a dish of crisps. 'We won't be long. I promise.'

Her mother sighed. 'It's always the same with you, Janey. Time for everybody else but not your own mother. We've barely had five minutes alone together since I arrived.'

'Mum, it's not that you're not welcome, it's just that we're busy at the moment.'

'Busy, busy, busy – always the same with you.' Audra pulled a face as pitiful as the last puppy in the shop window.

'Mum,' Jane protested.

Gary was the first one to crack. 'Oh, come on, what harm will it do if your mum just sits in here with us?'

Jane rounded on him. 'Are you completely mad? She can't keep quiet, she can't keep a secret and she can't—'

'Do anything right?' said her mother, all wounded and hurt. 'Is that any way to talk to me?'

Jane stared at her. 'Mum, normally you can't get away from me fast enough. If you remember, you're the one who told me that after you'd given birth you nipped out of the maternity home and left me there for the afternoon, because you had friends coming for lunch and didn't want the bother of having me about the place. And we both know if you'd got a man at the moment we wouldn't see your arse for dust. This is business. Ten more minutes and then I'll come through and we can catch up. I promise, cross my heart. Gary, give her another bottle of wine, will you? And, Mum, there's bound to be something dodgy on Five.'

'You promise? You said cross your heart?'

Really, it was worse than having a child. 'Yes, I promise,' said Jane. 'Now please, just go and let us get on with it, will you?'

Still looking on the wrong side of hard done by, her mother retreated back into the sitting room.

'So,' said Jane, 'to recap. Let's go through the plan.'

'Tomorrow night, I'll cook supper and leave dessert in the fridge,' said Gary. 'Maybe a lemon meringue? Or a fresh fruit salad?'

'I'll explain to Ray that it's Gary's night off, and that once the main course is over we'll have to fend for ourselves,' said Kit.

'Jane, I'll pick you up in the Mercedes and drive you over to Jayne's office, picking up Gladstone on the way,' continued Gary, nodding towards Gladstone on the far side of the table.

Jane added, 'I'll get us into Jayne's office, we make sure all this is being recorded on the CCTV cameras. Once we're in, Gladstone goes through the data logs to see if we can find out who did what when, and then he'll copy the information onto a spare hard drive – which we'll bring with us to prove our case. I'll take a couple of memory sticks too, to pick up anything that looks particularly important.'

'Meanwhile, after we've eaten, I'll take Ray round to Tony and Lil's party,' said Kit, 'and show him a good time.'

Jane's eyes narrowed.

'OK, OK,' he said defensively, 'so not that good a time.'

Gladstone looked around the table thoughtfully and nodded.

Jane turned to Gary. 'And you'll stay with us while we're in the office to see we don't tamper or fiddle with anything or change anything.'

'I'm not going to do that,' complained Gladstone, looking all offended.

'No, I know you won't, but it's good to have a witness there who Jayne trusts, and Gary can see what is going on and what we're doing.'

'And what would you like me to do while all this is going on?' asked Audra, popping her head back around the door jamb.

Jane narrowed her eyes. 'How long have you been there?'

'I just came back for some dip.'

'How much did you hear?'

'Oh, hardly anything at all and anyway, darling, these days I'm discretion itself. You always go on about how I can't keep a secret but you're wrong. I can. My lips are sealed. Look.' Audra mimed a zipper.

Jane lifted an eyebrow; her mother very pointedly said nothing. Gary got up and refilled everyone's glass. It was going to be a long night.

Jayne woke early the next morning. Bright sunlight streamed in through the open curtains of the hotel room. She rolled over, trying to close out the pain in her head that came with the light, and suddenly realised that she wasn't alone. She was a little surprised and then not so surprised and then smiled, savouring the sensation of Andy's presence, as the memory of the previous evening trickled back.

She remembered the long lazy supper, remembered sharing another bottle of champagne, remembered the slow walk along the beach, hand in hand under an unblinking ever-curious moon, when Andy had leaned closer and told her how very much he loved her and how he still thought about her every day. Yes, even after all these years, and how sometimes he imagined he had seen her on the street and then realised it was someone else and felt sad.

Jayne shivered, remembering how they had stopped in

the shadows and the way his lips had felt on hers, remembered the electric shiver of desire she felt as his hands slid up under her shirt, remembered the sensation of his fingertips stroking her skin, pulling her closer, consuming her.

The memories of desire past and the desire present mingled into a series of erotic tableaux where, looking back from the sober, if slightly hung over high ground, Jayne wasn't altogether sure what was now and what was then; vividly remembered, both were glorious, both had left her wanting more. Damn, why had she ever let him go?

Jayne groaned softly at her thoughts, desperately aware of the presence on the far side of the bed, and strained to remember exactly what had happened once they got back to the hotel room. She remembered sitting in the bar downstairs sipping Margaritas, remembered talking and laughing and talking some more, letting the booze carry her along, although part of her remained resolutely sober, and then she remembered Andy saying that as it was getting late, that maybe they should go up to their room. After all, they had a flight to catch the next day. And Jayne had laughed, because once upon a time it would have been her that said that sort of thing, not him. And then he had kissed her gently and she couldn't help reflect that without even trying her life had come full circle. Here she was, back in Kos with Andy, Beach Bum of the Year, and she still loved him just as much.

And then they had gone upstairs and sat out on the balcony under a waterfall of stars and moonlight, and then . . . and then . . . Jane screwed up her eyes and as she did, rolled over very slowly, trying to remember exactly what had happened next. Her headache complained at the change of view but she pressed on anyway. God, how bad was it that the first night she had spent with Andy in God knows how many years she couldn't remember what had happened? It had to be in there somewhere.

Jayne turned a little more so that from the corner of her eye she could just make out the lump under the bedclothes, and smiled; Andy was still sound asleep, undisturbed by her jiffling around and, thank goodness, he still didn't snore. She'd forgotten that.

It didn't matter what had happened last night, she sensed that whatever it was it had been the right thing to do, and turning, Jayne slipped her arms round the shape, curled up into it, and as she did laughed aloud. What she thought was Andy was in fact two pillows and her clothes. She sat up and stared at the lump, grinning and feeling such a fool, and then remembered now that Andy had said that he would put the pillows there to stop her rolling out of bed, cheeky bugger. As if . . .

And as if thinking about him conjured him up, the door between his room and hers slowly swung open, framing Andy, already dressed in chinos and a grey T-shirt. He was carrying a breakfast tray.

'Morning,' he said brightly. 'And how are we feeling this morning?'

Jayne laughed. 'You're very chipper for a man who appeared to be completely rat-faced last night.'

He grinned. 'Not every day the woman you've loved for most of your adult life says she adores you, wants to shag you blind, and spend the rest of her life ironing shirts, cooking rice pudding and generally making amends for breaking your poor heart.'

Jayne felt her heart sink. 'Oh God, I didn't really say that, did I?'

He laughed. 'No, of course not. Nor did you propose to me or offer to bear my children.'

Jane took the cup of tea he offered her. 'Well, that's a relief.'

'What you did say, though . . .'

Jayne looked up at him, trying to work out if this was another tease, and smiled. 'Andy, I'd like to say that I wasn't that drunk, but actually I was. Drunk and tired. But what I'm sure I did say was –' she paused, trying to pull the words back into focus – 'was that I love you. But that we've both come a long way since sitting on a beach on a rock under the stars.'

'So are you saying that this is all there is? That once we get back to England you're going to walk off into the sunset again? That we don't get a second chance?'

Jayne looked into his big blue eyes. 'How would you feel about that?'

'I was asking you. I suppose if I'm honest I wanted to see you one more time, make sure you were OK. I didn't come out here assuming that we could start over or we'd take one look at each other and leap into bed. I suppose I wanted to know that what we had back then wasn't some trick of the light.'

'Andy, I loved you with all my heart,' she said, feeling a lump in her throat. 'And I can't tell you how pleased I am to see you again.'

'But?' he said, watching her closely.

'But nothing.'

'That's all I needed,' he said, and set the tray down on the bed. 'Come on. You'd better eat, soak up some of the alcohol.'

'Did you mean what you said?'

'About loving you? That was a long time ago, we're different people.' He sounded defensive, hesitant, although she wasn't sure whether that was for her benefit or his. 'A lot of other things have happened.'

'I know,' she paused, and then said what was on her mind. 'Do you still fancy me?'

He grinned. 'Is the Pope Catholic?'

'Then maybe we could give it another try, see how we get on.'

Andy shook his head, eyes bright with amusement. 'You make it sound like joining an evening class.'

'We both deserve a second chance. Or is it that you're trying to let me down gently?'

'No, no, I'm not. I'm just being cautious, feeling my way – wondering, I suppose, why it took both of us so long to make contact. I've missed you so much.'

Jayne felt her eyes fill with tears. 'Me too,' she murmured. 'Me too.' And then she curled up against him, relieved and happy to feel him slip his arms around her, and let the tears run down her face. 'Oh, Andy,' she murmured, 'I must have been mad to let you go.'

'I know. You were totally and utterly mad,' he said, stroking the hair back of her face. 'Certifiable.' And then looking down at her, added, 'And you still look like a baboon's backside after you've been crying.'

'Fancy you remembering that,' she snorted.

'Who could forget? Now, do you want to eat breakfast or should we just go straight for the wild sex?' Jayne hesitated long enough for Andy to add with a grin, 'Obviously you remember that as well.'

In Buckbourne, Jane, still in her pyjamas and dressing gown, wandered downstairs through the sleeping household and out onto the deck, clutching a mug of tea. She hadn't slept well, torn between dreams involving being arrested by DI Rolf, and being chased by her mother. Sometimes both.

It was early, the immaculately clipped lawn was still heavy with dew, the shrubs tucked and tidy, and apparently asleep. By contrast next door looked like a mini festival, with tents and booths, and great trails of lights strung between the trees and statues, and along the ridge of the marquee, towards a bank of generators. Fortunately everywhere was still quiet, the only sound the breeze in the strings of lights, which tinkled like wind chimes.

Jane stretched. She was tired and tense and upset that her dream life – in both senses – had so very quickly turned into nightmares. Ray was expecting the money to be back by first thing Monday morning. If she couldn't prove she hadn't stolen it then Jane could see no other way out, although it felt as if transferring it back and accepting Ray's blood money was an admission of guilt. And then there was Kit. Jane sighed, her imagination conjuring him up like a genie. How on earth could she carry on seeing him if Jayne thought she was a fool – or worse, a thief and a liar?

Jane padded down towards the lake, feeling miserable and tired. Jayne's cat, Augustus, picked his way through the grass towards her, obviously on his way home after a night out on the tiles. She crouched down to stroke him, and he paused mid-stride, allowing himself to be adored while plaiting himself around her legs, purring softly. Jane smiled at his smug expression. Next time around she was coming, back as a cat, definitely.

'Are you OK?' The sound of Kit's voice hurrying down the path towards her made Jane jump.

He was dressed in a tracksuit top, trainers and shorts, revealing long lean muscular legs. 'I was going for a run round the park,' he said in answer to her unspoken question, 'before it gets too hot.'

Jane smiled. 'I couldn't sleep. Kit, you do believe me, don't you? About the money and – well – everything?'

'Yes I do.'

'Nice legs.'

He grinned. 'Nice of you to notice. Nice PJs.'

'Um, I wasn't expecting company. I have to get my stuff packed and go home today.'

He paused. 'It doesn't seem right you moving out. Jayne wanted you to stay here till she got back.'

'That was while I worked for her, and at the moment, as far as Ray is concerned, I'm out. And besides, I can hardly be here when Ray shows up tonight, now can I?'

'I suppose not. If this doesn't work out—' He stopped. 'I mean, if you and Gladstone can't find any proof, then I want you to know that I believe you and I'll try everything I can to prove it and explain to Jayne. I'll try and make it right, I promise.'

Deeply touched, Jane stared at him. God, he was gorgeous. 'You make it sound as if we won't see each other again,' she said, voice trembling slightly. She reddened. 'Or is that what you meant? Is this the get-out moment? I can see that things might be a bit difficult if Jayne thinks I'm either a total ditz or a lying thief.'

'That isn't what I meant at all. I do want to see you again. I suppose I was trying to let you know that whatever happens it will be all right, I promise.'

She smiled. 'Say that again.'

'Which bit?'

'The bit about it being all right and you promising. And you wanting to see me again.'

He laughed. 'You're nuts.'

'I know, but I'm not a thief or an embezzler or a black-mailer.'

Kit stepped a little closer, so close that she could feel the heat of his body, smell the soft scent of male sweat, see the soft rise and fall of his chest, as he breathed in and out, see the flutter of the pulse in his throat. Kit leaned closer still and kissed her on the end of the nose. 'I know. Stop fretting,' he said, and for an instant brushed his lips against hers. Her heart fluttered.

'I have to run,' he said.

'Before it gets too warm,' she replied. 'If I fret will you kiss me again?'

He grinned as he wheeled away, jogging backwards towards the path. 'In those pyjamas? How could I possibly resist?'

'I have to leave soon,' Jane said, as he turned.

'I know, but I won't be long,' he called. 'Don't leave without saying goodbye, will you?'

'No, of course not.'

She watched him jogging down the path, down towards the lake, wondering if he would come to find her if she just left without saying a word. Next door she heard the first stirrings of the party crew; it sounded as if they were emptying out the front porch of hell. As Kit became a dot on the horizon Tony appeared above the fence line. He had to be standing on some-thing.

'Morning, Janey. How's it going?'

Jane smiled. 'Don't ask. How's Lil?'

He grinned. 'Fighting fit. See you later?'

Jane's smile held. She didn't like to tell him that, come

party time, she would be breaking and entering or possibly being arrested. She didn't want to put a crimp on his day.

The house-warming party was in full swing when, several hours later, Jayne Mills and Andy Turner pulled up outside number 9 in his TT. The road, on both sides, was jam-packed solid with cars for as far as the eye could see, the air heavy with music and voices, and in the darkness by the lake they could make out the dull red glow of what looked like a fire.

'Sweet Jesus,' said Andy with a grin as he clambered out of his car onto the drive. 'What the hell is going on?'

'Hell might be the operative word,' said Jayne.

'Some sort of welcome-home party. Did you know about this?'

Jayne shook her head, completely bemused.

'Glad to see that you chose a nice quiet neighbourhood.'

Jayne, looking rueful, headed up to her front door, slipped the key into the lock and turned it. The lock gave but it was obvious that the door was also bolted from the inside. She rang the bell and waited. After a few seconds she rang again and waited some more. Nothing.

'Bugger,' she hissed. 'Let's just try the side gate.'

'You did ring, didn't you?' asked Andy.

Jayne nodded. 'Yes, when we got to the airport. I left a message, I would have thought someone would have picked it up by now.'

It took them about two seconds to discover that the side gate was locked too.

Andy eyed it up thoughtfully. 'I could probably climb up over it.'

Jayne laughed. 'Come off it, neither of us is up to getting

over that – and it's concrete on the other side. Last thing you need is a broken ankle.'

'Chances are everyone's gone next door,' said Andy, his voice raised against the barrage of sound.

'Either that or they're hunkered down in the cellar with emergency rations and bottled water, waiting it out.'

'Mind you,' said Andy, 'it sounds fantastic. Remember when we went to Glastonbury? And Knebworth? How about we give up on the breaking in and go round and see if we can see anyone you know?'

Jayne sighed. 'I don't see that we've got much choice.'

Hidden away from the main road, under the shadow of the porch outside Jayne's Waterside House offices, the other Jane Mills looked right and left, and then, holding her breath, tapped the security code into the street door – and waited. If Ray had changed the code they were in big trouble. As she waited Jane looked up squarely into the security camera and smiled grimly, wriggling her fingers in an approximation of a cheery wave. Meanwhile, behind her, Gladstone moved nervously from foot to foot, while Gary stood very still and stared out into the darkness. From somewhere close by, Jane heard a muffled click and then a soft whirr as the mechanism gave and the front door very slowly swung open. Inside the foyer it was dark, the only light coming from moonlight reflected in the water running by outside.

'I don't like it,' Gladstone whimpered.

'Neither do I but we'll be fine,' said Jane briskly, with a confidence she didn't feel. 'Come on, this way. It's on the first floor.' As they stepped inside a security light flashed on, making Gladstone shriek like a girl, the combination of ice-hard light and the sound making Jane jump out of her skin.

'Oh, for goodness' sake,' said Gary grimly. 'Let's get upstairs and get this over and done with. I've got a party to go to, and Lil is expecting me to give her a hand with the nibbles.'

Jane and the others headed upstairs, the beady eyes of the CCTV cameras following their every move.

Outside number 7 Creswell Close, a posse of fully fledged security guards were keeping watch over the front gates, a little huddle of men in dinner jackets whose shoulders suggested way too many hours in the gym. They were busy checking names from the guest list.

'I'm from next door,' said Jayne, pointing to number 9. If she was honest, the last thing she wanted to do was party. What she wanted was a nice cup of tea and an explanation.

One of the men, who had to be six foot six if he was an inch, from the bottom of his shiny Doc Martens to the top of his shiny bald head, nodded and then said, 'Name?'

Jayne noticed that he had an earpiece in, with a curly wire feed disappearing down into the tyre-sized neck of his collar. 'Jayne Mills,' she began, expecting to explain. 'And guest.'

The man nodded again and stepped to one side. 'Through you go, ma'am – if you'd like to follow the lights down to the marquee. Music and entertainment in the main arena, food and refreshments in the green tent. Little boys' room in the blue, powder room in the pink one wiv the flamingos.' As he spoke he guided her and Andy through into a marshalling area with an ease borne of years of experience. Andy meanwhile was eyeing up a little knot of guests who were standing by the main door to the house, sipping cocktails.

'I think that's one of the guys out of Status Quo,' he whispered in an undertone as they made their way down towards the tents.

Jayne looked back over her shoulder 'Really? Are you sure?'

She didn't catch his reply, which sounded like mumbled adoration. As they rounded the corner Jayne gasped in amazement. There on the lawn, leading down to the lake, were three marquees – one main one and two either side, decked out as circus tents. There were jugglers and strong men, each on a low dais, along with a fire breather and clowns, tumblers and what looked suspiciously like a bearded lady.

The whole place was heaving with people, most of whom appeared to be a few drinks ahead of the new arrivals, and apparently having a great time. Rock music rolled out from the main tent like summer thunder.

Andy hissed in Jayne's ear, 'That guy over there, I'm sure I know his face, isn't he on the TV?'

At which point Jayne saw a face she recognised too. 'Kit?' she called out and, grabbing Andy, elbowed her way through the crowd. 'Kit?' she called again.

This time her brother turned at the sound of his name, his face lighting up as he spotted her amongst the sea of faces.

'Jayne!' he said, grabbing hold of her hands. 'God, it's so good to see you. We've been so worried. When did you get back?'

Before she could reply he pulled her closer and Jayne

realised that the man standing next to him, ogling a leggy blonde who was dressed in a tiny cropped T-shirt and cut-off jeans, dancing with her companions, was Ray.

Jayne's smiled widened. 'Ray? I didn't realise you were here too.'

Ray swung round, unable to hide his surprise. 'Jayne,' he said in astonishment. 'I'm so pleased to see you. I wasn't expecting you back until next week.'

Jayne smiled. 'It's OK, I was rescued by Andy.' She turned to do the introductions. 'Andy Taylor, you remember my brother, Kit Harvey-Mills, and my business partner, Ray Jacobson. So', she continued, 'what exactly is going on?'

'Sorry,' Ray said. 'I'm not with you, what do you mean, *what's* going on?'

Jayne stared at him. It was such a simple question but it was Kit who picked up the baton. 'It's OK, it's Tony Butler's house-warming – your new next-door neighbour – although he's promised me and the rest of the estate that this would be a one-off.'

Jayne laughed. 'It had better be.' And then to Ray added, 'We need to talk.' She couldn't help noticing that he seemed uneasy. 'Are you OK?' she said, having to shout above the music.

'I'm fine. It's just been a long week. I'm really glad you're back safe and sound. Amazing party, isn't it?' he said, glancing around. 'Here, let me get you a drink.' He waved towards a waiter circulating with a tray of champagne.

'Where are Gary and Jane?' Jayne asked, as Ray pressed a glass into her hand and collected another for Andy, who still had his eyes fixed on the crowd.

Ray's expression flickered with something Jayne couldn't quite place. 'I have no idea. Gary's got the night off and

'I'm not sure where Jane is at the moment,' he said, eyes working the crowd.

'Is she here?' said Jayne, following his gaze.

'No, no, I think she might be at home. We need to talk but not here,' said Ray. 'I was just going to get some food, do you want anything?'

Jayne shook her head, although she had the distinct feeling she had just had the brushoff. Before she could comment Ray slipped away amongst the revellers, while on stage someone played the opening riff of 'Smoke on the Water', and a great roar went up from amongst the audience.

At which point Jayne's attention shifted to a rotund copper-brown man in a black silk muscle vest, black jeans and basketball boots, who stepped up to Kit and shook his hand. 'Glad you could make it, mate,' he said with a toothy grin, and an instant later Jayne found herself being introduced to their host, Tony Butler, who embraced her like an old friend, kissing her on both cheeks.

'I've heard so such about you from Gary, Jane and Kit,' he said with a grin. 'You must come in and meet Lil. She's inside, broke her ankle, and to be honest if it wasn't for the other Jane, God knows what we woulda done. Kit, why don't you take your sister inside and meet Lil – I've got to go sort out the ice sculpture and the bleeding vodka fountain. Apparently Elvis is acting up. Talk later. Ciao.'

On stage the music kicked in, so loud that Jayne felt the bass hit her in the chest like a friendly Springer spaniel. 'Can we go outside?' she yelled to Kit and Andy.

As they pushed their way out into the cooler night air someone else called her name. 'Jayne – Jayne!' shrieked a high-pitched almost hysterical voice on the periphery of the crowd. Seconds later Carlo elbowed his way through the crowd, his face a mask of mixed emotions.

'Carlo,' she said in amazement, 'what the hell are you doing here?'

Carlo sniffed. 'Oh, Jayne, I have missed you so much. I rang you, I wrote, I sent you flowers and still you didn't get in touch with me.' He sniffed again. 'I am desolate, broken, I thought I was going to die of grief.' When Jayne said nothing he continued, in a perfectly normal voice. 'Actually Tony invited me. But I want you to know how hurt I am. I was just telling Ray —' he looked back over his shoulder into the crowd.

'Carlo, this isn't the time or the place,' Jayne said firmly. 'We've had this conversation a dozen times. I'm sorry that you're hurt but it is over.'

Carlo bristled.

Alongside her Jayne felt Andy move a little closer and she smiled softly, touched by his show of protectiveness.

Carlo pouted and flicked his hair. 'You can't always ride roughshod over other people's emotions, and I also want you to know that it's your loss. I am a very special person, I deserve to be treated properly. My therapist said—'

'Yes, yes, of course you do,' Jayne said quickly, cutting him off before he rolled out his years of therapy speech. Carlo's idea of being treated properly mostly meant that Jayne picked up the bills, humoured his unpredictable mood swings and bought him lots of presents. Carlo was as hormonal as a thirteen-year-old girl and dating him had been a nightmare. God only knew what she'd seen in him. Six foot tall, with Latino good looks, hung like a donkey, and adored older women? Jayne grinned as he squared his shoulders defiantly, and let herself off the hook.

'What?' Carlo snapped.

'Nothing.' She shook her head.

'Well, I want you to know that, thanks to you being so cruel, I've found true love at last.' As he spoke he indicated a statuesque woman in her late fifties currently elbowing her way towards them through a group of dancers. She was clutching a champagne flute, and was dressed in a yellow and orange paisley kaftan, her hennaed hair twisted up on top of her head and secured with enough clips to build a small pylon.

'I want you to meet Audra. Audra, I'd like you to meet Jayne Mills.'

There was a flash of recognition on the other woman's face and then a smile, conveniently outlined in blood-red lipstick just in case Jayne missed it. 'Oh, so *you're Jayne Mills*,' she said. 'I'm Jane's mother. Obviously I was a child bride,' she continued holding out her hand in an approximation of a royal handshake. 'Delighted to meet you.'

'Really?' said Jayne, genuinely surprised. How had all these people ended up here, of all places? 'Where is Jane at the moment?'

Audra rolled her eyes and took another slug of champagne. 'God, she will be so glad to know that you're back safe and sound. It's been hell here. You know that Jane and Gary are—'

On the periphery of her vision Jayne saw Kit open his mouth to say something or to stop her but it was too late, as the woman continued, '– having to break into your office because she stole your money. Well, she didn't really steal your money. She was arrested, although I think that was about something else.' The older woman pulled a face as if considering the options. 'That's why Kit's here, isn't it, sweetie? To ride shotgun on someone.' She looked round thoughtfully. 'Is he here? Oh, and to stop Jane from stealing the family jewels – although obviously it is all a big misunderstanding. At least I hope it is. Mind you, her father was a bad lot.'

Jayne looked from face to face. 'What do you mean, Jane's breaking into my office? Are you serious. Is this true, Kit? What the hell is going on?'

Kit's face was ashen. 'Jayne, this isn't quite how it seems. I need to try and explain. The thing is . . .' Kit faltered and then raised his hands in surrender. 'Actually, I don't know where to begin.'

By the light of the monitors, Gladstone, his face a mask of concentration, copied the information from the hard drive of Ray's machine onto the external hard drive – the memory storage device that they had brought with them – and also onto a memory stick, which fitted into the USB port on the computer and was no bigger than a packet of gum, every move watched intently by Gary, who had a notebook and a digital camera with him to ensure that everything was recorded and double-checked as it happened. The atmosphere in the office was so tense you could have plucked it like a violin string.

'Have you nearly got it all?' whispered Jane, peering over Gladstone's shoulder at the screen where line after line of information slowly scrolled down. He nodded, without taking his eye off the monitor. She was barely able to bring herself to speak. They had been in the office for what felt like the best part of a week, although it couldn't be more than a couple of hours. Her head ached and she had a bitter taste in her mouth.

'How much longer do you think it will be?' she asked. Gladstone looked at her over his shoulder, his long pale face bluey-white in the screen's glare, his eyes widening.

'What,' asked Jayne. 'What is it? What have you found?'

'I could ask you exactly the same question?' said a familiar voice from behind them. Jane swung round in horror, as the office door opened, framing Ray, his face a grim mask.

There was a moment of silence and then Ray said, 'What the fuck do you think you're up to? I thought you were way smarter than this, Jane. You should have done what we agreed and just walked away. And as for you, Gary, what is Jayne going to say when she finds out you were in on the scheme to defraud her? Or is it that you've fallen for Jane's lies too? Maybe you were in on this from the start? Maybe the whole thing was your idea?'

Gary took a step forward but Jane was ahead of him. 'Ray, you know this has got nothing to do with Gary or Gladstone. This was my idea. I asked them to help me.'

'Oh, so *this* is Gladstone, is it?' said Ray gleefully. 'What did you want help with, for goodness' sake, covering up your little scam?'

Jane was confused. 'Proving that you framed me. How did you know about Gladstone? How did you know we were here?'

Ray grinned. 'Your mother told me. Carlo, Jayne's ex, was at Tony's party and introduced us. She's drunk as a skunk and was telling me all about how you'd come up here to break in. I don't think she has a clue who I am.'

Gladstone, who had carried on working, looked up from the machines. 'It's all on here, the dates, times, all the transactions, all the traffic.'

Ray nodded. 'I know, or at least I do now. Now just

unplug the hard drive and leave it exactly where it is and then get away from the computers.'

Jane stared at him. 'You can't do this.'

He sighed. 'Oh, I can, Jane, and I'm going to.' He turned to Gary and Gladstone. 'Move away from the desks, both of you. Now, get out. I want to talk to Jane on my own.'

'I've got nothing to say,' said Jane. 'You set me up.'

'Out, you two. Oh, and, Gary, just leave the camera and the notepad on the desk. This won't take a minute.'

They hesitated. Ray sighed and in the end it was Jane who waved them away. 'Go on, it'll be all right,' she said in a low voice. 'I'll be fine.'

'I'm glad you've seen sense, Jane. All I need to do is pick up the CCTV footage from the machine.'

'We've got the proof that I didn't steal Jayne's money, Ray.'

'So you have, but you've got nothing without the computer evidence.'

'I'll call the police.'

Ray stepped aside and indicated the phone. 'Go ahead. Even with the computers all you've got is circumstantial evidence. It doesn't prove my guilt and besides, I'm not the one breaking and entering.'

Jane picked up the handset and began dialling the number as Ray said, 'I'll tell them that you broke in – a vindictive ex-employee with a grudge. Possibly with psychiatric problems.' Jane could hear the phone ringing as Ray continued, 'I suppose you know that Gladstone is on parole, don't you?'

Jane stared at him.

'A real little newshound, your mother.'

The phone rang in her ear. Once, twice.

'I'm not sure how breaking and entering would go down with his parole officer.'

'Good evening,' said a female voice at the far end of the line. 'You're through to the police. How can I help you?'

'And Gary?' said Ray. 'I wonder what we could dig up on him? Trust me, there's bound to be something; there always is.'

Jane looked at him. Ray's face was an impassive mask.

'Gladstone will go back to prison, and I will see to it that Gary gets his comeuppance, and if you don't think I can do that, then try me. Let's look at the facts, shall we, Jane?'

'Hello,' said the woman. 'May I help you?'

'You were fired yesterday, and so technically you broke in here tonight – after all, what else were you doing here at this time of night? – and I notice that none of you is wearing gloves.'

Jane swallowed had. 'Sorry, wrong number,' she said, and dropped the phone back into its cradle. 'We didn't want to hide our tracks; we've got nothing to hide,' said Jane defiantly. 'You framed me and the computer records prove it.'

Ray sneered. 'Right, but the thing is, Jane, the computers won't be here when the police show up, and any CCTV footage that they can rescue after the event will just show the three of you letting yourselves in and coming up here – and before you ask, I came in through the consulting rooms downstairs – there is this annoying little blind spot in the coverage that we've noticed before and keep meaning to put right – and then I switched the system off. I was thinking that we could maybe have a little fire.'

Ray paused, his smile as cold and unflinching as a shark's, and as he spoke he pulled the waste-paper basket out from under one of the desks and, having taken a cigarette packet from his pocket, then produced a box of matches. Lighting a cigarette he casually lit a tissue from a box on the desk, dropped it into the bin and then threw in another tissue on top of it and then another.

'There are just so many flammable things in an office,' he said, almost to himself as the contents of the bin caught fire with an unnerving whoosh. It happened so quickly that Jane gasped in amazement. Almost casually he opened a desk drawer and pulled out a selection of the contents and started feeding them into the flames.

When the bin was ablaze he pushed it with his foot under one of the computer desks. Almost at once the heat began to melt the cabling, a steady drip of molten plastic feeding the fire. As they stood there the room began to fill with acrid smoke. Jane coughed, her eyes watering.

'Come on, my dear,' he said. 'Time to go.' And with that he guided her out onto the landing and pulled the office door to. As he did so, Jane heard the fire crackle and roar in complaint.

'So,' said Ray, holding her arm and leading her down the stairs towards the others, still apparently composed, 'we have you three showing up and then a little while later the office catches fire, destroying the evidence that proves one way or another exactly who moved Jayne's money. The computers, the hard drive, the camera, office diaries and records – all gone. I think the police will probably put two and two together and make—'

'And make what?' said a second female voice. Ray swung round, to find Jayne standing on the landing. By some odd trick of the light she appeared golden in the moonlight.

'Jayne,' Ray said, painting on a bright smile. 'How very nice to see you. I was just having a chat with Jane about some of the problems we've been having with the banking. All more or less sorted out now.'

'At midnight? You left a party to talk business?' said Jayne.

Ray's face hardened. 'I'm afraid, Jayne, the truth is that I caught your golden girl with her fingers in the till. I wasn't going to go public – we'd planned to put everything back in place by Monday – when I thought you'd be coming home. I thought she deserved a second chance. Are you all on your own?'

'Please,' said Jane, fighting back the shock and panic that was beginning to hit her, 'it's not true. Jayne, you have to believe me. The office is on fire. He's set the office on fire.'

Ray glared at Jane as if willing her to be quiet. 'She's a hysteric and a liar – though very plausible. I have to say she almost had me fooled. I caught the three of them trying to tamper with the computers. God only knows what she told them, but it's all sorted out now,' he said. 'I don't know about you but I think we should draw a veil over the whole thing. She's not a bad kid, I think the whole situation just went to her head.'

'And what about this?' said Jayne. She opened her hand. In her palm was a memory stick.

Ray stared at it. 'Where did you get that?'

Gladstone stepped out of the shadows, along with Gary, Kit and Andy. 'I took it when you ordered us out. We've got all the proof there that we need,' said Gladstone.

'Give it to me,' Ray snapped. 'Give it to me now.'

Jayne shook her head. 'I don't think so Ray.'

He took a step towards her, and as he did Andy tried to grab him but before he could make a move, Gladstone stepped forward and threw a huge haymaker punch that sent Ray sprawling.

As Ray struggled to his feet, Jane ran over to Kit.

'Jane,' Kit gasped as she stepped into his arms. 'Are you all right?'

'I'm fine,' she said. 'But we need to get out of here.'

From upstairs came the sounds of something crashing to the floor as the fire caught hold.

'Please,' yelled Jane. 'We have to go.'

'It'll be all right', said Kit, grabbing a fire extinguisher and before Jane could stop him he ran upstairs, followed by Gladstone. Gary meanwhile pulled out his mobile phone and dialled 999.

Across the landing Jayne and Ray stood facing each other, Ray rubbing his split lip.

'Ray, I don't understand why you're doing this.'

He stared her down. 'Doing what? Are you telling me that you believe a kid who has worked here for no time at all and your baby brother, the one you're always bailing out and rescuing? You said yourself he's not a shit's worth of good –'

'Ray please – I need an explanation.'

'That's bloody rich coming from you, the woman who works on instinct and flies by the seat of her pants.'

'Ray, tell me what is happening. I leave the place for a week and everything falls apart.'

'That's not my fault,' said Ray defiantly. 'It's yours. You hired a thief, Jayne, a loose cannon. You should have listened to me, listened to what I said. If I'd known you wanted an assistant I would have found someone to help you, someone who you could trust, someone we could both work with. I don't understand why you didn't let me take over the company if you wanted a break. This girl you took on is a thief and liar, and if it hadn't been for me, God only knows what would have happened. For Christ's sake, Jayne, I've got CCTV footage of her taking your master file out of the office. She had all the bank codes, everything.'

Jayne stared at him as if seeing him for the first time.

His expression hardened. 'Jayne . . .'

Jayne stared at him. 'Tell me about the passwords.'

He looked at her. 'I don't know what you mean.'

'What's Jane's password, Ray?'

He pulled a face. 'I don't—'

'I gave it to you before I left; you don't usually forget things.'

'Janetwo.'

'And how do you spell it?'

'J-A-N-E-T-W-O.'

Jayne stared at him and then pulled a Post-it note from her pocket. 'Jane gave this to Gladstone so he could access the computers here. He gave it to me with the memory stick.' She opened the slip of paper. On it was written 'Jane2'.

Jayne shook her head. 'Before I left I gave Jane the username password for administration on my accounts and the business site. She wrote down what she thought I said – such an easy mistake to make and neither of us checked. A misspelling. She could access things but not get to the next level to save or alter anything. The only person who had the valid codes for my websites is you.'

Ray stared at her. 'I don't believe you.'

'No, I didn't want to believe it either. It's the same with the bank account details, Ray. I'm not stupid. They're not in the master file, they never have been. It would have been stupid to have left them in the office along with everything else. Like leaving the keys to the kingdom. I left them with you, because I trusted you. I thought it was a bank glitch or something until I heard what Gladstone and Gary had to say.'

Ray sighed. 'Oh, come off it, Jayne, why the hell would I want to do that?'

She shrugged. 'I've got no idea, so the simple answer is I don't know but I plan to find out. Let me introduce you to my friend, Andy. He runs a company that investigates financial corruption – they call it forensic accountancy. I'm going to ask him to look at the company for me.'

Ray's colour faded as he looked from face to face. 'Jayne, let's not be hast—'

But before he could finish the sentence there was a shriek from upstairs and the sounds of a fire crackling and roaring above them. Jayne ran upstairs, followed by Jane, Andy, Gary and the others.

In Ray's offices flames roared up across the ceiling, while on the landing Kit was helping Gladstone away from the door, Gladstone was clutching his arm and hand, his finger blistered and raw, his jacket was still smouldering.

'Come on, we need to get out,' said Kit above the sounds of the fire. 'There's nothing we can do here.' As Kit caught hold of Jane's arm they could already hear sirens in the distance.

Jane glanced out through the floor-to-ceiling window with its view out over the canal and the car park. In the moonlight she could see Ray running across the tarmac and by some trick of the light, reflected around him was a mass of boiling flames.

Epilogue

'Jane, come and look. Seems you've got another dodgy email,' said Lizzie, glancing up from the screen. 'Ooo, and more pictures.'

Jane sighed. She was barely halfway through packing. Her lift would be arriving in Creswell Road in under ten minutes and she was nowhere near ready.

'Lizzie, I thought you would have learned your lesson about opening other people's post.'

'Oh, no, I didn't open it. I got one too. I've just seen that you've been copied in on it – along with everyone else on the library mailing list. You remember Anna?'

'The one who went to work in Shrewsbury?'

'Uh-huh. The one that everyone thought Steve might have . . . you know?'

Jane nodded. She didn't need to look up to appreciate the graphic gesture.

'Well, apparently he did. And we've all got the photographic evidence to prove it. According to this, apparently Lucy tried the same tactics with Anna and sent her a nasty little email saying that Steve was all hers now and that Anna should hold off – it's all here. Trouble is, apparently Steve didn't want to be held off. He's been spending his weekends driving up to Shrewsbury to play Mr Whippy the yoghurt king with Anna as well. And Anna decided when it came to photos she could trump Lucy's ace. Here, look I printed it off for you . . .'

'I hope you didn't use that shiny photo paper. It cost a— Oh my God.'

Lizzie handed Jane the image. 'See the date stamp, bottom right-hand corner?'

'Amongst a lot of other things. God, that man is so weird.'

'Her too by the look of it. Anyway, the date is important. Apparently, Lucy thought he was away on a reorientation course that weekend when in fact he and Anna were busy . . .'

The doorbell rang, which was probably a good thing.

'Oh, no,' said Jane. 'That'll be Kit and I'm nowhere near ready.'

'I'll go and let him in. There's no need to worry. Gladstone and I will mind the fort while you're away. Cats, plants, the whole nine yards.'

'I'll only be gone for a few days or so, and then it'll be back to the grindstone,' said Jane, folding a shirt in amongst the others.

Lizzie nodded. 'Smoozing Mrs Bottled Fruit and Mr Deliver-me-a-Decent-Dinner doesn't sound much like work to me. I've always wanted to go to Morocco.'

'It is work. I'm going as Kit's assistant,' said Jane. 'It's a photo shoot for Jayne's new line of household linen.'

'Sounds like a fix to me,' Lizzie said, heading for the door. 'Not that I mind. I'm glad Jayne let you keep the leather sofas. I like living here and my new job with Lonny down at the centre is going really well.'

'Don't get too cosy. I'll be back soon.'

Kit ambled in a few seconds later, looking gorgeous in cream trousers and a white shirt with the sleeves rolled back.

'All ready?' he asked.

Lizzie looked him up and down. 'Very nice, very Indiana Jones. Madam is still trying to work out which ball gown to take.'

'Take no notice of her. I'm more or less ready,' Jane said.

Kit grinned and kissed Jane lightly. 'Good. In that case I'll put the kettle on. By the way, they picked Ray up this morning.'

Jane stared at him. 'Really? Where?'

'In Holland, trying to board a plane to Argentina. Andy's company has already taken a preliminary look at the accounts and they stink. I think Jayne is stunned. All those years – and lots of money.'

Jane sighed. 'Should we still go to Morocco? I'm worried about leaving her on her own.'

'She'll be fine. Gary and Andy will take care of her, and Tony and Lil have taken her under their wing. We're only going to be gone for a few days and then you'll be back in harness. If it hadn't been that Ray was so furious about you being taken on, Jayne might never have found any of this out.'

'I don't feel good about that.'

Kit kissed her. 'Well, you shouldn't feel bad. The fire damage to the office was fairly minor, no one was badly hurt, and he's not going to take her for any more money.'

Jane looked up at him. 'Gladstone burned his hands, trying to save the external hard drive. I didn't realise that as long as we knew where the money had gone that the banks could trace where it had come from and when. I put everyone in danger.'

'Oh, stop it. He's fine,' said Lizzie, 'and he loves his new job.'

'Come on,' said Kit. 'None of this is your fault. Finish your packing, we've got a plane to catch.'

The phone rang. Lizzie picked it up and listened carefully for a few seconds, nodding, quite obviously unable to get a word in edgeways. 'Jane, it's your mum. She wants to have a quick word about Carlo – something to do with Tantric sex?'

Jane looked heavenwards and snapped her suitcase shut. 'Tell her I'm already on my way to the airport,' she said.

Over in Creswell Close, Jayne sat on the deck down by the summerhouse, Augustus the cat purring and rolling on his back, encouraging her to stroke his tummy.

'Penny for them,' said Andy. They were drinking coffee, and she was leaning back against his broad chest, relishing the sensation of his arms around her waist and the feeling of the soft rise and fall of his breathing against her shoulders.

She smiled. 'I was just thinking about how content I feel. I wanted an adventure – for things to change. You know the old saying about being careful what you wish for?'

He smiled. 'So you're planning to go off again. Looking for adventure?'

Jayne sighed. 'Not until I've got the measure of exactly what Ray has been up to all these years.' She paused. 'And I need to spend some more time with Jane, show her the ropes – she's a good girl. And then? Who knows?'

He leaned forward and kissed her shoulder gently. 'You know, I hadn't realised just how much I've really missed you,' he said.

Jayne looked up at him, eyes bright with tears of joy and of regret. 'And I've missed you too,' she said.

Gary topped up their coffee. 'Don't mind us.'

'Lovely spot for a wedding,' said Lil, adjusting her ankle on the stool.

'Yeah, we could have another party,' said Tony.

How romantic are you? Take our fun quiz and find out!

Q1 – What would be your ideal way to spend an evening?

A) A walk with your loved one on a moonlight beach, after a meal in an intimate restaurant

B) Your ideal night out would be spent in a bar with your girlfriends, dancing and flirting with strangers

C) You love a night with your man and your group of friends for a boozy night in your local – stopping for a kebab on the way home.

Q2 – What's your favourite kind of film?

A) You love a night in with a classic weepie from the golden age of cinema like *Brief Encounter* or *Casablanca* – back when men were dashing and women swooned . . .

B) Your perfect DVD evening would involve a high octane action flick, starring a musclebound, sweaty hunk in battle with the bad guys

C) You love any film that makes you cry with laughter – your perfect night involves having a giggle over a bottle of wine and a comedy film like *Borat* or *There's Something About Mary.*

Q3 – Which film star would you love to spend an evening with?

A) Your dream date would be someone with old school charm such as gorgeous George Clooney or the king of suave, Cary Grant

B) You need a sexy man who would treat you mean and keep you keen – someone like Colin Farrell or Russell Howard really floats your boat...

C) When it comes to sex appeal, your ideal man has to

make you laugh as well as lust after him – someone like Johnny Depp would be perfect.

Q4 – What's your favourite European city?

A) Your favourite spot in Europe would be Venice. Travelling down the canals in a gondola with your loved one, kissing on the Bridge of Sighs is the perfect way to spend a holiday

B) Your ideal destination for a mini-break would be Berlin, a cool city with great shopping and enough achingly hip techno clubs to see you through to the wee small hours

C) You're happiest visiting diverse places like Paris – you love to spend your days in the Louvre or buying the latest fashions and your nights over intimate candlelit meals with your partner.

Q5 – What gift would you most like to receive from a loved one?

A) You don't care about monetary value when it comes to gifts – what matters is the thought behind it. You would love it if your partner wrote you a poem or a song

B) You'd be happiest if your man came in clutching the latest 'must have' bag – your heart can be swayed by Balenciaga or Hermes!

C) You'd most appreciate a gift that you can share with your significant other – you'd be delighted with a surprise holiday!

MOSTLY A'S – HOPELESS ROMANTIC

You are unequivocally romantic and proud of it! For you, love is all you need, you believe in a thing called love and you have been known to call up your partner just to say 'I love you.' The world needs more people like you – just think how peaceful things would be if we all made love, not war . . .

MOSTLY B'S – ANTI CUPID

You believe love is a concept created by greeting card manufacturers to sell more stock and you gag at the thought of fluffy teddies and love song compilation CDs. You much prefer a wild night out with your girlfriends to a cosy night *a deux*.

MOSTLY C'S – PRACTICAL BUT PASSIONATE

You temper your romantic side with a healthy dose of cynicism – you're not averse to receiving hearts and flowers but you also realise that romance comes in the little gestures as well as the big statements. You're happiest with a home cooked meal rather than the fancy restaurant (as long as your partner doesn't burn down the kitchen in the process . . .).

P&O CRUISES

CRUISE
SPECIALISTS

the-cruise-specialists.co.uk

2 for 1 Cruises with P&O Cruises

2 for 1 luxury cruises with P&O! We are offering all purchasers of *Lessons in Love* a chance to ride the seas with P&O. This exclusive offer is available on cruises departing up to March 20th 2010.

P&O Cruises has a long and distinguished record as a British cruise line although it is now part of the Carnival Group. It maintains a high level of formality and traditional elegance although catering for all age groups. Cuisine is good and service is friendly and efficient. The fleet comprises mostly modern cruise ships offering a traditional British cruise experience. Ventura is a brand new family friendly 116,000 ton ship launched in 2008.

P&O Cruises offer cruises from 2 night party cruises to 100 day + full world cruises. Sailing to over 200 destinations in 90 countries, P&O offer the convenience of no fly cruises from Southampton as well as fly cruises from a range of departure airports. In order to claim your 2 for 1 offer, simply call "The Cruise Specialists" on 0800 027 5061 and quote "AVON BOOKS 2 FOR 1" in order to request a brochure or make a booking. **All bookings are subject to the terms & conditions and general information section contained within the P&O Cruises main brochure.**

TERMS & CONDITIONS

This offer is open to all UK residents aged 18 years or over for new bookings only. This offer is not available to employees of HarperCollins or its subsidiaries, TLC Marketing plc or agencies appointed by TLC and their immediate families.

1. The first adult fare relates to the Tariff (full brochure price) per person in the P&O Cruises, Main brochure 2009/10, First Edition, published July 2008.
2. Single cabins and single share cabins are excluded from the promotion.
3. 3rd & 4th person fares (including children and infants) will be charged at the latest current system price if applicable.
4. All cabins are subject to availability.
5. The Cruise Specialists are under no obligation whatsoever to sell a cabin under this promotion which would result in a loss to the agency.
6. The 2 for 1 fare applies to the cruise fare only and specifically excludes UK transport connections, taxes, gratuities, deviation fees, excursions, flight upgrades, pre or post cruise hotels, car parking, fuel supplements, insurance, on board spend of all description and any other cost not included in the basic adult fare.
7. The fare paid covers all the costs normally included in the fare such as international air fares,

meals, entertainment, children's clubs and facilities as detailed in the general information page in the P&O brochure.

8. The promotion runs for the full term of the current P&O 1st edition brochure – The first cruise will be in April 2009. The last cruise date is 20th March, 2010.
9. All bookings are subject to the terms and conditions and general information published in the P&O brochure.
10. All credit card payments are subject to a 1.89% credit card surcharge, Amex 2.75%, Debit cards no charge.
11. Only one offer may be used per person. The claimant may only claim one 2 for 1 cruise.
12. The instructions in the 'How to Use' section, form part of these terms and conditions.
13. Cancellation charges apply.
14. Neither TLC, its agents or distributors and the promoter will in any circumstances be responsible or liable to compensate the purchaser or other bearer, or accept any liability for any personal loss or injury occurring on the cruise.
15. TLC, its agents and distributors and the promoter do not guarantee the quality and/or availability of the services offered by The Cruise Specialists and cannot be held liable for any resulting personal loss or damage. Your statutory rights are unaffected.
16. TLC and HarperCollins Publishers reserve the right to offer a substitute reward of equal or greater value.
17. The terms of this promotion are as stated here and no other representations (written or oral) shall apply.
18. Any persons taking advantage of this promotion do so on complete acceptance of these terms and conditions.
19. TLC and HarperCollins Publishers reserve the right to vary these terms without notice.
20. Promoter: HarperCollins Ltd, 77-85 Fulham Palace Road, Hammersmith, London, W6 8JB.
21. This is administered by TLC Marketing plc, PO Box 468, Swansea, SA1 3WY
22. This promotion is governed by English law and is subject to the exclusive jurisdiction of the English Courts.
23. HarperCollins Publishers excludes all liability as far as is permitted by law, which may arise in connection with this offer and reserves the right to cancel the offer at any stage.

Avon Books / The Cruise Specialists – P&O Cruises Special Reader Offer

We are also offering a 17 night cruise visiting some of Europe's best destinations on P&O's newest ship designed for the British market. The ship is called the P&O Ventura and it will be departing on the 1st September 2009 for 17 nights.

The itinerary is as follows:

Depart Southampton. 2 Days at Sea. **Cadiz – Spain**. Day at Sea. **Ajaccio – Corsica. Rome – Italy. Naples – Italy.** Day at Sea. **Dubrovnik – Croatia. Corfu – Greece. Cephalonia – Greece.** 2 Days at Sea. **Malaga – Spain.** 2 Days at Sea. Disembark Southampton.

Full brochure price from £3259
Avon books offer price from £1699 + £75 per person on board credit

For more information and details of upgrade prices,
contact The Cruise Specialists on
FREEFONE 0800 027 5061

NB. Prices are subject to availability.
Price based on an Inside Cabin OH Grade.